PENGUIN BC

30,000 MORNINGS

Hiag Akmakjian was born in New York of Armenian immigrant parents. This is a first novel.

30,000 Mornings

HIAG AKMAKJIAN

PENGUIN BOOKS

PENGUIN BOOKS

Published by the Penguin Group
Penguin Books Ltd, 27 Wrights Lane, London W8 5TZ, England
Penguin Putnam Inc., 375 Hudson Street, New York, New York 10014, USA
Penguin Books Australia Ltd, Ringwood, Victoria, Australia
Penguin Books Canada Ltd, 10 Alcorn Avenue, Toronto, Ontario, Canada M4V 3B2
Penguin Books (NZ) Ltd, Private Bag 102902, NSMC, Auckland, New Zealand

Penguin Books Ltd, Registered Offices: Harmondsworth, Middlesex, England

First published by Viking 1999
Published in Penguin Books 2000
1 3 5 7 9 10 8 6 4 2

Set in Monotype Sabon
Printed in England by Clays Ltd, St Ives plc

For my

companion, lover, colleague, muse, straight man, amanuensis, nurturer –
and only joy and happiness –

my darling M.

I sat on a rock to rest and noticed a small cherry tree no more than three feet tall and only half in bloom – and marvelled that this lovely late cherry, buried deep in snow all winter, did not forget to blossom when spring finally came to these mountains . . .

Even though what I have written is little more than the babble of the intoxicated and the rambling talk of the dreaming, I jotted these notes hoping they could serve others who might set out on a similar journey.

Bashō Matsuo (1644–94)

Acknowledgements

A warm and deeply felt thanks to Margaret and Steven and Mish and Tim for their encouragement – and also because they make life so pleasurable.

And an affectionate thanks to my excellent editor at Viking, Kate Jones, for her verve and style – and to her assistant, Lesley Shaw, for her ebullience and enthusiasm. Thank you also to Annie Lee, for her copy-editing refinements, and to her son, David, for his percipient comments. And finally, much appreciation to my agent, Judith Murray, and to Antony Topping and Séverine Renaud, for their gratifying enthusiasm and support from the outset and their helpful editorial suggestions.

I

You can wake up from a bad dream but you can't wake up from life. Inge's *bon mot* for the day.

I'm sitting up in bed, which is to say my 'desk' – it's where I do my best thinking (my best everything in fact) – and I'm looking at the photograph of Karen, the famous one in which she is not nude so much as naked – and so vulnerable. It was the centrepiece of the famous Yves St Laurent spread in *Vogue*, calculated to give male viewers a testosterone jolt, and it did.

The image is already on its way to becoming as celebrated as the Marilyn Monroe calendar once used to be and for the past few weeks has been causing a sensation everywhere it's been reproduced. *Newsweek* and *Time* have run cover stories on it, a few of the glossies have mentioned it in their more gossipy columns, and even the Good Grey 'All the News That's Fit to Print' *Times* has alluded to it more than once.

And I think bitterly: all this would be fucking marvellous if only Karen were here to enjoy the unbelievable sudden renown.

A pair of blondes

With our Finnish model's looks, Karen and I can make quite an entrance – although I must say she's the true beauty, of the knock-'em-dead variety. It's not that people find me hard to look at – sometimes I wish some men would – but I'm not really in the same league with her. What helps my cause – a bit – is that people take me to be several years younger than

I am: they have even guessed that I'm a '*very* mature nineteen' instead of twenty-six.

I'm not exactly sure what the heavy accent on 'very' is supposed to mean, but people's reactions on meeting me are sometimes strange. When men first take in my Nordicness and blonde hair ('mythologically blonde and arctically pure,' somebody once described me – on the make, of course) and size up my 'butter-wouldn't-melt-in-her-mouth' look (another man in heat), they expect me to behave like a demure, wilting maiden in a nineteenth-century novel – all flower arranging and piano duets with *Maman* when not reciting Shelley or recovering from the vapours. I'm not at *all* like that. For one thing, with English being technically my second language and therefore not having the same reality as Finnish, I don't have the usual linguistic inhibitions, and when I open my mouth, people are not quite prepared for what pops out, namely language that isn't always suitable to Aunt Tillie's Sewing Circle. I sometimes lapse into Finnish so as not to offend a certain puritanical sensibility in moments when I'm good and pissed off, which is practically all the time these days, and go around muttering '*Paska*!' '*Paska*!' is infinitely more gut-satisfying than its English equivalent, 'Shit!' which is too thin a sound to be taken seriously. And as for 'Oh, *shoot*!' as the ladies of the boonies say, spare me: life is bad enough as it is. In fact, life is a very bad dream at the moment.

Sex if not love makes the world go round

The photograph was a shot taken just as Karen seemed to be becoming the fashion model most in demand in New York. The development had been so swift and so unexpected that she viewed it with humility and astonishment. In her own, self-effacing judgement, she is Bimbo Numero Uno, deflecting praise by claiming that being easy to look at is determined at birth, if not earlier, and posing for pictures, though it has exhausting moments, is not *work* work but more like play.

There's no use protesting that intelligence and talent are

required to do certain things well. Her arm usually waves away anything so rational – no no no.

'Talent? I have *deed*-ly-squat.'

Diddly-squat is the latest addition to her growing treasure chest of American-English, and I became a sworn believer that there's no accounting for taste when she told me:

'American slang give me the hots.'

She has received many 'hots' – and not just for slang – from our mutual friend Bill, the painter, who undoubtedly has taught her a few things. That's Bill Joachim, whose painting at Sotheby's broke all records last year.

When they first met, Bill took one look at her and developed a full-blown passion for her. It doesn't alter matters significantly that Bill took one look at me and developed a full-blown passion for me too. And while we're on the subject, he has a long-standing full-blown passion for Roz too, his 'official' lover, a designation that entitles her to priority whenever she blows in from Hollywood, between films.

'I know he's a tomcat,' Roz shrugs, 'but then I'm a pussy.'

I like Bill and I like his forthrightness (and Roz's too). Nobody is more honest, or more fun (until he gets high and gets into his metaphysical number, in which case, forget it).

He knows I'm involved with Hal but that doesn't deter him in the slightest. He resembles a male dog inhabiting a world that is permanently in heat (or as Roz says, 'It's really not a love wand he has, it's a heat-seeking missile'). It doesn't bother me as long as he doesn't pester me with it, and, in truth, he mostly doesn't.

Little mementoes for the rich

Bill and I are good friends and he tells me entertaining stories about artists – and if there's anything crazier than the photography world (my world) it's the world of art and artists. I especially like episodes in the goofy ongoing soap opera The Amours of Greenwich Village that he keeps spinning out. None of it is made up, however far-out it gets. He says that even if you left out the kinky stuff, life in the Village is so eccentric it makes fiction redundant.

'She was an attractive uptownik, chic clothes and all that, and thought Barry Hammer was me. Do you know Barry Hammer?'

'The "Neo-Minimalist"?'

'Yeah, if you can believe that. Anyway this uptown dame was dying to make out with him, that is, with *me* – you know, hot-shot new name in the art world, a painting at the Modern, and all that – and Barry couldn't believe his luck. They spent the night at his studio and she woke up in the morning all yawning and happy and said, "Oh, Bill, oh, *Bill*-Bill," and Barry said, "Uh, wait a minute, honey, my name is Barry." She was obviously a name fucker and had hopped into bed with him thinking she was going to bed with *me*. You never saw a woman spring out of bed so fast. She *lunged* for her clothes and dived down the stairs to the street and into a taxi. She took off in such a hurry she left her underwear behind – Bergdorf label, nice silky things. There are a lot of women like that, the hangers on of the art world – groupies except that these are sophisticated women with cosy little bank accounts. They want to have a fling with you and then hope you'll give them a modest little painting as a present – "Your work is so re*mark*able, I absolutely *love* what you're doing" – which will some day fetch a hundred thousand dollars at Sotheby's.'

Friendship and nightmare

But getting back to Karen.

Perhaps because of our shared Finnish origin and perhaps for other reasons not so apparent to me, Karen has become a close good friend. I've been showing her the ropes as I would to a younger sister. She came to New York from Finland to work but with plans from the start to return home eventually. It's nothing against America – it's just that she loves Finland more.

4

We've often gone out together doing things around town and when I'm not working (as in: when I'm not wandering, Leica in hand, up and down the canyons of Manhattan), she is an ideal companion (and I hope I am as good for her). We both think that if it's city life you want, it doesn't get better than New York – although Paris isn't bad either. But, as we freely concede (on comparing notes after individual personal research on both Banks), American men are preferable to Frenchmen, because Frenchmen treat women like Kleenex: grab one, use it, then toss it aside.

I thought that famous picture would be the making of Karen's reputation, but by the time that issue of *Vogue* hit the news-stands, two or three weeks had gone by since she and her lover disappeared from sight. They took a plane from Kennedy – and that was the last we heard.

At first everyone wondered what had become of her and who her companion was – did we really *know* the friend she had taken the trip with? Anxiety grew for a while but didn't last. The concern of her friends, the ones, that is, who showed any at all, turned lukewarm, began to cool to indifference and, unbelievably, within a mere few weeks vanished entirely.

All interest in her seems to have disappeared with her, as if she never existed, and I have never before experienced what I feel now, that there is a side to life that has the quality of an anxiety dream that you can't wake up from: friends disappear and, incredibly, nobody seems to give a damn.

That nude shot was the last one made of Karen before she was gone.

In the beginning

About her disappearing, there's very little to say: Karen met a new lover, Frank, and together they went on a jaunt to Africa and Europe and, as far as any of us know, she never came back – or wrote or phoned or sent word. End of story.

I'm surprised that nobody but myself thinks there's something wrong with this. No, not surprised – shocked. And

5

angry. My imagination runs wild, convinced as I am that for all we know she is suffering some hideous fate somewhere, hoping we will save her. One scenario is that she never reached Africa, or Europe, but was kidnapped to the Caribbean, where they killed Frank and drugged her and forced her into prostitution in some Central American banana port, a sordid film-noir brothel for drunken sailors on shore leave. In another fantasy, she was snatched away to Africa, raped and murdered in some isolated spot and her mutilated body flung into a ditch. Or she was forced into a Moroccan harem, where she dies a slow death every day.

The fantasies grow, and fester. The more I think about her, the more distressed I become, until I feel I can never rest until I learn what happened. How is it possible to know and love Karen and not care where she is – to so quickly forget her?

And when the fantasy font temporarily dries up I have another disquieting thought: what if *I* were to disappear? Would anyone know, or care enough to do something about it?

I keep waiting for some word, a sign. I wake up in the morning thinking 'poor Karen' and fall asleep at night with thoughts of 'poor Karen'. Hardly an hour goes by that I don't wonder what has happened, and I apparently keep on so much about her that I'm becoming a nuisance.

I've heard stories about innocent women being abducted from the streets of Paris or London or Brussels by white-slavers and never heard from again. I try not to think about such tales. My lover Hal – the fashion photographer Hal North (the one who took that famous nude of Karen) – gets irritated, no, *pissed off*, at my carrying on and as always, when he blows up, comes out with his inevitable blahblahblah speeches, or gibberish, really. He told me yesterday that I should stop being so melodramatic and over-reacting so much. You always know when Hal is on a furious kick – a whole stock of platitudes come trotting out.

'Women. Don't. *Vanish*. Life is not a Hitchcock film.'

Having unburdened himself of that, he deigned to explain that as for the so-called white slave traffic, there are places in the world where women, 'not enjoying our Western advantages', actually *aspire* to working in brothels and harems as their *only* escape from poverty ('*grinding*' poverty, of course) and 'consider themselves damned *lucky* to *have* such employment' – a long blahblah of unbelievable proportions.

In moments like that I come close to despising him – *haista paska kaikkialla!* (I'd translate that for him except that 'Smell shit everywhere', though it's as bad as Finnish cursing gets, sounds almost humorous in English.) I feel a tremendous outrage at his absolute insensitivity, his gross misunderstanding of what I said. The worst part is that, viewed in some *demographic* way, some *encyclopedia-of-facts* way, there is a kernel of truth in the crap he hands me, but only about certain local cultures, for God's sake, and not about the matter at hand, and certainly not about Karen. What did the background of poverty have to do with a fashion model jetting somewhere on a holiday? That doesn't make the *slightest* sense – has not even the *remotest* relevance to Karen's disappearance.

So, getting mad back at him – a new thing for me, and quite salutary and even ego-boosting – I called him a 'young fogey' (really scathing once I get going) and told him he had the compassion of a clam, adding cattily I hoped I wasn't maligning clams. (*Phew.* A *blistering* attack.) And of course he did what he always does: he laughed – no, *cackled*. Which cheered me immeasurably. Hal is the kind of person who thinks he's exhibiting comedic talent when he puts on a Count Dracula act and sprints chortling around the room with a hand cupping his mouth and cackling like an evil genius. I'm sure he was dropped on his head as a child.

2

New York, New York

Looking at the photograph brings home how depressing, how
doleful New York winters are – all charcoal snow, dog shit,
muggings, bus exhaust, grimy air – ugh. But winter is also,
to be fair, the season when you get Manhattan's true flavour
as it comes alive between Thanksgiving and Christmas, with
cocktail parties and gallery openings, the social fun spilling
over into January and February and cosy snowy evenings in
neighbourhood bars, soaking together in tubs, and fucking in
warm beds, all of it giving a charged excitement to being alive
in a wild and sensual Manhattan of the mind inhabited by
the young and untroubled.

Cover model

For me the shot of Karen naked was beautiful erotic art and
I understood perfectly what one of my art director friends
meant when he said he found in the image what he looked
for. He declared it charmingly phallic.

Although there is something androgynous about the image
that arrests the eye of both sexes, it is much more than
that. Hal has the ability to make a fashion photograph into
something moving. That's his signature.

So it didn't come as a surprise when the whole gaudy
editorial spread, and especially that talked-about shot, made
such a big splash in *Time* and *Newsweek*, where, in a dull
week for news, they blew things up into a racy exposé of some

jazzed-up idea of the moment. It began to seem ironic that, though she was missing, every time I turned my head, there was Karen again.

What people like about her is a peculiar expression of trust in her eyes. They, and I too, see in those eyes a strange yearning that stays in your mind long after.

As I say, the photo meant instant renown for her, which was much more than she had dared to hope for when she left Finland to look for modelling work in New York. And even just the other day, in an article on poor old murdered-in-Miami Gianni Versace, a reporter mentioned the famous Karen shot, confident that readers would remember who she is. And a considerable number of them did, including, interestingly, some who could no longer recall which Versace Gianni was.

I can't forget Karen and her life – neither forget nor forgive, as the saying goes (or the other way round). Hal, bless his constipated heart, in an effort to console me – O rare, rare moment – says that the only ones who are truly capable of forgiving and forgetting are terminal-phase alcoholics with Korsakoff's syndrome after a radical lobotomy. (Good grief.)

Forgive but never stop reminding – that's more his style.

The origins of despondency

That Yves St Laurent spread wasn't at all typical of Hal's fashion work but a concession, who knows why, to some of the stalest tricks of commercial photography: over-expose and print high-contrast to wash away Karen's face except for the mouth and her darkishly haunting eyes.

But what draws you in to the photograph, what fascinates you, is the surrealist black-and-white-striped necktie plunging rakishly between pale adolescent girl's nipples and suggestively pointing to a haze of pubescent bush – which you both see and don't see, you can't be sure.

Tricks or not, the photograph is unquestionably the best image anyone has ever made of Karen and it is that shot that overnight made her the talk of the trade. Everybody, even gay art directors, fell in love with it, one of them describing it as offbeat and mischievously vulgar yet conservative and classic (all rolled into one!).

I have several art director friends and like them all despite their somewhat flaky view of life (both the straights and the gays): if you scratch their surface, they're all members of a tribe that's convinced that if Rembrandt were alive today he would be an art director just like them – over at *Cosmo*, probably.

Anyway, as days have become weeks and Karen hasn't shown up and it has become clear (all *too* clear to please me) that very few people care whether she is back or not, or *where* in fact she is, I'm struggling against making it into another one of my great moral causes. I don't have much ground to stand on, though normally that has never slowed me down any, and maybe that's one of the reasons I'm plunging headlong into 'the Glooms' – one long *low* slump. Low and dark. My own private winter of discontent, and no glorious summer in sight.

3

Top model

I felt the photograph would be the making of Karen as a high-fashion model – 'tawp mo-DELL', as she would say whenever she put on hoity-toity swank to amuse her friends, describing herself in today's age-of-technology 'French' (*'le marketing'*, *'le comeback'*, *'le happy ending'*), the new lingua franca – lingua *anglica*, really – that now breezily accommodates *'le baise et breakfast'*.

Everyone loves her easygoingness. From the start, she didn't take the fashion world seriously – studios, posing, magazines – not any of it. She went into modelling for a purpose not connected with fame or glamour. Her friends describe her goals in life as based on tried-and-true old-fashioned storybook values. She wants (eventually, not yet) a husband and two children – a boy and a girl – and a comfortable house in the country, preferably near Karelia, the most beautiful province of Finland before the Soviet gangsters grabbed it before World War Two, and she saw no conflict between having those plans and being a feminist – with a small *f*.

You wouldn't suspect any of this if you were to see her easy poise in front of cameras, her quiet novice's obedience to photographers' coaxing commands. Aside from youthfully fresh looks, she displays an uncommon talent for modelling clothes and shows off even ordinary garments with such flattering professionalism that whatever she dresses herself in has a look almost of opulence. She doesn't wear dresses and suits – she enriches them. The joke among photographers is that if she were to wear bubble wrap she would give it enough chic that you'd want to run out and buy a wardrobe of it. Designers quickly noted this quality and began wanting her for their new creations, and after only a few months, as her image appeared here and there, there was talk of booking her for their autumn collections in Paris and Milan and especially London, which was at the new cutting edge of style.

All in all, everyone thinks she is a quite fortunate human being, and her friends know she is a very loving one, and are glad for her swift success. From the start we sensed she would make – when she felt ready – the hoped-for good marriage and satisfying family life. Our feeling was that Karen had so much drive and her dedication to work was so focused that it was only a matter of time before she realized all her dreams. My painter friend Bill Joachim says that if you yearn for an event with all the intensity of your being, you can make it happen, and many believe the idea has truth in it. And we all felt that would be Karen's case – in fact had no doubt about it.

Sex and love – with punch

Never underestimate the power of sex. The week the special *Vogue* hit the stands it sold fifty-four thousand extra copies coast to coast, and I watched Hal gloating in his most boyish manner at something that was at best a doubtful triumph – the shot was far below his gifts (a thought, however, that I keep to myself, for family peace).

But it had what art directors wanted, and in this field, that's what matters. As one of them described it, Hal's work has in it an indefinable quality called flair. I've heard the term 'flair' used so often that I tried one day to find out what it meant, and when I asked another art director, he explained it meant 'punch'. I asked him what punch was. Well, it was hard to describe but you knew it the instant you saw it.

Whatever that important but elusive quality is, it seems to

be all that art directors care about, and after lengthy reflection, I felt after a while I was close to making a breakthrough into the great mystery of flair or punch – but then dropped the whole subject when yet another art director told me, as we strolled through an Impressionist show at the Met, that he could like Pissarro more if his paintings had more flair.

'More punch,' I said.

'Exactly.'

4

It's a dismal drizzly evening outside and as I stare at that special issue of *Vogue* I can hear an occasional taxi whizzing by below as it speeds through the empty, ghostly lit Manhattan streets, with the background wail of a police siren – that faraway endless wailing that's practically synonymous with New York City. Right next to that copy of *Vogue* beside my bed is my journal, or notebook – scrapbook, really – with the somewhat formal inscription on an inside corner:

> NOTEBOOK BELONGING TO INGE SAARINEN
> IF FOUND – PLEASE RETURN –
> > TO: Hal North Studios
> > Lex near 58th (street no?)

The ledger of life

For weeks now I've been in a bad way, scribbling down everything I thought or observed, like some demented Kafka character eternally piling up material for a mysterious project that forever nears completion but never quite makes it – 'Karen's Disappearance and Its Implications for Life, Death, *la Morale*' – something totally insane like that ('Karen and the Polish Question').

Lately I've had hours of freedom, but no longer with that youthful (all-too-brief) feeling that life never ends – the irretrievable sweetness of that! Instead I've begun to have dreary moments when I can't find something to read that isn't trivial but (as I tell myself) 'has meaning'. Everything I've ever heard about the world is such a small part of my own experience of it that I always feel I'm missing out on things, and that even my reading doesn't supply the need. That was when I decided, a few months ago, that rather than hoping some day to run across published words that *maybe* offered a connection with my living experience, I would write down my own experiences – thoughts, observations, squibs, quotes, sketches, anything – just day-to-day stuff, as I went about doing photography. My plans for that project make me think of that eccentric Greenwich Village drunk I once read about, a mythic character named Joe Gould, who, in the legendary Twenties and Thirties, went around with a composition book clasped under his arm telling everybody he was recording bar-room conversations as part of his Oral History of Our Time (and if the manuscript should ever be found – if in fact any surviving 'manuscript' is more than cosmic profundities drunkenly scribbled on beer coasters – I would give anything to read it). Once, at Minelli's Bar, I was so high on an overflowing love for Manhattan, heightened, in a sentimental mood, by Finlandia vodka, periodically replenished by the ever-attentive and sexually undeterrable Bill Joachim, that I felt inspired towards closing time to begin a similar history myself – but decided, to the world's irreparable loss, to go home and get a good night's rest first.

Life's a gloomy joke

It's not of course surprising that I'm distressed about Karen (it would be surprising if I weren't). I *am* surprised that I (and apparently only I) feel down and angry when I think of her. And: just *who* is this guy Frank, whom we all thought we knew? And *where* did they go?

For some time now before Karen went away, I've had a feeling of great rage at life, wanting to hurt it in some way, hurt it *back*, despite all the brave advice I've been known to dish out to others. Absurd of course to fault life – for what?

I read at my dentist's, the other day, an old grin-and-bear-it joke in one of those dumb magazines that seem to exist only in waiting-rooms:

> *Philosopher*: Do you know why your life is so miserable?
> *Eager Young Student*: No.
> *Philosopher*: That's why.

5

According to Far Easterners, a sheet of paper is just a sheet of paper until you put your first mark on it, and then suddenly it's an empty page. It's the same with the ledger I started, and my life.

I started the notebook – the *scrap*book – just to record things in or merely to paste in cuttings from newspapers. I'm a bowerbird, except that my nest is mental.

It is, I suppose, a family tradition. My father is an inveterate journal keeper. He has always kept a lined notebook in which to set down his thoughts and observations – jottings, he calls them. But some are quotes from a wide and haphazard reading (we are a quote-happy family) and sometimes they're just squibs or fillers he cuts from newspapers and glues on to the page (which is no doubt where I get that from). All the scraps together form a hodgepodge that reflects some concern or state of mind at a given moment. He says the jottings help him sort out what's troubling him.

I used to love browsing through his notebooks whenever I came across one of them in my searches through his desk for a letter opener belonging to my great-grandfather or looking for my mother's ancient amber paperweight with the gorgeous mayfly imprisoned in it for eternity – we are not a secretive family and he would not have felt I was snooping – and I can still recall my pleasure in spending frosty Helsinki afternoons after school sipping my mother's good Russian tea and reading items like:

AP – NEW YORK. A man tried to kill himself by jumping in front of a subway train as it entered Times Square station. He lost an arm and a leg as a result of his suicide attempt. The New York City transit authority awarded him a settlement of $650,000 when it was decided that the motorman had shown negligence in not stopping the train in time.

My father had a deep-rooted liking for America. He never lost his own sense of wonder, the wonder that people were said to have had about the Great New World many years ago, before all the wars and cold wars. It was almost as though the discovery of that mythically marvellous continent lying beyond the sea was a personal find of his and truly an Eldorado. Even so he ('the ideal immigrant to the ideal land' I once heard him say) returned home to take up residence in Helsinki, where through books and periodicals he stayed more or less in touch with 'back there'. When I was very young I remember thinking of him as a great romantic figure. He wasn't just Finnish, he was Finnish *and American*, which to my childish mind made him something out of the ordinary, larger than life, and I remember yearning to follow in his footsteps and of some day actually going to New York and living there the way he once had. He encouraged me, his 'Inge-bird', as he used to call me, telling me it was a part of life that I should fly away some day. I wanted to be a poet (as he had once wanted to be a painter before he, sadly, gave it up), but I never liked my 'poetry' (no quotation marks were ever more necessary), and by the time I moved to New York I had made the more felicitous choice of becoming a photographer instead. (I put it that way but I doubt that we have much choice in these things.)

I hold on to those youthful attempts but keep them well out of sight. Once, a few years ago, I looked at the ragged-looking pages again, found the poems even more adolescent than I had remembered them, and rehid the stuff – or buried it would be more accurate. (And appropriate.)

A *new star or a comet?*

What I need to do most of all is sort out in my mind why I am so troubled by thoughts of Karen Bryggman (and what I can do about it). She is a still-gawky, not very experienced seventeen-year-old fashion model who one day a bare six months ago blew in to New York and landed at the Felicia Modeling Agency, and just as success looked like it could be within reach she disappeared. (Is there a connection?)

I'm concerned because Karen is a friend and I'm worried that harm has come to her. She has a very naïve side and needs protecting and I feel partly responsible for her. Seventeen is very young, and in some ways she doesn't know about life yet. We may be only a few years apart but I've been around the block a few times. Several blocks, in fact.

To be strictly correct, she hasn't 'disappeared'. She has only 'not been seen' lately. *I* say she's disappeared but no one agrees.

It was I who suggested she come to New York and arranged her meeting with the Felicia agency. Dawn Felicia, well-known as a shark of a businesswoman and whose models dominate the international field – she is said to be a genius at discovering top models, though some say Eileen Ford is both better at it and a far nicer person – took one look at the classic features and slim Finnish figure (almost anorexic compared with most Finns) and, to the astonishment of everyone, signed her on after a single interview.

'We'll give it a try,' she said cautiously to Karen, who was bowled over by her luck and attributed it to America. It's what happens here.

In the first weeks, Karen was given a few small jobs by way of breaking her in to the big-time assignments that Felicia hinted might await her if she proved herself. But it was the fashion photographers and the fuss they made over her that rocketed her career: it took Karen barely a month before she had leapfrogged her way to a couple of the more choice jobs normally given to name models. (Could there be a connection *here*?)

By word of mouth, she soon became the talk of the trade, and it made me happy that a friend of mine, a fellow Finn, a simple, unpretentious person, should make it so big in America: the American dream come true. Her looks were a sensation wherever she went, in a field where beauty is commonplace.

The stampede of assignments happened so soon after her arrival in Manhattan that she began to feel as though she were leading some kind of charmed life, as in a sense she was. Then – in January, just after Christmas and only months after she landed her first modelling assignments – Karen vanished from the scene without a word to anyone.

What is especially curious is that she disappeared just after she fell in love with Frank, who was a charmer of a hunk – 'haunk', Karen pronounced it in that Finnish-English of hers that turned men on (but the particular monosyllable sounding amusingly like a Bombay horn to me). He took her everywhere and they did things together. Then they decided on a holiday jaunt – go somewhere for a week of fun. She had been hoping to see Italy (had wanted to ever since childhood) but Frank suggested they go to Marrakesh first and then on to Rome, and Karen happily agreed. Which is her style – accommodate others always, being (in my opinion) far too trusting a person. We all assumed they went through with the plan. But then someone said Frank had reappeared in New York – and no Karen. And here, there *must* be a connection.

Some still don't believe she's really gone but think she will show up again. They tell me everything's fine, I'll see. But it's the middle of February now. It has been more than a month since her disappearance, and still no word from her and no sign of any kind. I used to see her several times a week, yet I haven't received even a postcard from her – not even a phone call.

There are many rumours now. One is that Karen has disappeared in Africa. It's possible but I don't know if it's true or not. But why do I have the feeling she will never be seen again?

That thought haunts me. I must see and talk to Karen. I need to be reassured that she's still alive.

And Frank. Where the hell is *he*?

And should I notify her family? Or would that alarm them unnecessarily? Why is no one else concerned?

A *death in Turkey*

My friends think I'm exaggerating and they may be right about my imagination running away with me, though I've never had this sort of feeling before. No one could say this is a pattern with me – it's actually more my style to make molehills out of mountains. But now I see her lying dead somewhere, a picture so ugly I put it out of my mind. Not so long ago I read of an English schoolteacher from Sussex who, hitchhiking from Ephesus to Istanbul, was raped and killed. A shepherd had found the woman's partially decomposed body at the edge of a forest. In reply to the British consul's protest that nothing was being done to apprehend the criminal, an official of the Turkish government expressed regret at 'this most tragic incident' and promised that whoever the guilty one was, he 'would not go unpunished'. Whether that ever happened or not I don't know. I recall reading a report two or three months later saying that her parents were asked whether they wanted her remains shipped to Britain or buried in Turkish soil.

So administrative and so cold . . .

Poor woman.

6

A paranoid delusion

My psychoanalyst, Martin Yeblon, also wonders if I might not be 'imagining this whole Karen thing'.

I both see what he means and don't. In either case, I also see it's going to be hard convincing him I'm not operating on as narrow a band width as he seems to think. He seems to have many doubts about me, and that's OK: I have doubts about him. Which is why I also want, as emotional back-up, to work things out on my own, the way my father used to: my own 'jottings', so to speak, even though mental.

It's a new thing in my life, a shrink: I decided to join the horde. It's not that I can't deal with my feelings and I hardly ever need outside help. But this is a different order of things and sometimes you need a neutral yet empathic environment for sorting things out.

That's one of my shrink's expressions, 'empathic attune-ment' (to be exact), a phrase he keeps using – 'keeps' meaning twice so far – which may only be the latest professional buzz word, it's hard to say. But I like the expression, and anyhow, a good listener is rare. My parents and grandparents are very good listeners but they live in Helsinki and Karelia, and despite phone company protestations to the contrary, overseas phone calls are not cheap – somebody has to pay for all that adver-tising.

At the moment, in my life there aren't many people for me to talk to aside from dear old Mr Maki, a very elderly fellow

Finn for whom I 'work' part-time (help him out is what I do). But he pays me to listen to him, not the other way round, as we continue working on 'the book of my long and interesting life'.

I love the absence of false modesty. He's a sweet old man and I enjoy his company. I'm the only one who calls him Mr Maki – out of respect for elders (as I'm sure my parents would be happy to hear). Everyone else calls him by his first name, which was originally Jaakko but he prefers Haakko. In his early days in America his friends called him Haakko the Finn, which got shortened to Hucko Finn, and it took him a while to understand the pun and in the end he liked it, wondering if some deeper meaning might not be intended. He explained it to me but I thought it far-fetched: 'It's life. It means "Life is a Mississippi" – you see?' But then I thought that was as good an interpretation as any, though I didn't believe a word of it, but maybe that's just me. I don't see symbolism in things and think it was just Americans kidding around with a foreigner, because most people in this country have trouble with unfamiliar names. Which is strange when you think about it, because the whole country is made *up* of foreign names.

Take two Prozac and call me in the morning

There is of course Hal to talk to. I get along well with him too, but he could not be described as a listener, good or bad.

'But it's *not*, *your*, *FAULT*,' he recently admonished me when I talked to him about Karen's disappearance.

I'm getting more and more down about the thing. We were in his studio and this time, as a switch, he was doing his supportiveness number to prop up my badly sagging morale. His idea of supportiveness includes urging me to ask Yeblon for a prescription for Prozac.

'Even if she *were* kidnapped, how could that be *your* fault?'

But unfortunately that's all he has to say on the subject, and I find that hard to take. Fault – mine or otherwise –

doesn't enter into it, but for some reason Hal seems to feel that that's the issue. Just in general, he has a low opinion of offering assistance to others. He says he likes Karen, but I can tell by his behaviour that it's out of sight, out of mind. But then, in our past forty-eight months together (good God – breaks all records), I have learned to keep my expectations low, certainly with respect to 'us', as I would with anyone who immerses himself in work to the exclusion of the world around him.

'But I don't like it that nothing is being done,' I tell him, honestly believing he is dense.

He doesn't have much patience with unhappiness. 'What *can* you do? Hell, what can *any*body do?'

Paska! It's not a real question he's asking. He's merely telling me to give up and shut up. It's his way of being kind, I think. Kind to himself, probably.

Hal can at times be fun and I like his work very much, which are two reasons I'm still with him. A third reason is that he's sexually very active and inordinately satisfying. To be candid, I enjoy what he has between his legs and think his photography is damned good, in more or less that order. But though those biographical details are large pluses, there are important gaps he doesn't fill.

Forty-eight months! Perhaps I hang on to Hal because I don't have anyone else, which, I remind myself, is not the best of reasons. And what, I ask myself, *is* the best of reasons?

I sometimes think I have settled for him. Not good. Browsing at Barnes & Noble's I found, in a book called *Reflections on Love and Life: Memorable Quotations*: 'Women, deprived of male company, pine. Men, deprived of female company, become stupid.' (Chekhov – obviously a man who understood things.)

Full of quotes these days, all going into my note(scrap)book. I tell Hal, putting him on (which is my surest clue – completely transparent to him – that I'm annoyed with him): ' "We live not as we like but as we can," according to Menander, who knew about life.'

'Man-*who*?' Teasing me.

But despite everything, I feel an immense respect for Hal. His is some of the best work being done in New York. They may be 'commercial' images but they come out of an intensely private world and stay with you for days. I can't say that about any other fashion photographer, not contemporary.

Still, it's his personal work, the black-and-white prints, that I prefer and that originally drew me to him. My photography is not as good as his – understandably: his work has few peers, maybe none. Many say he's in a class with Avedon, whom he admires.

What concerns me, though, when I let myself think about it, is that he flouts Stieglitz's remark: 'Have you ever been in love? Only then can you photograph.'

Yes – though that sounds portentous, for in truth Stieglitz nearly always sounds portentous, but I know of no truer explanation of how to make a photograph. It doesn't sound like it until you think about it a while. Then it becomes the only statement about photography that makes sense.

The problem with Hal is I don't believe he has ever been in love – that is, with someone other than himself, not counting (he *says*) a Persian cat he once owned and whom he imaginatively named Pussy. *I and My Camera* would be a good title for his memoirs, if he should ever write them.

But I still have hope and try not to let things like that bother me. Early on I learned from my father that it is the essence of wisdom not to want more from life than it can give – a simple lesson but one apparently that needs to be repeatedly learned, at least by me. Life doesn't mean much more than eating, sleeping, working, a sharing of knowledge and, during happy hour, reciprocal entertainment (which it dawned on me one day is what most conversations are) – and bed: I like bed enormously and could spend my life in one (and if you give me a pile of newspapers and magazines and a cup of tea – or a glass of wine or a vodka, if it's late afternoon – I'm in bliss). Put those elements together and it's called living, and that's the way the days pass. In fact that's the way the years pass, and we try to make whatever sense we can of it all and think of that as experience and sometimes, after the third vodka, wisdom.

7

I got up early this morning and have been watching a greyish dawn with a soft snow falling – thoughts still on Karen. Nobody is doing anything about her, including me (if you don't count worrying incessantly, and I don't). How can anyone just disappear?

A little while ago I started a fresh batch of my favourite soup, menudo. It will take all day to finish and will fill the place with rich smells. My mother would be happy that her (not overly enthusiastic) attempts at teaching me to cook have finally taken hold. She'd either be happy or shocked since neither one of us is much of a chef. She does enjoy eating and says the plumper she is, the better her singing voice. (She's an excellent soprano and is anything *but* plump.) She also says she sings best after making love and my father's joke is he shares her bed to help further her career.

At the moment I'm back at my 'desk', which is to say enjoying the comfort of bed and listening to a pittering of snow against the windows: a soothing sound when you're indoors and snug. Occasionally the wind makes a soothing moan, a *warm* sound.

Off and on it has been snowing for days. It's no longer a street outside the windows but a down comforter hiding the city. Sometimes at night I take walks around the smoothly blanketed sidestreets of Lower Manhattan, where, under snow, the decaying old buildings look like a darkened theatre set, mysterious and rich.

'Why do you like doing that?' Hal asks, gratuitously adding he can't figure me out these days.

I tell him: 'It's peaceful. The city looks like it has been stopped dead in its tracks.' (I pause, thinking about that choice of phrase.)

I'm used to his not figuring me out, and it's obvious he's not really interested in any answer I might give, but I explain anyway. I tell him that when it snows long and deep, noises in the snowy streets are cotton-soft and un-New-York-like and that there's something sweet about that. Usually, by that point, Hal has left the room. Figuratively if not literally.

My thoughts go to a Stieglitz platinum of the snow scene taken from his window at '291'. The daytime shot of the two versions is the one I mean: it has the same feel as the view from my loft. Though it was made in 1915, you *could* make an identical photo today, almost a century later. In certain parts of Lower Manhattan those old buildings still stand. (Which is surprising: I've noticed that Americans are always tearing old buildings down and putting up new ones.)

I have a reproduction of that photo on the wall. Karen would often stare at it and admire it and I always wondered what her Finnish imagination saw in it.

I'm becoming obsessed with Karen. My thoughts are never far from her. There must be something I could be doing. Should I look for Frank? He would know (I think) what happened. But how do you go about looking for someone in New York City? Or should I report Karen missing? (And *is* she missing?)

I wonder if I should call my father and get some advice. It's ironic: my best friend in New York disappears and I'm reluctant to act out of fear of appearing hysterical, or idiotic. *She* is in danger – and *I* worry about looking foolish.

I've always considered myself fortunate in having a father who for as long as I can remember spoke to me as though I

were an adult. Even when I wa[...]
artist, I later found out) would [...]

'Vermeer discovered the Impres[...]
dred years before Monet and the ot[...]

He would tell me things of that [...]
proven useful to my work even though [...]
photographs. He particularly admired T[...]
seemingly at first unconnected but both Im[...]
end.

'They had light in their paintings,' he wou[...] [...], a little
unhappily, I thought, because his own unsuccessful attempts
at getting light into *his* paintings so frustrated him (which
conceivably is why I chose photography, where everything
you photograph, no matter what the subject, is just light, light
itself as it defines form). Thinking of this brought to mind the
talks Karen and I had about painting, a subject of great interest
to her too.

Whenever I've reflected on my own life, I've noticed that
nothing much *has* happened in it, certainly nothing dramatic
– until Karen's disappearance, that is. It is one of our oldest
wishes to be somehow transported by life, live forever in the
magic of our early years. And then of course we grow up. Or
think we do. We grow older and learn that not much changes
from day to day except what we see on the evening news or
read in newspaper reports, and even those have a certain
quality of sameness about them: while we were asleep last
night or at work this morning, there was an ingenious jewel
heist on the Riviera, a hundred thousand more women and
children are starving in central Africa, a plane has just fallen
into a snowfield in the Himalayas, a famous actress, divorcing
for the fourth time, checked into the Betty Ford Clinic – life
as a series of large and small crises of which a mere few
(fortunately for sanity) become 'news' and fewer still *really*
touch us. And I know there'll be more of the same next week
and next month, and then one day I'll be as dead as everybody
else who has ever lived – and about dying too my father said

in worrying: when I die I will be the
n't know I've disappeared.

Time is the one thing you have plenty of –
for the time being

My father is not a Zennist or anything, yet one of his favourite quotes is from a Far Eastern thinker (poet?): 'Aside from thirty thousand mornings, time does not belong to me.'

That has always appealed to me, I think because of its concreteness: that definite figure – thirty thousand. Which isn't bad, in a way, when you do the arithmetic: something like eighty-five years. (Eighty-two years and sixty-nine days to be exact – not counting leap days – but we'll stick to the eighty-five.)

But that could sound like a downer if you think about it too long – I mean, life as finite. I try not to. It's best to take the motto merely as a warning, a *memento mori*.

If you don't think about death is that denial?

My shrink says I deny a lot and he might be right. In fact I know he's right, for the most part. (If I say he's not right I'd be denying, of course.) I wish I could talk to my father about Karen. I wish I could stop thinking about her. Is that denial?

Several days have gone by with no change on the Karen front. I called my father up – it's always good to hear his voice – and all he could advise for now was to ask around and aside from that wait and see. Maybe she would show up, but if not, I might call some member of her family in Finland, and depending on what the family says, call the police and ask them about the next step. After we talked about her for a while he asked:

'How's dear old Manhattan?'

'Fine. Apart from missing Karen, I'm having a wonderful time – although next summer I might come back home to get away from the incredible heat here.'

'And the photography?'

'Fine' – an answer based more on hope than fact.

'In the dead of winter . . . the airports almost deserted'

No one seems to care about Karen though everyone claims to like her. And now that I mention it, people are beginning to use the past tense anyway – 'I *liked* Karen . . .' To be truthful, I *don't* feel responsible for her, not really (it bothers me to say that, though). But I've decided to find out what happened, where she is. But where do you begin a search of this kind?

Hal says I'm caring too much about 'this whole Karen thing' (which is beginning to bug me – the idea of her being 'this whole Karen thing'). He says I should learn to relax. *Paska.* I tell him that no one simply disappears, that something has gone radically wrong.

'You're sure we're not being a teensy bit over-dramatic?'

'What if she's been kidnapped? Shouldn't we be doing something?'

But I don't tell him my fantasy that white-slavers have abducted her into some sweaty South American tramp-steamer dockside where, under threat of death, she services drunken sailors from around the world. Or she's locked up in Africa – Morocco – desperately hoping that we who know her will locate and rescue her. I remember the look on her face as we parted the last time, a naïve seventeen-year-old smile flashed at me and which troubles me now. I make every effort not to think about her, because there's no proof that any of this is true. It's far-fetched and dramatic. It's Hollywood. (But real?)

He says that maybe Karen decided to run away. Maybe she dropped out and is living a good life somewhere – Italy. Didn't she always want to go to Italy? Well, for all we know, she's having the time of her life and doesn't want to come back to New York.

Of course he could be right, but I would find it hard to believe. (And you'd think she'd send a postcard.)

The understanding is all. (Yeah, right.)

Disappearance again, comments shrink Yeblon when I bring up Karen for the *n*th time. He says my dreams are 'classic' when I tell him that lately I've been dreaming a lot about deer.

'And the word *deer*. . . makes you think of . . . ?'

He's hinting at a pun, of course, but instead I say: shy creatures in the wild – you barely glimpse them and they're gone.

'Disappearance seems to be a recurrent theme.'

I wait a long moment, hoping he'll say more. But he only asks:

'Anything else?'

I think a moment, draw a blank. 'No.'

I feel like telling him this is all just resistance, a word I've learned from him. But he's not big on humour, I've noticed.

Towards the end of the session he said my comments on life sounded pessimistic and asked if I got depressed often.

'I never get depressed,' I said with a brightness that wasn't there before he asked. 'Nor am I depressed now. What I'm feeling right now is sorrow, not depression, sorrow about not knowing what's happened to Karen.'

More silence – the great shrink response, or so I gather from friends. Shrinks take an advanced course called Silence As Communication.

8

Sorrow and hot dogs

I was still thinking of his remark about pessimism and depression as I left. In the waiting-room I passed the person who has the hour after mine, a casually dressed, fairly good-looking hunk ('haunk'). I noticed his beautiful butt going by and felt like following it.

This was about the third or fourth time we've passed each other in the waiting-room, and it wasn't until later that I realized his friendly hello was intended for me, not Yeblon. I *think*.

Feeling a pang of guilt at my unintentional rudeness (if I'm right about the hello), I ended up buying a hot dog at a street vendor. I told the man to pile on the sauerkraut, telling myself that's what people do when they're depressed – they eat lots of sauerkraut.

'No sauerkraut, lady. Just onions today.'

'OK, onions.' (They eat onions too.)

Moderation in all things

I have a weakness for hot dogs. You should be healthy up to a point. After that, nutritionally unsound noshes make life worth living. This is from Dr Inge's Guide to Health, Nutrition and the Happy Life (*not* yet a best-seller).

I stood eating the hot dog on the corner of Lexington, feeling strangely unconnected with the life around me, which though not a new sensation felt refreshing for a change.

Am I depressed – is that possible? I love life, and I even like myself most of the time. Surely shrinks understand that there is sadness, sorrow, grief, remorse, distress, despondency, weariness, gloom, malaise, discouragement, dejection, blues, lassitude, indifference, melancholy, disconsolateness and about sixty-five other emotions, including just plain being down for a little while, that don't all have to be reduced procrusteanly – Procrustes-like – to depression. Theory as steamroller. There is more to heaven and earth than is dreamt of in your philosophy, Horatio.

Life itself the MacGuffin

True, my statements on life may sound on the pessimistic side these days, but if they do, that only means I'm not saying them right, because it was thanks to my father that I learned to love whatever is ordinary about living.

I feel it is a gift to have the understanding, even if it's an imperfect one, that life is just something happening *through* us and through all other things. And it keeps on happening – and that's all there is to it. (Phew. Clears up *that* mystery.) Some Chinese guy once figured it out: he said life is a nothing going along with something and a something going along with nothing. Really inscrutable stuff. This report – part of our series in Life Moments – has been made possible by a grant from the Dingaling Foundation (and, uh, don't call us – we'll call you).

We have enough understanding to know we're in something but not enough to know what the something is that we're in. (And if we're *in* it, where's 'out'?)

When I put thoughts like these into words, they sound trite, or worse. Or at least so many people have told me that my thoughts are trite that now I shut up about them.

Last week I thought of a very clever *bon mot*: Everything that has ever been said about life is true.

I honestly think that's good. But that's probably trite also.

(But the triteness of truths is another truth. And another triteness.)

If I think about this stuff I must be bored. Or stalling about Karen.

Because I like the way it all connects with Karen. I wonder if her family has heard from her. Would it be cruel – selfish – to alarm them, maybe unnecessarily? But maybe they could reassure me. Would I be easing my anxiety at a cost to them? No. I need to know and so do they. (Or maybe she went back home to Finland and they know where she is.)

OK, a new resolve: I'm going to try to track down Karen's lover Frank. Of all people he would surely have some clue where she is – is probably the only one who does.

But a big problem right at the start – *paska*. He and I have met a few times and I know what he looks like but I realize now I don't know his last name.

But someone might know it. I can ask at the Great Scandinavia bar and also check out the small Upper East Side hotel where Karen was staying. And take my camera – maybe go photographing.

And this decision: if there is no word from or about Karen by the weekend I'm going to contact her parents.

I started a letter to Karen:

DEAR KAREN: Deeply worried about you . . .

'Worried' doesn't convey it. I stopped, not knowing how to proceed: 'Dear Karen, I'm sick at heart and feel an aching that won't go away'?

DEAR KAREN: Are you safe? Are you all right? Why don't you write?

Jottings

I did some photographing on my way to Yeblon's office. My visual jottings. The walls of buildings have jottings too, the graffiti in my neighbourhood proliferating like mad (The Flowering of Lower Manhattan). 'Show Superiority to Misfortune – Kill Yourself.' Also the inevitable, the eternal: 'FUC' (reflecting also the decline in education).

Many thoughts about Mother since her letter about her recent recital (the annual music bash in Helsinki, heavy on Sibelius of course). Among her songs was '*Kom Nu Hit? Död*', a family favourite. (More death.) The words are in Swedish (which none of us really speaks). I like Shakespeare's own words: 'Come Away, Death!' Shakespeare, death and Sibelius are closely associated for me. I love *The Swan of Tuonela*: a moving piece – about death.

And death = Karen.

I told all this to Yeblon, anticipating a comment like: 'Deaths and disappearances.' (Instead of deaths and entrances. He resembles Dylan Thomas so much, especially in profile, that I'm tempted to ask if he boozes it up and then writes lyric poetry.)

He surprised me. Or rather didn't surprise me. He said nothing.

Bodies pile up

A cemetery strike. Death, death, death. Bodies are not getting buried. Dead but not gone.

Lately Yeblon has 'begun to wonder' if I'm aware of my preoccupation with death. Maybe, he says, Karen is only a cover for deeper preoccupations. He has good manners and reminds me also of my father except that our views are so different. Which is not to say Yeblon is necessarily wrong.

' "Start as you mean to go on" – a phrase of my mother's,' I told Yeblon during a recent session, and added: 'How could anyone apply that to Karen's life? She was starting just as she meant to go on. And now what?'

No response from dependable Yeblon.

He told me several times recently that I keep 'blocking things out'.

'Well, isn't that what denial is for?' I kid him.

No response. He doesn't like humour. With him, it's all work.

I asked him for a Valium. No response. How about some Prozac for a human in distress?

I have heard about shrinky silences so I don't think he is being rude but 'working'. (*'Dis* you call *voik?*' my irrepressible landlord, Mr Nussl, would say.) Although if he was 'empathically attuned', he was empathically attuned to whom (or possibly what)?

These ruminations are a way of attempting to feel well again, and I understand my father's need for jottings in his notebooks, and understand also his liking for New York when he lived here as a young man. It was a special place for him – as it is for me. I like working in it and meeting all the terrible, rude, incredible people here – freaks, nobodies, once in a while a somebody and even a few rare good ones, all of them making Manhattan the purest poetry there is. Naturally, when I say things like that, my New York friends don't consider themselves part of any poetry (and they're certainly not pure) but consider me off the wall, not in possession of all my marbles – just plain whacko – nuts. A British acquaintance once described me as two sandwiches short of a picnic, a phrase I like so much I'm willing to be that even though it's her quaint way of saying I'm crazy. (But mad north by northwest.) I reflect that my obsession about Karen could drive me mad.

Speaking of which, New Yorkers think everybody in the world is mad – except themselves, of course – and of course everybody in the world thinks that New Yorkers are mad. Both are right.

The specialness of Manhattan, even now, during one of the coldest Februarys on record, is indescribable. But it's *the* city for me. New York is what life is all about.

9

TV: the news at noon

The cemetery strike is still on – eighteen thousand bodies unburied, piling up fast. You don't realize how many people die in New York every day until something like this happens.

This morning a wildcat garbage strike was called. And meanwhile there's talk that air controllers at JFK might again go on strike. New York is fast becoming Strike City, although it falls far behind Paris, which will always hold both the Oscar and the Palme d'Or on that. When Hal flies to the City of Light for a fashion shoot, he takes out strike insurance to eliminate uncertainty. (He has trouble with ambiguities, Hal does.)

News story

In the paper this morning (and in my scrapbook by 2 p.m.):

AP – SAN FRANCISCO. A 13-year-old runaway girl from Santa Clara County was beaten and tortured by four teenagers, two girls and two boys, and sold for $1 to a man who raped her in Golden Gate Park as several men and women watched, police reported yesterday.

The girl, described as 'homeless and living in the Tenderloin for the last six months', was taken to the Youth Assistance Shelter after being released by her captors. The police were searching for a number of other youths for more questioning.

The girl had been dragged from a coffee shop at approximately 9 p.m. by the two teenage girls, who took her into a back alley, where they assaulted her with a Coke bottle and when she fell to the ground kicked her in the legs and stomach. They claimed the girl was wearing clothing belonging to one of the boyfriends.

The police said the girl tried to escape by attempting to board a bus at the corner of Clement Street, but one of the girls prevented her, calling to the two teenage boys for assistance. One of the boys dragged the girl into the park and handcuffed her to a park bench and hacked off her long blonde hair with a Swiss Army knife. After that he burned her chin with a cigarette.

The boys, accompanied by their girlfriends, then walked the victim up and down Clement Street, offering the services of a 'nymphomaniac'. As a small crowd gathered, the boys announced that she 'gives it away', but they then amended that to 'a buck a throw'.

A man in his twenties stepped out of the crowd, threw a $1 bill on the ground and led the girl into the park and behind a bush, whereupon he proceeded to rape her, witnesses told police. No one in the group who had witnessed the scene moved to help the girl.

She was rescued four hours later by two sixteen-year-old boys, who fired a sawed-off shotgun into the air, thereby persuading the teenage gang to let her go. The two young rescuers then flagged a passing patrol car and Officers Denby and Macaros arrested the four teenage offenders.

The police are looking for the man who bought her for $1.

I really needed to read that. And all day long I was all too aware of just how long four hours is. And what if you're kidnapped and spend the rest of your *life* as someone's sex slave? Don't think about such things. Always opt for denial.

Quest

I keep going to the Great Scandinavia bar about every other day, hoping to bump into Frank, so maybe I won't need to contact Karen's parents.

Karen took him there a few times and the owner and barmaid got used to seeing him. In the past I used to stop in once a week, after my stint with Mr Maki and 'The Book' – the story of 'quite a few interesting adventures', Mr Maki says, dictating it to me. A very dear man. I feel sorry his wife died a few years ago and he lives alone now.

'Any word about Karen?' I ask Tuula, an au pair and one of the regulars at the Great Scandinavia bar on her days off (the blonde Tuula, from Riga – the Estonian).

'Ve heff no word.' I don't know if she understands what I'm talking about.

Frank hasn't been seen at Great Scandinavia lately, rumoured to be away on a new trip. Alone or with a new girl? They don't know. They don't, apparently, ask. But maybe he'll be there this weekend. Should I go back? Yes – *and* get in touch with the Bryggmans.

After leaving, I walked crosstown towards Fifth, heading ultimately for the Rambles, to see it under the thick snow covering Central Park. It's a sexual hotbed in warm weather but a frosty delight in winter.

But I got no farther than Park Avenue. I fell in love all over again with the avenue's broad expanse, looking downtown at it all covered in magic white (pre-soot). How to photograph it enveloped in a drizzly-powdery snow blowing wispily every which way? It would take a Gene Smith. Or a Clarence White. Or Stieglitz.

The afternoon darkened as I stood on a corner looking way down towards Grand Central, at the colourful traffic lights sweeping down in a double line, just taking in the scene, conscious of myself as being present in this time, now. I was alive – here.

Misty lights appeared through the falling snow as limousines and taxis whished down the browning slush of the broad divided avenue.

Photography as Weltanschauung

In Manhattan, promise comes as evening descends. And how do you photograph that? In any case, what*ever* we photograph, we're only photographing our feelings, takes of our experience.

On Park Avenue, if you leave out the skyline of the twin rows of apartment buildings, you sometimes feel you're in the heart of a European city, although many of the cities of Europe feel drab and unpoetic to me after New York – though not Rome, not ever Rome. Rome for me is Raffaello, and for Karen too. Raffaello used to call it an early day at the School of Athens and go home and fuck his girlfriend, until the people who were waiting for the mural to get done – Popes, dukes, whatever – decided to bed the girlfriend on some kind of futon arrangement next to Raffaello's scaffolding so the two of them could knock off quickies. Start as you mean to go on.

I know that Karen meant to go on to Rome. She told me that before leaving. And I can't help wondering if she really did get there after Marrakesh – or before – and I'm hoping she did and is fine – though, without news, nothing can persuade me to believe that.

No news is not good news. No news is no news.

Digressions: verbal photographs.

Digressions: self-protection against thinking about Karen.

I think denial plays an important part in life. So why deny ourselves it?

Kodak moments

I love love and I love love stories. The way to my heart is through love stories. I told this to Yeblon.

No comment. Before graduating, shrinks take a seminar in

The Role of Silence As Intervention (or something). The healing profession's supreme achievement is the art of not replying to questions. I told this once to my GP – GPs have it in spades – and he wittily told me to call him in the morning if I wasn't feeling better.

'"They made love as though they were an endangered species,"' I said to Yeblon, wondering if he would even ask who I was quoting. (Frankly I've forgotten. It's from my scrapbook but I didn't note down the source.)

No comment.

We tend to hide our tenderest feelings (which is obviously what I was doing) because putting them into words makes them banal, especially the deepest ones.

Triteness again – corn. But our deepest feelings are the ones we live for. And are not corn. Corn versus art.

'Don't let the word EROS bother you. It stands for "Earth Resources Observation Systems."' (Kodak ad)

I seem to have a thing about this – corn, I mean.

The problem of corn is everywhere, in everything we do – like a conversation I overheard in the Village, the wife gazing up at the sky on the one clear day we had last week and saying to her husband: 'How would you describe that blue?' Husband searching the sky with a wife-accommodating look and sounding supportive and interested: 'I dunno – a Sunday-blue sky?' But no. Even he's not satisfied with that (although it's not bad) and reflects further. I like them. They're middle-aged and obviously still in love. I feel a surge of happiness for them.

'*Kodak* blue,' he suddenly says and triumphantly she agrees. (I'm glad they have each other.)

The corn is in our thought, even the way we perceive. Is art the absence of corn? Blahblah.

More on love

I love love and the pleasure of mutual discovery – one of the great pleasures, and so rare. Like Hal at the beginning. At first you can't believe your luck and feel the happiness of loving this man you just met and want to know all there is to know about him. At this stage a new love is the promise of new life. The love grows and you want to see him often, be near him, do things with him – possess him. You can't stop thinking about him. You want to know what he's doing right now. Where is he at this moment? You restrain yourself from mentioning him to friends but hope they will ask you what's been happening in your life lately so you can bring him up casually ('Oh not much – there's this guy I met, and uh . . .'). You can't silence an inner jubilation. You love his hair, admiring it when you think he's not looking. You love the low quality of his voice. Hearing him speak stirs a heavy feeling that begins in your cunt. You want him to be inside you, to fill you up, lie heavy on top of you – and love you the way you love him. You like the smoothness of the skin on his back, his way of turning his head, the way his body moves when he walks. The most trivial thing takes on interest – and the first time you make love, you undress self-consciously but with a wild excitement, the momentary embarrassment of baring yourself before him while voyeuristically taking in his body – and hoping he will like yours . . .

Who is Hal, what is he?

That trip with Hal to Eleuthera, I was curious about how he would come. I wanted to hear what sounds he made during orgasm – to see if he was a grunter, a moaner, a held-back silent one (oh please, not that). I wanted to examine his body, the form and hang of his balls, feel their sponge of meat, admire the proud look of his stiffened cock head and its pageboy look, admire the shape of the upcurving muscly shaft and its girth and hormonal smell, burrowing my nose in the soft thick dark-brown furry bush at the base of the cock, wrapping my fist around the pole and jamming my throat down on it all the way to my stomach (would if I could).

We lay in bed and talked for hours until my body was achy and stiff but I didn't want to move and break the spell of the first time. (No, the second time – but it was the first *real* time, so slow and easy.) Everything he said echoed thoughts of my own, but different too and interesting, and we laughed over the silliest jokes.

'What's Italian foreplay?' – 'Eh: you awake?' (That ancient one was his, and I laughed merely over the way he told it.)

I said: 'In a woman who's obese, how do you know where to put it in?'

'How?'

'You roll her in flour and look for the wet spot.'

In a slaphappy mood we went through all the bad ones about women going to the Virgin Islands to get recycled, 'some requiring several trips', and the rock-bottom kiddy classics: 'The Tiger's Revenge' by Claude Balls, 'A Russian Tragedy' by Ibityourcockoff, things you would never in your right mind repeat to anyone except to someone you were falling in love with and feeling safely silly with – providing he loves you too or at least makes you feel you're going to be all right for a while (which is often the same thing and sometimes all you get). It's never the joke but the other's laughter that gives the pleasure.

When we were back in town again I felt like writing him love letters though I saw him every day, and that was a way I had never felt before. I didn't write of course – it was just a schoolgirl whim.

Actually I did once. I dropped him a fun card with only the word 'Hi' on it. I got no response. No acknowledgement even. But I had signed it '*Moi*' so maybe he didn't know it was from me. Which told me far more than I wanted to know.

He wasn't enough in love with me, if at all, and if I revealed too strong a desire for him it might have driven him away and even now I'm afraid it would. Men seem so fearful of the seriousness of life, similar to the surprising anxiety they feel at seeing the monthly crease of blood in our underwear. (My call-girl friend Iris says it evokes their primitive fear that women have teeth in their cunts.) I don't know what falling in love does to them but it does seem to crowd them or threaten them in some way. And if their feelings for a woman get between them and their work, it's goodbye love. They don't even have to think about it.

Hal at least is better than Malcolm, my handsome pal during late adolescence, a bad choice for me. But I hung on hoping – him too (a habit I must correct). My mother often said it takes effort to make a relationship work and of course that's true. But it can't be all effort and with him that's what it turned out to be.

I still feel terrible remembering being sexually frustrated by poor religious Malcolm and making myself come that time out of desperation, thinking, 'Oh Malcolm, oh my love,' and caring about him with all my being because he was so sensitive and so affectionate – really a dear but so much more devoted to Bible study and telling me he wanted to join a seminary and become a 'teacher of truths'. I was eighteen and the prospect of some kind of monastic marriage (as I imagined it would be) put me off. Our relationship was always being tested, I felt, by ancient strictures, or those chronicles of Mesopotamia, Old Testament places with ugly names like Og and Oz, until I began to think of the Holy Bible as the Holy Rival.

So here I am in the middle of my life (twenty-six anyway) finding myself stopping by snowy woods in Manhattan wondering why I have not yet found what I began looking for so long ago.

This is the quote-y way I used to think and then would say things to myself like 'O Frost! O Whitman!' and feel carried away for a moment.

Sometimes I feel I'm an anthropologist. I am a photographer

cum anthropologist cum diarist on Manhattan Island in the city of New York – heart open, spirit free.

But down.

> *DEAR KAREN: We all miss you. I would like to feel I'm writing this letter for nothing and will just throw it away when you're back, which I hope will be soon.*

I threw it away then and there. It sounded artificial.

10

I don't of course mean I'm an anthropologist in a South Sea, Margaret Mead sense – girl circumcision rites or second-cousin murder rituals (whatever – I mean, God only knows what nuttiness the late Neolithic mind comes up with – or ours). Or worse than rituals, headhunting. No, even worse than headhunting is kidnapping. Of girls into sexual slavery – not restricted to exotic tribes or Marrakesh: think Upper East Side, think civilization. Think New York.

Paska. Don't think. Act.

I went last night (Sunday) to Great Scandinavia and asked Mrs Jaaskelainen, the owner, if she remembered Frank. Yes, of course she did. Did she know his last name? No, she didn't. Did she know where he was? No, she didn't. Did she know anything about him? No, she didn't.

A terrific start.

She thought he lived in Harlem. How do you find a Frank in Harlem?

But at last Hal has an answer for me. He looks at me with gentle tenderness in his eyes and says: 'Give. Up.'

A letter:

Dear Mr and Mrs Bryggman: Do you know where Karen is? . . .

Paska.

Dear Mr and Mrs Bryggman (oh so casual): *As the self-appointed 'big sister' to Karen, I'm telling tales out of school but, well – she's gone to Europe and hasn't even sent me a postcard . . .* (No, no.)

Dear Mr and Mrs Bryggman: I'm sure I'm over-reacting, but Karen went to Europe a few weeks ago and I haven't heard from her since and . . .

(Better? Yes, but still dumb.)

The trouble with anthropologists

Hal says I would make a good gossip columnist. He's right if he means I digress all over the place. That's why I can't really keep a journal. So I think I'll divert gossip into letters to Karen. That would make more sense. There's something fake and stilted about diary-diaries. I read a Japanese diary once in which the author said, 'Nothing to report today.' The next day he wrote: 'Nothing to report today' – and so on, for several days in a row. I understood he *thought* he was trying to make it all sound real, but my feeling was, who cares about nothing to report? And in any case, unless the guy was in a coma, there couldn't *possibly* be 'nothing to report today'. (Talk about denial.) And anyhow, is it real to read about life in a way that sounds artificial?

Sometimes I bore myself.

(Now, for example.)

DEAR KAREN: What I don't like about anthropologists is that they leave out the daily important things, like how do the people of tropical forests select a good spot for shitting? . . .

Would I really write to Karen about that? Absolutely.

Karen and I used to compare notes about American toilet habits and even thought of doing a guidebook to the women's johns ('comfort stations'!) of New England, expanding the series across America as our guides became runaway bestsellers. *Places to Piss and Places to Miss.* Instead of stars, we'd award three spiffy toilet seats to indicate a highly recommended pee place, and a broken toilet bowl for johns where you wouldn't even *think* of lowering your ass (and I mean just to *squat* over without touching anything – *megayuck*).

We used to talk about things like: Does the tribe in the tropical forest have a powwow about the site of a dump, or does a clearing get established in honour of an ancient chief's hurry call before breakfast one morning after that funny-looking fungus in his dinner the night before? And who determines behind which bush only the women go for a midmorning pee klatsch? Hal says women's peeing customs differ greatly from men's. He says in a business office, when men want to take a leak, they go to the john and piss, but not women. Women gather up their handbag, confer with a friend, form a toilet-convoy of two (sometimes more) and make the pee break into a social event. They reappear ten minutes later refreshed and cheerful, their make-up redone, and able now to get on with their work.

All this may seem ridiculous but it's really of cutting edge interest, apparently: Karen and I recently read that the French have put out a Michelin-style guide to the johns of *la ville lumière.* Hotels like the Crillon get top rating, with, in place of stars, three air-freshener symbols, meaning that *le* can (*le,* how you say, wat*air*) is not only *propre* but refined – an experience *absolument* not to be meesed.

What got us was that if an anthropology report ever *does* get into anything interesting like genitals and sex it seems obligatory that it be about courtship rites and the tribe's sixty-two restrictions on instincts that most Kansans – hell, even John Calvin – would approve of and you wonder how those people put up with it. Also they never seem to tell you whether Polynesians or the Kalahari get tired of the missionary position and for a change of pace go down on each other for some satisfying sucks (which I happen to know that Karen digs). Only Eskimos receive the full treatment, but there I suspect it's because in the frozen north there's a lot of Wife Swapping in the Old Igloo (but nothing about anybody going down on anybody, though). Wife swapping, from what I gather, is a high-interest topic in sophisticated North America. In civilized France nobody swaps: you just go out and cheat and sophisticatedly look the other way when your mate goes out and cheats, and the score remains about equal in the long run. At least that's the illusion (sh) the men hang on to.

Why don't more anthropologists go into customs and mores *outside* rain forests or deserts or islands – I mean, around the world more familiar to us, one that we think we know? Like the mores of Prague as compared with the mores of Los Angeles, or Hollywood. I seem to be among the very few people interested in comparative everyday activities, the things that hardly get a mention in anthropology books.

Karen and I talked a lot about that too. Her interest is not in anthropology but ecology. Her goal is to go back to Finland and get involved in the ecology movement and preserving the environment. It's amazing to think that even Karelia can feel threatened, but she assures me it's true.

Tribal customs of different places fascinate me and help me understand (I *think*) why some New Yorkers find me immoral: my values are not theirs. My values are Finnish (both parents' side), or Finnish-personal, and in no way immoral. I'm amused when American friends tell me I have a dirty mind, but that's because New Yorkers are puritans, something they can't see. But this is a whole subject that it's best not to get into, although I almost always get into it.

I have nothing personal against Kansas. After all, Topeka has the Menninger Clinic in it (even in Kansas there is a need for mental health), but Kansas evokes for me places like Philadelphia, which for the longest time when I was growing up in my home town of Jyväskylä I used to think was the brand name of a spread cheese whose silvery package I liked and once begged my father to buy thinking it would taste like Eskimo Pie ice cream. The only thing I know of that's worse than Philly is Salt Lake City (unless you need to trace your genealogy back to Alfred the Unwashed or Ethelred the Lint Gatherer, and then you're in clover). And speaking of washing, it was against the law in colonial Philadelphia to take a bath – to just lower your ass into a nice warm tub on a cold winter afternoon. Possibly the British colonists were afraid they'd discover that underneath those debutante cotillion gowns and Louis XVI culottes they all had – *genitals*!

The random nuttiness of life

That sort of thing would make for interesting anthropology, and I once had the thought that somebody ought to do a Guinness Book of Archaic Laws, meaning regulations still on the books that are no longer enforced. There's a law in the Bronx that says you're not allowed to shoot deer from the back of a tram, and in Tulsa, Oklahoma it is illegal to go to bed unless (fussy fussy) you first remove your boots. And in California, 'America's cereal bowl' – full of nuts, fruits and flakes, all right – until recently in a place called Pacific Grove you had to leave your window shades open a few inches so that a passing police officer could see you weren't playing cards. (Horrors.) In contrast, in Little Rock, Arkansas there's a quaint city ordinance that sounds like it *should* be archaic: after the wedding ceremony, the county clerk presents the newlyweds with a bag of mouthwash, a deodorant and – I kid you not – some window-cleaning spray. (Either Little Rock has an enormous amount of dirty windows or – don't dwell on it – the window-cleaning spray is multipurpose.)

DEAR KAREN: There are many assignments floating around and it's too bad you're not here. Hal has been busy day and night with summer wear for Vogue *and* Harper's Bazaar, *with the result that I'm not getting boffed as often as I would like. I hope you are.*

That beginning of a letter hasn't seen the inside of an envelope yet, but I did mail my *very* tentative and (I hope) tactful inquiry to her family this morning.

DEAR MR AND MRS BRYGGMAN: Let me introduce myself. I'm a friend of Karen's and not having seen her for a while I wondered if you might have news of her. If you do, could you please forward her address to me? I would be much obliged. With my warmest regards, Inge Saarinen.

11

Hal has begun to bug me. He makes out with all the models he photographs and then claims it's their idea, they seduce him. When I comment on his suspiciously high acquiescence rate he gives one of his happy little fuck-you grins, to which I feel like replying 'Up yours', having learned most of the art of American cursing from him. (I learned the rest from Iris – though with Iris Stavropoulos, it's graduate-level vulgarity, or the Feast of Pure Sleaze.) But I hold off saying anything back. Later I wonder why I always do that. Something else to take up with Yeblon.

These are mental jottings, or jottings as drivel depository.

And speaking of the drivel, that makes me think of Saul Perilstein, my friend Roz's shrink (and definitely *not* mine). There are shrinks and there are shrinks. Perilstein is one of the latter. At a party, once, he said I should have no psychological problems. Why? I ask. Because, he says, I get along well with my father and my mother. Well, I tell him loftily, I don't in fact have what you call problems, except that I drink too much, though only Monday to Friday and on weekends and holidays. He didn't even crack a smile (which is probably what it deserved).

He came back with a quiet, non-judgemental 'Hmm' and I felt bad. I made a note to ask Yeblon why I felt so aggressive towards Perilstein. (Why I *feel* so aggressive.)

Most of the time I feel sorry for him. Somebody once described him as an advance man for the decline of the West.

He's a divorced psychiatrist from Park Avenue and Quogue (and inevitably known as the Quack from Quogue) and goes around wearing an olive-drab parka to look like one of the boys and you can tell he bought it at J. Press or Brooks Brothers and paid three times more for the same thing than he would have at an Army and Navy store. The other night (at an opening at the Modern) I heard him say to a woman that when he saw her his heart 'felt like it was off on holiday', and the same night to another woman I heard him say that when he looked at her his heart felt like 'a speared fish'. (He was all heart, you might say.)

The same night, leaving the Modern and feeling champagne-babbly and out of late-night taxi-ride boredom, I chitchatted away about Perilstein to a driver named Nathan or Nelson Goldstein. He replied, 'Go figure.' Ten per cent of the taxi drivers in New York are from Brooklyn and half of them are named Goldstein, which they pronounce Goldsteen. Anthropology: all taxi drivers in New York say 'Go figure' (or its longer equivalent 'Go understand').

La Forza del Destino

There are many subcultures in Manhattan and I'm surprised at how few of them New Yorkers know about. For example, a taxi subculture. I'm a taxi freak and so is Iris. Iris has been known to pay her fare in trade even for a short hop if it's in the early-morning hours. There are taxi drivers who work the graveyard shift to get fares like Iris and it surprises me she's not more careful – I don't mean murder but disease, though murder too. She does it, she says, because her father once yelled at her that she was a goddamn whore – this was back when she had reached the advanced age of thirteen (and was already set in her ways, right?) – so she did the obvious thing, deciding then and there to grow up and become a prostitute to prove he was right so he'd hate himself and his misfortune in having raised such an immoral daughter. 'Being the cocksucker that he is. "See? I *am* a whore! Squirm, motherfucker!"' She routinely describes her father as a dickhead and names of that sort, really shameful things to say about your own father, and hopes he'll have the good grace to commit suicide, ideally while she watches, even handing him the weapons and mopping up the floor afterwards.

I once asked her, 'Don't you enjoy sucking cock?'

'Depends on who the meat is extending from.'

'Then how could you possibly use that expression as a put-down?'

'Context – it has nothing to do with sex. When you understand the context, it becomes a description of character.'

I understand, but still. It's like men calling each other 'cunt'. I could never understand using that word as an expletive. It's such a nice word and such a nice part of us, something that both men and women love.

It was easy for Iris to become a prostitute. In fact, she practically *fell* into the teenage escort business (which I hadn't even known existed – another subculture). Someone in a limousine approached her on the street one day around the time her father was doing wonders for her self-esteem, and although she told this stranger to fuck off (probably in so many words), she kept his phone number on the all-purpose ground that you never know. And as things turned out, she was glad she had.

As a kid she was so emotionally distraught by the crazy home life provided by her father that her classroom behaviour went to hell and they transferred her to some special education thing in the wilds of the Bronx, like sending her to Siberia. But after an IQ test, they entered her at Hunter High, just across Central Park from her parents' place over on Columbus (and even closer, as it happens, to the escort service she eventually began working at, which is off Park Avenue, near the Russian Consulate). Partly because of her IQ score and partly because of her new height and almost a regal physical endowment (since ripened further) they jumped her a year or so, she said, 'to a grade where the boys jumped whatever held still long enough, with me presenting youthful but easily overcomable objections, feebly expressed the first time' – which is the way Iris has learned to talk through her upper-class clients, or does when she's not in her more usual cursing mode. One reason I like Iris is that she bears a certain resemblance to Karen. (But the idea of Karen becoming a prostitute is one I don't want to think about.)

The moving finger . . .

It was when Iris (about a year or so later) met a classmate named Brian, a Kansas creep – a little redundancy there – that The Event happened.

One day Brian and Iris were meeting for lunch at a drugstore on Madison Avenue. Brian was supposed to come alone but he showed up with Frank, a friend he bumped into on the way over. A person of colour (as some describe him). As the three of them sat there eating their BLTs, Karen Bryggman walked in, a ravishing sight she was but looking as lost as an orphan.

She was Iris's new acquaintance, 'the new model from Finland'. I had earlier introduced them to each other, and after that they met one day buying clothes at Henri Bendel's, where Iris, feeling an unusual (for her) access of kindness, had helped her out with tips on shopping.

It turned out that Karen was *supposed* to meet Iris at this 'd*rr*awg store on Madeeson', except that it was to have been later in the afternoon. And it was supposed to have been just Iris. But Karen's spoken English was not on a level with her reading and she had misunderstood Iris's message and arrived for 'launch'.

Which is how it began.

And having writ . . .

When the group broke up, Frank asked Iris for a date.

That amused her. To begin with, Frank is, probably, in his late twenties, which to a seventeen-year-old is early middle age. Besides, Iris by now gets hundreds of dollars an afternoon through the escort service. And she said no. I learned the truth a few days later, at least Iris's version of it, when she told me she took one look at Frank and found him so drop-dead handsome she had to have him or die but turned him down because it was obvious that Karen was the one he had eyes for. In fact, she said, Frank couldn't stop staring at this new girl in town.

'You don't know anybody?' Frank asked Karen. He would be glad to show her around and take her places – it would be a real pleasure for him.

Although Iris couldn't have explained why, she said (several times in fact) she felt something happen between Frank and Karen, something she felt would lead to deep friendship and even love, and although she herself didn't want any part of the 'usual man-woman crap', she didn't want to stand in the way of it for Karen if that was what would float her boat. (I think she was also smart enough to know when she couldn't compete.)

And that was the fateful event.

There is never any distress signal when an event happens that turns your life around – no light that switches on or some signal that's fired off. The principal person, Karen, was not even aware that something unusual was happening because nothing unusual *was* happening. Fateful events are uninteresting in themselves: a series of banal circumstances coming together in an unremarkable way. It's only afterwards that you see significance in the person's stare, or a smile, or detect a plan (if there is one) behind an apparent coincidence. Or you connect things up in some new way – the misunderstood message, the too-early arrival, a friend's friend bumped into on the street: the events of ordinary daily life that no one would pay the slightest attention to but that seem to build with inevitability. For me, in retrospect, the horror of it all is precisely in the triteness of the elements as you look back and see them fit together.

All this assuming I'm right, of course. If my worst fears about Karen turn out to be true, then now that it's done, there's no undoing any of it, no second take, no running the film back from the ending – except in my mind, where I continually rewind Iris and Brian's meeting for lunch and reshoot the afternoon – the three of them meeting *without* Frank's being there or *without* Karen's showing up (she's unable to make it because she's home nursing a cold, or is out on a fashion shoot, or even perhaps is back in Finland, anywhere but in that Madison Avenue drugstore between one and two on a freezing December afternoon).

The romance followed swiftly, with me and all of Karen's new acquaintances excited for her, and then the short remainder of the story – what we know of it: during a hiatus in assignments, Karen and Frank went off on a jaunt to Marrakesh, a destination spontaneously proposed by him in place of Rome, and accepted by her because North Africa was another Helsinki dream of hot sun and days of love. And besides, she was at that intoxicated stage where she would have gone on a long weekend to anywhere Frank suggested. He knew a place where they could be happy for a short stay with friends who – rare in that part of the world – were unprejudiced enough to enjoy the free and liberated spirit of women from Europe and America. Northern women were like unbridled horses, a special pleasure for men in that part of the Arab world. She would like his Marrakesh friends. They led a life that no one dreams exists . . .

She told me all this and didn't share my suspicion over women as 'unbridled horses' and a 'special pleasure' and a 'life that no one dreams exists'. I must be paranoid but the phrases gave me the shivers – which made her laugh. ('*Paska*! Aren't you *afraid*?' I asked. 'No, no, no,' she said, laughing. In moments like that I felt like an old maiden aunt out of touch with youth. Or reality.)

Then the day after I mailed the letter to the Bryggmans, I

bumped into a girl I've seen many times at Great Scandinavia. She told me that *she'd* heard that some of the Finns who frequented the bar saw Frank returning some time later, the colour of his face even darker and richer-looking, and asking Mama where Karen was, had anyone seen her. And good-hearted Mama – the sixty-five-year-old barmaid and mother hen to Finnish au pairs – replying in her interesting English, 'I dassent know.'

Hearing this I raced uptown to see Mama, but she told me no, she had never seen Frank after he and Karen disappeared. So either it was a false rumour or he had dropped in to the Great Scandinavia on a day when Mama wasn't on duty.

12

'Mama', or Carita Amssi, recently celebrated her sixty-fifth birthday. Her husband is seventy and sturdily built and still so handsome in her eyes she proudly refers to him as Mr America. But she dearly wishes he wouldn't look at other women so much. (High acquiescence rate there too. Hm-hm-*hmmmmm*.)

Women as men's fantasies

Mama is instructed by the owner of Great Scandinavia, Mrs Jaaskelainen, to charge half price to the Finnish au pairs who gravitate to the bar from all over the Upper East Side. They make it their headquarters because it is the only place in New York where Finnish is spoken – mostly among themselves when they congregate (and also with Mama). Drink prices are reduced for them, not for humanitarian reasons – for example, that au pairs are wage slaves – but to induce the women to act, unwittingly, as customer bait: some of the bar is teasingly visible from the busy crosstown street, and the sight of two or three girls perched on barstools, observed through a glass darkly, entices men who would not just wander in if they could see from the street that the place was a quaint but empty bar. Mrs Jaaskelainen knows that when male fantasies about women, which are mysterious enough to begin with, get darkened by expectation, all the lonely drinkers, from Yorkville to East Harlem, come out of the woodwork. Accordingly she arranges it so that the bar is not very brightly lit – not so incidentally offering a 'goot' saving in electricity. I more than once heard Mama, in that incredible Åland English of hers, explain: 'For ven is too much light, it's no be go have good beez-nez.'

Obviously there was an art to running a bar (as in all things), and the system makes everyone happy. The au pairs as a class are sex-starved. If your social life is restricted to Thursdays off, there is no way, at eighteen or twenty, you can have a sufficiency of boffing. And this way they were assured of encountering men at Great Scandinavia in large enough numbers to provide them with a range of possibilities during mating hours, ten-thirty to midnight (mating *season* being confined to those months that begin on the first). And Mama acted as a screen, to warn them against certain men she has a barmaid's (and very experienced woman's) intuition about.

But though the au pairs are glad of Mrs Jaaskelainen's self-serving generosity, they prefer Mama because she goes Mrs Jaaskelainen one better: behind the owner's back the girls' drinks are free (typically vodka and cranberry juice) and Mama even sneaks in a double vodka if she judges that Paula or Ulrika or Leena is in a mood to enjoy it and a condition to hold it. The extra kickoff amount, poured with a wink so conspiratorial you'd think KGB files were being smuggled from the Kremlin to the Finnish border, is occasionally accompanied by the advice that they keep their money for their return to Tampere and Savonlinna and Jyväskylä and Rovaniemi. The role of den mother to girls living alone in a big city comes naturally to Mama. From before she met Mr America, she still remembers, years ago, how little she liked living as a single woman, lonely and often broke, in the big city of Turku, which after Åland was a metropolis.

Mama the barmaid

Mama has the kindly Elderly Uncle look of the giant tortoises that live in the Galápagos Islands. And she's that big around too, tall and robust as a Viking even at sixty-five (but Finns are not Vikings). Her kindly eyes, with an ineradicable humorous look, are sleepy-lidded, and the deep lines below that half-eyed look are open feed bags – the kind that lead to corny jokes about bags having bags. But when you get to know her you see in those homely eyes a concern for her charges and also for certain customers – the ones who show an obvious respect for women.

And the Wicked Witch of the North

Mama is in great contrast to the owner, Mrs Jaaskelainen, who could pass for a fairy-tale witch and is said to put up with anything as long as it brings in money. Even Mama (not so) secretly dislikes their brief changing-of-the-guard meetings, when the owner comes in to relieve her post. Late Sundays Mrs Jaaskelainen regularly drives in to Great Scandinavia from Bucks County, Pennsylvania, by consensus a fairly impressive achievement at seventy-seven years of age (with pancake she can look surprisingly fiftyish in a kind light). Sunday night is when business is dead and she doesn't want to hire a relief 'beembo' who will make money for doing no more than 'stand around and to be scratch her ass' and maybe sneak in drinks and, who knows, possibly even dip into the till. When I happened by that recent Sunday evening – the time when Mrs J. stonewalled me about Frank and Karen's disappearance, or non-reappearance ('I don't know,' 'I don't know') – I was impressed by her evasiveness, although it *could* have been ignorance (unlikely) or an expression of boredom with anything in life lacking economic interest.

There are many stories about her greed for money. There is the sad but true joke that in the last year or so, she has made money even from the dead and dying.

In one case it was her husband. On a beautiful August day he went out to their Bucks County barn and hanged himself from a rafter after leaving an open shoebox full of cash on the kitchen table, a copy of his retirement pension agreement newly signed over to her and his last will and testament that made her his sole beneficiary. The point that caught everyone's attention was that she thought she should have gotten double indemnity because of his death by suicide. There was no clause to that effect in her husband's policy, and that pissed her off for weeks, and resulted in everybody's disapproval and amusement in about equal proportions. She didn't close the bar on the day of her husband's funeral because there was no funeral, only a cremation, and she told the crematorium staff they could keep the ashes and do whatever they liked with them, startling them with the suggestion that they might even flush them down the toilet for all she cared.

Her eulogy for her husband: 'He vas Svedish. In Sveden dey commit suicide.'

Nascentes morimur

The other case involved Lasse. Lasse is a middle-aged Finnish seaman, who shows up at Great Scandinavia many evenings a week. Not long ago, for safe keeping, he gave Mrs J. his savings of eight thousand four hundred and eighty-five dollars, and three days later she reported that a burglar had broken in the night before and the only contents of her safe she had found missing the next morning was Lasse's money: she had forgotten to lock the safe for just that one night.

It was she herself who told everyone about the theft, I think to demonstrate her honesty: if she were the thief, would she go around telling a tale that nobody could believe? (To remove any doubt we might feel, she supplied us with the correct answer too: no, she would not.)

Everyone knows Lasse. He's always at the bar late at night by himself (by choice) and if you try talking with him or saying hello (I used to and even Karen, out of Old World politeness, did the first time she went to Great Scandinavia), he never manages more than a forced murmur that you learn to interpret is a greeting. It seems obvious he's at a point where something like the gain or loss of a few thousand dollars no longer matters to him. Possibly Mrs Jaaskelainen knew her man. He was known to talk of suicide as a peaceful and legitimate option at his age (forty-nine or fifty, at a guess), and Mrs J., who once reported this detail, maintained that if he talked about suicide it meant he would never do it, so we needn't be concerned. ('My husband never vunce mentioned suicide.') Someone even suggested that that was why she had taken the money: to her it seemed a waste to see it just sitting there – although in what sense it could be a 'waste' and after only three days of 'just sitting there' was never made clear.

On those evenings when Lasse leaves his furnished room at the southern edge of Harlem and drops in to Great Scandinavia he sits hunched over the untouched drink that entitles him to a place at the bar. He sits in the middle of the semicircular bar, right where the nipple would be if the bar were a breast. I have often seen him like that right up till closing time, elbows planted before him and eyes, half-shut and lifeless in the manner of depressives, staring at something neither near nor far nor anywhere.

'He's waiting to die,' Karen said.

I find him interesting because his wish not to live sounds genuine and I feel has to be respected, but I hope he won't act on it. There's something sweet about him that brings out pity, though when I mention this to others they can't see it: they think he's just someone who has cracked and those things happen in life and more commonly than we think. He merely sits at the bar, immobile, and Mrs Jaaskelainen, brazening things out because she has all the time in the world, waits patiently for him to die of heartache, or whatever it is he's dying of, so she can be free of guilt (if any).

Some of the girls at the bar don't think Lasse has cracked but has been broken by life, the way older people sometimes get, and they feel it's sad but that nothing can be done about it. Some think he's mildly insane since he suffered cardiac arrest off Honolulu as his Finnish tanker approached port and the crew had him helicoptered to shore and moved swiftly to an operating table, where, after administering adrenaline

64

or whatever 'heroic measures' they take in such cases, he gave a sign of life and doctors got his heart going again. As Lasse was reviving in intensive care, the director of the service, anticipating his patient's joy at the rare experience of being brought back from the dead, turned away in shock or sorrow (or possibly anger) from Lasse's reproach: 'By what *right* did you bring me back?'

> *'I tell myself I can't go on any more and then I go on some more'*

DEAR KAREN: *I would like to bring you back. How about a sign of life?*

Yeah, sure. There is now almost a permanent feeling of emptiness in my stomach.

> *And meanwhile, in the land of the living . . .*

Once you understand the economics of the fashion world, it is very believable that Hal gets seduced, but I can't altogether accept that it's always the model's idea, not entirely.

I very much doubt, for example, that Karen, in one of several shoots she had with him, talked him into going to bed with her. Far more likely it was the other way round. My view of what transpired (trans*pires* – present tense) is that he has a hefty dong and males being what they are, it gets Hal into things, in his case fashion models. If the ancient Greeks were right that each sex act shortens your life, Hal should be ready for Happy Valley Rest Pavilion around the age of forty-one.

But whatever he does doesn't seem to diminish my interest in him, because in many respects he has a view of life I like. A right view of life, right values (leaving out infidelity) and a good dong are the essentials of an average one-sided love affair, which, let's face it, is what we're having. At least he's not into drugs, like Catherton (not to mention that whole entourage) and somebody else I could name (Corelli).

Not exactly the stuff of tragedy, or comedy, for that matter, though in moments it feels like both to me. Which raises the question of why I'm still with him.

Of course to him it's not one-sided. We're just a modern couple making it together in an open relationship – open at his end, not mine: I attach like a barnacle if I care for the man. Part of the one-sidedness is that he's most of the time off somewhere in his head, even while we're hugging in bed. Though *he* is obviously only enjoying an ongoing fling with me, *me*, I'm crazy-ass in love, or have been, or maybe just was. Or maybe just crazy. (Or maybe just ass, Hal, the ever-witty, would say.)

I couldn't and can't help it. A quickie romance we started in Eleuthera, on an assignment for Revlon or Elizabeth Arden, some biggie, is currently completing a four-year run. The affair was really my own doing, for two reasons: first, I was seduced not by him so much as, if the truth be told, by his photographs at the Waldenheim Gallery, which exhibits his personal work, not the magazine stuff. And second, I just plain like humping a lot and he eats vitamins by the pound. So I went along as gopher, primed and panting.

And impatient – champing at the bit even.

Life is short, art is long, the occasion fleeting,
experience fallacious, judgement difficult and the position
ridiculous – but what the hell

I was champing at the bit because that was not our first time. The first boff was almost an accident, both of us high from a very liquid corporate luncheon and doing it standing up in Central Park over near Daniel Webster, whose pedestal reads: 'Liberty and Union / Now and Forever' (the first half, I thought, appropriate and the second half, I hoped, a prediction). I loved it – the boff, that is. It was spring and the trees had tiny apple-green branch tips, with just the very earliest buds peeping out and the barks all beautifully blackened by rain. The trees were dripping with soft raindrops that clung to the branches in the unseasonal chill and fell – *tip* – to the soil below – *tip* – a cold languorous dripping. A gauze of mist surrounded the distant trees like visible air. It was a very moving sight, reminding me of childhood years in Finland. There was no one in the drizzle except, far away and moving away from us, a thin old man in a black coat, the top of him enclosed in an enormous black golf umbrella. We stood under a tree, me happily slammed up against the trunk by his battering-ram hips, orange slicker falling open, a tear in the crotch of my pantyhose enlarged by that surprisingly filling cock, carried away in lust for each other, humping rhythmically and me idiotically saying, 'Never done it in Central Park – standing up – daylight' and coming fast, him right behind, and a wonder we weren't caught and arrested. The Eleuthera assignment was right after that, and Hal was mad for me then and couldn't get enough. Said he was going to start a diary devoted exclusively to me, saying he had become a changed man, I was opening new doors for him, and blahblahblah, none of which I believed. (Right.)

But, when all was said and done – 'sad and done', you might say – he was like most men and I don't know what it is about them. You think you're talking to a rational human being lying next to you between the sheets, with that marvellous skin smell that men have that's faintly metallic, like copper, and him occasionally making nice grunting sounds in response to what you're saying. And then you notice the smile is frozen in place and actually he's climbed back inside his mind and is somewhere else and you might as well be talking to yourself, which as it happens you are. How some men accomplish that I'll never know. Possibly it's a little-understood aspect of testosterone.

13

Mrs Bryggman didn't waste any time replying. Within ten days I had a short note from her saying not to worry, probably Karen was having a marvellous time and *much* too busy to think about writing postcards. Obviously Mrs Bryggman is fairly enlightened about what young couples in heat get up to on jaunts to Europe, but. But. But.

Meanwhile, Hal keeps coming up in therapy. Martin Yeblon thinks I'm preparing to get rid of him ('disengaging my libido,' he says: how clever of me).

I need to work out my feelings about a lot of things. I seem to be involved with hordes of creative people and sometimes I'm not sure I like it. Bill Joachim is a special case, of course, as Roz's lover – though that never stops him from trying to make out with me or with anyone he so much as imagines as boffable (or considers a challenge). But I put up with people's shenanigans if I like their company.

About Hal: Martin – that is, Yeblon (he wants me to call him Martin) – intensifies my doubts about our relationship, not unintentionally, I think. Martin *should* ask me why I settle for so little, because I think more and more that I do. The only reason I'm not yet convinced is that everybody I've ever talked to in therapy thinks they're making terrific progress when they start going around saying, 'From now on I'm going to start thinking about *me* for a change.' I always feel like saying, 'How's that different from what you've been doing all along?' I don't think Hal is *that* bad, and besides we have a long history now, and some of it quite pleasant. In fact, *very* quite pleasant.

The best love is the love that grows slowly, and it's that thought that inspires me to be patient with him (maybe too much so), that plus, as I said, a truly inspiring dong: Superman's cock, if he were ever to flash it at Lois Lane (I can see her going all dreamy-eyed as her body turns into oestrogen mush), would resemble Hal's. It ain't the meat, it's the motion, true, but face it, the meat has its importance. It's a myth that size doesn't matter. A cute acorn, however captivating it may be to chuck one with your pinkie as you shower together, would not be the hottest of turn-ons in the sack. The only women who think size is unimportant are those whose partners are well-endowed and, not acquainted with men more modestly hung, don't know how dissatisfying a teeny dick can be. Or else they're people from Philadelphia, who never think about such things except in fantasy as they while away an afternoon in bed reading their favourite turn-ons in Nancy Friday while hubby, who lost interest in boffing them two years into the marriage, is safely out of the way at work and will come home too tired for a roll in the hay anyway.

Hal's own nickname for his frequently upright friend is Studley, which seems appropriate enough. Little-known anthropology (little known, though, only to men): some men actually baptize their cocks, as though it were their child. That surprises and amuses me every time. I have so far known, or have heard about from friends, a cock named Dooley, a Willie, a Buddy, a Prince Rodney, and a very redoubtable Percy – the last belonging to my friend Perry J. Pierce of Sydney. Also: Slim, Humphrey Bogart, Junior, Baby Jim, and Wallbanger, the source of these five last being Iris. She also told me about a young guy who sported an elaborate tattoo and inscription on his cock: 'The Bearded Lady.' ('This,' she said – I believe without irony – 'is a man with problems.')

I've heard of a few female counterparts too, my favourite

being from my English friend: she calls her pussy her 'Merry Christmas'. (So many cheerful connotations!)

It's interests like these, openly expressed, that have (I *think*) earned me a reputation for immorality. (If anyone ever taught the silent majority how to read and if those good people actually *read* the classics – Chaucer, Rabelais, Catullus, whatever, *dozens* of others, ancient and modern – the great literature of the world would be burned in huge bonfires outside public libraries across America.) This reputation has acquired for me the nickname of Humper Inge – behind my back, of course, to spare my feelings. (But then my friends, to keep me informed, tell me what's said about me behind my back: what are friends for?)

'Humper Inge' is mostly envy, of course. Other women at Great Scandinavia would *like* to enjoy humping, I mean more than they pretend to (especially 'da Svedish'), and it does something to them to know that I *do* enjoy it, a helluva lot in fact.

And I'm easy too, sometimes coming while Hal is still slipping it in (sorry I took so long), followed by a baker's dozen or so of the leisurely spaced-out variety except for orgasms three, four and seven (more or less), which, thanks to the energy level of vitamin-enriched Hal, can be seismic.

Hal's thumbnail sketch of me though not flattering is *fairly* accurate: I drink like a fish (on occasion), eat like a horse (when famished) and hump like a rabbit (always). (And I hope forever.) It's a question of values, he tells me – Hal the philosopher.

Which is what he almost became, a philosopher, until he regained his senses. He dropped Philosophy 101, the usual Heidegger inscrutabilities – what is time, where is it happening, how do I know I know that? not to mention who gives a *fuck* if a falling tree makes a sound when I'm not in the forest to hear it – and decided instead not to get even a BA but become a fashion photographer. This is known as a midcourse correction, or wrench. Not all midlife crises happen in midlife.

(In fact hardly *anything* happens in midlife, from what I gather, so it's not the worst time to have an occasional crisis: keeps your interest going.)

Of course you don't just step into being a fashion photographer any more than you just become a philosopher. It takes years of wading through high-octane ad-agency crap, in the case of fashion photography, and besides, it's photographs you want to make, not photographs of pantyhose. But to survive, you need to have, in Hal's charming expression, an income coming in, so you look for something, and if you're lucky enough to get into the fashion world, the revenue can be dizzying – if you're willing to make an initial investment of ten or fifteen years of hard work and also have talent and luck. Hal originally was an assistant to Frontera, who, from what I gather, had earlier been a sidekick to Avedon back in the days of a legendary art director called Alexey Brodovitch, and watching Frontera work, Hal picked up the ropes. After a couple of years he branched out, taking with him a humongous account (it's a cut-throat field) thanks to his agent Roberta (that friendly and rare kind of lesbian who adores her dead father and therefore likes men, but in the end it's women who have the milky boobs plus one other feature). Anyway, the point is, what I like about Hal is he chose photography over whatever he might have done if he had gone for a BA or, worse, an MA. What gives me the right to say this is that I *got* an MA. I took seminars in the philosophy of art (I was young), and then, as though *that* weren't bad enough, I went on to get an MFA in the history of photography – starting out as I meant to go on, right? I then . . .

Cut the crap.

14

If I doubt myself it's because in Hal's view my mind jumps all over the place as every new thought sizzles through my synapses. (He doesn't talk much but there's a zinger factory inside his head that works overtime.) I told him that things have begun to turn me off and reminded him that that state of mind doesn't induce clarity of thought. I said I didn't know what was bugging me (a lie: Karen) but sometimes talking to someone about things helped sort out feelings and I appreciated his being there and listening – and so on, unburdening myself before going to sleep. Or so I thought until he asked me in a quite cheerful tone how it would be if I just piped down for a while, it being pretty late, so please shut up, and then adding, 'Just kidding about shutting up' (right, Hal).

Hal, Hal alone, is an excellent reason for seeing a shrink.

And what does shrink Martin Yeblon say? 'But nothing keeps you in the relationship except yourself.' Thank you, Martin – and let's stay in touch.

The bedtime habits of a creative artist

I'm (sort of) living with a guy who at bedtime gets in and out of the covers five or six times before he finally settles down – out of bed and back in again just *getting* things: water, a sleeping pill, plus calcium tablets, *plus* passiflora, *plus* Melatonin – enough sleep-inducers to knock him into a week of hibernation, except that he wakes up at dawn with a start, after six unrestful hours. And last of all, a final pee before bed – sometimes so brief you know it could have waited. But I have to say, on the plus side, at least he sits down when he tinkles and the john seat *chez* North is always nice and clean. (Probably thanks to his mother, who must have done quite a job on him, though: more than once I've turned on the kitchen tap for a glass of water and then heard his footsteps padding obediently to the john followed, sure enough, by peepee sounds.)

But he's right, Martin is – was right even before he knew the half of it, which is that Hal, the man I think (thought?) I'm in love with (have been in love with) has nightmares. In addition, he's a hypochondriac and is plagued by a heroic portfolio of phobias. Moths and tunnels I can understand (without sharing), but he has a fear also of crowds, closeness, the number eighteen (?), ice cream (??), sneakers and West 110th Street (go understand). Aside from that, he thrashes around in bed despite pills, calcium tablets and whatever, twitching and thrashing around so much I have trouble falling asleep or staying asleep. And not only all *that*, he gets petulant (in and out of bed), becomes very demanding and gets violent when his work is not going well. He sinks into depressions and then becomes dismissive of my efforts in photography. And this is just the short list (I'm leaving out things like his wanting me to apply vitamin E oil to his very tight asshole, which is a first for me and – trust me – a last). Yet with all this, even with his bedding other women down, I don't bear him malice, not to any noticeable degree. Why? I ask myself (aside from masochism).

'Good question,' says Martin, a modern-day master of repartee.

But at least he didn't ask me (didn't have to – I thought of it for myself) why I'm harbouring a fantasy that I (and only I) can save, change, rescue and straighten out poor old fucked-up Hal.

But Hal is also helpful, at times shows concern and would like to be better than he is but doesn't know how. And to be honest, he has in moments been kind to me and shown me pointers in making fine prints. I can't leave that out. And has been generous in creating my portfolio and getting an occasional modelling assignment (as for example another mail-order catalogue soon! – which promises to pay well because of the sheer quantity of the work), though God knows I hate modelling, especially ready-to-wear middle-class house-wife stuff. But I can't complain: I'm still living on the assign-ment I completed six months ago.

So far, seeing a shrink is not helping with 'this whole Karen thing'. Ever since I told Martin how much I enjoy boffing, he nudges my 'free' associations toward sex. I told this to Roz the other day – in town to attend Bill's upcoming retrospective at the Whitney Museum – and she said: 'Sounds like he's empathically attuned to your Merry Christmas.' (I told her about that – we compare notes about sex.)

And sex reminds me. I have decided to go see Iris. It's just possible she can provide a clue about Frank's hang-out when he's not at Great Scandinavia.

Besides, I need to see her again. We may be worlds apart in practically every respect but there are some things we can talk about and she does cheer me up. And her resemblance to Karen has a comforting effect.

15

After Iris

I felt strange looking her up, as I always do. I feel like the Mature Older Woman in the Life of a Young Person.

She is extremely attractive but also for a 'call-girl' extremely young: just seventeen, an age I barely remember. With her precocious body, a sculpture by Phidias, as I judge through her clothes, Iris began leading a double life of school and work in her sophomore year in high school, declaring as her sole income the tips she gets as part-time hat-check on Saturday afternoons in an East Sixties French restaurant, La Chartreuse de Parme (where she lies about her age).

(Parenthetically: She says, 'Skip the Shar-truce: its "gourmet cuisine" and "organic" veggies are frozen food packages bought in bulk from one of the Brooklyn families.')

She's working there only until she can conjure up some other cover story, one she would not find distasteful. The share of the tips she gets for a night's work are not enough even for a homeless person to survive on, although that's not her reason for working. Most people don't know that hat-checks don't receive the tips the customers think they're leaving them. At the Chartreuse de Parme the customer inserts the tip into a locked mahogany box inside which there's a metal box, and on Monday afternoon some leg man in his sixties, probably a small-time retired hood from the old days, goes around the territory established by the local family (another interesting subculture) and empties various weekend takes into an old shopping-bag with a canvas-bag lining: the daily take gets heavy by the end of the Upper East Side run.

Iris makes so little money legitimately that she declares triple her 'honest' earnings to keep the tax people happily ignorant. The reality is that Iris's income as a teenage call-girl has from the beginning been fairly upper-bracket. If you include her Wall Street investments, paternally counselled by her favourite stockbroker client-friend, a man named Harrington, she has saved this past year alone one hundred and fifteen thousand undeclared dollars, thereby creating two problems for herself: one, where to stash the swag that keeps piling up, and, more immediate, how to replace the boring hat-check cover. Imagine earning hundreds of dollars for an afternoon boff, then going to work later and having to say '*Thank* you, sir' for a cheesy dollar tip, which you then have to split with management. I mean you can sympathize with the way she feels held back by her job when all she wants, as she says, is a life dedicated to prostitution: a boff makes better economic sense, and here the feminists are right, God knows. (At least this is Iris's reasoning, and I bear in mind that she *is* seventeen. You would have to be that young to speak of it as '*honest* prostitution'.)

I phoned her at her parents' place, having her permission to do this, and got her just as she was about to go out (to call the Presidio Escort Service for messages from a street phone). I asked if we could meet that afternoon. Lowering her voice to a whisper, she said she would love to but can't. She would be seeing her supreme court judge (Lonigan, Logan, some name I didn't quite catch) later.

What did I want to see her about?

About Karen, I said – and she made a small, not too happy sound.

'Another time. Tomorrow I have to see Gil.' Gil was Harrington. 'Maybe next week.'

She also mentioned that Bill has been pestering her. Energy is eternal delight.

A *father's balls*

I am always surprised by how mature Iris is for her age. I suppose it comes with the territory. And maybe too out of her associating with her financial adviser and steadiest client, Father Figure Harrington.

'He shows me how to make wise investments.'

For a while she had considered buying real estate and asked him what he thought about acquiring a small abandoned lot in the South Bronx and maybe another parcel in Nevada, or perhaps Utah. He told her to wait a bit, she needed a cushion first, and also she was probably not legally old enough in some states to sign contracts. To say no more than that.

He buys and sells stocks under the name of a fictitious company he set up for her and through his accountant pays her taxes for her. In gratitude she has offered herself to him for a 'lifetime all-expenses-paid no-holds-barred honeymoon' whenever he feels the urge, which is a fairly safe offer given his age – eighty-*eight* (forgot to mention that). But that's for when she pulls out of the 'life'. Right now he pays. Business is business.

I said I had to hand it to the old boy, to have a body in good enough shape to make love at his age (or does she get the prize for Magic Fingers – or the Palme d'Or, so to speak?). I asked how he was in bed.

Her face got a little cloudy as she said, 'He's a gentleman and all that, and very considerate, but have you ever seen a pair of eighty-eight-year-old balls?'

She doesn't say so but I think she loves him a little (despite that small detail). The man is an honest kind, it appears, and deep-dyed paternal – a common-enough story: youngest granddaughter Darcy is the 'apple of his eye' and a slightly older version of Iris, and he 'wouldn't feel right' if he didn't pay Iris the going rate for his afternoon sessions ('Worth more to me than any shrink') as his earnest contribution to her nest-egg. He really wants her to get ahead and encourages her to think about going to law school some day, with the gentle pressure that she give up any thought of ever quitting school.

There's a great bond between them and he keeps saying to her, 'Think of your retirement years,' and in fact has told her that so often she had to remind him once, about a year or so ago, 'Look, I just turned six-*teen*, fuck rice sakes' (he's still working on her diction).

He says he is crazy about her and she believes him, not because of the not-to-be-believed cellophane-wrapped steamer baskets of fruits he sends her at the escort service but by his behaviour when they're together: even out of the sack he can't keep his hands off her and some afternoons she has to remind him that the stock exchange has closed (he still works, incredibly enough) and it's time for him to go home to Beekman Place and wife and din-din (they sometimes play at his being Iris's baby).

Iris says, 'To really know a man, you have to see him when he's over seventy-five and has a hard-on.'

I'm not sure what that means, but if it's a life lesson, I think I'll leave that one on hold. (Eighty-eight-year-old balls?)

16

I went down to the bottom of Manhattan while more thick snow began falling. I mostly wanted to clear my head of Karen thoughts – a hopeless effort.

The snow has been falling heavily for a week – March coming in like whole *packs* of lions – and I went down to the docks, thinking in a singsong way how I like all things down, down to the sea again, downstream, down the hatch, go down on someone, eiderdown, put-down, up and down, downtown, don't let me down . . . the last leading right back to Karen again (guilt, the gift that keeps on giving).

You can't think about being down when you're down because when you're down you're too down to think objectively about it. This is a sample of the ripeness of my thoughts in the twenty-sixth year of my journey through life. *Nel mezzo del cammin.*

The graffiti in a women's john: 'Thighs so wise and golden fur.' The universal preoccupation. How poetic, sound here mattering as much as sense: 'Thighs so wise.' Evocative, rhythmic, conveying life: I enjoy it as I pee, reading the wall and swaying my ass slightly raised above the disgustingly untouchable seat that had previously been tinkled and sprinkled on. What are such thighs? I imagined men – in bed, not here – kissing and burrowing their snout in a muffy pungent golden fur.

I peed so long I almost developed a cramp in my legs. A half-hour later I was still repeating obsessively, 'Thighs so wise and golden fur.' The things that people put on john walls. I once spent a week in Amsterdam and in one women's john alone gathered three winners, all in English:

> Life is a dick.
> I love Bennie's penious.
> Nothing is harder than her cock.

What Inge did next

But then there are the cold, dead-of-winter thoughts too, with snow everywhere, more snow expected, drifty sidestreets like snowy meadows in which buried cars are hummocks of snow. It's an urban Finland. In certain streets of Lower Manhattan the inhabitual absence of moving vehicles makes the place feel as if it had been invaded by Quakers – except not a horse in sight either. No pictures. Bummer.

I get recipes from Iris, who gets them from her mother, Medea, an interesting woman, descendant of Athenians (as she tells you any number of times), who comes out with mysterious things like, 'There's no spring without autumn.' (Go figure.) Hal says I know nothing but crazy people and that's what's disturbing me these days.

Hal's a helluva nice guy but should stick to photography. If I so much as mention Karen to him, he tells me to forget about her, she's one of the crazies. He doesn't believe she's disappeared. He said the other day: 'What are you going to do, stop living and straighten out the world? If she doesn't show up and you're *really* worried about her, do something constructive, like call the police, or call the Missing Persons Bureau. Or write to President Fuck-Face-Whatever. People don't just vanish except in films.'

Hal has spoken.

I was shocked the first time, but that's not an act he puts on: he honestly is not *sure* who the current president of the United States is. Well, so he claims. (He's only voted once in his life. 'My candidate lost.' 'Who was that?' 'I forget.')

And if I only know crazy people, what does that make him?

Pretty bad weather and I've been doing a lot of reading. Mark Twain lately. Enjoyed this: 'Uncle Abner said that the person who had took a bull by the tail once had learnt sixty or seventy times as much as a person that hadn't, and said a person that started in to carry a cat home by the tail was gitting knowledge that was always going to be useful to him, and warn't ever going to grow dim or doubtful.'

Five minutes after I read that I ran across this in the paper:

A pet Persian cat suspected by vets of having animal schizophrenia was put down after attacking Miriam Harrow, 57, of Avebury, Wiltshire, and her daughter Mathilda Malachy, 32, who suffered 90 cuts and scratches. Nurses at first thought the pair had been in a car crash.

Probably Miriam and Mathilda had carried the cat home by the tail.

And that made me think of sex slaves. What do they do when they're captured and kidnapped – do they scratch and claw like cats? At what point do they succumb to their captors, give up any hope of escape?

I was still reading when Bill called, wanting some photos of his paintings. It's not the kind of work I enjoy, but I said yes. I hoped he wouldn't make a pass at me – vain hope probably.

It's my fault, really: I don't discourage him enough, especially since I keep going to his studio to see his work.

For a fleeting second I wonder if *he* had anything to do with Karen's disappearance. But highly improbable.

But I love Bill – love the way he acts and talks. I can see why he and Roz get along so well. One time Bill was seated at the bar in Minelli's next to a well-stacked bimbo with a blank look on her face and he turned one of his unctuous smiles on her and said:

'How would you live if your life *had* meaning?'

Legends

When Bill drinks he insists on paying everyone's tab, a habit that over the years has attracted dozens of drinkers whom he knows when sober only enough to greet 'Hi.' One night Bill and Roz tallied up what he had spent in the past year at Minelli's. It came to eighteen thousand dollars, which of course is chickenfeed these days. Sue Damson was selling Bill's paintings for five hundred thousand dollars apiece now, and he had a tax consultant who advised him to limit the number sold each year for maximum tax breaks. The Met recently acquired one of his early paintings for one million, eight hundred and seventy-five thousand dollars, a 'handsome example of his middle period' (his late twenties!) that was sold to them by none other than Rupert Damson, Sue's husband. Bill had sold it to Damson before he got connected with Sue's gallery at a time when he was having trouble paying four months' back rent on his loft. That was six years ago. He had asked Damson for a thousand dollars for the painting, the amount he owed, but Damson wouldn't give him a penny more than six hundred and Bill took it.

Part of the trouble I have is that his tales, his gossip of the art world, are byzantine and quite fun to listen to. He calls them his 'Fur and Feather Reports'. Once he caught on that I liked them, he kept providing fresh instalments, outrageously embellishing as he went. He told me I looked like one of those people who have never given much thought to American toilet bowl design but in fact it's pure sculpture. He said there was a sculptor who used to work in terracotta and then got so involved with glazes he began doing ceramics and then one day switched to making dinner plates, and finally ended up doing toilet bowls for a living and became 'one of the finest toilet bowl designers you'll ever meet'.

I never look for relevance. I just enjoy the flights of fancy. But I always feel there's sadness in this humour, that he's profoundly unhappy. It doesn't help when he says: 'Let's have another round if we want our lives to have any kind of structure – and those are my dying words.'

As he becomes more and more cynical about life, his paintings get bigger and better and more colourful. He has fallen into the unhappy-but-successful artist's trap: 'If I drink and kill myself and that enables me to make these paintings and enjoy success, I'd rather drink and kill myself than go on living and *not* be able to make these paintings and enjoy success.' A sort of Mephisto thing except that it remains unconscious. At least that's what I think. Sometimes the whole art world seems that way.

The feeling of pain and rage that leads him to go out and get drunk every night has made him so profoundly alcoholic that I sometimes think the only emotion he can feel any more is the pain and rage that make him go out and get drunk every night. He seems aware of the irony because when I once commented on it he replied.

'Self-defeating, sort of.' His voice, when he said that, sounded little-boyish and soft. My heart went out to him.

He said, facetiously, his sole ambition was to appear one day on a postage stamp: 'First-class mail, of course, none of this nineteen-cent Susan B. Anthony shit.'

When he talked like that he was back to his old self.

Turning now to the simple life . . .

It was from Iris, the champion curser of the Upper West Side (East Side too, and Brooklyn – hell, the champion curser of our time) that I learned to live simply. I eat cheaply and well. Most of the time I cook anything that can be made by slow simmering – stew, for instance (usually meatless).

Basically I like soups: lentil, soybean, yankee bean or my favourite, menudo (hominy and tripe), the cheapest and most nutritious of all. And the tastiest when the menudo behaves well.

I once got a really great Mexican recipe from a doorman on Park Avenue. He was actually a Panamian who had lived in Tehuantepec, where he was married to an Aztec. She gave birth one day to a yellow-skinned squinting baby greatly resembling the local Chinese Bible salesman, and that was it: it was off to Manhattan and the life of a doorman and goodbye *Meh*-hee-co!

A recipe for good cheap food

Anybody who knows food knows that corn, which is what hominy is, combined with beans (which I personally add in) is richer than steak and healthier. I buy my supplies in a Puerto Rican bodega, soaking the beans in water for a couple of days before starting a soup. I get the tripe from a butcher on Second Avenue, shred it all up and mix it in with the beans and herbs and garlic. When I make menudo I make a gallon at a time to have food for a week, dumping in chick peas as I go along, or split peas or navy beans or anything that's handy. The gallon costs less than ten dollars for a week of good food, and I have never felt physically healthier in my life.

Karen asked me to teach her how to make it, she liked it so much, and the two of us once polished off a gallon and a half in three days.

'Better than herring every day,' she said.

This concludes today's food report and we return you now to our studios. Any breaking news about Karen's disappearance? No, no breaking news about Karen's disappearance.

17

Actually, nobody ever guesses I'm Finnish, or Finnish-American, because of the bigness of my appetite and things like menudo. But they don't know Finns and their love affair with the stomach. Finns eat and drink with a passion.

Another thing about Finns (Byron here, bless him): 'Finns make love a lot and assassinate hardly ever' – an observation I particularly like: emphasis always on boffing. I wouldn't have minded a roll in the hay with Byron, club foot and all.

And another reason people don't guess I'm Finnish: I don't have the typical Finnish accent: 'I thought I voot call to see if I coot come op for a leetle while and maybe ve cook a fiss?' Their idea of a fun date: get together and cook a fish. (Better not forget the vodka, though.)

That's the way Karen speaks English. But less coherently when excited.

'Fiss': it's difficult for Finns to make the *sh* sound, as in *fish* – although they get around it pretty easily when they want to put you down, as in 'I sink you are fool of sheet!' (Practically the worst thing you can say in Finnish is 'Smell shit!' – which they know how to say in English too: 'Smell sheet!')

I'm almost always taken for Norwegian or Danish until I start talking about bodegas and kosher delis and Hebrew National. And then when I tell them my name is Inge, they ask whether I'm Swedish or Dutch. Nobody ever thinks Finnish. There must be something unexpected about being Finnish. Karen too: she was always being taken for Swedish because of her Swedish name. But she's Finnish, from Åland. (She's from Turku but she's also from Åland. Like Mama.) Funnily enough, Finland's most famous name, Sibelius, isn't Finnish at all, there being no 'b' in the Finnish alphabet – a piece of trivia I sometimes drop on people, thus enjoying their profound lack of interest.

Actually, as I was telling Martin (after he told me I don't free-associate enough), few things surprise me nowadays. I'm getting used to unexpectedness, life's contrasts, people's imaginings. The whole thing, the whole *shebang* ('sexist phrase', I point out to him, 'but also sexy'), seems like fantasy to me. Uptown and downtown, for example, is a contrast (and a fantasy). Lower East Side bodegas may be fine but I also like Lex and Third in the Sixties and Seventies, where I also sometimes go shopping when I'm uptown doing something like seeing Hal. I'm not a snob but the Upper East Side is an area of town I like because it exudes comfort.

And it has its own form of unexpectedness: it is the only place in America where you can be waiting at the supermarket checkout and looking at a model on the cover of *Elle* and turn around and see the model standing behind you on line – a shocker the first time it happens.

Keeping one's shrink happy

This gets us back to Martin's favourite subject. I hear him shift in his seat when we approach sex. He tries to sound clinical but the male comes through, poor fellow. Actually I sympathize: the good news is he's not a eunuch. (I wonder how many times a week he boffs Mrs Yeblon and whether she's happy with the ration.)

Like all provincials, I tell him, New Yorkers pride themselves on being superior to others and quite special in their degree of sophistication, in fact supercool. I have to smile at that. I remember on one of the dog days of August seeing a six-foot gangly model walk into Gristede's wearing regulation blue-jean hot-pants with obligatory frayed edges and a blouse unbuttoned down to her ankles, with one 'unruly' nipple (a little romance novel here) of a peekaboo breast doing a lively little jig. Life ground to a halt. The customers were so supercool that the only ones who stared at the dancing tit were the manager, the assistant manager, four checkout persons, an inventory clerk, the butcher, the butcher's assistant, four women shoppers near the checkout counters and a male customer. There was only one male customer in the store at the time.

Who am I, what is me? – like

A sign of life: a letter from Mrs Bryggman. Do I know where Karen is? Would I be kind enough to tell her, when I next see her, that her family is concerned about not hearing from her?

Paska. If I weren't so down I could get furious at this late awakening of anxiety. Besides, I had looked to her for reassurance for my *own* anxieties.

Progress so far: nil.

I've been in this down state for a while now (an accumulation-of-gloom mood), fighting off the feeling that my life would forever stay as it is at this moment (the gloomiest of glooms). The search for Karen is going nowhere and my plans and projects (such as they are) do not inspire me to think that anything will be resolved at all – though I may learn something about myself, with Martin's help. (I make fun of him but what's a shrink for?)

I want a breather to think my life out, not just live it on the run. (I'm getting profounder by the minute.)

Gloom attacks used to go away with a little Sibelius, or a bowl of menudo. Now they sit like black ice in my feelings. It's a case of heartsickness.

I keep remembering the feeling I had way back when I was twenty-two that the world, which was just coming into focus as the place I was alive in, would be there forever . . . the security of total innocence. I wanted to shake things up and thought maybe for starters I needed to get away from men and sex for a while, a resolution that lasted well into the afternoon, when I got the hots for Hal and went over for a quick boff – his term originally (meant affectionately).

Being hot-blooded and not at all prudish, I don't mind 'language'. I think of four-letter words as forceful sounds, or sometimes just an affectionate manner of speaking. To me 'pussy', whatever it may mean to others, has affection in it. I like 'cunt' as referring to my pussy. 'Cunt' has softness in it. 'Twat' is funny. But aside from 'gash', which is a little sadistic, men obviously love what we have, to have so many names for it. (Quim, crack, slit, pie, honeypot.)

Some words are quite amusing. The first time I heard 'box', whispered in my ear by a classmate, it broke me up, and I thought, oh, so that's what I have. Later, when I learned about 'tonsil hockey', it knocked me out. That one is still funny to me: in retrospect, so were my first attempts – poor dear Alvar (father of four, I hear, and he's only twenty-seven!). I don't know why, but the word is so unlikely that I think it's funny (and to have thought up 'she lost her cherry but still has the box it came in' took imagination).

18

Though it may officially be my second language, my English passes as fluent, but with occasional breakdowns. My father, whose family had taken him to America at the age of two and who is a naturalized American, insisted that English be spoken at home when he returned to Finland years later, as an adult. He had taught briefly at CCNY, and returned to Finland to marry my mother, who was Miss Finland that year. They decided to live in 'Feenlondt', as my mother would say, which is the size of Pennsylvania but has (you had better sit down for this) one hundred and eighty-seven thousand eight hundred and eighty-eight lakes (and a hundred and eighty thousand islands), and, although beautiful country, the idea is too *Walden*ish for me, at least on a permanent basis.

I like their story and have heard it so often I feel I practically attended their wedding, which my mother says I did. She was four months pregnant with me and happy as a clam. (Or a herring. In Finland everything is herring.)

According to Hal, I'm a newspaper freak. He recently said:

'Here's a quote for your quote book. "A person who reads nothing is better educated than a person who reads nothing but newspapers." That's Thomas Q. Jefferson, in case you're interested.'

I sometimes read two, maybe three papers in the morning, ranging from the *Times* to New York's sleazoids, depending on my mood. I even occasionally get the London *Times*. That bit about the pet Persian cat scratching the two women so much they looked like they had been hit by a car was from the London *Times*. I put it in my scrapbook. A harvest from this morning's papers:

AP – LAS VEGAS. Police searching through trash bins and a disposal site found the head and arms of a woman yesterday, hours after her severed leg was found in a trash container. Police continued 'the search for the woman's missing leg and torso,' homicide Sergeant Ed Schaub said. 'That way we'll have a complete woman.'

AP – FABRIANO, ITALY. 'A long thicket of billions of caterpillars' halted a freight train at a crossing near this central Italian town, officials reported Friday. They said the engineer did not see the 'procession' nearly two miles long and 33 feet wide until the train hit them Thursday and came to a halt. 'I felt we hit something mushy and suddenly the wheels started spinning,' Romolo Duca, the station manager, quoted the engineer as saying.

No word on the survivors.

Meanwhile, according to the *Times* (New York), the cemetery strike has entered its third week: some fifty-five thousand bodies have piled up and are being kept refrigerated so they won't freeze outdoors or rot indoors. All corpses are in excellent condition, a spokesperson for the gravediggers' union reassured, apologizing to the public for any inconvenience 'as might be caused with regard to this matter of respect for the dead.' (Phew!) He added: 'We can handle quite a few more bodies in this cold weather. Fortunately the weather is on our side. We just have to make sure the dead don't freeze.'

And (you mean Freud was right?) . . .

There was this item, a 'heart-rendering' story, as Iris would say, of a Los Angeles judge who ruled that a woman could go ahead with her claim for damages for

emotional pain caused to her grandchildren, aged four and nine, who were allowed to see Mickey Mouse undressing. The children had been invited to visit staff headquarters in Disneyland as a special treat, and while there they witnessed several Walt Disney characters removing their costumes. Seeing Mickey Mouse suddenly become headless caused great distress and emotional trauma, the woman claimed.

In its motion for dismissal, 'Disney called the case ridiculous.'

This morning I realized that I was reading newspapers partly to see if Karen's name would appear.

The heroine's living quarters

I'm moving uptown, and my new quarters are going to mark a new me. Possibly I'm going through some kind of nest-building stage. In any case, domestication is a new sensation for me. It might pass, of course, but lately I have started finding it fascinating to study different qualities in bedsheets and discussing with clerks at Bloomies the down content in feather pillows and the price-quality ratio in wool blankets. Hal could probably use one more sleeping aid, for to him that hath shall be given and he shall have abundance (for them as has gits), and softer pillows might just do the trick. Maybe for Christmas I'll give him a gift certificate to a Sleep Clinic, come to think of it. (Hmm, and maybe they'll provide support counselling for bruised-in-the-night partners.)

Another curious change: to turn men off, I have begun going around with my hair sticking out all over the place, like a fright wig except more messy. I look like a comic strip character shrieking, or who stuck her finger in a socket. And I have started leaving off the only make-up I ever wear, the faintest amount of warm eyeshadow that most men don't even notice. But of course men are strangely unobservant creatures. They think my eyes have a 'special' quality. They always describe it as 'something indefinable'. (Flair, probably.)

Am I pissing up a rope?

About Karen, nothing. Which, I sometimes think, is worse than almost anything. Most people have (already!) forgotten about her and think I'm strange for worrying. Hal, of course, has always thought I'm strange (I think it's what attracts him). But he says I'm more so now, since Karen.

'Maybe you like them "more so",' I said.

'More or less "more so" – yes.'

Hal says I'm Don Quixote. I'm on Mission Impossible. He also says, 'Forget her and get on with your own life.' But getting on with my own life includes *not forgetting* her.

Men. Go understand.

19

A lentil lifestyle

About the move. As squalid as it is, I like where I have been temporarily holed up but despite that have for a long time been wanting to move out. My income has gone up, thanks to Hal and the super portfolio he's been beefing up for me, and I can afford to live uptown. Also uptown brings me nearer to Hal and some good nooners when in rut (as is frequent). American men turn me on, and if you want to know why, go to Finland and talk to the men there. Hint: find one over eighteen who's sober half the time.

I plan to move around the middle of March, or two weeks from now. Meanwhile I had another letter from Karen's mother. Karen's brother plans to come to New York. He wants to fly Finnair and is arranging for a booking. The Bryggman family are grateful to me for writing them because having had no letter from Karen since before Christmas they're deeply worried. (Better late than never.) They hoped I wouldn't mind if the brother looked me up.

I replied immediately: no problem. I don't know when he will arrive so I've given them the new address I'm moving to and my current address also. I have the feeling that something is beginning to happen at last.

How to live

The place I'm leaving is a loft in a commercial building near Chinatown, not far from the Bowery. It isn't the kind of SoHo loft that socialites decorate with tasselled swings hanging from velvet-covered ropes, carved-wood carousel horses with flaring nostrils and all the well-to-do collectors' junk that skyrockets key-money when tenants sell an 'artist's loft' to uptown lovers of downtown bohemia, who believe that to produce art requires living artistically.

Even the galleries are leaving now, driven out by the prohibitive rents of posh shops selling imported wear and expensive cosmetics. You would think they were all vying with Rodeo Drive. The very latest 'Village' is not even SoHo or NoHo any more (or even Uh-Oh). Those new 'Villages' have degenerated into the picturesque, or what Manhattan realtors *imagine* is picturesque. The 'new SoHo' is West Chelsea, already looking more chic than it did last year. But Tribeca will probably still hold out for a while. Artists: the great raisers of real-estate values. Artists raise values, landlords raise rents – and artists raise hell (well, send letters to the *Times* anyway) before moving out and then raise rents elsewhere. They're unwilling pilot fish for shark landlords.

Anyway, my own private space is not Haute SoHo at all, being too far off all the beaten paths. The loft has just attained that lived-in look after a couple of years of dedicated wear and good honest filth – to dignify it a little. (In other words, my friends tell me, it's cruddy.) I like what Walker Evans once said about Agee: 'His clothes were deliberately cheap, not only because he was poor but because he wanted to be able to forget them.' Right – and the same goes for shelter. This is the Inge School of Right Living. And another thing, I tend to dress down when I don't want to attract men. I enjoy sex too much for promiscuity to have appeal. Hence the current shriek look.

My studio is one half of the upper floor of a derelict two-storey building. The in-name-only tenant of the other half is Iris, which is how we first met.

The plot thickens

Iris dropped in to see me. She likes dropping in, I think out of a need for a kindred spirit. The only thing wrong with her life, she says, is that she feels cut off from people to talk with. I welcome her visits because she temporarily replaces Karen, and if Bill's Fur and Feather Reports and his Amours of Greenwich Village are pretty wild sometimes, Iris's tales of her trade lean towards psychopathology, which is always interesting.

After several months of acquaintance, cautiously at first, she began to trust me and gradually opened up about her teenage ring when she saw that I don't give a rat's ass about morals squads and the Mesopotamian morality boys (read Fundamentalists). Iris's colleagues are 'senior' teenagers: over the sixteen-year legal limit. I don't *like* it that she's a prostitute, I think it's a lousy life, but I don't like it for *her* sake: I feel sorry for her and what must be going on in (and to) her feelings, starting with her father (his name is Aristotle!). But how she lives her life is none of my business, and I'm a firm believer that, as Martin says, everybody at all times is doing the best he or she can. (We grow and develop, he said the other day. Me: 'Isn't that a redundancy?' 'You can grow physically and not develop emotionally.' Oh.)

Iris refers to our building as Le Dump, but one of her clients – the superior court judge Lonergan or Logan – likes filth in every meaning of the word, and they hold their trysts, as he refers to them, in the loft, where it's also more anonymous. (*He* thinks. He's not aware of the escort service's Rolodex in a locked desk uptown, reputed to be worth two to three million.) The more 'slovenly', he says, the more 'appealing', for which 'privilege' (the terms are all his) she makes him pay dearly. She hates him, refers to him as 'Shit-for-brains'.

She's funny about her descriptions of him and tells me everything. He yells, 'Mush! mush!' as he humps her on the bed from behind on all fours in his freshly laundered white drawers, Paris garters and white lisle socks, which he never takes off. Every once in a while she goes down to the courthouse on Center Street to watch him preside over a trial (especially enjoying prostitution cases – Iris: 'Revolving-door hypocrisy') and likes making him warm under the collar and shift uncomfortably in his seat when he sees her – and then demands and gets more money from him the following time for the kinky pleasure of her embarrassing visit. And he pays her. An ornate form of blackmail, I suppose. Go understand.

Some of what she tells me is hard to believe and when I tell her that, she says, 'Are you kidding? As a novelist, Krafft-Ebing was ahead of his time.'

She knows a lot for seventeen (in some respects).

20

I'm fascinated by her explanation of the operating mechanics of the Presidio Escort Service. The ring returns the girls by car to their neighbourhoods – the West Side, the Village, East Harlem – in time for homework and dinner: most of them still live at home, no doubt part of their charm. They're treated with courtesy, not to say appreciation.

Especially Iris, who feels zealously protected by the service as its rising 'star' (she was told this not long ago – to insure loyalty?): when the market is up, some of her stockbroker clients don't mind paying an extra thousand, or even two, for 'specials' that involve her, that is, doing a trio with her friend Juanita Maldonado as the third. The clients, satisfied customers all, are delighted that the girls apparently enjoy their sessions as much as they do (and Iris assures me there's no faking their own orgasms: 'I never dreamed I could *have* so many orgasms in one day').

In these meetings with Iris we talk about Karen, but always, before long, the conversation drifts to her work, about which she is like a child who can't keep a secret. Her repeat clients include a child psychologist ('He's got this minidick is why') and a millionaire who has the same illustrious name as one of the Founding Fathers of the fledgling United States – a fact and a name that I feel sure would interest Mr Nussl. The name figures in an American history course she's currently taking called 'Problems in American Democracy', the conjunction of school curriculum and extracurricular work giving her a pleasant jolt for its link with 'our national heritage'.

Iris has been writing a 'pretty interesting best-seller' about all this, *The Confessions of a Teenage Call Girl*. A Hollywood agent (through Harrington) claims – she says – to be interested, but she won't be getting it published until retirement, which she places at about age thirty. The profits from the best-seller would be used to bankroll a cologne, Iridescence, and a perfume, Iris ('goddess of the rainbow'). She wants to be another Paloma Picasso.

She says being a call-girl is the most fun she has ever had, which is certainly easy to believe, given what she has told me of her father. Mr Stavropoulos forbade her to talk to the boys on the block because he says he knew the one thing they were after and, goddamn it, he'd better not catch her giving it away to those scumbags. Iris assured him that no neighbourhood boy *had* ever or *would* ever touch her: she was not interested in 'a bunch of kids who are losers, with no ambition and no money', and her father was pleased with this wisdom coming so early in life and reinforced it with the suggestion that it was just as easy to date a wealthy man on Park Avenue as 'some little neighbourhood shit'. ('Even easier,' she thought, and that was probably the first and last time Iris ever agreed with her father, and more than he knew.)

She had begun to accumulate an expensive wardrobe at places like Henri Bendel to please her wealthy clients, who had suggested the shop. Her obviously accelerated sophistication made her father suspicious about her 'part-time work as a model', even though she almost always remembered to put her ordinary clothes on before returning home for dinner and homework. And then one day, just as Mr Stavropoulos had bought a copy of *USA Today* and was walking up Columbus, engrossed in reading about the most recent Central Park rape of a teenage girl, he saw the limousine dropping Iris off a block away. With dread, Iris saw her father furiously fling the paper to the pavement and rush at her in a paroxysm of eastern Mediterranean cursing, disowning her as publicly and as brutally as he could, at the same time savagely yanking her long hair. He stiff-arm marched her ahead of him along Columbus Avenue, loudly proclaiming his formal malediction of her sluttish ways, saying she had sullied the great name of Aristotle Stavropoulos and dragged the family honour through the mud. He called on neighbours, shopkeepers, passers-by and a busload of German tourists, stopped at a red light at 73rd Street and wilting in New York's summer heat, to bear witness to the truth about Iris:

'*See* – my daughter, the Whore of Greece!'

In retrospect, Iris said, it was a 'two-Oscar performance' (acting and directing?) and that was the last time she planned ever to talk to her father before his death, when she would *maybe* forgive him but only if, *a*, he got out of his deathbed and crawled on his hands and knees to her, and *b*, knelt before her with his forehead touching the ground, and *c*, *begged* her fucking forgiveness ('the prick, the cocksucker, the slimy goddamn fucking *scum*bag shit-filled *mother*fucker!').

She had to go off to work. I watched her leave, a young woman chicly clothed but with a stilted walk that verged on flounce and betrayed her youth – the marketable quantity. Her make-up was too seriously applied to be artfully casual, and I imagined her in bed, eye-linered and with lipstick-encrusted lips, servicing a moneyed client who loved this curvy, sensuous, bouncy girl whose enjoyment of sex irrepressibly broke through a cool exterior of hired lover.

Maybe because they were the same age, I also thought of Karen, but forced myself not to go on with that thought: kidnapping, prisoner, slave, brothel, sex – no. *No*.

Karen is in Italy and will show up soon.

21

Karen's older brother Paavo telephoned from Finland. He's in Helsinki and wants directions to my place. I glanced at the loft with the hopeless sense that it was too late to start the massive tidying up it needed, but that was followed by a more cheerful oh-fuck-it attitude (more typical too). I told him to call me from JFK when he got here and gave him Hal's number – to leave a message if he couldn't reach me at the two numbers I had sent his mother.

I liked the way he sounded. It was the voice of a caring person.

For a brief moment I wondered what it would have been like to have grown up with a big brother, as Karen had. I imagined a brother would have been fun to be with, and protective. A bit like Hal in his better moments.

Even in a palace one can be happy

After I hung up I tried to see my place through the eyes of someone from Europe, especially Finland.

This can be a downer.

To Europeans, the Lower East Side is a shock. New Yorkers are not aware of the filthiness of life in Gotham. Guide books don't include it. When they think of New York they think of the Museum Mile, that nice stretch of Fifth Avenue in the Fifties, Sixties, Seventies, or the skyscrapers, or Wall Street and the World Trade Center, or the Statue of Liberty, or even Brooklyn and the Brooklyn Bridge sometimes, and as a concession to reality they might drag up the South Bronx (but that's way up to hell and gone somewhere and nobody in his right mind ventures that far).

Europeans see those things, of course, but that's not what they come over for. They come to New York to be bowled over by the glitter and the skyscrapers, by the height and sheer number of them – and then they get bummed out by all the dust and filth. They notice trash-filled streets with potholes the size of the Sea of Tranquillity. They see yellow air turning darker with black soot and hear deafening express trains roaring underground as if they're out to break the Olympic speed record on the non-stop midtown-to-Harlem run. They see, and hear and plug their ears against, the thousands of snarling and screeching garbage trucks making a fearsome racket. And with all this, they encounter literally thousands of the one or two million people daily zooming across each other's path in so skilled a choreography that it seems a miracle they don't smash into each other. In this respect, New Yorkers are extremely polite, *chiefly* (if not uniquely) in this respect: they accommodate their walking pace to the steps of the one approaching them and adjust to it out of the corner of an eye, intermeshing their strides so intricately it sometimes impresses even the New Yorkers themselves. (New Yorkers are often impressed by themselves in any case, purely and simply for being the inhabitants of *la Grande Pomme*.)

All of that is on my mind now – the trash and filth, I mean – because in my building the entryway's 'white' tile floor, piss-pungent, is an accretion of a loose soot that drifts lazily back and forth with every breeze. Spelled out in the middle of the tiles is the date of the building's construction, 1883, composed artistically in jagged small hexagonal tiles of red, white and blue: artisan's pride, I suppose, although maybe back then the place was less cheesy than now.

The ground floor is the world's second dustiest shop and sells 'Orthotics and Prosthetics': the two large windows straddling the entryway are a depressing clutter of anatomical supports, fake limbs, wheelchairs, four-legged canes, bedpans, plastic piss bottles – a cheerful sight each time you go in and out. (Iris is convinced that the judge gets a secret sexual charge out of it all, which is another reason he prefers their trysts to be at Le Dump.)

On a clear day you can see the rear windows

Upstairs, my studio is ballroom-size and spaciously empty and has such a vasty feeling you sometimes imagine it looks foggy at the far end. On grey and rainy days the place has a lost feeling, as though it had long ago given up the ghost and was waiting for a compassionate wrecking crew and the peace of oblivion.

It previously housed, according to Mr Nussl, the landlord, a small printing plant, the Liberty Press, whose name is still stencilled on the hall door in black enamel, along with the Stars and Stripes, also in black. It specialized in wedding and communion announcements and business cards until the police raided it on a tip and discovered the 'printer' and one male and two female employees cranking out porn flicks in an improvised rear room behind a door wallpapered with a photo mural of the Statue of Liberty (curtained out, no doubt, during filming).

Mr Nussl's description of the operation was a veiled pass at me but I didn't mind as long as it stayed veiled: covert passes are easily ignored. The printing press and other prop equipment were sold to pay a calculatedly ruinous fine plus back taxes, with the alternative of several years of prison lending the option persuasive force.

I was new in New York in those days and found such stories fascinating. I felt sorry for the film-makers, that they had to film sex to make money, and for the customers who bought them. It's not that I don't understand them or that I mind watching porn flicks (once in a while) but that they were making a living at it – all so joyless. At least Iris enjoys herself (for now anyway).

When I moved in I knew I'd be living there only a short while and didn't mind the moulded-tin ceiling or windows fronting the street and rear only (but with a huge, redeeming skylight in the middle.) The windows looked like they hadn't been washed since the Spanish-American War and on a sunny day still make you feel like you are living underwater.

Some of the century-old floorboards move up and down when you walk on them and the floor feels wavy, and there is one queasy stretch where the planks surge upward and sink down like a heavy sea, and after a drink or two you get almost fluttery crossing over to what Mr Nussl optimistically calls The Kitchen. (Landlords have revenue-inspired imaginations.)

What stopped the place from depressing me after Finland's forests and one hundred and eighty-seven thousand lakes was that I was temporarily forced to live somewhere that cost hardly any money. The loft's rent was cheap, and I can't think of a more important statement to make about rent.

The house of Nussl

No further word yet from Brother Paavo. His phone call was Friday – two days ago, and I'm wondering what the hell is wrong. What *is* it with these disappearing Bryggmans?

I could be wrong, though. Maybe they're more actively involved than I think.

The loft. It gave me a chance to get to know this Mr Nussl, whose stories fascinated me as much as he did – as most Americans do, in fact, naturalized or unnatural. He doesn't own the leased land the building sits on, just the building. According to Mr Nussl, the owner of the land, the owner of half of Manhattan and the whole of the Bronx in fact is the Astor family, living in England in baronial splendour and peace – and safety. (And if Iris thinks she can buy even a sliver of it away from them, lotsa luck.)

Mr Nussl liked me from the start because, as he explained, I'm Finnish and he's Polish, and that makes us both Baltic and therefore related. Gallantly he has always overlooked my living arrangements – bed, refrigerator, a clothes-line of drying 'scanties', as he calls them, strung across the back end of the loft near the translucent windows – pretending to believe my explanation that the place was being used purely as a studio and that I lived elsewhere, residence in a commercial loft being illegal.

Birds of prey

Nussl hates officialdom and ordinances, and as his family's only survivor of Auschwitz (at the age of three, he told me, Christian neighbours kidnapped him with the connivance of his mother on the morning his parents and his sister were trucked from the ghetto to the train), he has values not typical of building owners. Many of the nuisances of day-to-day living seem to bore him. He is not interested in municipal regulations, which he feels only embroil property owners in minor points of obscure safety codes. His life too has been permanently altered by a disappearance act. The war experience left Nussl with reduced interest in civic concerns or really anything not tied to matters of life and death.

Not counting, of course, sex: there he may have been an ageing gent but his interest in sex wasn't ageing but getting deathless – true of a lot of older men, according to Iris, for whom they are lucrative prey, not to say a capitalist enterprise.

But of course it works the other way too, with the girl the prey in another, similar kind of enterprise. I hope I am wrong about Karen, but so far nothing convinces me of that.

22

It's Saturday and from Karen's brother Paavo there's still no word. Should I contact Mr and Mrs Bryggman about *him* now?

Unfortunately Mr Nussl's relaxed attitude extends to needed repairs. My living there illegally, although the fact is always tactfully avoided, encourages him to permit himself an occasional pass at me in blackmail. He fondled my bottom once, but a decent man at bottom, as they say, he accepted my no philosophically but in revenge adopted a policy of a friendly ducking of any responsibility for maintenance. He began countering all requests for repairs (a leaking toilet, *an entire step* missing from the hall stairs, rats entering through a hole in the back) with diversionary flattery.

How *fortunate* I was, he told me, to be both talented and educated (he dreamed, in the early days of his New York expatriation, of going back and attending Jagiellonian University in Cracow) when I reported to him – the point at issue – that the building was a rat's maze and could something be done about it. 'Rat's maze' provoked a long tale about the psychology studies of a brilliant older cousin, Ignacy, who was dead now, poor fellow, and he would have made such a fine scholar, and here *he* was, Isidore Nussl, in the New World, his life as fortunate as Ignacy's had been unfortunate and blah blah blah *blah*.

All true, I'm not making fun of him. But the digression to

Eastern Europe, the Nazis and World War Two ended in an irrelevant denunciation of political life and 'so-*cold* civilization', and the complaint about rats or a leaking toilet was effectively derailed.

In fact I ended up offering him sympathy and a few vodkas in Baltic fraternity over at Minelli's, an artists' hang-out near SoHo, where, it was reported to me the next time I went in, we made an otherwise dull Tuesday evening into something that still enlivens conversation. I must have had a good time because I don't recollect much of it, and until my next period, I went around hoping I hadn't democratically boffed one particularly aspiring candidate (whose face I thought I could even recall later, dimly).

He called my complaints a 'qvetsch session'. I learned the word 'qvetching' from him, but of course everybody in New York speaks Yiddish, sometimes without knowing it (*tsuris*, for example, and *khutzpah* and *schlep*). (I also like *yontiff*, *chochka* and the all-embracing *ganz vershtunkunuh*.) The present 'qvetsch session' ended with his telling me I was the one tenant he never worried about and admiring the head I had on my shoulders, though that was not the part that drew his glances.

'A smart cookie like you,' said shrewd cookie Nussl, offering a warm smile and a beam of comradeship, and concluding my audience with a '*Sei gesunt!* my friend,' which was his polite way of saying shut up.

The toilet still leaks, of course.

'Vy dun't you esk how I am?' – 'Oh! I'm sorry, Mr Nussl.
How are you?' – 'Dun't esk'

'Dun't esk' could be Mr Nussl's middle name. It makes me think of Dantesque.

As used by him, 'dun't esk' is a two-word wrap-up of disgust, dread, melancholy, blighted hope, cynicism and world-weariness – a marvel of economy. Ask Mr Nussl about floods, about El Niño and crazy weather patterns or strikes or CIA blunders, and he shrugs away these trivia of life, which are not worth a more amplified answer. Ask him about banks and white-collar crime or New York City's imminent bankruptcy or dishonesty in the White House, and he dismisses this social detritus with a muttered 'Go understand.' But *hint* at terrorism, or racist fundamentalists, or Arab peace promises, or mention any part of the globe between Greece and India, and a darkness descends over all the land and he pronounces quietly (emotions visible only in the eyes):

'Dun't esk.'

In an uneven swap, I taught him 'blivet', as in 'to get hit with a blivet'.

For the first and only time I saw him look blank and I thought, aha – I'm one up on him. Taking whatever pleasure I could derive from the puzzled look that came over his face (*Blivet? Was für ein . . . ?*), I informed him:

'A blivet is five pounds of shit in a one-pound bag.'

I even had the vanity to think he might seize on the expression and make it part of his repertory. But there wasn't even a laugh from him. He only said, gloomily: 'Life in a nutshell.'

I wondered if I should tell him of my suspicions about Karen but decided not to. He would offer no sympathy, I felt, but would tell me that such events only confirm his *vershtunkunuh* view, which, in the maturity of my years, I would some day come to adopt.

Little old New York

Mr Nussl is an unusual landlord. He is a source of far-out bits of information he would casually let drop – that detail about baths in colonial Philadelphia I got from him (the subject coming up when I was discussing the absence of a tub in the loft). When Virginia City, Nevada wanted its cathouses moved out of the neighbourhood of a primary school, the local paper ran an editorial that said: Don't move the whores out, move the school out. So they moved the school out. He's an authority on New World trivia and a walking library especially of Curious Facts About the American Colonies.

He's particularly a freak on the subject of New York. It was he who told me that the Bowery was once an Indian trail. The Indians used it in their expeditions against New Amsterdam. I loved hearing these details. Later on, the northern end of the Bowery became the place where Brueghel Dutchmen got drunk and unhitched their codpieces and fucked joyfully in the green meadows of Greenwich Village. The Village was cut in half back then by the meandering Minetta Brook (it's there still but subterranean, near where the Minetta Tavern is, which was Jay Gould's hang-out). In those days the woods were part of Pieter Stuyvesant's farm, *Bossen Bouwerij*, the Farm in the Woods. Mr Nussl knew Greenwich Village's Indian name too, Sapokanican, which he wrote down for me in his curious spidery Middle European handwriting.

'And Manahatta, which we get Manhattan from, means place of drunkenness,' he said. 'So it hasn't changed much.'

There was a man named Mullins, or Allen, the name isn't important, who operated a brothel in colonial New York. (Mr Nussl's history places heavy emphasis on cathouse documentation, another way I can tell his sexual urges are alive if not exactly kicking.) Like his three brothers before him, he had wanted to be a minister but he didn't have the call, he explained to the family, so he went into the *call*-girl business (a little Baltic emphasis there for humour extraction). However, he managed to carry on in the family tradition by furnishing each girl with a small Bible for her tiny bedside table, a homey fact that brought a cryptic smile to Mr Nussl's face and an elbow jab to my ribcage. The story was, to me, interesting anthropology. The elbow to the ribcage was just poor aim. (Iris's name for him is David Copafeel.)

23

I suppose it's because I'm a foreigner, technically a half-American immigrant, that Americans and New Yorkers intrigue me, especially someone like Mr Nussl. This is my country (dual citizenship) and he too is a compatriot, although like me he's a foreigner and from a country different from mine. From what I piece together, Nussl and his wife Sarah lead a life of tranquil Polish exile in Bedford Hills, far from what Nussl calls 'the gnomes and drones of Neanderthal New York' (pronounced pedantically correctly *nay-onder-tahl* – very liquid *l*).

One of my very few possessions (by choice) is a framed version of the ancient Chinese quotation my father gave me: 'Apart from thirty thousand mornings, time does not belong to me.' I'm leaving behind the old Goodwill bed I've been sleeping on. This morning I took down from the walls a few prints given to me by friends and some small watercolours of Karen's. They're lovely things, with a spontaneous feeling and nothing of any art movement in them, unlike most of the stuff in galleries, which is all gimmickry and mimicry.

I like the erotic too – it has special appeal, like a photograph of Hal's of a sensuous rose whose petals are primly shut and looking like the pudgy frill of a vulva.

After many moves over the years, I have reduced my belongings to survival level. One heavily loaded taxi trip is all it will take for the move uptown. The hard part, during a late March blizzard in the Chinatown-Bowery area, will be finding a taxi.

It's snowing like a motherfucker (to borrow Hal's descriptive powers).

A moving experience

Tuesday (writing this in Hal's kitchen as he works). And *still* no word from Karen's brother Paavo. *Paska*.

The big move: there were no taxis visible on Moving Day, no moving vehicles of any kind, in fact, and I just enjoyed the scene in a mental-photography way, seeing the streets as silent as a theatre set when the curtain goes up and before the actors begin to speak – a magical moment or two.

I waited for five minutes at the kerb, hoping a taxi would stray past and feeling like an idiot watching the falling snow and a lone Sanitation Department truck that improbably appeared around a corner, clunking around with an emergency snowplough out front, piling up a six-foot-high mountain range of dirty snow on top of a row of parked cars that will probably not get shovelled out till spring. Well, at least their owners won't have a parking problem.

On the outside of Nussl's building I noticed someone had written: 'Something Terrible Is Going To Happen' and below that, in another hand, 'You.'

Despite my parka and black woollen body-stocking and thick black sweater, it was colder here than Lapland, where winters don't get so ferocious, and I decided that my chances would be better up around Astor Place. I shlepped past snow-drifty sidestreets to Cooper Union, where, as I got nearer Eighth Street, the graffiti took a literary turn: 'Moby Dick is not a form of VD' and below that: 'What's wrong with it then?'

But most were sophomoric: 'Make Love, Not War' and beneath that: 'Do Both – Get Married.' 'Impotence, where is thy sting?' and (maybe an answer?): 'Better latent than never.' 'When you're down and out / Lift up your head and shout, / '*I'm down and out!*' 'I'm dying, therefore I must have been.'

One disquieting one: 'Kil', the spelling giving pause.

*

A new beauty salon has opened across the way: Cutting Corners. Start as you mean to go on. I saw one the other day called The Pony Tale. You sometimes see very inventive names.

24

A taxi came sloshing through the crosstown-traffic mush at St Mark's Place. I read 'Herb Mendelsohn' in block letters on the chauffeur's ID card, and together we went back and picked up my stuff at the loft, after which the trip from the Bowery to East 61st Street turned into a memorable tour of Mr Mendelsohn's digestive tract.

More oral history of our time

'So I went t'roo like this GI series. I had these cramps and some days I couldn't eat nothing. I mean I never had trouble with my stomach before, so go understand. Next thing I knew, I had an ulcer and my colon started acting up, which added to this irritating bowel syndrome I'm supposed to have. Then I developed diarrhoea, and when you're driving a hack all day and you have diarrhoea, it's murder, believe me. I mean, where can you stop? You learn where every public john is in Manhattan. Between my stomach, my intestines and my colon I was pretty busy for a while. But if you think *I* got problems, let me tell you about my brother-in-law Melvin. He's been, like, going through depressions and midlife crisis and he told me he finely couldn't take it no more. He sez, "It's driving me crazy, Herb. I don't know whether to go out of my mind or move to Florida." I sez, "Go out of your mind. It's cheaper."'

Upward mobility

I gave him a fifty-dollar tip for helping me in and out of elevators and service entrances. Upstairs at my new place – thirty-fifth floor no less, six floors higher than Hal's studio, with a view of the cable car to Roosevelt Island – I just threw everything inside the door of the apartment with the intention of unpacking later and tramped through the snow to Hal's studio over on 58th. Maybe we could get in a cosy boff, work permitting.

On my way over I noted down four more hairdressers: March Hair, Wigged Out, Headquarters, Mop Crop.

On Lex I passed a man and a woman walking arm in arm, once again demonstrating that you hear everything in New York. The man said, 'He went to France and bought a château,' and the woman replied, 'A real one?' 'No,' he said, 'this one was built.'

How the other half lives it up

Hal's place is a penthouse on the twenty-ninth floor and as different from a SoHo loft as you can get: a terrific view, brilliant light and the convenience of being in the heart of midtown, where you can shop for practically anything – plus there's the Modern and all the film houses and foreign delicacy shops on the Upper East Side, and also Central Park just a short walk away. An ideal location if you have to live in New York. And have a healthy income.

Hal was working with Clarissa Moore, the Miracle Model (this year's), for an assignment for Young & Rubicam. Clarissa is famous among the four or five commercial photographers I know for always trying to get herself photographed as super-sophisticated Glamour Woman, when she photographs to perfection if you just catch a certain Georgia peanut farm glow about her that the mysterious chemistry of emulsion and developer transforms into *Vogue*ish elegance.

You can't help liking her innocence. She says things like:

'It was when I discovered modelling that I felt myself propelled to the forefront of my career.' You have to look twice to make sure she's not kidding. 'It's something that's just in me.'

It's hard not to smile (and hide your face) when she carefully says '*ek*-cetera' obviously thinking *she's* saying it correctly, unlike others. But I really don't believe that in Paris she once asked which model agency Marie Antoinette was with (and probably the joke about Beethoven's Erotica Symphony is apocryphal also).

People can be quite mean about models, who're easy targets. What most people don't realize is that some models have enough brains to become lawyers, and do so later on (which, in Hal's view, doesn't say much about lawyers). Last year during a break she told me she had majored in comparative lit during her first semester at college, which really impressed me, and then she decided that for her second semester she should give another major a try, namely psychology, but during vacation she quit school to become a model. 'You have to know what you're looking for in life,' she explained. 'It can't be all study.'

It was Clarissa who told me about the new sumptuous German bimbo Gretel (covers of *Cosmo*, *Vanity Fair* and so on), who had a cut-and-dried arrangement with photographers. She was married, which she told you up front, but before or after the shoot she gladly hopped into bed with the photographer. But if the photographer thought he might be getting somewhere, or if he tried to interest her in dinner and a night on the town, she would go out with him, all right – no problem. But no bed: bed didn't go with dinner. Bed went with work. He would call her up about another fashion assignment and – it was hop-into-bed time again. She had worked out an unemployment insurance programme with specific labour rules.

Which Hal confirmed (the bastard).

25

Willing to do almost anything to get my mind off Karen for twenty minutes or so, I watched Clarissa go through the fashion model's two-step, swirling her dress butt-high (pantyhose ad), a smile of high intensity climaxed by a strobe flash, repeating the choreography dozens of times with infinite variations. Motor-driven Hassy for this, thirty rolls of Kodachrome 25, which was about twenty rolls more than needed, but Hal, or rather his agent Roberta, would show about half the shots to the art director and the agency would choose the ones it liked for the agreed-on sum of twenty-five thousand dollars. But if the art director was not altogether satisfied with the batch shown he (sometimes she, sometimes both in one) would order a retake for an additional five thousand dollars. Sometimes the agency ordered three retakes before feeling satisfied, and of course the trick was, all the 'retakes' had been made at the very first shoot and held in reserve.

These are the ins and outs you have to know in order to survive in this trade and meet your studio overhead, which is usually horrendous. But you have to have a dressed-for-success studio or you don't get these fat assignments in the first place. Commercial photographers pay as much as two hundred thousand dollars a year rent to get the kind of space they need for their equipment and at an address that fits a certain image: their studio has to have a certain grungy/classy look but not *too* grungy – up-market faux bohemian. (A certain 'flair', no doubt.)

You have to be better than good in that world. It's very competitive. But once you're making it, you can occasionally get away with murder. ('It all depends on whether the art director is lusting after your ass – and you keep him lusting.') I once saw Hal make twelve and a half thousand dollars on a simple fashion assignment that took him about thirty minutes in Central Park with a hand-held camera, with me – the (unpaid) Gopher-in-Residence – holding a reflector.

The models make out too, that is, the top ones. There are something like fourteen hundred models in New York City in a fashion and commercial photography business that's a billion-dollar-a-year industry. For a TV commercial, a top model can get fifteen thousand dollars for a day's shoot, hell, more, and a commercial's thirteen-week cycle could bring an immodest fortune in reruns: in a twenty-one-month period it's possible for a model to make more than fifty thousand dollars for one day's work. It was that level of modelling Karen was working into.

Karen is almost an anagram of Frank.

You know what that proves? Absolutely nothing.

(*How* can I find Frank? There must be something I haven't thought of trying.) *Paska.*

PASKA.

The underwear's the thing

I enjoy watching Hal work – the way he has of getting intimate with the models. He will bend over and concentrate on the viewfinder and then there'll be a sudden concern in his voice:

'Clarissa, has that tear in the crotch been there the whole goddamn time we've been shooting? *Shit!*'

A look almost of intelligence suddenly transforms Clarissa's face for the microsecond of a strobe flash – *click* – and dies.

'Great,' Hal winking – 'my mistake. Crotch fine.'

(Probably a good shot, that one.)

Clarissa was lit from the sides by two banks of strobes, a

pair of umbrellas that filled in more light and a gobo in front shielding the lens from flare. I've seen stock-in-trade scenes like this many times: model and photographer working quietly, with a leitmotif of praise – 'Great, perfect, good, yes, mm, like that,' all of it breathed excitedly, encouragingly, to incite them to perform – with a camera in hand speaking to a woman with words you usually use only after horizontal acquaintance, 'Mmm, ah, oh' and so forth – sounds you make when boffing.

He was pouring it on with Clarissa: 'Suck the lens, you beauty,' and Clarissa suddenly bending over silently guffawing, hand shooting up to mouth – click *zEEZZZ* click *zEEZZZ* click *zEEZZZ* . . . in rapid succession. I guessed that those photos would be some of the better ones of the session. The unreal made real.

He was good at that, Hal, and there were some agencies who wouldn't use anybody else. He never did the typical stuff you see, like Messinger's attempts at chalk-and-charcoal abstractions, which you get by dodging on high-contrast paper (he sometimes works in black and white too), and *especially* not like Dick Catherton's work. Catherton would photograph Clarissa with one hand snappily cupped over her eyes peering down Park Avenue in a hearty welcoming smile at absolutely nobody on an absolutely empty street (shot at 6 a.m. on a Sunday), leaning forward a half metre at the top of her body as though that's the way people naturally stand. It's the kind of fashion shot your eye doesn't register any more except to note its unreality, and also except to note Clarissa – and then magically the whole tasteless unbelievable photo becomes effective because of that: purely because of Clarissa. Her face could sell anything. Women love her because they want a face like hers and men love her because they want to possess that face (and the body they imagine goes with it).

At the end of each series, a hairdresser and his assistant led by the magazine's associate editor fussed around Clarissa while her eyes became infinitely expressionless in high-assed chic. The hairdresser tried to run the show too, impatiently snapping his fingers for hairspray from his assistant, who gratified each wish almost before it was expressed. The associate editor gave the impression that she was *ordaining* the model's look. All three touched her and adjusted her clothing as though she were inanimate, the way you would handle and turn a window mannequin – or a chicken you're preparing to roast.

Cheesecake epiphany

Clarissa took it in good grace – munificently paid to take things in good grace – still, a real pro, which is why you see her face on half the billboards in town. A stunning model really, each cheekbone an unripe plum and her cheeks like landslides – no exaggeration. I remember one time seeing her entering the Plaza from the Fifth Avenue side when a movie star, a drop-dead knockout from Italy world-renowned for her *mamma mia* ba-*zooms*, strode in on her Swedish-amazon legs and was immediately swarmed around by a feeding-frenzy of photographers tipped off in advance by her publicity agent. A member of the star's retinue, rushing up to whisper something in her ear, grabbed her by her sleeve and we all looked on in stunned disbelief as the top of her dress fell from her shoulders to her waist – like breakaway furniture in cowboy movies. She fumbled to cover the jackknifing breasts, but with enough expert clumsiness to give the electrified photographers time to record those celebrated boobs in all their resplendent glory. During the prolonged lightning storm of flashbulbs I looked at the group surrounding her and noticed a man looking on with peculiarly intense concentration, and it took me a moment to realize he wasn't staring at the jiggling breasts: he wasn't even looking at the actress – he was gazing at Clarissa.

The warm winter clouds of Suomi

I could tell by the sounds that the session was going well. I poured myself a cranberry juice and vodka as Finnish fortification (New York Finns drink cranberry juice as though there were an epidemic of cystitis) before going back to my new place and unpacking, then decided it was too early in the day for vodka, and besides, I didn't feel like unpacking, or even going back. Or anything at all, actually. I was in my goof-off mood and wanted to hang on to it.

Behind the partition I found a pot of what Americans have agreed to call coffee and, sipping it, looked out through the floor-to-ceiling windows at the sky, which was getting darker by the minute. The winter clouds reminded me of Finland except that Finland is warmed by the Gulf Stream, which winds its way up to the top of the world, and you never get the freezing weather that poor New Yorkers have to suffer through.

Wonderful town

Proverbially, New York doesn't have a climate, only weather, and you get two seasons: winter, when it's so cold that any attempt at speech outdoors gives you lockjaw, and summer, which makes you so soppingly hot the sweat meanders down your cleavage even if you sit in the 'cool' shade and don't move. In between you get a week of balminess that you might miss if you're down with either Asian flu or spring fever.

New York, New York, it's a wonderful town . . .

26

It felt strange peering down from the twenty-ninth floor at the hundreds of snowy black-and-white rectangles of buildings like a bleached patchwork in which doors were slamming, lovers were meeting, johns were flushing, babies were crying, stores were being robbed in crimes too petty to make the evening news . . .

One of those nondescript buildings was Karen's small but comfortable hotel (I checked it out three weeks ago: 'We've no idea where she went on leaving here,' and no, they did not know Frank's last name, and I left them my phone number) – and still no report of her disappearance on the evening news. Which was to be expected: her abduction or disappearance is pure conjecture, 'this whole Karen thing' being the product of a febrile Finnish imagination, namely mine. If you hang around midtown Manhattan for a while and then simply don't show up at your usual places one day, you can't really expect CBS or ABC to headline it.

I was sinking further into my winter seclusion (doldrums, duh Glooms) but it didn't stop my pleasure in viewing the Queensboro Bridge and its baroque spires spanning the East River, paling away at the far end, way off in Long Island. Through the girders of the bridge the headlights of cars flashed rhythmically towards Manhattan like an endless stream of fireflies and I loved the beauty of that. New York: no city in the world like it – not London, not Paris, not anywhere.

Of my origins

To appreciate how beautiful Manhattan is you would have to be from a town like the one where I was born: Ii, which is pronounced not *ee* as in eek but *eee* as in easy – a long sound. It's in northern Finland, not far from the Arctic Circle, and my mother, who was eight and a half months pregnant with me, was supposed to be spending a weekend with her sister, my Aunt Leena, who lives in Ii. She ended up spending it instead in the local hospital and left town the following Wednesday with a small, warmly wrapped bundle: little Inge. *Moi.*

I once went back to Ii to see what my birthplace was like. To have a good time in Ii, you get in your car and keep driving south till you come to Haukipudas, down the road. If Haukipudas isn't hopping that night, and you could probably bet the farm it isn't, you climb back in your car and return to Ii. And that's about it for northern Finland – leaving out Oulu, further south, or Rovaniemi, the capital of Lapland (where you can even go bowling, if you should ever be overcome by a desire to go bowling at the Arctic Circle). Compared with those two places, the town I grew up in was a metropolis: Jyväskylä. (Now *don't* tell me you've never heard of Jyväskylä.)

Ii – no relation to
Llanfairpwllgwyngyllgogerychwyrndrobwllllantysiliogogogoch

Correctly spelled. (Hal's atlas. Why does he have an atlas where models go to change their clothes?) According to Hal, Llanfairpwllgwyngyllgogerychwyrndrobwllllantysiliogogogoch is where all the best proofreaders come from. He says the last three syllables sound like you're being choked to death.

Killing time, I saw that there's a place in the French Pyrenees called Oô. According to the pronouncing gazetteer, Oô is pronounced *oh*. Ii (*eee*) and Oô (*oh*) should think about twinning themselves. Signwise it would certainly make more sense than twinning Ii with the wonderfully named village of Llanfairpwllgwyngyllgogerychwyrndrobwllllantysiliogogogoch: the road sign would be a hazard, sticking half-way across the road.

I looked at Poland on the map and thought of Mr Nussl. I once said to him, fighting off some of his charming bullshit with a little of my homegrown (fight fire with fire), that the unexamined life isn't worth living, and before I could supply the credit line to impress him with my classical education, he came right back with 'The unexamined society is not worth living *in*,' proving once again he was a step ahead of me (not difficult). In a philosophical mood (and because platitudes are not only excellent bullshit fighters but good conversation concluders), I told him: 'Life is change, Mr Nussl,' and he came right back with: 'Small change.'

I pored over Cracow and Poznan and the whole of Poland and thought about Mr Nussl because I didn't want my eyes to keep going back to Marrakesh. I'm getting Moroccophobia.

Of course there's no certainty that Karen's in Morocco.

Voi ch'entrate

I picked up a tabloid from a whole pile of them on the floor and read that a father had been convicted for poisoning his son with arsenic-filled Hallowe'en candy. A twelve-year-old girl, injured in a train wreck, died in hospital, where the morgue attendant was found sexually abusing her.

A man with two artificial arms has been charged with murder, and the American Civil Liberties Union was looking into the matter because the police have been holding his arms for eighteen months as material evidence.

A bomb in an office building was disarmed by a bomb squad cop who when interviewed later about his goal in life said, 'To get through the next twenty-four hours.'

So much for thirty thousand mornings.

Some time fairly recently I read a Human Rights Watch article in the *Times* about Mauritania. Mauritania is a vast desert republic stretching from the Atlantic to the western Sahara – a country of choice if you like spending your life up to your neck in sand. According to Anti-Slavery International, in London, which has been monitoring activities there for the past twenty years, it's a country with a hundred thousand slaves – 'and probably a greater number than that'. A place called Chinguetti is 'one of the most important oases on the slave route from Timbuktu . . .'

That pushed a pause button – the matter-of-factness of that: the 'slave route'.

('You take the slave route to the first oasis – it'll be on your right – and swing past McDonald's until you come to a . . .')

A thousand years ago Chinguetti was one of the great holy cities of North Africa. Today it is largely a ruin as the desert slowly consumes it. Then this sentence: 'In Mauritania it is illegal to discuss or mention slavery or even talk to foreign journalists.'

I read that again. *Illegal to discuss or mention slavery or even talk to foreign journalists.* A death sentence.

I flashed on Karen's eager face turning towards me with that smile when her eyes met mine as she and Frank were leaving Hal's studio the last time.

Is *that* where she is? How would it be possible to learn what happened? Illegal to discuss or mention . . .

Tears welled up now just thinking of the article, but I told myself: 'No, you're imagining things. *Nothing* has happened. Karen was abandoned by Frank, went to Rome and will be back soon. You haven't heard from her – and that is all. She has a new lover, whom she's wild about, and doesn't want to leave Italy just yet.'

Which wasn't very satisfying because (interior monologue): 'Have you *heard* anything on the evening news about a kidnapping?' 'No.' 'Well, then shut up. Maybe she's not "missing".'

Except of course that she's missing.

And Brother Paavo – if he ever shows up – will sort it all out.

I told this to Martin this afternoon. And just when I thought he would praise me for finally seeing things a bit less para-noiacally, he quietly muttered something that sounded uncomfortably like 'More denial.'

Go understand.

(His speech is sometimes like a soft humming. They must take murmur lessons too.)

27

Of harems and dead bodies

Out in the studio Hal was still working with Clarissa, so to find out how long the snow would keep up, I turned the radio on and caught the end of the weather report and its wind-chill discussion, the importance of which I will never understand. The announcer explained we were experiencing a lowering subsidence inversion – which was what, snow or no snow?

'And now, back to the cemetery strike' and whether it would be settled by Easter: the body count is at sixty-eight thousand. The Jews were being permitted to bury their own. A report on funeral customs of different faiths. More anthropology. The announcer spoke of 'cur-TAHJ-es'. There has been much theft from cemeteries recently of bronze memorial vases, metal doors and even headstones despite the law that makes it a felony to receive items stolen from cemeteries.

Another New York story in Hal's newspaper pile: the city built a new sewer line. It excavated so much dirt that a house, owned by an elderly couple on social security, threatened to collapse. The city itself, 'in recognition of its error', put up support beams at its own expense to prop the house up. Then another city agency served an eviction notice to the couple unless they took the beams down. They were blocking the pavement.

I clipped that one to send to my father. I'm only surprised the elderly couple didn't sue the city for giving wrong advice and causing undue stress. Should be worth a couple of million right there. What's a headless Mickey Mouse compared with that?

I stretched out on the couch in a little room at the end of the studio behind the partition where the models relaxed during breaks – a really comfortable chaise-longue thoughtfully provided by Hal. (With forethought?)

The model's changing-room has a stage-set feeling just short of garish. It feels like a small den in a harem. (I see harems everywhere now.) The colour motif is saxophone gold, complemented by the jade green of a shaggy rug with a pile deep enough to be scythed. Moroccan (Mauritanian?) rugs and zebra skins are strewn on its opulent shag, with immense and luxurious cushions scattered here and there over the fur.

In one corner there's an ostentatious-looking turn-of-the-century ball-and-claw bathtub, for use as a prop, though it's generally not usable, being filled to the brim with boxes of 8 x 10 negatives in plastic sleeves, proof sheets, contact prints, blow-ups – the overflow of Hal's crammed files. Next to the tub is a peacock chair that appears in some of Hal's earlier black-and-white (gallery) work, and next to that is an Eames chair.

As I lay down I noticed that the ceiling had what could only be dried champagne spots, a sight that did not fill my heart with joy, Hal and I never having toasted anything there that I can recall. (A good time with Karen? I can't help suspecting they made it here.) I once commented to him on the bordello quality of the scene, and in one of his more loquacious moods he said, 'It keeps out the wind.'

Not wanting to dwell on what might have given rise to a champagne party, I got up and made myself a cup of instant tea that you could easily argue was better or worse than the coffee, eased back into the studio and sat discreetly in the far background ready to watch and learn. But no luck. Before long, Clarissa and entourage wrapped it up.

Artists and models

When they had left and while the equipment was still in place, Hal took a few quick shots of me for my portfolio, as an update. I didn't see myself in *any* sense as a fashion model but I thought I could make as good a glove or shoe model as anybody else, or for aprons or nurses' uniforms, something where you don't have to be a glamour puss. Hal thinks I could do better, but I'm not interested. As a 38C I am slightly too bosomy, at least so I've been told, to be a bra model or even do limited fashion work – though ironically the first 'major' assignment I ever got was for that recent series of bosomy-looking Icelandic sweaters in a Midwest mail-order catalogue and that I'm still living on (and relatively well). Also some lingerie shots (underwear pays double, the only benefit that prudery confers) that wound up in *Vogue* and led to several small but lucrative jobs (my *vogue*, you might say, beginning with Hal).

Being looked at in the nude doesn't bother me, as it doesn't most Finns, who hop in and out of saunas all the time without having to wear some clammy bathing suit merely to hide an innocent triangle of fur. But posing in front of a camera is different. Even with clothes on I feel like an exhibitionist and don't enjoy it.

I must say, in this respect, Karen and I are different. She doesn't mind flaunting it a little. But then she's quite a sexy number.

Calling it a day

We knocked off after a very short session. Hal didn't mind, in fact he doesn't mind anything, being, like most American men, easygoing and something of a pushover, except where feelings are concerned. Coming from Europe, you always feel you're each man's first sexual experience and that he's grateful to you – unlike Frenchmen, who think you owe them your body and each of its openings and then after they've dropped their load they drop you. (Karen and I in full agreement on that.)

'So you'll have a thin portfolio,' Hal said and shrugged the implication that I'd get work anyway. I like his unflappability.

Which is a quality about him that Karen liked too, as she told me the last time we met, during her last shoot with Hal. I had arrived as she was leaving the studio with Frank to go to Great Scandinavia for drinks, then dinner somewhere.

As she left, Hal (Hal the Indiscreet) kidded her: 'You don't waste time.' To which she replied something about feelings having a life of their own and then something blahblah love (the blahblah being her excited and therefore – intentionally – not easily decipherable English) and . . . 'Well, *you* know, the een-evitable eez always,' she finished and gave him a smile as reward for whatever he may have gotten from her explanation.

I don't think any of us quite understood what she had said, maybe not even herself, the words having passed through a sieve of Finnish guide-book English of '*Où est le bathroom?*' variety plus a heavy charge of teenage embarrassment. But her eyes met mine briefly and I could tell the conversation had made her uncomfortable. The embarrassment made me like her more, revealing as it did that she and Hal had – well, you know, the inevitable is always. Especially with him.

As she passed through the doorway, she shot a shy final glance at me, making me think of a wild animal, a doe perhaps. But the look was also a smile of camaraderie – hands across the sea in friendship forever – blahblahblah, a teenage thing.

The smile breaks into my thoughts, though, at night.

That was the last time she worked. Well . . . at least in New York.

Start as you mean to go on

After Clarissa's shoot, Hal suggested Rory's Bird in Hand for a bite although I really wanted to be somewhere else – in bed with him, actually, with his arms around me to make me feel young and in need of protection for about three minutes and then boff for about thirty – that mood.

The girl-in-need-of-protection was a part of the gloom I was in, but even aside from that I could spend the rest of my life in the right man's arms. I like men, driven as they are by their balls (or testosterone, if you're from Philadelphia), and I especially like Hal and his body, which, after a shower, feels like satin, and I enjoy being held in his arms as we lie in bed and talk.

28

Worth two in the bush

The Bird in Hand is the kind of place that only Americans understand. And put up with. It's a restaurant-bar-coffeehouse over on First, but during the day it serves fancy hamburger platters with names to titillate the middle-class mind, like Bah Humburger and Haremburger. (There we are again.) To me it's just McDonald's with aristocratic pretensions (chintzy red-velvet walls) and late at night tries to be mistaken for Elaine's, which it resembles (well, physically anyway, if you leave out the red-velvet walls), except that Elaine's is an eight double-parked-limousine place, with meals, atmosphere and prices that go with it.

The Bird in Hand has upward strivings to be that way. After midnight the after-theatre crowd drops in to the Bird in Hand along with the occasional Hollywood minor celebrity, not name-above-the-title people but six-hundred-thousand-dollar-a-year prematurely balding forty-year-old execs living in the Platinum Triangle or Malibu or Venice (California) and accompanied by women who give the impression of being more enjoyable to sleep with than live with and whose style of dressing leaves very little to be guessed at.

'Arm candy,' Hal calls them.

I would have liked a hidden camera to photograph a behaviour schooled in a rapacious striving for big money. Oh those casual public touchings of each other's arms in the Beautiful People's facsimile of spontaneity: the flashed smile, the women languorously caressing the necks of carefully groomed men who show so little emotion at the display that their casualness betrays their pleasure. The women can play their roles of women of the world (*not* of course call-girls) because they narcissistically feel each time they notice your observing them – which they periodically reconfirm with a blasé turn of the head in your direction – that you share their splendid fantasy of themselves.

(Now that I've got *that* off my chest . . .)

Put it this way: by continental standards the Bird in Hand is a crappy joint. Having lived in Paris and eaten in ordinary around-the-corner restaurants, I don't consider the Bird in Hand a real restaurant but an eatery. Roz rates it lower ('You can tell by the limp-dick bread that it has unattainable pretensions'). In any case, you know a place is lous-*ay* if its menu card is almost as large as the tablecloth and you can't see your partner's head over the top of *his* menu card unless you stand on your chair.

Hal was studying the el cheapo side dishes, his idea of a festive dinner being his mother's Thursday night meatloaf, the festive part being Jello for dessert. (Lunch for him typically is peanut butter and jam, a regime unchanged since kindergarten.) He would have made a cheap date, but the trouble was, he was the host and I was the date.

'I don't know if you realize it,' I said, 'but you're paying forty-five dollars for an adjective. Why do you come here?'

'Hubris Burger,' Hal read. 'Homo Burger.'

'Isn't that what gay rights people call offensive?'

'Rory's lesbian, so it's an in joke.'

He was in one of his more talkative moods and told me Rory created a drink called Gangria, or Orange Death, and another called Slow Screw, which was classic sloe gin and orange juice. And there was the Thigh Opener – actually only a vodka gimlet but with a dollop of cognac in it that was said (by Rory) to give it eerie power. But she hyped everything, life without hype being dull. She even said there was no such thing as a boff, that making love between men and women was either rape or a mercy fuck, so obviously (at least in my opinion) she has her head on wrong.

'What's Linguini Machiavelli?'

'Long thin rubber bands in spaghetti sauce.'

We ordered the Tortellini Cellini.

Hal was famished, and in the absence of menudo or maatjes herring I'll eat anything. The Tortellini Cellini was dog food bits in about three cents' worth of wimpy noodle chunks annealed to the bottom of a copper scallop shell in which the concoction was reheated so as to melt the deep-frozen sauce. That's the polite description. What made it Cellini was that the ornate cover of the pan was topped with a silver-plated reclining nude. The waiter lifted the cover with a ceremonial twist of the wrist and a smile that expected you to fall all over yourself in rapture as he then proceeded to serve the four tablespoons of gunk.

The alternative to Tortellini Cellini was the Chicken Pterodactyl dinner. It was formerly Chicken Teriyaki but a customer once said it tasted more like pterodactyl than hen and Rory immediately changed the name, slapped an additional twenty-five dollars on the already outrageous price, and in the first night sold two hundred and twelve Chicken Pterodactyl dinners.

Go figure.

29

Back at Hal's place, his answering machine had the usual two dozen messages on it – nothing from Karen, though (hoping against hope) – and while he answered the Extremely Important Call Me Back Immediately messages – there's always about nine of those – I showered and got into bed and was dozing by the time he joined me. But then we boffed a good long while in a lazy dozy way, which is my idea of a completely pleasant evening. I remembered the next morning that I still had not unpacked in my new place but then I also remembered that first I had to locate a comfortable but inexpensive bed and not be tempted to splurge at Bloomies.

What I *think* I really want is to move in with Hal, but the idea has to come from him even if it's only because he thinks I'm a good boff – to start with. Things like that don't bother me. Men get to like me slowly, *then* fall in love with me. Then their temporary insanity gradually passes, and as they start to feel normal again, we become even better friends. At least that's what has usually happened, but what I want now is love. A man, not thirty-year-old boys – no more of *that*.

You keep hoping the opposite sex (or 'opposing sex': Roz) will catch up to you, I mean in age, but it never happens. I remember telling one boy, a few years ago, I wished *some*body *some*day would find me deep and interesting and he leaned towards me and said he thought I had a very deep and interesting chest. I consoled myself that in another few years we'd all be grown up and then things would be different, I'd be around men at last. But I know better now: with rare exceptions, men are boys and stay boys, and if you knock around the world as long as I have, you begin to see that if you have a lover and a few friends, you have all you will ever need (if your work is something you enjoy). So there.

After breakfast I left Hal and went to see dear Mr Maki, the retired elderly Finnish frame-maker I was helping put together The Book, 'the story of my life'.

A widower, he spent his days living in his underwear, which in wintertime meant warm woollies. At first it bothered me, but I got used to it.

'It is so much less trouble.' I understood what he meant.

He said he enjoyed old age. When you are old, he said, life has less disappointments and fewer ups and downs.

I feel in no hurry to put that to the test.

Laughing together

Mr Maki's hand is too shaky now for writing and he doesn't know how to type, and that's where I come in. And because his English isn't as good as his Finnish, we've ended up speaking a kind of Finnglish to each other. He even went out and bought – for me to use – a personal computer for the project, he was that serious about it. By coincidence he too was from Jyväskylä but didn't know my parents (a long shot – population over fifty thousand – but you never know).

I started The Book in the days when I was willing to take on any odd job to buy film supplies, but I was learning so much about Finnish life and generally life up north that even though I no longer need the income I continue to work for him. It takes only a few hours a week and comes as a break from everything else I do. I also go food shopping for him on my way up to his apartment. When I get there, I make him a cup of tea and read him something for a while, and after that we sit and have lunch together and right there in the dining-room get down to work.

He likes me to read to him from Whitman (and it surprises

me he even knows him). He says Whitman is easy to understand. His favourite quote (maybe mine too) is: 'But where is what I started for so long ago? And why is it yet unfound?' He decided to make that the inscription to his book because 'that's my life – it's your life too'. He knows about Karen, and when I mentioned that the inscription inevitably makes me think of her, he smiled. He seemed quite pleased at the connection.

First feed the troops

I like his idea of lunch, Finnish all the way (but with a touch of France and the Continent for relief): herring and the inevitable boiled potatoes with dill. Or maatjes herring in spiced sauce. Or red snappers, or striped bass, or lobster tails. Or tins of elk meat bits and asparagus with Finn Crisps (without caraway – 'When you get one of those seeds under your dental plate life can seem not worth living' – another experience of old age that can wait). And some pâté from the Pyrenees and camembert and chablis (for washing down vitamins) and a large bottle of Apollinaris. Top these off with strawberries or a chilled rhubarb pie. Or kiwi and whole-milk yogurt. And double cream. He's a freak about double cream.

Not all of this of course in one lunch, but that's the range. Ideally there would have been a sauna following that. Or a boff. Or a sauna followed by a boff (or a boff followed by a sauna). This time we had Strasbourg pâté and real camembert washed down with Löwenbräu. And of course the inevitable dill potatoes. A Finnish meal without dill potatoes is *une jeune fille sans tétons*.

I was surprised to learn that Mr Maki had for a while been an island keeper. You don't ordinarily think of that as an occupation (like lighthouse keeper also) and I found it fascinating. A small island had been made into a Finnish nature preserve and he lived alone on it during the warmer half of the year. His job was to meet tourists coming in on the morning boat, see that they enjoyed themselves hiking and doing nature things without getting lost, and make sure they all got off to the mainland again on the evening boat.

He liked the solitude when no tourists showed up, which happened on some weekdays. He eventually married one of the day tourists, moved her in and decided he liked living with her even more than he liked solitude, so he went back to school and studied botany before discovering there wasn't any money to be made as a professional botanist. So he and his bride came to the States, where he established himself in a sideline he had learned, frame-making. His skills were so appreciated that in a remarkably short time he was working for some of the better galleries in town, as he continued to do until he retired.

He had been married forty-two years when his wife Marita died, and after her death he said he became impotent overnight, just like that. I'm not sure why he felt he had to supply me with that tidbit, especially as he sat around in his underwear, the two of us practically side by side, but, to give him the benefit of the doubt, I think it was intended to be reassuring. He was all courtesy when I was with him. About a year after his wife's death he tried a boff with an old friend who had doggedly but unsuccessfully pursued him while Marita was alive, but it turned out to be a no-liftoff, he said, and he never tried it again or even felt like it.

I appreciated his getting that subject out of the way, if that was what he was doing, because it kept our relations comfortably uncomplicated as I cleared away the food and washed and dried the dishes (part of the deal) and we sat down again at the dining-room table side by side like two reasonable and non-incestuous family members concentrating on The Book. One time I *thought* I saw him getting a hard-on but then I have a rich fantasy life and I'm sure I was mistaken. Thanks to Iris, I'm curious about the elderly (and, I have to admit, eighty-eight-year-old balls).

The top of the world

He was a nice old man and there was always a fresh smell of Arctic snow about him, which maybe is my imagination after listening to all the stories he told about the great north, including the Canadian tundra, where he had once gone travelling as a young man. He told me about an Eskimo woman he had met whose teeth had been worn to the gums from years of biting hides to soften them to make clothing for her family. Her husband had died, her whole tribe had disappeared and both her sons had been killed while hunting. She was some indeterminate age, probably around sixty, he thought, but entirely unwrinkled, and lived alone in an igloo of her making and survived on a couple of fish a day which she caught through a hole in the ice in the water not far from her igloo, a small bay connected to Hudson Bay. She still sewed skins together for her clothing and even stitched intricate designs on their outside to make the clothing look pretty even though there was nobody around to see the handiwork.

She said to Mr Maki, 'How good life has been to me! How lucky I have been!'

The way he described her, her way of life was not unlike the way the Lapps live, up north of Ii, but without the reindeer. I enjoyed hearing about her and he enjoyed telling me.

Love under the midnight sun

The Eskimo woman talked about many things and apparently did not mind answering questions about sex, although she didn't call it sex. She called it 'laughing together' and said it made her eyes feel fresh and sparkling and she could feel her cheeks glow every time she laughed together with a man.

She liked Mr Maki and offered him a fresh fish:

'You are hungry.'

He understood this to be courting and felt flattered but he also couldn't help thinking he could be her son or possibly grandson. There was nobody else around for her and he understood her loneliness because by then he'd been up in the frozen north for a couple of months himself.

She hadn't laughed together for a long time, and the hints got broader and broader in case she wasn't getting through to this peculiar paleface from Europe, going so far as to peer up into his eyes with the hope that maybe he would understand at last how things were with her.

As an added enticement she would be glad to rub tallow in her hair, grease her face, scrape herself with a knife and rub fresh blubber over her body if he wanted her to smell all fresh and clean. She knew men liked fresh blubber smell and she liked it too: having fresh blubber all over was good for the skin and it also kept her warm.

Mr Maki managed to convey to her through about twelve words of Inuit and a few universal gestures and some elaborate miming that she was irresistible just as she was. She didn't need a coat of blubber (he privately thought it would probably make her love handles too slippery to hang on to). Hearing his reply, she considered the courting phase now over and smiling contentedly pulled down her sealskin pants and lay back and awaited his attentions, expecting him, as my English girlfriend says, to give her a good seeing to. He said she had an irrepressible smile, and from his description I could just see her shiny bronze face and Eskimo-squinty eyes gazing up at the top of the igloo in happy expectation of rubbing noses and laughing together.

He told the story well and I took down nine pages of notes on things he learned from Asiak – that was her name – and liked Mr Maki for it because, even though it happened many years ago and was only a one-week stand, it obviously had meant something to him (to the point of remembering her name). I find that touching. Also I guess I identified with the woman and thought of the pleasantness of a nice afternoon igloo boff. (Your ass must get cold, though.)

'She took me as a sex object,' he remembered happily,

enjoying the irony of the put-down phrase. 'I would have stayed longer and laughed some more but . . . well, you just don't. You're young, you move on. Before I left she offered me a fish – one for the road.'

The detail appealed to him. I could tell he loved telling the story and he added that if there had been postal service between Jyväskylä and Inuit territory he would have dropped her a note when he got back home. I told him I doubted she could read, but he said he would have sent her a photo of himself with a big smile on his face attached to a postcard of a fish.

Eskimos pay no rent

I enjoyed seeing Mr Maki more than usual these days: it took my mind off Karen. I told him how much I enjoyed anthropology and could never get enough of it (leaving out my sexual interest, not wanting to encourage wrong ideas: impotent or not, he's a man and men are men). He told me about the annual wife-carrying contest in northern Finland, in which husbands race over the snow carrying their wives on their shoulders over a 780-foot obstacle course – about a seventh of a mile. It involved a lot of spills in snowbanks and accidental skiddings down slippery slopes and whooping and yelling and notable amounts of vodka. Sounded like fun – and an excellent prelude to a bit of laughing together.

'I want to get in my stories about the Lapps too. I lived among Lapps for a while, you know. Fine people.'

'Certainly, let's put them in.' He counted on me to help shape the book too. 'I personally would be very interested in Lapps.'

'They're nomads, you know, and each year they drive their reindeer from the lowlands up to the mountains. Then with the changing of the season they drive them back again. In the lowlands there's a special lichen that the reindeer like and in the mountains there's a special grass. Many people say that Lapps don't drive their reindeer, they follow them – after all, a good-sized reindeer is stronger than three men. Actually the two groups depend on each other, but the Lapps need the reindeer more. They get their meat, their fur, their milk and their cheese from the reindeer. And bones and horns for their tools and scrimshaw – a lot of things.'

'And what do the reindeer get?'

'Protection from predators. Reindeer don't get hurt with Lapps taking care of them.'

'Except of course to lose their fur and meat, not to mention bones and horns.'

He took it nicely. 'Only when they're old, of course. But then at least all those good things are not wasted.' He was protesting a little – ah the old school.

'Only the aged really love life – the young merely live' (Mr Maki)

Working with Mr Maki and hearing stories about life not too far from the Pole was guaranteed to dispel The Gloom – at least for a while. Partly I think what made my work with him enjoyable was that in New York the elderly all seem to grow into stand-up comics. (Like Mr Nussl.) They all turn into Woody Allens. Mr Maki would occasionally come out with a one-liner like: 'You know you're getting senile when at your clinic check-up they stop asking if you have an occupation.'

The 'joke' fell with such a thud I was sure it was original. But telling it knocked *him* out of shape, so much so that he had to stop and hold on to a bookcase to breathe. I laughed politely so as not to offend him – but I got worried about what might happen to his insides if he wasn't careful.

Sometimes the conversation would go off on loony tangents. I suspect this was to relieve our tension after talking about Karen. He would ask if there was any news about her or from her.

'No.'

A sigh of sympathy from him. Or maybe just a philosophical sigh.

So then we would talk about life in America. I would regale him with the fact that in America some cows are fitted with false teeth so that they can eat more grass (really true). That cracked him up some more and he tried to top it with the pet shop he once found in Brooklyn that sold diapers for parakeets. I had already heard about that one, I think I had read it long ago in some column in the *Times*, but laughed anyway because he was cracking up again, and I didn't want him to feel lonely. But then, on the other hand, not to encourage him too much, I kept the laugh brief (easy) because I was afraid he might choke to death. I've never met anyone who laughed so hard.

He asks me often about Karen. I told him the other day that in my tracking down Frank I had concluded he didn't live in Harlem. Or Bed-Stuy either, for that matter. In fact, according to one of the au pairs at Great Scandinavia, Frank wasn't black – part African, true, but not African-American.

'Ah,' Mr Maki said. 'Karen wanted to think he was black and maybe the man encouraged it?'

'Why?'

'Certain Nordic women are attracted to blacks. But if he wasn't black, what was he?'

The au pair had told me that according to a friend of Frank's who just dropped by one day, he was half Egyptian and half Polynesian, a blend that might account for his exotic appeal. Mr Maki said that was sad.

'Why is that sad?'

'He's making it so that the blacks get blamed.'

So Mr Maki doesn't think I'm so crazy. He takes it seriously that Karen has disappeared. I could have kissed him.

'I'm convinced she was kidnapped,' I told him.

'Oh yes,' he said thoughtfully. 'It's very possible.'

I kissed him. On the cheek.

The itch in anthropology

On the way home I bought a pound of peas and stopped in at Great Scandinavia, where I ordered a chablis and began shelling the peas at the bar.

I held the open bag of peas in my lap and was shelling them and putting the peas and the empty pods on to two napkins on the bar and thinking about Asiak. Down at the end of the bar, Mama was knitting another sweater for Mr America, silently taking in what I was doing and, being from Åland, thinking it natural to shell peas at a bar before going home and cooking them.

The only other person there was seated at the middle of the bar, on Lasse's stool, an attractive and tastefully dressed woman slightly older than me. I thought her regular features and definite eyebrows would make her a good cosmetics model. She appeared to be waiting for someone. I could see her watching me in the bar mirror, there being nothing else in Great Scandinavia to watch, and after a while, she turned to me and said:

'Mind my asking what you're doing that for?'

'The peas? Shelling them for dinner.'

Reflective pause.

'Why don't you buy them frozen and ready to cook? That way you wouldn't have to go through all that.'

'I like doing it.'

I popped a bright green pea into my mouth and offered her the rest of the pod. She shook her head a vigorous no. Then to soften the blow to my ego, she said:

'But *than* kyou.'

She actually said '*than* kyou', not 'thank you'. Hoity-toit.

I kept on shelling peas and Mama kept on knitting the sweater and I didn't need to glance over to verify that my neighbour was still gazing at Weirdo Me-o in the mirror shelling peas.

Gradually I became aware that *Than*-kyou was trying to scratch herself and at the same time conceal that she was doing so because the itch was apparently in her crotch, judging by her discomfort. She had her legs unnaturally jammed together and was rubbing her right hand against her groin in an awkward rhythm, palm *upward*, and that's impossible.

That apparently didn't work too well because then she tried a genteel flick – a brief discreet flash of thumb, like an accident in case anybody was watching. The itch evidently went away and everything was all right, it had been just an insignificant passing itch. But *no* – *damn* – the flick hadn't been enough – and the right hand went back to scratch position, again palm up, desperately massaging the crotch area. To put her out of her misery I almost said to her, 'Why not just scratch it?' But the trouble of course is that when you think you're helping people you sometimes only embarrass them more. They want you *not* to notice they have an itch, certainly not *there*. (Nobody *ever* gets an itch *there*, right?)

The peas were podded (depodded? unpodded?) and so as a diversionary tactic that might allow her a decent shot at one solid satisfying scratch, I made much of noisily gathering up my things and saying goodbye to Mama. *Than*-kyou looked suddenly relaxed and cheerful as she gave me a goodbye wave. Ah – sneaked in a direct rub, all right, and I felt relieved myself. I had started to feel itchy all over just watching her. The Eskimo woman would have scratched her crotch while calmly handing you a herring for the road. That's the sad part about studying anthropology: the reminders of where you are and how you're allowed to act according to whatever tribe you're born into, or stuck with. Still, Manhattan is better than New Guinea, which is better than Philadelphia, and even Philadelphia is better than Kansas. (I said this once to tease Roz, who was born and raised in Kansas, and she said, 'Never speak ill of the dead.')

Still slogging through the Karen doldrums and general blah feeling of these days, I wasn't in the mood to go to Hal's studio, so I went over to my new place, despite my good intentions to goof off the rest of the day, and was unpacking when the phone rang – Mr Nussl. I had given him my new number in case of problems but of course I never expected to hear from him again and I was surprised. I had swept the studio clean and left nothing behind except the Goodwill bed, which I had done with his approval, so I knew it couldn't be that.

'Mr Nussl,' I said into the phone. 'How are you?' And to keep things on track, 'And how's Mrs Nussl?'

'Ecch, dun't esk.' Mrs Nussl had gone to the funeral of her cousin Natasha in Fall River, Massachusetts, but she was not what he wanted to talk about. He wanted to talk about Iris, The Other Tenant. He asked if we could meet and he suggested Minelli's.

'That place where we had such a good time.'

I took the IRT downtown. Out once more on the street, I saw it had started snowing again, creating a feeling of tranquillity – trafficless peace in certain parts of town. At that hour Minelli's was empty and I sat at the end of the bar farthest from the door and ordered espresso.

Last winter I had dropped in there so often, to warm up after photographing downtown, that Sam, the daytime bartender, remembered me now even though it had been a while. He was one of those handsome barmen just under forty with a well-married look who don't bother you if you're a woman sitting alone at the bar. When he saw my Leica, that first time, he told me he was thinking of getting an Olympus for his wife for Christmas and asked if that was a good investment. I told him she would be thrilled with it.

Aimez-vous baseball?

He brought over the espresso and went back to the front end of the bar, watching a baseball game in some kind of taped sports classic that Americans freak out on: 'Two men on, no strikes, top of the seventh . . . Hector at bat, Hector oh for three. Now Mason looking at first . . . Mason doesn't throw a screwball as such.' The scholarship of baseball. 'It's more a curved fast ball.' Pause. 'Mason's just called time. Actually a ballplayer cannot *call* time. He can only *ask* for time.' More scholarship – hard to believe this stuff – then pause. 'Hector disdains the bunt.' (I loved the 'disdains'.) Finally old Hector apparently connected and slammed one into the centrefield stands, three runs in, followed by the orgasm of baseball: '*Man! What* a *ball*game!'

I sipped my coffee and waited, my mind drifting to other snowy nights when I would be drawn to the darkest quarters of backwater Manhattan, walking in the hushed moonless gloom of Coenties Slip, where fleets of seagoing schooners once docked, to where the old Fulton Fish Market's ramshackle smelly buildings used to snuggle below the elevated FDR Drive before the renovation. Once I saw a Finnish tanker cruise by, with the home port of 'Helsinki' on its stern. And that made me think of Karen again – Karen – home port – going home. I wondered for the umpteenth time that day alone what was holding her brother up.

I tried not to think about her but about the dockside areas of Manhattan: comforting thoughts.

What makes me different from most New Yorkers is that I love walking. More than once, feeling especially energetic I've taken a marathon walk beginning at the sombre Custom House (where Melville, after writing *Moby-Dick*, checked bills of lading as inspector of cargoes) and walking north along the river (in the summertime smelling like boiled laundry) and rotting docks and Moran tugs all the way up to Little West 12th Street and the Gansevoort Pier – Revolutionary Army country. Washington and his bedraggled troops slept and pissed here, where derelicts now sleep and piss on the cobblestone street named in honour of the leader and founder, with rotted-meat smell coming from the wholesale butcher warehouses where at night drag-queen hookers in fishnet-hose provide meat of another sort. I always wondered if I could draw deep moral lessons from this but never could.

The art form called photography

I had brought along a copy of *World Photography Newsletter* to look at while waiting at Minelli's and I read a review by E. F. Hartmann of the work of 'newcomer Meryl R. Geist':

'Hers is a shared world, in which a dispassionate distance is forced on the viewer by the impersonality of the lens. It is not an angry but an inquisitive lens. Her photographs are statements as questions: they are visual opinions, a vision that tests. The images are dispatches from the front.' He especially liked her 'Peoplescape Series' and the new 'Eggplant Series II', the latter 'stunning' him. Jesus H.

In a review of Atget he used the word 'automaticity' not once but twice and added that the 'evolving, inundating tones of the grey scale shimmer the senses into an apprehension of emotions too submerged to be summoned by superficial imagery', and I was still puzzling that one out when I noticed the time: I had been there an hour. Suddenly restless – and unnerved – I decided to go on my usual East River walk. I waited a little while longer just in case, but Mr Nussl never showed up and I wondered if I had maybe misunderstood.

30

The way is near yet men seek it afar

It was the walk I take whenever I feel a need for change. Finns never get too far away from water. I feel drawn to piers, rivers, ships – New York is for me, first and last, a good working port.

With my camera along as always, I went over to the waterfront not to photograph necessarily but to look around. It was a low-contrast day, with a slight mist and the air warmer than it had been all week. I walked towards the snout of the island, where the East River veers towards the bay and flows peaceably out to sea. A freighter was riding downstream through the brown and violet river murk, sombrely lugging cargo to the Atlantic and the open sea, probably Europe or faraway Africa (bloody Africa again). Seagulls, sounding like rusty hinges in the sky, soared upward through the wettish tumbling snow, following the old boat at a distance, the flakes falling faster and finally obliterating the departing tub. In the falling-snow silence there was no longer a horizon, only indeterminate middle distance – space destroyed. It felt like early evening all afternoon long – time destroyed. The only thing moving was the sky full of gulls and flakes. On the ground every flake lay where it fell.

There was a faded-edge-photo look about the oldest downtown streets and buildings with black fire escapes scaling their sides. A smell of spices and roasting coffees came from aromatic warehouses in colonial buildings. Some of the very old buildings had grillwork like frilly black lace exaggeratedly highlighted by the falling snow that was piling on them in round white tufts. The darkly pitted façades were specked with old white powder from a week of snow.

I was startled by a 'Hey!' and an elderly bearded drunk with what was once no doubt a nice face took off his hat in an exaggeratedly gracious manner and smiled. His yellow-red eyes stared out of dirt-caked cheeks, and his lower lip, with a blue welt on it, hung down and revealed grey-white gums. Chained around his neck was a toy barrel, meant to be funny, making him into a St Bernard dog. He tried to move his mouth and say something but instead shuddered in hideous slow motion. Then finally, with difficulty: 'Want, picture o' me? Don't, charge much.'

'How much?'

'What's today, Wednesday? Wednesday, special's ten dollars.'

'Today's Sunday.'

'Sunday special too.'

I took a snapshot and gave him a tenner. He wafted a formal kiss in my direction and bowed from the waist, tilting a little, and left.

All of a sudden a luminous fog drifted in from the direction of the sea and a pale sun began breaking through as I walked past some boarded-up iodine-smelling structures under the FDR Drive. Dots of misty sunlight shone languidly on the water between the piers, gelatinely stretching apart and back. The water was so quiet you could hear slats of wood at the river's edge gently tapping against each other as they softly rode up and down, down and up, going nowhere in the pier-trapped water, and with everything smelling of tar.

Out on a heavy-timbered pier, at the far end of it deep in the river, the water washed and slapped against the pilings, and somewhere in the bay a boat hooted its way. Close in, in a slow swash of water, a tug loomed suddenly and hugely out of the mist and chuff-chuffed past me just yards away, its foghorn making a hoarse moan ending in a high-pitched squeal like a dog crying. Through the brilliant mist I could make out a portion of the Brooklyn Bridge standing monumentally aloof against the mauve Manhattan sky.

Later I saw the bearded old man again, lifting up a pint bottle in a long pull. He spotted me and we waved to each other.

Jotted-down graffiti: 'I want to live too.' Not a joke (I don't think) but of course next to it the inevitable wisecrack: 'Take and you shall receive.'

More graffiti, in a series: 'Hooray, hooray, the first of May, / Outdoor fucking starts today!' 'To the vast majority of us nothing ever happens.' 'Especially not outdoor fucking.' (Mm. Check out Central Park.)

In an alley two bums were drinking cheap sherry from a shared bottle, one of them wiping his mouth off with the back of one hand while loosely gripping his cock with the other, pissing an amber (sherry-looking) fluid against the brick wall of a building. They were arguing about the names of the seven seas. The Caspian Sea, the Black Sea and the Sea of Galilee were valid but not the Atlantic, which 'is not a sea, it's a *notion*'.

I caught a last-second glimpse of the other one parking his very liquid lunch on the pavement, a wine-dark sea. Ugh, charming.

I decided to go back uptown but first passing by Minelli's to see if Mr Nussl had showed up.

No Mr Nussl, but Roz was there.

Bill Joachim: 'If you bring out the worst in Roz, you see her at her best'

About Roz: she likes to say Roz is just her *nom de bar* but that's also the way we knew her in school. Besides, who would want to use a movie-star name like Lorna Beach? I don't know what gets into movie people. She claims to dislike it, but actually I think she likes it a lot.

She had just arrived and was taking off a fur stole and installing herself at a booth as I walked in. Dressed as flamboyantly as ever, she was like something out of the Sixties: white blouse, chestnut suede gaucho pants, thirty-calibre bandolier belt with bullets that looked almost real (and conceivably were). She could look chic in old faded farmer's overalls, which is what she wore at home.

There's something brave and at the same time sad about her. But an amazing woman, physically – I have to hand it to her. At twenty-seven, she has a place in Big Sur, a modest house in Bel Air and a *garconnière* in Paris, all of it paid for out of her own work, not family wealth: seven films in seven years, really as meteoric a rise as Karen's. She also sublets a *pied-à-terre* in SoHo for shacking up between films with Bill.

One glance and it was obvious she was on a bender, with the eager oral look of a navy commander's wife pub-crawling with him on shore leave, all boozy and wet-lipped. She has a tough-sweet personality and untrusting eyes that beg to trust. You can see her early beginnings in her looks – privileged but starved. I like her breezy view of life, especially when she gets outrageously high, which despite analysis (with Perilstein, though, good grief) is whenever she's not working. Even on the set she has the ability to work when mildly smashed. Some day, my guess is, she will cave in all at once.

'Hi,' she said, seeing me. 'What's *que-pasa*-ing? Every once in a while I have to come back to God's concrete.'

When I'm with her I always have the feeling I've accidentally walked on to the set of a Marx Brothers movie and at any moment the stooped figure of Groucho will come long-leggedly loping into the room with Margaret Dumont oh-so-bra-*h-ave*ly in tow as Groucho dances his eyebrows up and down and flicks cigar ashes around.

'It doesn't matter what you do in the bedroom as long as you don't do it in the street and frighten the horses'

I called over to Sam for another espresso as Roz began telling me about a funeral she had just come back from in Beverly Glen or Malibu or one of those places.

'Remember Mimi Haviland?'

'You told me about her crack-up.'

'Yeah, she'll do it in any position. She was the original double-breasted mattress thrasher, with the intellectual depth of a cucumber – through osmosis – and an IQ only slightly above room temperature. Well anyway, she finally did what she always threatened she would when she died – lie in state topless so everyone could admire her breast-enlargement surgery. She was the original good time had by all. No husband was safe around her, so at the funeral nobody was wild with grief. The embalmer put a nice smile on her, being possibly a member of the club, maybe even posthumously, I mean who knows what might happen with an unhappily married Hollywood undertaker? She was a born-again Baptist but then died again and became a born-again agnostic, then really died and this time got cremated. *After* lying in state so we could admire her bazooms. She tried to show them once on Oprah.'

'They were large?'

'Darling, they were the original World Cup. Listen, I'm a little more than pissed but less than shit-faced, Hamlet, Act One, Scene Four.'

She's still too young for the alcohol to affect her looks and you can't help admiring her sleepy languorous thick hair that looks like it's never set ('My wind-tunnel effect'). Surprisingly women like her as much as men do. Competition with her is so hopeless there's no point hating her for what's not her fault. They identify with her and enjoy seeing how men feel when they look at her. The women feel it too each time they see her.

Once long ago, in our sophomore year at Bennington, Roz wrote in a men's room during a weekend trip to Greenwich Village: 'Men (all sizes) wanted by nymphomaniac,' with the dorm phone number. No calls. Which reminded me of the time when Roz and I were stretched out in the dorm one long peaceful twilight, just quietly reflecting on life and death, and she suddenly came out with: 'Jesus, when you think about it – Bennington, and all that *cunt*.' She once had China bowls moulded from her breasts after someone told her that Catherine the Great had had that done. (Which of course is not true: it was Marie Antoinette, the famous Paris model.)

Anatomy may be destiny but there's anxiety in it too

Sam brought over the coffee and gave Roz a respectful fan's discreet smile of recognition.

'You serving lunch?' Roz said.

'Yes, Miss Beach.'

Squintily she focused on the chalkboard hanging next to the bar.

'I'll have the fettucini al dente – I mean, Alfuckinfredo *por favor*, or whatever, with extra oregano, or whatever. *Per favore.*'

'Will that be with the lunch or à la carte?'

'It's with the veal parmi-john. And hold the mayo.'

Sam smiled as if hearing such nonsense for the first time and moved away. Roz began a lengthy monologue that, summarized, meant (I think) it's better to live alone in New York than be surrounded by people in L.A. because loneliness has nothing to do with people or their absence. Even when she was with Bill she felt lonely, and that proved it. But at least there was the Manhattan scene for the two of them to be lonely *in*. Something like that. All this rapid fire.

'But right now it's OK. Bill's having one of his attacks of love, which last about a week, or six orgasms, whichever comes first. You know the old joke. "Why do women have cunts? So men will talk to us."'

'How's Bill?'

'Bill's Bill. But we get our revenge on men. There's an enzyme in pussy that's detrimental to the enamel of your teeth. My dentist told me that, Marvin Glasscock.'

'Ouch.'

'Yeah, well, think of his wife's anxiety. You'd think he'd get his name changed.'

'Where's Bill now?'

'At the shrink's. His "Soak-high-a-tryst", Bill calls him.'

The fettucini arrived as I was trying to think of an excuse to get away from Roz. The only way to be with her when she's drunk is to get high also and for that you have to be willing to throw away the rest of the day – which means drinking even more than Finns usually do, which is a lot.

'Excuse me,' she stage-whispered, 'I've been dying to go peepee. I can say that in French too. Pee-*pee*.'

Her round trips to the john were so swift you couldn't help worrying about her (in school we called her Thimble Bladder).

She returned and plunged into the fettucini. I started thinking about Mr Nussl again and wondered what could have gone wrong but then decided to hell with it. I also thought about Bill and the last party we all went to, a boozy affair in which we milled around a lot. Roz and Bill had been tanked up enough to be in top form and were enjoying themselves. I heard Roz talking to an airy-fairy woman from Los Angeles, who said, 'The light in me sees the light in you.'

Roz: 'You better fucking believe it.'

With the amount Roz drinks, people wonder what I see in her. But it's her high wattage and offbeat understanding of life. High jinx and humour are akin to intelligence, and I enjoy her hit-and-run statements, like the·one she once made to a drunken lech at a party, who asked her:

'How do you spell Roz?'

'With two *t*s.'

I loved the dismissal, boredom, a wish for a higher level of discourse and an implied hierarchy of values, all compressed into three words.

I liked Bill too, and the two of them together. Bill once told me: 'Alcohol distorts your senses but then that's *why* you drink. You look at the same old things but you see them now in a new way and feel stimulated. Read Aristotle.'

'*Ari*stotle?' Roz said – both of us a little surprised.

'He said nothing great in politics or the arts has ever been achieved by anyone who didn't have a melancholic temperament. And there's a close connection between melancholic and alcoholic and I don't mean the rhyme.'

'Where did you read that?' I asked.

'You know those little *Reader's Digest* things?'

'I didn't realize you were so learned,' Roz said.

'It's the only reason I drink,' Bill said. 'I know too much.'

Bill is less subtle than Roz. But then, without, I think, being chauvinistic, most men are less subtle than most women.

Which, interestingly enough, is not an opinion shared by Roz. But I think it's only because of a few feminists who recently got on her case in some trade journal or other. She describes them now as 'the thought police'.

I watched Roz wrestle with her fettucini for a while. Then I came up with an excuse that sounded, I hoped, plausible and made my escape. We went through the usual parting speeches about getting together for dinner some time and in any case promising to meet at the opening of Bill's Whitney retrospective in April, which was already the talk of the art world. Apparently Hal and I were invited to the party that his dealer, Sue Damson, was throwing right after the opening. Roz said we could go as her friends, there'd be no problem. I said fine and told her that until then to say hello to Bill, and she said to say hi to Fellatio. (Felicia, of the Felicia Agency.)

I noted that nowadays you got a museum retrospective at thirty-four.

As I left I heard her ordering a 'Grammar Yay' and Sam the bartender saying, 'Yes, Miss Beach, one Grand Marnier.'

I feel bad about what she's doing to her body. But there's no way I can stop her. Or him. I give him ten years to live at the outside.

31

Periodic seizures of Finnish gloom: northern, hardy perennial variety. Now in addition there might be a Seasonal Affective Disorder, according to Martin last week. Which I can believe: every Finn has some. That's one reason they hit the bottle, I told him, to raise their *spirits*. He didn't get it – at least, he didn't comment. Again.

I developed some film, mostly old rolls, and made contact sheets: disappointing results. Not surprising. I've been putting off film development these days half expecting the results to be nothing.

Have been to the Great Scandinavia many times, and of course no sign of Frank. A few of the regulars remembered Karen and half-heartedly wondered whatever became of her. Was she just another flash in the pan? That made me angry. It's evident their interest in her is not real, especially when the talk drifted to other subjects, as though all subjects were of equal value.

Evidently it hadn't taken Karen long to get into the habit of going to the Great Scandinavia and taking Frank with her. On nights when it was hopping, Great Scandinavia was like Helsinki but with Frank's company as added pleasure.

I know the place's appeal. Like all ethnic groups in New York, Finns live in a world within a world. But what New Yorkers are not aware of are the Finns' Rabelaisian bar-room scenes on Friday and Saturday nights (if in fact they're aware at all of Finns in New York). The scenes are of an order and nature not associated with Finlandia and Sibelius or the timber forests of the Lappish north.

Sometimes, for fun, or for its shock value, I've taken an American date there, or did in the days BH (Before Hal), or whenever Hal got too busy to see me. The night before Karen's disappearance, a friend named Quentin suggested having a drink somewhere. He needed consoling, he said, being on the verge of divorcing his wife of seventeen years. Madder wine and all that.

The higher nowhere

Quentin is an author – as distinguished from writer, I suppose – and uses the word *libation* for drink and says things like: 'A writer is benignly afflicted with the need to comment on life while engaged in the act of living it.' And: 'It's discernible – to the discerning.' He once told me: 'Women keep men from getting too abstract. Women hold us to life,' and when I asked if that was the reason he enjoyed going to bed with them, he said: 'At a profound level, yes.'

Quentin, who cutely, or quaintly, says he was originally from Asspin, Colorado, has written another book since his novel *A Stab at Mater*, which he says is about a boy who kills his mother but is secretly a requiem for his own dead mother. Why it's a secret I have no idea, but I send not to ask for whom the bell tolls: it tolls for Quentin and his Mom. His books are well-regarded but sell anyway.

'My new novel is about time, time as protagonist. I know that's been attempted countless times, but I have to have *my* say.'

When I looked at him blankly (also politely, to the best of my ability) he added:

'It is not easy to convey the "so-called dance of life" through words.'

That kind of talk is always a little over my head so I tried looking intelligent by not saying anything and maintaining a solemn air, a trick that works surprisingly often.

We have seen each other once in a while ever since we got acquainted through one of his showoffy pieces on photography for the *New York Review of Books*. He's a novelist, he says, but he's also a man of letters (dun't esk), and I don't want to put him down in any way that singles him out and picks on him. As far as I'm concerned, *all* pieces on photography are showoffy. They get this pious tone. They sound like they're writing Ph.D. theses at each other.

That was the article in which he mentioned me and four or five others out of twenty-three photographers, some of them well known (I felt good about being included in that company) in the big anniversary show the Nièpce Gallery put on last year. He said that work like ours 'provided justification of the photographic enterprise'. That's the way he writes (and talks!): he can't say photography – it's the photographic enterprise. Quentin says he's 'inclined to credit the assumptions that underlie the imagery'. Jesus.

(After Roz's first meeting with him she said: 'He probably drops pin-striped farts.')

I have mixed feelings about him: nice guy but creep. (Which is another thing. Whenever I have thoughts about leaving Hal I think of all the creeps out there.) Quent once taught creative writing at Harvard for a year but quit to write an 'Updikean novel'. I'm not sure what that is (maybe Updike doesn't know yet either) but Quent's 'style' is to keep introducing 'interesting' people to keep readers from getting bored and no longer buying the books he cranks out each twelvemonth (his word). Another thing: he always tries to sound in conversation the way he thinks philosophers sound in conversation. He says 'thus', as in: 'Thus everything changes except everything changes' – which is actually not bad, when you think that one through, although I doubt it's original. (Maybe he read it in Updike.)

I asked him if it was true, speaking of time, that he was writing a novel called *And the Sun Also Sets*. He laughed and said no but that that wasn't bad.

Quentin also writes pieces and reviews for magazines. This is his *style* of writing (reconstructing a piece I read once about cockroaches, of all things):

New Yorkers live in a city that's so far in debt it can no longer physically maintain its schools, plough away snowfall in less than two weeks, clean its air enough to render it invisible, settle its utility bills less than three months late, pay all its employees *every* payday, patch up axle-breaking potholes, collect its garbage unfailingly, or reduce its rat population by a modest thousandth of one per cent. But all these are as nothing when compared with the orthopterous insect of the family Blattidae [*that's a cockroach – I had to look it up*], whose local lineage can be traced back to Pieter Stuyvesant's landing at the tip of Manhattan, when he opened the lunchbox provided by Mrs Stuyvesant for his maiden New World voyage and unwrapped New York's first pastrami on rye. At that critical moment, he unintentionally released one roach, female, the equivalent of nine months pregnant and the progenitor of sixteen dectillion descendants, counting only those below Wall Street and only during the first year of the Dutch colonial settlement. The residence of these *concitoyens*, otherwise *las cucarachas*, is openly accepted by New Yorkers on the unassailable ground that they have no choice. Therefore roaches are not a 'problem': problems have solutions. Roaches are a *presence* – like corruption, like potholes, like uncollected garbage, like the Dutch colonists themselves who brought them over. You could *try* to reduce the cockroach population by a millionth of a billionth of a nano per cent in what might seem like a realistically attainable time span, but you would not make a dent in an exploding population that defies Malthusian reckoning in a species that reproduces that number every night in the East Sixties alone.

Ek-cetera. Except that it sounds a lot like me when I read it over, but his writing is *something* like that.

When Quentin first met me he thought I was an ignorant pinhead (a name I have been called before for reasons that mystify me), which turned out to be, in his case, merely his way of making out: he looks like papa's boy in designer jeans and adopts the treat-'em-like-dirt macho approach to women, a winning combination that perhaps explains his batting average of around .003, and possibly his impending divorce.

I don't like maligning him, though. He has a likeable side, and I don't *usually* feel that Quent has, in Roz's stale joke about him, delusions of adequacy.

Anyway I told Quentin that the only thing that interested me was what made something into what we call art. And of course right away he started to smile with a superior writerly smile – the way writers suddenly get a cryptic look as they struggle to come up with a *lit*rary reply. I tried to explain to him: not how you *do* art – that's not what I mean. I do photography and there's no problem about doing it unless I'm stuck, which happens to everybody at one time or another. But what *is* it that we do that we call art? It's hard for me to make it any clearer than that, which is ironic because it's the only subject that has *constantly* interested me since adolescence. Why does it make us feel good to look at nature and also feel that extra something that makes us grab a camera and start making pictures of it? When I told Quentin that that's a subject worth writing about he smiled the way adults will smile at a child as they pat the little kid on the head (*good* girl), yet to me, personally, that's the only subject worth considering in life. Something in us enables us to produce art, and it's that something, whatever it is, that makes life worth living.

Got nowhere, of course, but I hope, as I get older, to acquire some understanding on my own. But some day I'd like to meet someone I could talk to about things that interest me. Apart from sex.

32

So anyway, there we were at Great Scandinavia, and when I tuned back in to Quentin he was expounding on how women have always had it easier than men. This came as news to me.

'Consider all the great women writers and artists, if you will. They stayed *home*. They didn't pursue careers. Look at George Eliot, Edith Wharton, George Sand, Mary Cassatt, and what's-her-name Virginia Woolf, not to mention Berthe Morisot – and all the others. They didn't have to report anywhere at nine in the morning and wait until retirement before doing what they *really wanted to do*, do you see? Their husbands and their fathers and grandfathers *slaved their asses off* so these women could stay home and write and paint.'

'Right, Quent. And so they could instruct the governess and maids and cooks and wetnurses on all the work that *they* had to slave *their* asses off doing.'

'Well, thee uh . . .'

An oral history of our time (Part CXXVII)

Mama was on duty, and the usual Friday-night festivity was in the air. I could hand-hold Quent by myself for only a limited amount of time. My spirits picked up when Mama said Ulla might drop in that evening. I looked forward to the kookiness that would ensue – when you get to know Ulla, Roz sounds like Mother Superior – and maybe that would catch old Quent off guard and shock him into unaccustomed happiness ('He

once studied philosophy but cheerfulness keeps breaking in'
– that kind of thing, whatever the exact quote is).

Three women drifted in, first two, then another, and I
introduced them to Quent as they came in the door and went
down the bar past us. It was a little confusing because all
Finnish women (nearly all) are named Paula or Marita or
Leena (which Americans pronounce 'Lay-ner', putting an *r* at
the end), with an occasional Ulla or Karen, or Carita or Ulrika,
thrown in for good measure. The first two that evening were
a pair of Leenas.

When you have only about ten or twelve women's names
in Finland you end up assigning numbers or epithets to distin-
guish them: Paula One, Paula Two, Leena Four, 'No, *not*
Washington, D.C. Leena but the one with the gap in her front
teeth.' 'Oh, Bay *Ridge* Leena.'

Paula and the two Leenas, happily looped, were talking a
machine-gun sultry Finnish, loaded with trilled *r*s in that
staccato gutsy sound that give men erections. (Source of information: every man I've ever met at Great Scandinavia.) Somebody down the bar yelled for accordion music and somebody
else temporarily detached himself from his drink (after gulping
most of it down) and went somewhere in a taxi, came back
in ten minutes with an accordion and disappeared into the
pocket dancehall in the back, where somebody switched on
a blasting loudspeaker system and a polka got stridently going.
Polkas don't begin, they get launched.

The door opened and in came two able-bodied sea-women,
if that's not politically incorrect – anyway, women crew
members of a ship – one a short brunette and one a tall blonde
and both probably from the old Gripsholm, or Stockholm, or
whatever the name is of the Swedish ship in port nowadays.
They ordered 'Yeenan tawneek'.

Mama (coolly): 'Vat?'

Tall Blonde: 'Yeenan tawneek.'

Mama (muttering): 'Oh. Yeenan tawneek.'

She served their gin and tonic.

I recognized Mama's style. She had understood the first time, but in her view, Swedes only look down on Finns while drinking themselves into comas and the cold 'Vat?' was Mama's 'subtle' way of saying, 'Have your drink and then beat it.' The only people she ever got surly with were Swedes, and Mrs Jaaskelainen did too. Finns and Swedes don't get along too well, although I could never understand why. I like Swedes.

The invisible dancehall behind us slowly began to fill with moving bodies occasionally glimpsed through the open doorway. There was hand-clapping at intervals to thank the accordionist, and Mama behind the bar smiled now with non-avaricious pleasure at the upswing in business, glad that the evening was not going to be the usual deadly stretch till 4 a.m. closing time.

Ulla the Legendary

Leena Three walked in – between jobs as au pair and free Friday nights lately – and came over to say hello and have a drink with Quent and me. She was annoyed by a report in the *Post* about two feminist Cherokee women who had been in the papers recently over some Oklahoma land claim and getting a lot of press.

'Can you believe dot? Indians. Sue gauverrn-ment for meellion dollars.'

She gave the Swedish women a dismissive glance.

'Bullsheet dykes, I dink,' she told us, more or less softly.

Who were dykes – the Cherokee women or these two Swedes? But with a more furtive second glance it became clear the statement was intended for present company, not something generic or ethnically prejudiced. It was common knowledge that Leena Three was bi and possibly she was trawling.

A couple of Finnish seamen – crew members – walked in and ordered beers, 'Carlsbeddi' and 'Tuboddi', already high from fuelling stops for Carlsbeddi and Tuboddi along the way, and one of them started singing to Leena Two, further down the bar, sounding like an off-key Bing Crosby, which is probably the way he learned to sing – from ancient World War Two records. The other one, oh, you know, very casually idled towards the Swedish women and somehow, entirely by chance, you understand, ended up at their side, discreetly looking off into the middle distance and silently pondering his next *sub*-till manoeuvre. The two Swedes, ready in any case to shove off and taking this in, maintained amused radio silence until the Tall Blonde said to the hopeful Finnish Lothario, calmly, breezily:

'Piss off.'

In a coordinated movement, the Swedish women gracefully slid two Scandinavian rumps off butt-warmed stools and heartbreakingly headed for pastures far from hoi polloi.

As they walked out the door, the short brunette paused in the doorway and shot back: '*Vy* you call dis Great Scandee*na*hvia? Feenlondt is *not* Scandee*na*hvia.' Slam!

'Bullsheet dykes, all right,' the disappointed Lothario said to Leena Three in retroactive agreement and shouted at the door, 'Don't pissing me off!' He put a coin in the jukebox, from which 'Finlandia Hymni', with one-hundred-piece philharmonic orchestra, swelled to life and vibrated the four walls and floor. A reverent hush passed like a wave through the crowd – and then the stereo jumble of Finlandia and crazy polka music from the back moved one of the regulars to reach behind the jukebox and temper the volume of Sibelius.

Mama was glad to see the women go.

'I dassent like Svedish vimmin,' she said and as she gave the bar a disinfecting wipe in case they had deposited any staph germs, she looked up with a sudden warm beam at the door.

Because there she was: the legendary Ulla, tall and with patrician swagger, came in wearing a below-the-knees heavy black overcoat completely unbuttoned even though it was storming outside and exposing the two long columns of her sheer-tighted legs. She was a six-foot blonde ex-Finnair flight attendant with pistol-packing thighs that zoomed to the cheeks of her flamboyant ass, which was barely covered, despite the weather, by a leather minidress so mini it could qualify as cummerbund. It was a skirt you didn't dare bend over in in mixed company. Which wouldn't stop Ulla.

The V-word

She arrived in a scornful rage, some of it pure Ulla theatre, with rapid-fire Finnish and English, talking about the 'mother-fucking American' she had just left and apologizing to Quentin that the remark was not meant for all American males ('whom I absolutely adore, dahling') while liberally using the words 'prick' and that horrible Finnish no-no, *vittu* (cunt). Mama, who is normally Carita the Imperturbable, began to get red in the face and considered throwing Ulla out (not liking the v-word). But she remembered just in time that with Ulla there the place would jump and the liquor would flow, or more to the point, money would agreeably pour into the till, and the next morning Mrs Jaaskelainen, the owner, going over the receipts, would feel what in her passes for happiness.

I turn to the suit next to me, a well-dressed Finnish business-man eyeing, inevitably, Ulla and say, 'I could never settle in Finland. The late hours and the vodka would kill me in a year.'

'Maybe less,' he assures me.

But he's barely aware of me. All he can see is Ulla: she's all non-stop fast lane and men can't get enough of her. It has been said that she can't get enough of men either. But selectively.

The Finnish subculture of New York

Toronto Paula comes in and heads towards Ulla. Ulla is the magnetic north of the bar: everyone gravitates towards her or revolves around her.

After a perfunctory exchange of hellos, Ulla, already bored by this deadbeat Finnish world that it is her fate to live in, and knocking back a Teacher's scotch to brighten up her little corner of it, takes in Toronto Paula's humdrum get-up and mentally dismisses it as pathetic. She inquires whether Paula's breasts are for real or are they getting a little help – in the half-interested idle-chitchat way you might ask a friend where she found that pretty little handbag while not really giving a damn.

But Toronto Paula – who has been in the country four months now and likes to show off her command of English – is 'with it', as she occasionally informs you.

She says: 'You mean, vat nature had forgotten I stuff with cotton? No, dese babies are for real.'

Breast contests yet. She grabs one in each hand and gives the round globes an affectionate fondle as though without the massage we wouldn't believe she was telling the truth.

You could *feel* Quentin's blood pressure rising.

'Vat about those mountains you got?' she asks Ulla – Quent smiling now (at this 'interesting Finnish dialogue' probably).

'You better believe they're real,' Ulla says and nonchalantly undoes the top of her dress to reveal a blindingly white lacy bra that supports two handsome size 40DD bazooms-and-a-half.

Quent looks electrified, blood pressure shooting up.

'Not bad,' Toronto Paula says, but with such genuine feeling you can hear the envy. 'Too bad I'm not a dyke.'

'Yeah, it is too bad,' Ulla says. And by way of bored small talk to keep the evening moving along: 'You sure now you're not?'

Mama, getting anxious at the direction the conversation is taking and in anticipation of the worst when Ulla is knocking back scotches: 'Vy you vant to talking like dat?'

Ulla accepts a fresh Teacher's from the Finnish business-man, who has moved up the bar to be near the action. On her arrival she had routinely eyed him to see what the cat had dragged in and now downs the shot he has just offered and orders another one through him.

'Like all Finns,' she explains to us, staying in English out of courtesy to Quent, 'I'm shy and backward unless I drink. That's why I tank up and that's why I get hostile too. I'm basically fucked up.'

She goes back to a conversation she had apparently had with Toronto Paula the last time about a dismal failure of an experience with a drunken Swede whom she wrongly guessed would turn out to be good in bed.

'It was too bad. Very handsome young man. So I told him to go home and have his milk and cookies and go to bed – fucking was not for him yet. But he wasn't as bad as the one who wanted to smell my panties to get his rocks off. These guys, all of them, are so wrong in their lovemaking. They do fast frantic movements, nothing slow that maximizes the friction around your box area.'

The Finnish businessman feels quite interested in this discussion of sexual technique, and Quent seems to have forgotten he's unhappy about his wife's leaving him.

'How long since you lahst fucked?' Ulla the Survey Taker asks Toronto Paula.

No comment from Mama, keeping her own counsel. Quent and I, neutral onlookers, politely wait for Toronto Paula to tell us when the last time was she boffed. I personally don't think she boffs at all, being a loner, but I could be mistaken.

'I never "*fuck*",' Toronto Paula announces, implying that what she does is 'make love'. She's easy but she has a prudish streak that would make Philadelphians proud to claim her as their own. But then she's not a hundred-per-cent Finn either but has Estonian blood and is known behind *her* back as The Rolling Estonian. Someone once told her that and she took it as a nice compliment.

I decide to come to Toronto Paula's rescue. I say to Ulla, 'If you were asked that question, would you give an answer or would you be evasive?'

'Dahling, I haven't been fucked in twenty-nine days and five hours. But I needed a break. My pussy couldn't take it any more. I have a Norwegian-American boyfriend who is forty years old and a mama's boy, and wealthy, and his mother calls him every other day to see if he's eating his lunch and wiping his ass properly and to make sure he doesn't actually move *in* with me because she's sure I'm a fortune hunter, and so this mama's boy cahn't fuck me enough. He absolutely requires four times a day, twenty-eight pieces a week, and we're not even going to discuss blow jobs. This has been going on for four months with no let-up – until he went to Norway to see his Mommy, where he is currently no doubt fucking keyholes, knotholes lined with liver, broads, doughnuts, maybe even (God only knows) Mommy, anything round and open or will hold still long enough or that can be wrapped around his shlong. My weirdest boyfriend yet.'

'You like him for his money,' Toronto Paula says.

'Dahling, I do not sell my ass. If I like someone I fuck him into a state of blissful contentment any time he likes, and like any Finnish woman who *really* loves her man, I will never look at another man again. But if I *don't* like someone, then he can just forget I exist.'

Toronto Paula and Mama, the chorus of this Finnish drama, both murmur that it's true that Finnish women are loyal to the death if they really care for someone, and through some mysterious private association, Ulla is reminded of her current job, at Trans-European.

'The fucking phone is always ringing with people wanting to know how come Flight 294 from Lisbon is overdue. As though I know just because I work at Trans-European. So I tell them, "Mechanical trouble." I mean, how would *I* know why Flight 294 is late? Or I say, "There's a gasoline strike in Lisbon." Then before they panic I say, "But the strike is just ending – it's appearing on my screen now." And dahling' – she turns to Quent – 'don't fly Air Cosmopolitan. The pilot *and* the co-pilot are always either slightly high or in the back fucking flight attendants, who get discreetly tipsy while the passengers sleep. I *know*, having been a not-so-discreetly tipsy flight attendant and getting fucked over South Africa, the

Azores and points north. And enjoyed it. There's something about forty thousand feet and a series of updraughts just as you level off into an orgasm.'

The Finnish businessman edges closer to Ulla by one and a half centimetres as he silently computes intoxication levels and investment-in-scotch interest payments – but with a single glance, and a couple of decades of experience, Ulla blocks his next five moves.

'Listen, dahling,' she says to this supernumerary of the Friday night Ulla show, 'I know you're getting turned on at the prospect of having a roll together, but [*sweetly*] please go away and save us both time? It would be only fair if you ahsked for a refund, but it so happens I'm broke.'

She gives the guy a saccharine smile as he experiences simultaneous turn-on and rejection and obediently goes to the end of the bar and watches from a distance. That doesn't mean he's given up. The scotches – you can still see his wheels going round – are an investment for another time. But he might as well be back in Helsinki or on Mars as far as Ulla is concerned. Men always make that mistake with her. They think because her speech is racy she's a pushover. No way. On the other hand, if she likes you, fasten your seatbelt.

33

Mama is beginning to mutter something about my 'date' getting the wrong impression of Finnish women.

'He's getting exactly the right impression of me,' Ulla says, 'when drunk, that is. And he wouldn't want to know me when I'm sober. I'm a drag. I'm as backward and dumb as any Finn. I crawl into a shell. Finns are not to be believed. And the men cahn't fuck as well as Americans can. With a Finn, who is of course always drunk, it's all furious pelvic movements, an early orgasm, a limp prick and deep slumber, with me lying there waiting for the curtain to go up on Act One. But Americans constantly munch their vitamins like good little boys, it's almost an article of faith in this country. They believe there's more to life than just eating dill potatoes and strawberries, like maybe a virility-producing steak, and somebody has told them – maybe a sex manual and of course a four-colour *ill*ustrated sex manual – that not only are women passingly interested in sex but they have actually been known to have an orgasm now and then, and I mention this only in case anybody wants to know why I don't live in or near dear old Hell's-sink-ee. Besides, I could never make twenty-eight thousand a year in Finland answering dumb questions like "How come Flight 105 from Delhi is delayed one hour?" I once told the caller, "The pilot is getting his preflight rim job, part of Teamsters regulations." The boss overheard me and threatened to fire me and I said, "Hey, do me a favour, fire me. I could use unemployment compensation and put my feet up for a while. Besides, there's a guy at Finnair who's been lusting after my ass for ten years and would rehire me whenever I want." True too. Said he'd leave his wife for me, but I don't break up homes.'

Sex for the horizontally challenged

Mama is back in approval mode. Ulla hasn't said *vittu* in at least ten minutes. On our fifth round of vodkas and scotch, Ulla, now buying her own, is telling about a friend who has cerebral palsy.

'His hands and feet flap and flutter all the time.' She pantomimes his gestures. 'So he was dying to get laid and I suggested to him this tall willowy Chinese call-girl who is the girlfriend of an ex-boyfriend of mine, reasonably priced and beautiful. She operates on East 57th Street near what's the name of that French restaurant? (Which reminds me, La Toque Blanche is OK again, they must have changed chefs.) So we got him upstairs and stretched him out on her bed, with somebody trying to hold his legs still and with his hands flapping away over his head, and this Chinese call-girl blew him for a hundred dollars. It was over in less than ten seconds, he was so ripe, and he wanted to know how much all night would be. So I said to him, "You're *kidding*. Listen, if I know you, that blow job will put you out of action for at least two *weeks*. What would you do "all night"? He didn't take that too well and in a way I could see his point. In his case, it amounted to ten dollars a second. He wanted more for his hundred bucks, but for a hundred dollars all you get is one straightforward blow job and no trimmings. A fuck is two hundred dollars with her. Hand jobs – well, those you negotiate. So he finally left, arms and feet flapping all over the walls and floor, and when all was said and done, he didn't exactly look sad and he probably felt around five pounds lighter. He seemed to walk a little straighter too for about a week after that.'

And so to bed

It was quite late when we left and I was uncomfortably aware of lacking talent as a consoler of divorcing husbands. Not my *métier* at all.

As we went out, Ulla was still knocking them back and we heard her jabbering on.

'Of course when I was a child, I was dirty, sloppy, lazy, ugly and clumsy. But I got away with it because I was an only child and my parents had tried for *years* to have a baby. And I was too fucking adorable for words, so they put up with me.'

Outside, as Quent and I parted ways, he thanked me and hoped I had enjoyed myself half as much as he had. I walked away quickly to provide him with the opportunity he was probably looking for, to double back to Great Scandinavia and Ulla – like a bee to an overripe melon. Ulla is easily impressed by intellectuals and I think Quent stood a chance with her – for a weekend that would leave him drained dry and happy.

From a phone on the corner, I gave Hal a ring before going over, but he was out, or else he was busy and not answering. Or I don't know what. I left a message: 'Hi' – to match his chattiness, or rather because, on reflection, I didn't have much to say. Sometimes talking to him was like leaving messages at the cave's entrance.

So I called it a day and headed back to my place.

34

I crawled into the bed I had bought at the Brand New Bed Emporium, on Third, which, naturally, specializes in second-hand rebuilt beds. I had cosily tucked it into a corner of the bedroom, under the framed 'Apart from thirty thousand mornings, time does not belong to me.' I had put that up first thing, partly as a pleasant reminder of my father and partly as a *memento mori*, one he would approve of, and that was something I needed always but these days especially: I'm always planning to live next week, as soon as I get a few things done first. I pondered Quent's remark once that I live as if I were going to be around forever. He was right. I should be more careful. After all, not everybody *gets* the full thirty thousand mornings – and no refund on any unused portion.

Annihilation's waste

As I lay relaxing I drowsily pondered Quent's new novel and its theme of time, reflections that lasted about three whole seconds (perseverance being my middle name), and arrived inevitably at Marrakesh and Karen. (Martin thinks I have a masochistic streak. I don't like the word as applied to me but I'm beginning to think he's right.)

Quent had once passed through Marrakesh and had described it to me earlier this evening. I think I had asked him what the place felt like. It has been a market town for over nine hundred years, with little change since medieval times. In the town's principal square, among swarms of people, is one of the larger souks – the traditional Arab bazaar – consisting of dozens of covered stands clustered together and selling nuts, oils, fruits, sacks of olives, earthenware pots, hammered-brass art objects, rugs, leatherwork, marquetry. You see beggars on the street and men in sky-blue jellabas and turbans, and passing camels, and smell cool mint flavours in the dark alleys, and from far away hear the muezzin's wail rising up from a hidden mosque. In a clearing an acrobat performs gymnastic tricks, or a solo dancer accompanies himself on a tambourine, or a storyteller, with stock dramatic gestures, recounts ageless Arabian tales to thirty or forty rapt listeners seated on the ground at his feet. There are hordes of flies everywhere, and hanging like a haze over the souk is a spicy smell and the smoke and charcoal fragrance of grilled kebabs.

It sounded interesting but a place where I wouldn't want to live for very long despite modern hotels in the classy *zone touristique* and handsome sidewalk cafés. Once you got away from the centre of town, there was only the monotony of low sun-parched dwellings extending to the town's edge, and after that there was the shifting sand of dunes drifting aimlessly away for as far as the eye could see.

' "One moment in annihilation's waste and the caravan starts for the dawn of nothing," ' Quent said. 'That was pretty much the feel of the place for me.' He described it with a smile of reminiscence over his pleasure there and I shuddered – and wished I'd never asked him.

Art is long and life is just one of those things

There were some newspapers and magazines, including a very old Sunday *Times* I had used as wrapping for the move, and to get away from thoughts of Karen and try to sleep, I read a review of a photography show by Frank Thompson called 'Twelve Post Offices, Six a.m. Summer'. I was glad the boys were still at it. E. F. Hartmann was pleased with the exhibit, although I wasn't sure how the criticism connected with the subject: 'Self-destructiveness can have a positive value in that it might be a subtle fulfilment we do not yet understand. It at least has authenticity. What appears bizarre in Thompson's maturing vision might simply be a disjointedness between the photographer's unconscious drives and the sublimity of his ego – a *negative* commitment. In this connection we might recall Weston's authenticating statement (however removed from this context his particular oeuvre might seem) . . .' Jesus.

I clipped that out for the scrapbook and pasted it on the same page with a bit about a photographer with a show opening at the Watkins who was quoted as saying: 'I love the encounter with issues that inform my work. I am absolutely enthralled by events I attempt to describe in my work while not understanding them.' The critic of that show – not Hartmann – commented: 'He enriches us with his native vision. His perceptive imagery gives us an incisive measure by which to evaluate our sensibilities.' Right.

That reminded me of an exchange I once had with Quent. He wrote in one of his pieces on the millions of photographs we see nowadays and spoke of 'our world, which has been made ordinary by the camera', and I believe he thought that was an insight and I don't. So to deflate him a little, and in the interests of accuracy, I said it was the other way round: 'our world, which has been made *extraordinary* by the camera' (which I do believe). I have to admit he was gracious and conceded the point. I'm waiting to see now if he swipes it for one of his reviews, although probably not: the statement is really quite trite.

Reading through various reviews, old and new, I ran across this marvellous bit (stirring up hope even though it was about painting):

'We are at present surrounded with art of depressing triviality – the detritus of late postmodernism; with art that lays claim to remedial social virtue and yet "addresses" social issues in a depleted conceptualist language that is as socially ineffective as it is aesthetically boring. Artists are scared by the past and don't believe in the future.' (Robert Hughes: in an ancient yellowing *Time* I was still hanging on to – because of the review?)

A *few things off my chest*

I'm also compiling, in a special section of my scrapbook, a list of banned words, phrases that recur in photography criticism, like 'dissolves into light', 'insubstantiality of the material world', 'the world and [*something*] become one' (especially 'the world and *man* become one'), and all abstractions like 'enigmatic luminosity' and 'the still one hundredth of a second in a world of flux' and the ever-popular 'beyond the visible'. Criticism and pseudophilosophicalism. (Say that fast three times and win a Kodak Brownie.)

The word *beyond* should be retired from general use world wide for the next two hundred years.

I've become aware that a lot of art 'criticism' consists mainly of descriptions of what you're seeing right before your eyes, with dollops of metaphysics to spice up the dull prose wrapping. 'Peter Wanker's way of rendering the sea of grass as long, resplendent strands of light refreshes the eye. The image hovers between the tangible and the imaginary, an outcome effected by the precariously placed central bush and overhanging foliage that emphasize the "empty" space surrounding them. On the right can be seen a meandering stream, and in the upper left and dominating the photograph is a tree. There are no sheep or cows in the picture, unlike its companion photograph, which is of a crowd of barnyard animals.' It's as though you can't see for yourself that there are no sheep or cows (and as if you were looking for them). Art criticism amounts to: 'I have observed more details and can make more connections than you.' Or else it's the kind of writing that points out resemblances, as though they added to your understanding or love of a given work: 'Jackson Pollock's "Blue Poles" are similar to Monet's poplars in their vertical division of space.' (Well, I'll be damned.)

It's like the time Hartmann said about Hal's first show that a certain landscape had a 'Japanese floating quality'. We had to laugh when we read that. The truth was that in those days Hal worked in 35mm and any 'floating quality' came from the unsharpness of the horizon in a mist he had incorrectly read as darker than it was and in the dim light had shot at f/4. That review became one of our private jokes and from then on we would talk about the 'floating quality' of his work and concluded that critics never talk about what really matters, which is that the subject of a photograph is a *feeling*. Ultimately all we ever photograph is a view of life that comes out of our feelings, but critics talk about form and rhythm and the treatment of space. To deal with feelings you must speak naturally, and they don't. I've never read a critic who said he or she was *moved*, which is what art is all about. Great photographers do work that *moves* you – and each in a particular way, which is how we know at a glance that this photograph is a Werner Bischof or an Emmet Gowin, and that one's a Lewis Hine or a Cartier-Bresson – or a Fay Godwin – or a Paul Caponigro.

Many art shows are impressive but few are moving

In reviewing exhibits, Hartmann gets technical too, overly technical, as though photography were no more than a craft to be mastered – grey scale, reciprocity departure, parametric curves. He even speaks of lens characteristics and apertures as though they have any importance at all to the print, and so frequently mentions f-stops that when Hal learned that the 'F.' in E. F. Hartmann stands for Fitzgerald, he began referring to him as 'f-stop Fitzgerald'.

The back alleys of the mind while awaiting sleep

I tossed the newspapers and magazines aside and picked up an old *Vogue* – it's an addiction – and there was Clarissa again, three times in one issue: two ads and a six-page editorial spread by Dick Catherton. It was his usual stuff, accompanied by a sparse text in children's primer, voyeuristic prose: 'Here's

Clarissa in the morning!' '*Look* at what Clarissa is doing *now*!' 'And here's Clarissa, kicky supergirl!' 'All girl – and spit and polish!' 'What fun! Clarissa prepares to go out on the town!' Elsewhere: 'Though serious about her modelling, Clarissa doesn't rule out acting as a career.'

She recently signed a contract with La Vie cosmetics for an astronomical sum, or as she told me, a 'stupendously bullshit fee, but then, I don't make the rules'. No, but I'll bet she didn't fight it too hard either.

La Vie was willing to pay that kind of money for a special quality in Clarissa's face that photographs to perfection (given the right corrective filters). In fashion work it's the clothing that has to look good. But in cosmetics ads, what's being marketed is the model's face, which is reproduced life-size, close-up, full-colour, straight-on. It has to photograph convincingly natural-looking for the cosmetics not to appear like the fake goo that everybody knows they are: a greasy batter of pulverized minerals given a scent. It's civilization's equivalent of Asiak's blubber (although the blubber at least keeps her warm, and it's free).

Though it seemed a strange world to me, it was one Karen wanted to get into for the money that could be made, and with that the freedom to enjoy life and follow her dream.

By and by the reading had the desired effect and I got drowsy as I remembered Hal's photographing Clarissa once as cold and impersonal as sculpture. He had induced her to pose in the nude, which she didn't mind doing, but only for him and only for personal work. The best shot was part of her head, one shoulder and a full breast, a Bill Brandt bleached-flour look against a bleak menacing sky of falling snow seen through the skylight and glass wall of his studio, making it look like a Puccini *La Bohème* Paris. Most of the picture was of snowflakes, big lazy flakes shot at a slow enough speed to make them register, so that the nude in the lower corner of the photo gave it a feeling of an unfamiliar reality, a peculiar moment of time and nature because not quickly understood. It was a photo he had a feeling for, which was pretty evident.

He was very talented, all right. And I was glad he was getting the recognition he deserved, and from two directions, the world of fashion and the world of photography, straddling them in his life, not his work. His work, in both areas, remained inviolable, and I admired him for that – for being able to keep the two separate and balanced and not contaminating each other.

Reality check

My thoughts switched back to the evening and Ulla's orgasming high over Africa and I wondered how much of her you could believe – and with Africa my thoughts naturally went back to Karen and the shimmering immensity of the Mauritanian desert broiling in the sun. As I closed my eyes I wondered how the people who lived in that furnace bore it for thirty thousand mornings . . .

35

Yesterday afternoon, since Brother Paavo *still* hadn't shown up, I was toying with the idea of going out on a good old Finnish bender to clear the cobwebs. I had loads of time and little urge to do anything. Then at six-thirty yesterday evening he phoned from JFK for instructions to give the cab driver.

While waiting for him I became aware that it was snowing again (and we're practically in April!): a brief snowstorm, which momentarily deepened the unnatural New York silence. (Any silence in New York is unnatural.) In a few hours the streets, which had been a winter-wonderland-of-slush, wore a new frosting of white, which softened all contours and made the air brighter.

I prepared a casserole and waited for him – waited until midnight. No Paavo. Was it the snowstorm or The Case of the Disappearing Bryggmans? More disappearances.

But he was there the next morning. The bell rang and filling the doorframe was a rather attractive, interesting-looking hunk – Karen's older brother. The family resemblance was obvious but his fierce eyes were not Karen's. Hers were softly beautiful. (*Damn*! – *are* softly beautiful.)

He had spent the night at a hotel because he had not wanted to meet me while feeling tired. I would not have been seeing him at his best and he didn't want me to form some poor impression of him.

I took that in for later processing. What mattered now was Karen.

He was an architect and told me about himself to help 'place him'. He spoke with pride of Finland's architectural achievements. ' "Modern is our tradition," ' he said (a quote I like, by Eero Saarinen – unfortunately no relation). All in all he sounded intelligent, as I would have expected a brother of Karen's to sound, although his ego would never be in need of bolstering.

I recounted what I knew about Karen's disappearance and he listened quietly enough. I asked what had delayed his arrival. He said Finnair has only one New York flight a week (which surprised me, if it's still true) and he flew only Finnair. It piled up his frequent-flyer miles, and besides, he owned shares in it, 'you see'.

I told him of course I saw (saw what?).

He had missed last week's flight by only twelve minutes and that meant either going back home to wife and family in Turku or holing up in Helsinki with an old girlfriend. There was a seven-day wait for the next plane to JFK and when the old girlfriend invited him to pass the week for old times' sake in her Helsinki apartment – she had become a successful interior designer since the days when they had been teenage lovers – he let himself be tempted, you see. He smiled and said he felt sure that as a woman of the world I would understand. (I did, all right.) Anyway, he thought Karen was probably safe, wherever she was.

His sister's keeper or what?

Ignoring the lead weight sinking towards the bottom of my bowels somewhere, I asked if he had a plan.

Oh yes, de*FIN*itely, he had – several plans. First, he wanted to visit the Guggenheim – to see the work of the great Frank Lloyd Wright. Then he wanted to go look at the façade of the Hotel Ansonia and after that study the Seagram Building, Mies's triumph of modern classicism. He would give the Chrysler Building a miss – it was being over-studied these days. Then a brief check of the Modern, to see if there had been any significant design changes since his first visit, back in student days.

He said he would stay in touch and I should not worry about Karen. He knew his sister too well and I could trust his intuition: he didn't think she would just disappear.

He prepared to leave.

'She *has* disappeared,' I reminded him.

'Perhaps we should know-tify the police,' he said, pronouncing the superfluous *k*: kuh-no-tify.

I told him that maybe one of us should report her to the Missing Persons Bureau. (Actually I had telephoned the Bureau but they had made it sound so red-tapey I was putting it off for a while.)

'And they would – ?'

'They'd put out a report.'

'A "report" means?'

'They'd start looking for her.'

'Excellent. I'll do that. After all, just in case.'

Oh – he almost forgot: 'The Louis Sullivan building, with the intricate façade.' It was a famous though minor specimen of something or other and the only example of the great Sullivan's work in New York.

'Perhaps you are familiar with it? It says in the guide book the building is on Bleecker Street, number sixty-five.' He said it was 'in Green Witch Veal Lodge'.

But he didn't know which subway would take him there. If I would be so kind as to explain please how to get to Green Witch Veal Lodge I would make him delightful.

For ease of getting around I thought I had better tell him it wasn't pronounced Green Witch; and while I was at it, though less important, corrected Veal Lodge. He got them both correct after only one try.

I lent him my *Outsider's Guide to the Insider's Greenwich Village* and meanwhile drew the subway route to Washington Square on his map and gave him directions from there. I waved away a profusion of Finnish thanks, telling him I was happy to meet Karen's brother and do my small bit towards making him delightful.

The prick.

Portrait of the artist

DEAR KAREN: It's a cold April and still no word from you or about you. Life continues as usual. I've been seeing a lot of Roz and Bill. I told them I was writing you because I hadn't seen or heard from you recently, and Bill said to send you his best. He even said something complimentary about my worrying about you (almost the first sympathetic thing anyone has said yet).

Bill can be trying at times. Unfortunately he got bitten at some point by a Buddhist bug and you have to learn to ignore him when he gets into his 'karmic investiture mode' and spouts things like 'We live in illusion, in the mere appearance of things.' Fortunately he's used to people not listening, which is a saving grace, although I sometimes wonder if his brain is intact after years of a consumption of alcohol that outdoes even the Swediest Swede. (Outdoes even old Sibelius.)

One time Roz and I and his dealer Sue Damson had lunch with him, and as we ate and peacefully chatted, Bill, who was getting martini-ed out, held forth.

'That's not reality,' he said apropos of God knows what. 'Reality is you – *you* are reality but you don't know it. So what you have to do is wake up and realize reality, realize that you are not *you*, which is a simplistic view, but that you are reality itself. You are nothing, and since you're nothing and since you're also reality, you are everything. And that's the whole story. Everybody's everything.' (Pause.) 'See?'

To which Roz says: 'Pass the salt, please.'

Sue nods her head, acquiescing to passing the salt, not to anything Bill's saying.

'The invention of the mirror spoiled everything. Until we

had mirrors, whenever I saw you, I thought I looked like you.'

Sue: 'Where's the pepper? Oh thanks.'

Roz: 'Steak's good.'

'You haven't been given just a body, which you will soon leave behind, divesting yourself of some outer garment so as to live in a purified nonmaterial nirvana way.'

Roz to Sue: 'Your steak OK?'

'You have also been given a personality that is unique. That uniqueness is as much you as your body is.'

Sue: 'Mm, *very* good, but not *nearly* enough. I'll need another one after this.'

'We may all have much in common, we may all be one, but also we are all unique and different – that too is marvellous.'

'I didn't realize I was so hungry.'

'Dissolve boundaries. You have to interpenetrate with the cosmos, live utterly naturally. But *utterly – totally.*'

Me (feeling sorry that he's conducting a monologue): 'How do you do that, Bill?'

'You get rid of the false overlay.'

'I don't even know what that means.'

'Get rid of whatever's not fundamentally natural.'

'Then how do you make a photograph, which isn't something natural? – although I could argue about the fundamental.'

'You don't.'

'How do you make a painting?'

'Well – you don't' (slight pause there, though).

He doesn't know it but what I liked most in everything he said was that slight pause. Life was in that pause – and he passed over it quickly: how do you tell a person that?

The inevitable gulf between people.

Fur and Feather Reports

Roz has confided in me that Bill's EEG is going flat. 'His dong too, which is worse. The suffering we women go through.'

The big opening (the Whitney retrospective) is coming up

soon, so we were in Bill's studio to look at the work that would be hanging in the show and maybe do a few candid shots of Bill – for the press or maybe for just some day. I liked the acrid-sweet smell of oil and turpentine in the overheated air of the studio and all the mammoth stretched canvases leaning against the walls. There were boxes, rags, a pair of stepladders, a huge paint-encrusted table, cheap wooden chairs, gallon paint cans, rollers, brushes.

Bill saw me looking around and said, 'The place isn't picture-postcard-perfect.'

He pointed to a painting in progress. It stood in isolation in the midst of what always to me looks like an urban disaster area. It had been commissioned by Diners of America, Inc., for a restaurant on the top floor of a new skyscraper in Houston. It was ninety feet long and twenty feet high, a deadly mauve and dark terracotta. The two colours were painted in a thin acrylic wash of two giant horizontal bands of equal width, and very hard edge – as far from de Kooning as you could get.

'This painting I particularly like.' He squinted at it with interest. 'It has all my hatred in it.'

He said he was selling too well to be good and considered himself a failure as an artist. I think he was only partly kidding.

'On your way up you think if only you can make it every-thing'll be fine. If you can make it up to the next step on the ladder it will lead you to some kind of answer – but it doesn't. And the same with the next step. Then when you get to the top you find *that's* not the answer either and there *is* no answer, but at that point, as they say in Wyoming, that's all the further you can go.'

A celebrity interview

The next day Bill phoned to say he'd like me to be present at an interview by some reporter. Roz had to go meet some new PR person. He hates interviews and doesn't know how to handle them without getting nasty – unintentionally. He said my presence would have a calming effect. He's actually quite shy, I've realized, and as vulnerable in his own way as Karen.

The reporter was garbed, or attired, in an Ivy League suit and school tie, had a Mark Cross pen and a Crouch and Fitzgerald attaché case – and a name that completed the image: James Laurence Parker.

'I'll have a perfect Manhattan,' he instructed Sam the bartender.

The interview began with formality.

'You're from Green River, Wyoming originally, Mr Joachim?'

'Yeah. Call me Bill.'

'Studied in England?'

'Yeah, the Slade. And Italy. Belli Arti, Florence.' Bill begins sketching on the back of an old subpoena.

'Mr Joachim – Bill – what do you think of painting?'

I thought he would reply something scornful to a question like that. But he stared intently as a thought formed somewhere in his noggin and said: 'To do it at all you have to not give a fuck.'

'Of course, that could be our lead right there. With editing.'

'It has to not matter. Otherwise you spend all your time worrying about what you're doing.'

'I see.' Writing it down. 'How did you start, Mr Joachim – Bill?'

'First I studied, see? Studied for years. Went to the Belli Arti in Florence. The British Fucking Museum, the Elgin marbles, the whole bit. I drew feet, like they were *joined* to the leg, a knee that when bent looked like a *knee* and it was *bending*. Then I painted and it all came out the most constipated fucking crap you ever saw. So I gave up. I decided I was not going to be a painter, fuck it. Maybe I'd go back home to Wyoming and get into the lumber business or raise sheep. So just for the pure hell of it, as the last thing I was ever going to do as a painter, I nailed a big piece of canvas to the wall, the remainder of my last roll, and since I was no longer an artist, see, I was going to put on that final canvas a monstrosity, any goddamn thing I wanted, just slap the sonuvabitch on and have fun. I started by throwing a leftover can of paint against the wall, you know, as a joke, and kept going from there. That became my first painting – the one up at the Modern: "Totemic". Once you decide, fuck it, then you're doing it.'

Reporter, head bent, writing: 'I . . . see . . .'

Bill was relaxed now and at his charming best. The more he hated, the more charming he became and began hamming things up to entertain the interviewer.

'You know how you can tell if a girl is ugly?' The interviewer looked up to see a friendly wink.

'No.'

'If you're stoned and you've got your dipstick in and you're in the home stretch and she's *still* ugly – face it, she's ugly.'

'I see.'

'Coming back to art,' Bill said, 'which I can tell is where your heart is – you're not gay, are you?'

'Huh? No.'

'Fine. I've thought a lot about art and the thought I keep coming back to is that most painters aren't.'

'Aren't what?'

'Painters. They're just self-created myths. They're involved with galleries and sales and museums and *Art News* and that whole load of shit. A real painter is a rarity. A real painter is a failure – by definition. You haven't heard of him yet. He's creating something different, and nobody wants it. A real painter not only creates a painting but he creates the people who will appreciate what he's doing. *But* he loves what he does without giving a fuck whether or *not* it creates a stir, and it's certainly got nothing to do with Sotheby's. He *loves* what he paints. And he hates it too. He thinks, is *this* all painting is? Painting starts to get good when it stops really mattering to you.'

'I . . . see . . . "Painting gets good . . ."' (writing)

'For a change of pace, would you like me to tell you some of my views on life?'

'Why, yes.'

'My human interest side. Well, the way I look at it is we're all let out on a personal recognizance bond issued at birth, see. It can be revoked at any time.'

'. . . a personal . . .' (writing)

'Perhaps if I talked more slowly.'

What I like about Bill is that he honestly doesn't give a rat's ass about what might eventually be made of the interview. Of course he can afford that now, but even so, there is a love of honesty in all that nuttiness, a not-so-subtle 'fuck you' to the art world and its deep-grained phoniness, which is something the public is oblivious of. Bill goes directly to some core idea, which, like as not, disconcerts people, and pursues it relentlessly, but underneath it all, there's a terrible sadness and I don't think anyone hears it.

And sure enough, the published interview, which appeared a few days later in the *Times*, described him, as usual, as one of the ten greatest painters in the history of American art. This was pre-Whitney-opening hype. It was all upbeat, with no hint of any sadness, nothing about Bill that I found more than superficially recognizable. It was an official Bill Joachim, the icon, the celeb: in a class with the old modern masters Pollock, de Kooning, Kline, Rothko and the rest of the 'Cedar Bar gang' – in their tradition of action painting though less expressionist and of a later generation.

I've been an interested observer at other Bill interviews. Once, at Minelli's – with Roz there this time – a doe-eyed psych major from Vassar (maybe Bard), interested in art and artists, wanted to interview him for the school paper, and Bill was explaining to her she could do a whole master's thesis on him.

'That way even when we're in the sack you'd be doing research.'

Roz: 'Ahem.'

Bill winks at Roz and continues reasonably with Doe Eyes:

'You see, God actually created two whole universes, separate but identical. The other universe we have no inkling of, of course, but that's where he is right now, trying an experiment to make improvements in life. He interferes constantly, shows up here and there and makes changes and refinements, jots down complaints on a little pad he carries around with him, asks about living conditions or if maybe the amount of pain should be adjusted downward, and in general helps out people in jams rather than have them suffer unnecessarily, and he promises never to let them get unhappy again – ever. *And*: there's no evil, see? The whole thing is fantastic and you can tell he really cares about people. He wants to be a basically benign deity, and everybody is just tickled pink with life, and they all have a life expectancy of a hundred thousand years minimum, so no term insurance is needed (unless you're very insecure) and everybody receives a continually rising income to keep up with inflation.'

Doe Eyes takes all this in. Wheels slowly go round in a very sweet-looking young head. A thought surfaces:

'But what about our universe?'

'Well, that's just it, you see. We're the control group.'

It's men who drive women to drink

I'm really enjoying this jotting things down. Mr Maki said I should write the story of *my* life too. He said he has never read an autobiography of a young woman. I said I'm not writing an autobiography, just anecdotes. Sketches – moments in time. In a sense, they're snapshots, grab shots. And they're private, just for me.

I had to explain 'grab shots' and launched into their unacknowledged importance: Stieglitz's 'Steerage' was a grab shot, as was Ansel Adams's 'Moonrise: Hernandez, New Mexico'. But it was over his head, as I suppose it would be to anybody who's not a photographer. Very few people know anything about photography, even those who say they're interested in aesthetics.

I was getting philosophical – on the strength of two Löwen-bräus with lunch – and told him that everything we do, we're doing *against time*. The winged chariot is with us every second of every minute of every day. (Getting really profound, here. But it was all coming out of grief, I could see that.)

That thought, which was probably one of the oldest in human history, apparently intrigued him, and as we got into a discussion about O time! O life! I could hear myself getting carried away. I was saying we're all Scheherazade (I don't know where *that* came from), but me especially, I'm Scheherazade, telling my daily story (these jottings) to hold off not my own death exactly but the death of a friend, or at least her disappearance. Or maybe my own death too.

Maybe it's all hormones

I may not be any closer to finding out about what happened to Karen, but I am discovering a few things about myself. Even Martin commented the other day on 'a new clarity' in my thought – half-kidding but serious. (I *think* that's what he said.) I told him I write to Karen even though I don't mail the so-called letters. Everything I jot down in my scrapbook nowadays is really a letter to her. In fact I told him I have finally come round to agreeing with most women that it's great to have a man-woman relationship, but when the chips are down, I mean really *down*, and you need more understanding and support than usual, you find it only in a woman friend. Sad but true. It must be hormonal, because all men lack it.

I'm beginning to feel a little more clear about Hal. I think I know how that movie ends. It's hard to acknowledge mistakes, but of course it's doing things like that that stretches us. Even while it hurts. (I'm full of pep talks these days.)

An art opening

Meanwhile, at Bill's retrospective, he wore his usual artist's uniform, which *Art News* once described as 'prevailing nonstyle': an unironed yellow plaid shirt (clan Campbell?), violet-and-cobalt-blue knitted tie loosely hanging from some-where near his collar at a gravity-defying angle, white-pencil-stripe mustard linen jacket with mother-of-pearl buttons, paint-spattered blue denim pants and a pair of black para-trooper's boots. I think he thinks he blends in with the back-ground.

He arrived at the Whitney drunk out of his gourd, of course, so Roz gently parked him at a table in a rear serving area, away from the crowds of admirers standing in obligatorily appreciative poses in front of his giant canvases. His eyes stared in apparent fascination at the black plastic surface of the table before him. It had to be its high shine that held his attention because there was nothing on the table. He came out with 'the only complete sentence he can speak without slurring any of the words' (as Roz once described it):

'Drink.'

He didn't make a pass at me – *not* a good sign: usually he's so undiscourageable his persistence reminds me of our huskie when I was growing up. I'd stretch out on my bed doing homework and Vanka would burrow his head into the bed-sheets and nuzzle his nose into my crotch. Impossible to keep him away. When I shoved him away, his tail would slowly wag and he would single-mindedly and not very subtly burrow his nose right back in again. Of course at twelve and thirteen I could not admit I found it exciting, but I remember having fantasies that he was a secret lover who came to my room every night while I was being a 'good girl' and reading and studying. Adolescence! *Sturm und Drang.*

Bill's persistence is that same kind of male thing: he's as rejection-proof as Vanka. Even with Roz in town he phones me up and wants us to meet or he drops in unexpectedly and stays until I finally have to ask him to leave. He goes away but in another day or two he's back again. (Those hormones again, or as Roz says about sex: 'It's all moans and hormones.') Sometimes I think the whole world's behaviour is governed by women's crotches.

36

Party notes

One way to view the party at Sue Damson's is that it was an illuminating piece of social history. Another way is that it was a bummer.

It was the usual case of the dreary leading the forlorn – a drag, however opulent the setting. And the Whitney opening that preceded it, though impressive and pretentiously super-gala, managed at the same time to be Dullsville – or maybe it was just me, the eternally unthrilled at openings and parties.

As it turns out I got three invitations to both events. One through Roz, one through Bill and there was of course Hal's. Sue wanted Hal to attend and Hal wanted me to go with him. (Hal told me: 'Don't forget to invite Karen too, if she shows up.' That both surprised and pleased me, making me think there was hope for him yet.)

Hal doesn't like parties and he doesn't like 'aristocrats', as he calls them, so I go as his buffer. That at least is what he says, but when we get there, he always drifts away to mingle with the ladies, as he calls them. Trawling, I call it.

Walking into Sue's, we saw her talking at (not to) some fat-cat who clearly regarded himself a kind of grand fromage. She was complaining in world-weary tones:

'What do we look for? Love. But what do we find? Loves.'

Each time I see Sue I'm impressed all over again by the size of her (reminding me of the old joke about the five sizes of bras: small, medium, large, *wow* and holy-*shit*!). And spread out all over the upper portions of the vastness of her front, or frontage, was so much gold jewellery she sounded like a mobile Fort Knox. Seeing us arrive, she clanked over in a fluttery embrace of greetings and a cloud of expensive perfume that was almost visible (if you *could* have seen it, it would have been an emerald-breeze green, or some such Japanesey colour), simultaneously instructing her butler to see that we all got drinks and complaining to us about 'staff nowadays'.

'He took me into his library and showed me his books, of which he had a complete set'

Sue Damson's place: a thirty-six-room triplex on Sutton Place South and furnished in French and English period pieces – whole gobs of furniture – a châteauful. I was told that the floor of the ballroom, when uncovered, reveals an Olympic-size swimming pool, though I find that hard to believe. The master bathroom has a small marble Roman pool for a tub, with elaborate gold faucets shaped like flying dolphins. The tub area is surrounded by a wall-to-wall rug of waterproofed white velvet. There are nine other bathrooms and johns of greater or lesser ornateness. One bathroom had a library of uniformly bound books: Ring Lardner, Mark Twain, S. J. Perelman . . . I peed in that one. It was comfy, warm and peacefully satisfying for a reflective pee before joining the fray. The bidet looked like the latest super deluxe model from Paris. Much too elegant for actual use but I used it anyway.

Sue Damson's party A-list includes three hundred people – movie actors, socialites, Senators – drawn to the smell of money. There is no B-list. For their annual bash, the Damsons have ten thousand fresh flowers flown in from the Bahamas, mostly lupine and what looks like trillions of daffodils, and replanted in boxes scattered throughout the three floors. Out back, a few hundred of them, in some lunatic décor, were freezing their last few hours on earth in the snowy garden behind, making sad little yellow splotches in the grey-white bleakness, just in case anyone thought of peeking through the gaudily curtained windows. (No one did of course: it was night.)

To give an idea of Sue's wealth: when she realized she'd left a pair of earrings in a London hotel safe on her last theatre trip, she flew one of her maids back on the Concorde to retrieve them because she wanted them the next day for a gala at the Met (Museum).

The very rich really are *different from you and me –*
when it comes to tax breaks

Her wealth isn't all in art, only a small part of it. The bulk of it comes from husband Rupert's financial ventures, which are apparently under perpetual scrutiny by government agencies. In the course of a lifetime, honest-john Rupert has been indicted, enjoined, delisted, suspended and fined by the Justice Department, periodic irritations that so far from bothering him are a source of pride, not to say status and community standing. The Securities and Exchange Commission likewise has adopted a watchdog attitude towards Rupert's thriving empire. (Or is that thieving empire?)

Rupert has a sentimental side. He still feels close to his former mistress, who keeps having private-room nervous breakdowns at Payne-Whitney (said to have begun ten years ago, on an African safari, seeing her twin brother eaten alive by a crocodile), these regular hospitalizations of hers compelling him to turn to other mistresses, both serially and simultaneously (as he enjoys boasting).

Sue's upstairs bedroom, with a secret entrance (which everyone knows about, including old Rupert), is called Gigolo Hill.

'That's just a rumour,' a friend once said.

'Yes, but it was Sue who started it.'

The party. Sue was dressed in pink from head to foot – in a pseudo harem pants suit: filmy bloomers and a gossamer top that floated above her enormous bare midriff. I half expected to find the Koh-i-noor's twin sister ensconced in her navel. If it were, it would have been lost in flesh. I don't like to make fun of her, but you have to see such bulk to believe it. She has been described as shaped like an egg but thirty thousand times heavier. She was floating around the room like a Turner sunset on one of his very widest canvases: 'Sunset over Manhattan – and New Jersey and Long Island and Connecticut'. So much of her top was exposed in the back you could see the bottom fold of her breasts where they joined each other at the spine.

She was holding her lap dog, a pink-bowed chihuahua named Wendell, affectionately suffocating him against her mammoth bosom – not bosom, flesh tsunami. Wendell had a permanently beseeching look in his eyes, as though he deeply regretted being himself.

People were prancing around drunkenly from canapé to canapé. One forty-year-old-looking guest said to a friend that he was living on two million a month now. He bought paintings and had his eye on a Joachim he had seen at the Traherne-Castiglione.

Mixing, I heard a girl in her twenties explaining to two young men, whose libidos were clearly showing, how she had been one of the producers of a Broadway musical that had recently been made into a film. Protected by an ample narcissism, she thought they were engrossed in her story of investing a hundred thousand dollars of the five hundred thousand she had come into on her twenty-first birthday and how the investment had sextupled.

'In all sincerity,' she told them, 'you have to admit that at twenty-five it takes a degree of skill to have earned six hundred thousand dollars all on one's own.'

One of the young men agreed with feeling, 'Lord, yes.'

Me, I got another very necessary vodka and tried out a different floor as part of my anthropological research into how rich Upper East Siders live and in no time at all was lost. I wandered through several eerily silent rooms, encountering not even a servant, and tried a closed door – which gave on to a study. There, behind a magisterial desk I saw an El Greco portrait of some Spanish don in a seriously gilded frame and next to it an absolute jewel of a Holbein (the Younger? the Older?). If these paintings were copies, it almost would not have mattered, they were so marvellous. The windows had a gorgeous black filigree grille, Spanish-Moorish-baroque (it was either iron bars or no art insurance, no doubt) – *and*! on the facing wall, a Sisley *and* a Pissarro! Side by side! But (hard to believe) also a crappy Boldini, one of those society portraits of his that some wit described (accurately) as gypsy-violinist painting.

But the Sisley and the Pissarro – I stood staring at them for a long time.

37

I found some stairs and descending them passed an ageing platinum blonde coming up. She had diamonds splashed all over her bosom and was thin and sagging everywhere except her bulbous middle. Her eyes were squeezed shut from alcohol and I could smell the gin from three feet away. It was only as I was passing her that she became aware of my presence, stopped, turned her head and squinted her eyes to slits as she tried to catch up with me (focusing at least a foot behind my head). A family member, I suppose.

It's a dog's life

'It's so crowded I'm afraid someone might step on Wendell' (Sue to me, back downstairs again). 'I'm going to lock him in one of the upstairs rooms, *poor* little Wendell – it's for your own good, my little cookie' – kissing and hugging the life out of old Wendell, who keeps staring at you with that bug-eyed beseeching look.

I drifted in and out of conversations. ('He went off to bond with himself.' 'Where was this?' 'California.') In a doorway, effectively blocking my escape to more interesting bits of oral graffiti, Rupert and a crony were discussing ways of assassinating Ralph Nader. ('What has he done to you person-ally?' 'Nothing, but one has principles.')

An elegant middle-age jock was crooning 'O beau-ti-ful faw spa-cious skies . . .' and said *la-la-la* for the rest. 'Don't r'member all the words.' 'Sing it, baby,' the smart-looking dish with ageing cleavage who was with him said. She was wearing an engagement ring the size of Half Dome.

An ancient relative of Rupert's informed a small group of us that Siberian wolf's urine is the foulest stench known to man (and here I had always thought it was *pissoirs*), that the streetcorner mailbox was invented by a novelist (Smollett or Trollope), the wheelbarrow is *said* to have been invented by Pascal (ah, the famous doubt), and roulette was invented by Descartes. (I am, therefore I hope I break even because I need the money.) A system for writing in the dark was invented by Lewis Carroll, though I can't imagine for what reason except maybe darkroom purposes while printing up photographs of Alice for which he would be denied entry into the United States today. Start as you mean to go on.

I broke away from them and from another group (woman's nasal voice: 'He was a very tall dwarf, like a short *hu*man – you know?') and bumped into Roz, discussing insects with a producer who was saying:

'What gets me about Mother Nature is that she creates something called an io moth, which has two enormous spots on its wings that look like eyes to frighten away predators. Then she makes a predator who *knows* that the spots on an io's wings are only spots, not eyes, and goes ahead and eats the io.'

'Go figure,' Roz said.

'Of course, we don't know all the facts,' the producer said. 'The io moth might have some compensating feature. Perhaps its pleasure potential is unusually great.'

'Great but brief,' Roz said. 'Good god, I can't believe these conversations.'

'Well I suppose there would almost have to be some compensation if you're going to go on being an io moth for very long.'

'An io moth has a choice, right?' Roz said.

As Bill and Sue joined us from somewhere I began to edge away. Obviously not wanting to get stuck with the producer, Roz insisted I stay.

'I can cope with a lot,' she said, without lowering her voice appreciably, 'but I need moral support to handle conversations like these.'

I told her that some conversations I couldn't take even *with* moral support.

'Where there's life, there's dope,' Roz said, wink wink.

Reflexively I looked around for Hal and saw him in earnest conference with someone more bimbesque than usual, no doubt being 'seduced' by her.

'Shit,' Roz said to Bill, 'or words to that effect. Pilot to co-pilot – let's fuck off.'

The loophole wealthy

'You know what's heartbreaking to millionaires?' Bill began to Sue.

The producer chimed in with 'Millionaires don't have hearts to break' but the rest of us, being more discreet, chose to ignore him.

'Millionaires have all that money,' Bill went on serenely, 'and yet they only get the same lousy lifespan we do. Which is carrying democracy too far.'

'Well,' Roz said, 'maybe they can get Congress to work out a life-depletion allowance, get some money back on it.'

'Trouble is, that could benefit the poor too.'

'Yeah. Needs more work.'

'My family's *always* been loaded,' Sue said, 'not like the Whitneys or the Vanderbilts or those Rockefellers. I mean, dis*gust*ingly so. And eminently screwed up too, which is the down side. They sit around feeling *terr*ibly superior to everybody and then go to Morocco –'

– [that damned Mo*rocc*o again] –

'– and then take a rest from all that terrible exertion. Their whole life is superior feelings and junketing. And watching their money like hawks.'

'I didn't know your wealth was so over the top,' Hal said, cruising by on a break from Travels in Bimboland.

'Oh, filthy. My father's side of the family goes back to the

Mayflower and is now totally alcoholic and my mother's side of the family was so fucking blue-blooded it died out.'

'The ultimate in selective breeding.'

As ever, Roz ignored any conversation not focused at least in part on her and picked up where, apparently, she had left off with the producer.

'So this prickola from London, Cliveden, *some* asshole place, Lord Sniffcock, I believe, got so drunk he thought I was a boy and began mauling me.'

Sue chuckled happily. 'Oh dear.'

'I mean, with these boobs the guy had to be blind drunk, right, to think I'm a boy, right?'

'Drunk as a lord,' the producer said.

'I wish I had said that – you will, Oscar, you will. So anyway, *mean*while he kept talking about Lord Satchelass and Lord Blue Balls and at the same time kept squeezing my ribcage in this clever London way of his that copped a feel of my boyish boobs with his lordly wrist. The pressure mounted with each lordly named dropped –'

'Peer pressure.'

'– so finally I told Lord Prick-Ass to royally shove it and unfortunately he loved the royally part, or possibly the shove-it part, it's hard to tell with creeps what turns them on, especially with boyish boobs size thirty-seven thousand triple D, if I'm a day . . . Men have sex on their minds so much it's the only thing they talk about when they get you alone. You'd think it was some fabulous new country they had just discovered – Outer Genitalia, or something.'

'Labia Minorca,' Rupert said.

Sue Damson snorted and howled. It didn't take much with Paralysers. That's a drink invented by Roz and it's what they were all having. It combined whisky, brandy, rum, ouzo (I *think*) and one other ingredient (vodka?) – totally insane. ('You keep hoping it'll induce amnesia when all it does is paralyse you.') Paralysers have a way of sneaking up behind you and decking you, and it's obvious it doesn't do much for your sense of humour either, though unfortunately you're the only one who doesn't know it.

'A hard man may be good to find, but a good fuck is at least an *or*gasm,' Sue Damson interjected, feeling at this point totally painless. Hal wiggled his eyebrows at me and took off again. The present company didn't make it for him even though Roz was delivering a talk now on dipsticks and love pumps and making the observation that 'when we're tortured we yell and scream and when we have an orgasm we yell and scream – so go understand. Talk about weirdo wiring.'

Then for some reason she got on to houseboats, telling Rupert that for as long as she could remember she had wanted a houseboat in the East River. When she got drunk it was hard to believe she was a movie star. When you looked at her you recalled her vivacious screen image but her voice had none of the plummy sexiness it had in her films. Unamplified electronically, it sounded flat and characterless.

'Do you know about houseboats?' she asked Rupert.

'No, I don't know about houseboats, my dear,' Rupert said, 'but don't ever buy a yacht.'

'Oh, I would never buy a yacht, I want a houseboat.'

'When you see a yacht you think of speed, you think of cruising, you think of cocktails on deck, but don't ever buy a yacht because that's not the way it is.'

'I would never think of buying a yacht. A houseboat is what I want, just to sit in and rock up and down in the river right at the damn dock. You're going to tell me I want my mother, that it's my mother's womb.'

'My dear, I wouldn't presume. The truth of the matter is a yacht is so uneconomical and so cramped and damp that it's like sitting under a waterfall and tearing up banknotes.'

'Rupe, I promise I'll *never* buy a yacht. If I ever get an uncontrollable urge to go out and buy a yacht, I'll call you from the nearest phone so you can talk some sense into me.'

'Here's to houseboats,' Rupert said.

'And here's not to yachts,' Roz said.

'Hear hear.'

'I know an artist who lives on a houseboat in the basin off 72nd Street. Really cool. Very talented guy and comes on very superior. You know what I really hate, though.'

'What?'

'I hate the kind of, you know, *aloof* creative person, very ivory-towerish. I know, I know, it's maybe envy on my part, but I always feel like telling him that I'll –'

'Telling him or *her*,' Rupert said.

'– I feel like telling him or her that I'll kick the son of a bitch in his or her balls.'

Hollywood story

There was a lot of film-industry talk for some reason. I stumbled into a West Coast cluster of men surrounding a famous débutante whose name I don't remember, if I ever knew it, found that boring and moved on to another group of men, engaged in high-powered Wall Street jabberwocky about earning expansions and quarterly price ratios, or whatever. I began to wonder why I was there but that's what I wonder at every party and keep going to parties anyway.

Then it happened. I moved away from a group of middle-aged adolescents trying to work out which London Underground station doesn't contain one of the letters in the word *mackerel* (so now, *damn* – I'll have to figure it out myself) to a group talking about an abduction that had apparently happened fifteen years ago.

'It's not just Hollywood but all over. Right here in New York too, and all the time, no exaggeration. Women disappear and you never hear about it.'

'Disappear?' a woman asked. I moved in closer. 'Where do they disappear to?'

'Well, there are places, you know, where slave traffic is a part of life. It's hidden, obviously nobody is going to document it, but it goes on all the time.'

He continued in awful, fascinating detail about a woman

from the Midwest who vanished one day. She and her family had gone to L.A. and were sightseeing along Sunset Boulevard or somewhere, when she got separated from her husband and children in the crowd and some guy (later described to the police as a 'fatherly type') appeared from nowhere and wanted to know if he could help. The woman was never seen again. 'And it happened in broad daylight.'

'That's very scary,' a woman said.

Hal had to pick that moment to come over.

'You OK?' he wanted to know, prompted no doubt by conscience, but fortunately did a fresh bimbo-sighting across the room and without missing a beat kept going. Women go for him because they think he will make glamorous photographs of them and put them in *Vogue*, a fantasy he pretends to be unaware of and therefore feels no need to discourage.

But then, regrettably, Roz and Bill came over. I don't know if Bill was sobering up or was on some new level of high, but he was slightly more coherent than earlier and gave me one of his unctuous smiles as he approached. I hoped he and Roz would go away also.

Bill, affably: 'Would you like to hear the story of my life?'

I made no reply, trying to hear more about the woman who was never seen again.

'Or would you prefer to wait until the movie comes out? It's a very innaresting life once you get past the opening – though not anything a good editor couldn't tighten up here and there – maybe delete the incest with my sister.'

Roz: 'Skip the preliminaries, Bill. Everybody likes a good climax.'

Meanwhile, the man was saying:

' – to this con artist. He had to deliver her to some place in Asia, I believe, or Malaysia, to a palatial residence of some sort and – and that was *it*: mission accomplished. The con man got his money, twenty-five thousand bucks, I believe it was, and took off. End of transaction.'

I opened my mouth to ask where this guy got his facts but

Bill said: 'Actually my life is still in process and I really shouldn't talk about it because that way you talk it all out and lose it.'

'What do you mean process?' Roz asked.

'What they do to cheese in Wisconsin.'

'I had an aunt in Wisconsin,' Roz said, 'whose ass was so vast for her size – The Great Vast Ass they called her – that they referred to it as the county seat. On Sundays people would come from all over and stand outside her house hoping to catch a glimpse of her famous ass. She had to keep her blinds drawn all day and finally began taking Prozac. The locals said she was their town's equivalent of Mount Rushmore, and the Chamber of Commerce tried to figure out ways to attract tourists and was in touch with the *Guinness Book of Records*. No, hey, really, I'm serious.'

A case of hysteria

By this time I have no doubt that I was wearing what Hal calls my deer-in-the-headlights look – sceptical about the man's story but intensely fascinated at the same time – as, meanwhile, Roz and Bill kept up their Pat and Mike routine. I couldn't think how to get rid of them.

'The surprising thing about the story of my life,' Bill said, 'is that the ending is foreshadowed by a very important event I can no longer remember.'

I couldn't help grimacing at him to shut him up and turned back to the story of the woman who disappeared.

'. . . but the Malaysian was quite pleased with the kidnap victim. She was attractive and twenty-three years old – actually a little too old for that part of the world but she had the extra spice of being American. The abductor, or rather the recipient of the goods, if you will, explained to her, the way you might discuss the weather, that she would never see her world again, so it would be best if she acted reasonably: the sooner she got used to her new life, the easier things would be for her in the long run.'

'New *life*?' a woman in a black gown next to me said.

'Her-*ream*,' the man said. 'It's how they recruit white slaves.'

The woman caught her breath audibly, and me, I gulped – I think just as audibly.

But old Roz, she never gives up: 'Tell us about the time you committed a public nuisance over at Lincoln Center, Bill.' She turned to me. 'It was his thirtieth birthday and I think he thought he was doing a Scott and Zelda.' Now I gave *her* a look and she tried placating me: 'We've got diseased minds, what can I tell you?'

'I'll drink to that,' Bill said.

The Roz and Bill road show *finally* departed as Roz led the way in search of one of the bars set up to resemble a stall at a bazaar.

'He wasn't a brute,' the man was saying, 'this prince or whatever. He told her she would learn from the other members of the her-*ream* that he was really a kind man and provided his women with a comfortable life and security. He showed them every consideration and they felt well cared for. Everyone who knew him said he had never struck a woman in his life or in any way caused them harm.'

Probably he should be given the Humanitarian Award of the Year, be fêted at the U.N.

The 'her-*ream*' had a good reputation, he went on. 'The women led a more pleasant life and in more pleasant surroundings than any of the local women did.' (I wondered if Hal and this guy had been in touch with each other.) 'The male attendants – the eunuchs – always reported back on how the members of the her-*ream* enjoyed each other's company. A kind of a sorority, you might say.'

A friend of Rupert's, who had been listening in silence, said that such a fantastic story would make a great film – something along the lines of *Midnight Express*.

'It's a natural best-seller.'

'And no one *did* anything?' the woman in black asked.

'Like what?' the man said.

'I don't know, send troops over, rip open the harems, free the women.' She glared at him accusingly: 'What do you mean, "like *what*?"' She turned to me, an instant confederate in the gender wars, to see if I mirrored her outrage. 'Can you believe this guy?'

Actually, I could.

'Right, the American solution,' the man said, 'send in the Marines. It may interest you to know that her-*reams* are a way of life in many parts of the world. Who are we to dictate –'

'*Kidnapping* is a way of life? You abduct an innocent woman and keep her imprisoned like an animal? And keep her there *forever*? I wouldn't even keep an *an*imal locked up, for God's sake. And then use her sexually? That's a life des*troyed* – not some fucking *way* of life.' *Pissed off* and outraged, she was, then again turning to me, to provide the expected corroboration: 'Is this guy nuts or what?'

I was feeling pretty angry myself. *Midnight Express*, I was thinking – best-seller – *shit*. Novels merely pretend to be like life when even *life* isn't like life.

On the verge of losing it I decided I had better get away from the conversation. Anyway it was getting late and it wasn't much of a party to begin with. But at the same time I couldn't move. The story fit precisely my fantasy of what's happening to Karen and I wanted to know more. Most of all, I wanted to know what finally became of the missing woman.

My neighbour, the woman in black, was still bawling at the man, and Hal, hearing the commotion, came over. I hoped he wouldn't say anything, not needing any sage coolness right now – his remoteness and cynicism disguised as 'calm judgement'. He was always quick to come out with a 'Don't get involved' speech (those words would be on New York's coat of arms if New York had a coat of arms).

'It *is* sad,' the storyteller was saying, trying to appease the woman next to me, who was still extremely agitated. 'No one ever heard from the woman again, and if you put yourself in her husband's shoes, or the children's . . . you know? They still don't know where she is. It's as though she had been swallowed up by the earth. And the worst of it is, in all these disappearances of women, they happen so *easily*. It's always: 'She was here just a second ago. I turned around – and she was gone!'

'What about the police?' somebody asked.

'Oh, the police know about these things and they know they happen all the time. But they're powerless to stop it.'

I found my voice finally and asked him how he knew all this.

'It was in the papers a few years ago. The kidnapper confessed and told the story. Which was funny. The way they got him was by accident. They picked him up on something unrelated and were nailing him on another crime – a heavy drug charge that had a paper trail leading to some higher-ups in the C.I.A. I don't remember all the details now, but under questioning, this whole *other* story came out about the kidnapping, and the druggie's attorney plea-bargained and got him off with only fifteen years – but still a pretty stiff sentence.'

'And he's still in prison?' the woman in black asked.

'No, he was released a few years ago. He has a new life as part owner of a steak house on Long Island.'

'He's *free*?' she said – or screamed.

As a precaution, Hal's grip on my arm tightened a notch.

'Yes. He served his time.'

'Served his *time*?' This woman was ready to kill someone now. 'Served his fucking *time*?'

And that got the *storyteller* irritated: 'What do you want, for God's sake – have him pay forever? You want his balls on a skewer?'

'Even *that* wouldn't be enough,' she said.

'He paid his debt to society – he did time. And I believe that's what the criminal justice system is all about.'

This statement was addressed to the rest of us, the reasonable if not totally silent majority.

'His debt to society?' The woman looked around at us to bear witness to the level of stupidity she was contending with and then turned back to him. 'What about his fucking debt to the *woman*? He's running some fucking steak house and she's still a prisoner. What kind of fucking justice do you call that?'

'Look, I didn't invent the system,' the man said, desperately grabbing high moral ground to exonerate himself.

But *she*, of course, had a point. Even if the victim were some day to be reunited with her family, how could you make up for the emotional misery she's enduring? How do you undo psychological torture? How do you eliminate it from your psyche? How do you restore a person's potential after you have destroyed much of it? And that's if she got *away*. The woman, wherever she was being held, was being transformed by degrees into someone who, even if liberated, could never become what she had set out to be, what she had once set her heart on. And if freed by some miracle, she would at best live out her life as some ghost of her former self. And meanwhile the con artist who destroyed her was running a fucking steak house out on Long –.

Christ, now I was as furious as the woman and felt Hal's arms gently edging me away from the group – prying me loose, actually – while murmuring in my ear, 'Boy, this is some party.' I caught one last statement from the man:

'I can understand still being angry at something like that, but you know, people do begin to forget.'

Hal said grimly in my ear, 'Let's go now, he-e-re we go now,' hugging me from behind, and making it appear like an affectionate wrestler's lock, and without quite breaking my arm, he gently walked me into a john (one I had missed earlier), smoothly greeting various acquaintances as we went, 'Hey, hi, there.' Once inside and alone, he locked the door behind us.

He looked hard at me to see if I was OK, and I assured him, yes, I was fine, perfectly fine, goddamn it. Surrounded by polished white marble and dazzling mirrored walls and ceiling, I saw a dizzying number of Hals calming infinite replicas of me with cold-water compresses applied to my numerous foreheads. I felt, but hadn't the energy to say, that the compress was a melodramatic touch and he should save that stuff for his bimbos.

'Wow! Look at the taps in this sink' – wily (but kindhearted) Hal distracting me. '"Hot", "Cold", "Salt", "Pure", "Iced". Can you believe people actually *live* this way?'

I tried to say something on the order of 'Well, I'll be god-damned' in some tepid effort to hold up my end of a humorous exchange. But all I could think of was harem and harm, her-*reams* and Harem Burgers. I was finally able to muster, in a voice that sounded even to me like something from the tomb: 'Uh-h-h' – and gave up even that with a token moan.

'So. Feeling OK again, eh?' Hal: beaming at the suffering young friend he had brought back from the edge of hysteria.

'You looked like you were about to go berserk,' he told me with cheerful reassurance.

'Although he is a bad fielder he is also a poor hitter': in other words, you need Ring Lardner at a time like this (and Perelman does no harm either)

Berserk is what he *meant* but he pronounced it *BEZ-er-ick* to make me laugh. He was only cheering me up – although probably the whole episode was amusing to him.

'I've never seen you this way. It's a whole other side of you I don't know.'

The bastard was being *so* cheerful I had the uncomfortable feeling that this was making his day. No, I thought. The truth is he's probably about to score with one of the bimbettes he'd been talking to, or at least has her, or *them*, booked for a shoot (in a manner of speaking) next week and is feeling high anticipating his 'acquiescing'.

'Hal,' I said, 'you're a prince.'

*

Princy left me alone once he was sure I was not going to backslide into BEZ-er-ick mode, dying, no doubt, to get back to the party, or get away from me, at this point I couldn't decide which. And if the truth be told, I was beginning not to care.

I do love men but they just don't seem capable of sympathy. I've recently begun thinking that only a woman can give the right kind of understanding or empathy in critical moments. That's a sad comment and I don't like making it, but it's a fact of life. Men our equals? Sadly no.

I doused cold water on my face. It felt late – at a guess, one in the morning. I wanted to go home and hoped Hal would be ready to leave soon.

Emerging from the glitzy *Architectural Digest* bathroom, I spotted him talking to Roz and Bill. Rupert and Sue were there too and I joined them all – the crew, as I was beginning to think of them. I wondered how old Wendell was making out upstairs, with a lot of years still left to go, poor bastard. Fortunately, he *doesn't* have thirty thousand mornings.

Roz said not to worry about the time, it was still very early. She sounded chirpy, almost too happy to be real. It must have been a combination of New York trip, Bill's retrospective and about a pint of Paralysers (more or less, and not counting champagne chasers).

'What do you say we get the fuck over to Minelli's and close the frigging joint,' Roz said.

'Yeah,' Sue said, smashed, crimson roses in her cheeks that I didn't remember from before. 'Let's frig the fuck – thee uh, let's frig over – the fuck over to thee uh –'

'Paralysers, boy,' Roz said. 'Closest thing to a stroke.'

'Thee uh . . .'

'Yes, of course, darling,' Rupert reassured his wife, adding tactfully, 'but don't you think we should, ah, stay here and, ah – this *is* our party and our guests might find that –'

'Well, if it's *our* party, then it seems to me we have the right to *leave* it if we want to.'

After a quick and confusing discussion of manners and propriety, we found our coats, wrapped scarves around necks and put on boots, and frigged the fuck over to First Avenue. Only on the avenue would we have a chance of finding a taxi at this hour, especially since another snowfall was just starting. It was coming down in earnest and threatened to turn into another blizzard. Maybe it was another lowering subsidence inversion.

Goals

Bill spotted a lone cab slowly cruising away from us, far up the long avenue, and in the strange (for New York) night-time stillness – that eerie winter hush I like so much – we whistled, stamped our feet, yelled, started singing crazily until the cabbie finally heard us. But he had to halt immediately at a traffic light. At that hour of the night and with the weather the way it was, I wasn't surprised he was willing to make a U-turn and come back for us.

While waiting, what had begun as arm-waving and foot-stamping ended as free-for-all clouting each other on the back and helpless giggling as we hurled snowballs at anyone who made the mistake of cringing in anticipation and ducking away.

Except Rupert. Safely on the sidelines he twirled his snow-flake-shedding umbrella smartly and cheered us on, saying that all this fun reminded him of his youth at Phillips Exeter more than a half-century ago. While waiting, he exuberantly read a scrawl of graffiti on the door of a classy delicatessen (*'Delikat Essen'* a turquoise neon sign read). The graffiti exhorted in large white letters: 'Speak Without Bullshit!!!!'

'One would not argue with the sentiment,' Rupert said, 'although it's discouraging to conjecture that it was almost surely first inscribed on a cave wall, don't you think?'

I noticed he didn't mention the message scrawled right next to it, 'cunt', along with a small handsome drawing of it. I thought Rupert's selective view of the graffiti was a garden-variety example of what Martin would call denial.

I have never seen the word *cunt* so often and so publicly displayed as in New York. It seems almost an icon. You see it everywhere. I wondered, what is there in the male imagination to make men, or boys, write it on walls? An appreciation of women's anatomy? A yearning for the part? (Just that part of us?) Is it fear of the unknown? Is it male fear of women?

Or is it perhaps love – in grotesque and distorted form? Writing it on walls revealed, I couldn't help thinking, a desire for women, a great reaching out for them. With that lovely abstraction, Ψ, the graffiti writer magically made them appear. A woman's crotch as peach tree. Cunt, the softly downy rosy-sided clefted fruit perched at the union of crotch and warm thigh, naturally fragrant, hiding a fleshy core of crimson slit, a cerise flower of pleasure (a *delikat essen*). It was meant to be loved, fantasized, undressed, touched, fondled, looked at, sniffed, wetted, fucked, tasted, licked, admired, respected, dreamed about . . .

'I don't mind snow,' Roz was saying, 'snow is nice. But what falls on New York is brown shit.'

Ways of viewing snow.

A cruising squad car suddenly appeared and stopped beside us. The near cop rolled down his window:

'You folks O K?'

'Marvellous,' Sue said. 'Thank you, dear, for asking.'

'No problem, lady.'

Sue (apparently even more smashed than I thought): 'You've just made powerful friends.'

One of the cops looked at the other, whose eyes rolled upward as the squad car pulled away.

'Well, Bill,' Sue said, turning to him. 'I must say, that was some opening.'

'Opening?' Bill said. '*Oh* yeah, the opening. Yeah, that was some opening, all right.'

The Whitney seemed far behind us now. I didn't even want

to think about it. Besides, I was beginning to feel cold and was grateful when the taxi finally pulled up. It was an ancient work horse of a taxi, the only kind, in view of Sue's tonnage, that could accommodate all the members of the crew. After some discussion about the order of boarding the vehicle, based on hip-spread factor (a point not overtly mentioned), I, being the thinnest of the group, climbed aboard first and was followed by a massiveness of Sue incompressibly filling the door-frame.

With much breathiness, she squoze in and eased herself down, steered by advice of dubious helpfulness from those outside. The cab perceptibly sank under her bulk and in the rearview mirror I noticed the driver staring back at us in controlled alarm. Sue jammed herself into a position that was adequate or at least endurable, sagging me downhill against her softly yielding body as she, maintaining poise, shyly ran through her standard repertory of diet jokes and getting a tan from the light in the refrigerator.

Bill and Rupert inserted themselves into the jump seats, while Hal slid in up front and offered his lap to Roz, who, in jabber mode, jauntily accepted the invitation and asked the driver about the incidence of haemorrhoidal problems among New York cabbies. The cabbie, not recognizing her and ignoring (perhaps pointedly) the opening she had democratically offered as friendly chitchat between two equals about to set off on a journey, craned his head towards us in the back.

'Excuse me, but would anybody here mind telling me where we're headed?'

'Ah,' Rupert said, 'a teleologist.'

'Last summer already I should have retired,' the driver murmured. He glanced at the rearview mirror again, eye-balling Sue – and no words could equal the eloquence of that face scrupulously devoid of expression.

The scene ought to have been funny, but I was only partly present. I was struggling not to remember the story of the woman who had disappeared, but every word that the man at the party had said was like acid on my skin – etching a track from New York to Africa, a one-way ticket to oblivion.

And at the same time I realized (with a small shudder now) I was trying not to think of giving old *Hal* a one-way ticket.

One trauma at a time.

38

Love-shmove

The day after the party I felt mildly hangoverish but immensely relieved to be alone, therefore unlaid (even by Hal – keep forgetting to buy pills). Hal and I had had a sudden change of mood in the taxi and opted not to go on to Minelli's but get ourselves dropped off, Hal at the studio and me at my place, an escape (and separation) that turned out to be easier than I would have expected.

I woke up with a groggy thought that nagged (one of my 'cleverisms'): Life is a near-death experience – which, I felt certain, would not be a candidate for any World Anthology of Great Thoughts.

I lazed in bed, doubly grateful not to be with Hal given his propensity for a raucous wake-up fart. It was the cock's clarion call announcing the dawn of day (never smelly and sometimes actually comic when it turned unexpectedly long and musical). Lying in bed also gave me time to think about him, or us – about *me* is what I mean – and seeing Martin and thinking about where all the shrinking was going. Mid-April and I'm still not feeling better. Actually I'm feeling worse.

About a month or two later I slid out from the covers and made some espresso, showered, put on fresh underwear and felt immeasurably better. Silk panties are the greatest morale boosters ever devised. I don't know how the Kalahari do without them.

I rearranged the sheets and blankets and fluffed up the two

enormous cushions I got at Bloomie's last week – and then bedded down again to enjoy the coffee in comfort. A *grasse matinée*.

By and by, the morning-after fuzzies passed, and I found myself remembering another waking quote, I forget whose: 'Love is the exchange of two fantasies and the superficial contact of two bodies.' Something like that. (Probably by a Frenchman.) I didn't need Martin Yeblon to figure that one out.

I put on *The Swan of Tuonela* and listened for a while. We think we hear with our ears, but all our senses and our whole bodies hear too. I don't know how else I would be able to explain that when I listen to *Boris Godounov* my skin crawls pleasurably and a shivering starts going up and down my spine and across my solar plexus, joining in my crotch to go all the way down my legs to my toes.

Words don't carry all the feelings we feel. Music is a subtler language and does the job better, reaching into feelings that have no words, including and maybe even especially the feeling of being excited at being alive. Music even makes you *think* – as though in some mysterious way it has *thought* in it – or anyway it *conveys* thought along with feeling. Difficult to explain.

I lay there thinking about dear Suomi and missing it a little and recalling my adolescence and the intense ardour of my 'Sibelius period', when all day and night I listened to his symphonies and tone poems and felt so swept away that once, as I stretched out on my bed listening to the slow prolonged finale of the Second Symphony and the tension of its languorous steady rhythm, I felt the music caressing my arms and legs and passing through my body in waves and suddenly making my breasts and nipples tingle in a spasm of pleasure that erupted into a powerful orgasm. Surprised the life out of me at sixteen (losing my virginity to Sibelius!).

When *The Swan of Tuonela* ended, I leaned over and stopped the tape, not wanting to hear anything more than just that for now. Enjoying the espresso jolt, I picked up the world almanac, always within reach of the bed for distraction purposes. Usually I get things like: 'Albert Einstein had an unusually small brain.' Or: 'It was 78 degrees Fahrenheit in Lapland on 16 July 1997.' (Once I even found: 'Philosophy has played an important role in the scholarly and cultural life of Finland.') But it was just the kind of luck I've been having lately – synchronicity, they would say on the West Coast – that it fell open to: 'The male emperor moth, *Saturnia pavonia*, of Europe and Asia, can smell the sex stimulant of the female moth seven miles upwind from her.' Downwind, I suppose, he'd smell her in a salt mine in South America.

The authoritative *whomp*! of the Sunday *Times* crashing against the hall door called for a second espresso, 'synapses' now firing on all eighteen cylinders (or however many cylinders I possess). And, as a great believer in extending pleasures, I burrowed back under the covers again.

Twitching with espresso and speed-reading several sections of the paper, I saw that according to the *Times*, the cemetery body count had reached eighty-three thousand. A city official expressed concern that New York might be at the point where it needed to consider burying people vertically to accommodate the growing number of dead. Why not? The whole city lives vertically. Why not die vertically?

Death all over the place. I lay there thinking about love and death and about how Iris's talk was often on such themes. 'When you fall in love with a man, you have fantasies about him and about yourself and the life you will have together. If the man crushes your fantasies instead of allowing them to grow into a wonderful new reality for the two of you together, then he's not the one for you. He's a life-limiter. And I don't want to live limitedly.' Words to that effect. 'It becomes not a relationship but a death-in-life trip. Marriages like that are the pre-divorce shit we see everywhere.'

Roz once said something similar: 'Love is joining my fantasy of myself going through life with your fantasy of yourself going through life.'

Pretty good, although I sometimes think the only real life we have is a fantasy we're having about life – that there's no 'real' out there any more than there's an 'out there'. (Because if there's an 'out there', then where's 'there', and if there's a 'there', then where's 'here'?)

The return of the Glooms

Too deep, all that stuff, so I thought about men instead. I realized with a shock I've never lived alone – without a man somehow in my life. That might seem too obvious to have escaped notice but I had honestly never thought about it till now.

But if I were to live alone, I don't know what I would do for boffing. I'm not into sport fucking nor am I an aficionado of one-night stands, if they're just to keep from climbing the walls, even though most of the men I met before Hal were dillweeds, best enjoyed in small quantities. (Hal too, now that I think of it.) And I don't like briefies or weekend stands either, or summer affairs or flings. I don't know how some women spread themselves so thin with their maintenance-oriented dates (the current euphemism for need-fucking). Nor do I like vibrators and dildos and My Secret Garden paraphernalia, preferring, in extremis, the ancient solution – providing there is no other option and if the glands have been on overdrive for an uncomfortable amount of time. It's King Cock for me (if I care about the person that Wee Willie or Prince Rodney is attached to): a part of sexual pleasure is having someone you can put your arms around, or better yet, be in arms that hold you.

Paska. And I had begun to think the Glooms were behind me.

'The FBI is powerless to stop oral-genital intimacy unless it obstructs interstate commerce' (J. Edgar Hoover)

I made yet another coffee and hopped under the warm blankets again to read a story about a prostitution ring on the East Side operating out of several apartments.

Much effort had gone into gathering information for what turned out to be an engrossing article. The cottage industry in question (why do they always call it a 'ring'?) employs twenty-five to thirty-five high-priced prostitutes, who were described in the article as superior in looks to the average streetwalker. Many of the girls were solicited from neighbour-ing states and were taught to dress well and behave with a certain gentility – shades of Iris.

All of them, according to the reporter, said they enjoyed 'the Life', a protestation I was not inclined to believe, and a number of them said they were feminists and spoke of their having a stronger economic power base than most women. They charge from a hundred and fifty to three hundred dollars per short visit and split the earnings evenly with the house.

I had never read the mechanics of brothel management before (yet another subculture). Each of the apartments has a beautifully furnished waiting-room, and the other rooms are divided into cubicles to create many areas of activity while keeping a degree of privacy. Each of the women of the organization makes between five hundred and fifteen hundred dollars a day or night, working in shifts. At any given time there are as many as twelve girls in each apartment, although the usual number was five or six. In the hours before dawn, a skeleton crew of two is all that is required to handle the trade.

The report said the brothel operators pay particular atten-tion to public perception of their activity. The owner-managers are 'mindful of the distaste they occasionally engendered in the legitimate tenants'. ('Hey, Angie, to what do you, like, attribute your continued success?' 'Like, I and the girls try to be mindful of the distaste we occasionally engender in the legitimate tenants – y'know what I mean?') Whenever a neighbour's anger becomes vocal, the local operation closes down for a few days and the women work out of another location until the crisis blows over.

The women get their clients through permanent ads in sleazy tabloids, porn magazines and periodicals for the wank trade. The newspaper reporter, as part of his research, answered one of these ads and over the phone a female voice, sounding like the product of elocution lessons that weren't going too well, quoted him the price for oral sex and a slightly higher one for 'standard no-frills' sex, with a time limit in either case of thirty minutes. She gave her address on East 34th Street and the number of her 'suite' on the fourth floor. The reporter realized that one of the places the police had raided and shut down just a few hours earlier was on the eighth floor of the same building.

A leading expert in sex

I wondered if Iris and Mr Nussl ever compared notes, I learned so much lore about prostitutes from her. But in her case it was mostly contemporary data and habits. For example, prostitutes in Ethiopia are proud of their calling and respected by the men they serve. In their society, since they supply a recognized need, and in an activity that everyone enjoys, they're not considered inferior to anyone else.

I frequently press her for information. She may be years younger than I am but she's an expert compared with me.

'You know that sex interests me,' I say as a prompt.

'One or two of my clients actually don't care to do fucking, which surprises you at first,' she said. 'They just want somebody to talk to, or maybe play with their wee-wees, as one of them calls it. A lot of our work is really about dealing with emotional problems – doing therapy, when you think about it.'

Of termites and murder

I thought of Mr Nussl, not just because of his anthropological interest in sexual transactions, particularly in colonial Gotham, but because of another article that caught my eye on the same page. It was about termites and their biggest enemies, assassin termites.

An assassin termite eats termites by sucking out their liquefied innards (charming). It does this in a clever way: by camouflaging itself as a termite's nest. The ordinary unsuspecting termite returns home after a day's work, coming back to what it *thinks* is the nest it left in the morning, and the assassin termite grabs it and eats up all the good parts. It dangles the empty corpse out of the nest to attract more termites – although how that attracts termites is something known only to termites and a question not addressed by the article. Another termite happens along, falls prey and gets eaten, and then another and another. The assassin termite's function in life is to eat termites: the simple life. You would think *non*-assassin termites would have wised up by now, maybe even starting about, say, a million and a half years ago, especially when they come home and see *corpses* dangling out of goddamn windows. But go figure.

It reminded me of the story of the io moth and the complicated Darwinism in that, but even more, it made me think of Mr Nussl and our occasional discussions about New York's cockroach population. The cockroach is a species he claims to admire:

'They're survivors.'

There was deep respect in his voice when he said that, but to be honest, I think some of his 'respect' (typically) is a way of evading the roach problem (like the rat problem). An inconsistent respect too, as I found out. I once saw a roach appear from a crack in the wall as he and I were talking and when I said 'Ugh' he calmly reached over and squished it with his hand (eliciting from me a more heartfelt '*U-u-u-ugh!*'), to which he responded with wise-ass Nussl reasonableness (A Quip for Every Occasion):

'If not I, who? If not now, when?'

(And that was the last time I ever shook *his* hand.)

Thinking of that reminded me of the day I waited in Minelli's for Mr Nussl, the time he didn't show up. That day and the next I kept wondering what he had wanted and I felt a small frisson at the thought that he too had disappeared. Life as the great disappearance act. (Which it is, of course.)

But in this case there was a sequel. He had phoned again a few days later – this would have been back around the beginning of March – and explained that what he had wanted so urgently that day was someone he could talk to. He said he needed a woman's point of view and Sarah wouldn't do because what he wanted to talk about was one of her rivals way back (and not about Iris, as he had pretended to me). The rival was the woman he had not married when he had chosen Sarah. He often thought about this other woman, Rebecca, and the 'unlived life' he might have had with her and felt moments of regret: the door not opened, the road not taken, and so on. He said he has begun to believe that most people have that feeling, that their life feels as if it had many leftover bits, or maybe even whole unused portions.

'A universal condition,' he added: 'Like nostalgia.'

I could see some truth in what he was describing and made a mental note to ask Mr Maki if he felt that too.

The life not lived was an interesting thought, but, typically, Mr Nussl had to spoil it by making it into a joke. Like most cynics, he hates showing a beautiful sensitivity he keeps buried. I flattered him that he was a philosopher, and he scoffed at that. He said if *he* ever were to write a philosophy he would call it *Life as a Near Miss*. Then he *really* startled me:

'You know, life is endless murder.'

He certainly had a way of expressing things.

A *lifetime achievement award for just getting* through *the thing*

'It's all murder. We eat three times a day, eat everything we can get hold of, cramming it into our mouth and destroying it, and then one day *we* get eaten. So what is life, then? – a huge mouth, a thing that never stops chewing. And what are we? Food – everything that lives is food. And what is food? Potential shit. So [*rising now to the great summation*] we go through life as food and end as shit that our relatives have to take outside and bury it someplace. So forget *Life as a Near Miss* – I was joking. What life is is a fairy tale about eating. Eat, get eaten, kill, be killed – all death. But you want to know what's so funny about eating and shitting and killing and death? We say life is beautiful. Go understand.'

I decided to spare him the ancient joke about the pessimist whose doctor advised an emergency optorectomy to sever the central nerve between eyes and asshole to get rid of his shitty outlook on life. If I had thought it would make him laugh (it was his kind of joke) I would have told it, but he was so horribly down that day, bitter, even, that I had the sense he was entering some new phase of his declining years ('going into reclusion,' I said, 'or, no, going into *se*clusion,' which he topped with his usual ease, though wearily, 'No, no, *con*clusion').

He had confided to me once that fellow property owners were buying up tenements in the Bowery-Chinatown area to resell to an uptown realtor with plans for putting up a showy highrise somewhere near SoHo. Three of Mr Nussl's fellow property owners, after hearing stirrings of uptown interest, had banded together to buy up the area one building at a time, all hush-hush to keep prices from being driven up before they made their grab. Through discreet inquiries, Mr Nussl uncovered the scheme of his hypocritical colleagues and the real reason for their el-cheapo offer to him for 'that old beat-up loft building' – the place where Iris and I had been living above the prosthetics and piss-bottle place. The offer was made through one of the owners, pretending to be a lone principal and saying he only wanted to 'make some minor improvements and clean up the run-down neighbourhood a little'.

Mr Nussl didn't disguise his pleasure in telling me that their acquiring *his* loft building was essential to the success of the sneaky plan: it sat smack in the middle of the block of real estate, at the very heart of the contemplated buyout.

Hell hath no fury like Mr Nussl hoaxed

He of course played dumb. If they were in alliance to swindle him, then he would adopt the role of a naïve, nebbishy, *pesky* little hold-out, someone who looked like an ageing sucker but would turn out to be a thorn in their side that they would slowly grow to fear, hate and then (heh heh) dread. The tawdriness of their attempt at a coup at his expense appealed to his view of the human race as a *shtinken-von-alle-seiten* mob. In response to what was supposed to be an irresistible offer, Mr Nussl explained that though it was only a broken-down old loft building, the income from it was his family's mainstay, the extended 'family' that he now specially created for this occasion including, along with Sarah, his cousin Ignacy and Ignacy's (fictitious) wife 'up in Tarrytown' – the same unfortunate Ignacy, of course, who many long years ago had perished in Auschwitz.

Patiently, the dissembling delegate approached him again with a sweeter offer, and Mr Nussl, a master at the waiting game (as I, his tenant, can easily attest to), told him he had solemnly promised Sarah he could never sell this 'prize property' knowing how much it meant to her: it was the first 'bite' they had taken out of the Big Apple – the first property in the New World they had bought and could claim as their own.

The scheming property owner had the relaxed perseverance of someone who feels certain of eventual victory and casually, coolly approached Mr Nussl a third time about 'that paint-peeling dump', but Mr Nussl stuck to his story of sentimental attachment, though announcing that a recent (unexplained) change had created a slightly new 'sitoo-ation': he hinted that we all have our price (after all, if the truth be told, which of us is entirely free of greed, blahblahblah?), and it was conceivable that an amount of money having an impressive number of zeros could persuade Sarah to change her mind, hinting to them that he just happened to know she was teetering. But – *but* the amount would have to be great enough to console her for what would be a very sad loss for her, and God knows she had been through a lot already, poor woman. But she was a very stubborn woman, you know, very stubborn . . . Their plot fell through, and now that I think of it, he's damn lucky they didn't just bump him off and drop his body into the East River.

Life the way we live it – rhymes with blivet

His bitterness was connected not just with these *goniffs*, these hick Machiavellians who led their squalid lives plotting against neighbours, but also with his fondly remembered older sister Hannah. In Wrocław, the infamous truck, the one from which he had been saved by Christian neighbours, took away Hannah and their parents to the cattle cars whose destination was Auschwitz and their (mercifully swift) murder. He was understandably bitter about that, but lately the bitterness had been spreading over his whole being. When he spoke he exuded a quiet revulsion at life.

'What if my sister *had* lived? She would have come to America and paid rent to some schmuck landlord like me only maybe *wois*. She would have gone to see Shakespeare in the Park. She would have taken her kids to Disneyland on her vacation. She would have taken out a car loan from the bank and traded in her piece-of-junk old car for a piece-of-junk new car. In the end she would have gotten shovelled into the ground in Brooklyn instead of in Silesia.'

I told him that that missed the point, that her life had intrinsic value and, like everyone else, she deserved to live it fully.

'Ha!'

He wasn't having any of it. In his best grand-opera manner he hurled his head back and glared at the Simpleton of the Isles. He stopped as if readying himself for an epigram, or as I was beginning to think of them, Nusslgrams.

'*You* miss the point,' he yelled. 'Sure her life had abso-*LOOT* value. I don't need you to tell *me*. But the "fool life" she deserved was what? – rent, Shakespeare in the Park and *facockta* car loans? I mean, *shit!* And kielbasa with sodium nitrite that you can't even tell from *trafe* hot dogs? *What* fool life?'

In truth, I didn't know how to answer that.

But then, on further reflection, I thought perhaps he was experiencing what my grandfather once called end-of-life feelings, that he was both sad and angry that life ends (in particular his, of course). Life doesn't wait for us to reach some point where we might feel at least a *degree* of satisfaction, a small bit of contentment that might come from having done *some* of the things we once set out to do. There was never closure in life. Almost always death came as a midcourse interruption, but the 'interruption' lasted till the end of time. I could understand his unhappiness.

I had what felt like a new insight: we don't 'die' but it's more that we're *torn away* from life. (Not a great insight, if an insight at all, but an accurate feeling?)

DEAR KAREN: I have been trying out my new discovery of the perfect cure for the common cold. OK, it may not be perfect for everybody but it works for me: mugs of hot red wine, plenty of bed rest (now there's a switch) and Sibelius quietly in the background. Or maybe Crusell, whom I'm beginning to like – a little, so far. (And Purcell always.)

I caught a cold the night of the party and have been taking it easy for days. Bill dropped up to see how I was doing – and surprisingly was on his best behaviour. He came over with a big bottle of brandy to warm us both up and sat and drank it all himself. Amazing capacity. Not very healthy, though, to have that degree of tolerance. He only stayed a couple of hours, and it made me almost sick to watch him putting it away. When there was none left, he went home. He told me his accountant and Sue had both told him to make fewer paintings, limit his production to drive prices up. They felt he was ripe now to triple and quadruple his prices. He also told me he had started dating his work four years ahead 'to fuck up future art historians. I want my paintings to be a health hazard to curators.'

Recently I told Roz she should try to encourage him to drink less. Didn't she know any way to stop him? It was a killing pace. She agreed, of course, but guiltily said that something happens when she's with him and before she knows it, they're both boozing it up again. Of course what saves Roz is that she returns to Hollywood and is pretty much off the hard stuff for months at a time making a film. I never thought Hollywood could be good for your health.

39

Is this life as we know it?

Phone call from Karen's hotel. The manager had some luggage belonging to her. On instructions, he had been holding it in storage. Karen had told him she'd be back in a week, maybe a bit longer, but so much time had passed he was wondering.

'How did you get my number?'

'You gave it to me.'

That's right. I had called the hotel not so long ago for news.

I told him I didn't know how much longer she'd be away and I'd be by in a while to pick up whatever she had left.

Fine except blahblahblah, he hoped blahblah I understood the responsibility, and so forth blahblah – and I said fine, fine, OK. Mr Blahblah said I would be required to pay a small sum that remained to be settled, and after that he'd be glad to let me take possession, providing I could produce ID. I said sure, no problem, I felt sure my ID would prove conclusively that I was none other than me, and he said *what*, and I said never mind – just clearing my throat.

The call had come as I was about to leave for Mr Maki's so I rang him up to say I'd be late. He hardly noticed – he was all jazzed up about some computer software called Viva Voce, and he wanted me to investigate it for him. It was a great device, apparently. You spoke some words and they magically appeared on the screen. That meant Mr Maki could do some work on his own in between our sessions, and that would speed up progress on The Book.

'I can't *believe* how wonderful are the inventions they have now.' He sounded ecstatic.

I hopped a taxi to Karen's hotel and rang the bell at the front desk for the manager. A suave gent appeared, almost a caricature of a Continental type with a ridiculous resemblance to President Jacques Chirac. He seemed pleased to see me and even more pleased when I took out my cheque book and scribbled out what I hoped was not too rubbery a cheque, aka ransom money. After I signed a piece of paper, we exchanged hostages: I handed him the cheque and he surrendered the goods (both, I think, releasing our grip at the same time).

I ran out and grabbed a cab to CompuMania, desperately pushing away the thought that I might be holding all that remained of Karen.

The swift completion of her appointed rounds

At CompuMania I asked the geekier-looking of the two men working there about Viva Voce.

'No problem.'

He sat us in front of a PC to give me a demonstration.

'You're going to love it,' he said, smoothing down his Macy's tie with a caress of his hand and flipping its end up.

'So. What would you like me to type?'

A flyer on the desk read: 'The factory parts are made according to the highest technical standards.' I didn't think anything Mr Maki might dictate would ever be more complicated than that, so I pointed to the words.

'This OK?'

'No problem.'

He sounded so happy to be demonstrating this latest technological wonder that I felt a small twinge of happiness for him.

Slowly, distinctly, he read the words 'The factory parts' into a small microphone clamped to his head. As he spoke, the screen typed out 'Saddam Hussein'.

Maybe I had missed something, and said with a laugh, 'Huh?'

He too laughed. 'Just a glitch.'

Very slowly, a word at a time, he said to the machine: '"The . . . [*pause*] . . . factory . . . [*pause*] . . . parts . . . [*pause*] . . . are . . . [*pause*] . . . made . . ."'

The words appeared on the screen: 'Her . . . [*pause*] . . . cracker . . . [*pause*] . . . hearts . . . [*pause*] . . . are . . . [*pause*] . . . taint . . .'

'Just a second.' He smiled reassuringly and again smoothed down his tie and gave its tip another upward flip. 'No problem. It's my fault, not the computer's. I omitted a simple test. The software needs to recognize *my* voice. Carl's been using the machine – he's on vacation.'

He sat still for a moment, then said: 'The.' He pronounced the word with care and surrounded it with silence. After gazing at the screen he repeated it: 'The' – and then whispered to me that he was training the computer to *his* way of pronouncing a few key words.

I mentally conceded that the word *the* qualified, I suppose, as a key word in English, though it seemed to me that at this rate, if I had to train the thing to *my* voice for a vocabulary of just basic English alone and then train it also to Mr *Maki's* voice, pen and pencil would be quicker.

With the third careful enunciation of 'the', I saw it flash on the screen: 'creeper'.

Damn, I thought: poor guy, everything's going wrong.

There was a pained look on his face as he whispered (to himself this time), '"The" doesn't even *sound* like "creeper".'

I waited, hurting for him. He studied the screen, turned and studied me without seeing me, or for that matter taking in anything. Patience personified now, I politely waited some more (but at the same time was treacherously completing my report to Mr Maki: Ixnay on the immickgay).

'Well . . .' this earnest geek began – and immediately ran out of energy.

I offered a gentle 'Yes?' meaning to show that the truly

open mind is always prepared to hear the pros and cons of Viva Voce.

He leaned towards me, a strange new smile suggesting we were in cahoots about something – you and me against the world, babe – although for an instant I was afraid it might be (please: no) testosterone time again.

But it wasn't. He gave his tie another one of his caressing tugs and beamed a confidential, friendly wink at me. 'Don't buy this thing.'

'I used to be Snow White . . . but I drifted.' Mae West

'Oh, that's too bad,' Mr Maki said when I gave him my report.

So we went on as we had been doing, he talking his story to me and me typing it up as we went. Sic transit glorious Viva Voce and a brief moment of excitement in our lives.

We were deep in Canada's eastern Arctic, in Inuit territory, where I was learning that it takes less than an hour to build an igloo (called *osuitok* in Inuit). I was loving it that although the Inuit language has no words to describe many ordinary things we consider an important part of everyday life, it has thirteen words for snow. When Mr Maki lived among them, the Inuit survived mostly on seals, each seal the size of a cow and enough to feed a family for a couple of weeks. There were stretches after Asiak had lost her family when she couldn't hunt seals on her own and she was forced to live on gulls' eggs – if she was lucky enough to find any.

The Inuit used to make stone sculptures and do bone carvings but in recent decades Eskimo sculpture and scrimshaw had grown into practically an export industry. Drawings too. I was shocked to learn that the Inuit sell three hundred thousand drawings a year (!) to dealers in Montreal, Toronto, New York and Chicago. The Eskimo way of life begins to lose some of its charm when you hear things like that, although it would be unreasonable to expect it to remain forever Nanook of the North up there. It depressed me to hear that a few years back, the Inuit built a four-million-dollar school and basketball gym. *Paska*. I tried to square that image with my picture of the tundra. But despite changes of that sort, old habits persisted, especially in resourcefulness: when an outboard engine broke down and they needed a new part, instead of sitting around and waiting a few months for the part to arrive, they carved one out of bone and got the motor running again.

And I liked listening to Mr Maki and all his stray facts. In a sense it didn't matter what he talked about. I was a school of one and in part a solace for the loss of his wife. I learned that in Savo, a place near the Russian border, the farmer's wife makes a rye bread baked around a filling of small, whole freshwater fish, which is flavoured with pork and onions, a dish Mr Maki's wife used to make.

'You bake it for five hours, then eat it hot or cold. You wash it down with ice-cold buttermilk. It's called *kalakukko*.'

In the country, the farmer's wife buries the *kalakukko* in a deep pile of hay in the barn. The hay insulates it, preserving it cold but not frozen. (Like New York City corpses!) Later when they want to eat it she unwraps it and lets it come up to room temperature and serves it in thick slices spread with butter.

Sometimes I feel I am being given the privilege of hearing the views of someone who had lived a long time and thought about many things about which I hadn't formed an opinion yet. One time he told me that people make their lives too complicated. But he went back on that, because another time he said he didn't like the Noble Savage trap of looking down on progress. He felt the Eskimos were surviving better now, they had longer lives than before, and who were we to criticize them for going crazy over snowmobiles? (And hell, I thought, why not? We had bowling alleys in Rovaniemi, the capital of Lapland.) He privately thought that snowmobiles were probably a mistake for the environment and wildlife, but on the other side of the coin, Eskimo children were learning that the cultural horizon was a wider one than their parents used to think, that the world beyond Inuit territory was bringing more of life to them and pushing back the limits of their interests. I suppose he championed that because of his own modest origins, especially his job as island keeper, which must have felt quite confining. And of course there could have been other reasons – I don't know.

His stories combine history and anthropology and I can listen to him sometimes for hours. He makes me want to live until I am very *very* old, older even than he is right now. He sounds so reasonable about everything and of course it would be impossible to tell until I *was* that old whether that just came with age. Thirty thousand mornings: I wondered if I would be lucky enough to get that many. And if I did, would they feel like enough. Is *any* amount of life enough?

Lemminkäinen's homeward journey – but forgetting his American Express Card

Like smog, muggings are so much a part of everyday life in New York that after a while you don't think about them – which is why it's a shock if it should ever happen to you finally (a mugging, not smog).

This preamble is by way of saying that on leaving Mr Maki's I underwent the experience I had heard so much about: I got mugged. Where the mugger appeared from I can't truthfully say but it took a longish nanosecond, possibly two, for me to become fully conscious that I was in the middle of the kind of dreaded thing I've heard people describe as a defining or shaping experience (although what gets defined or shaped, I don't know).

To restrict myself to the physical circumstances: everything was fine and then suddenly there was an open switchblade slicing the air back and forth three inches from my eyes – eyes now taking things in in slow motion – before the point of the blade went down, down, down and put a very cold, very pointy dimple in a tender part of my throat.

Next, appearing slowly from the left side of my face, a pair of eyes slid into view as, peripherally, I took in their owner, a tall and surprisingly handsome jock despite an unkempt beard that was not enhanced by a yellowish memento of breakfast or lunch (or a contribution from each). He was neither clearly a white dude nor clearly of African origin nor was he Far Eastern but could have been anything – and at that, a handsome, though not recently washed, example of whatever it was. As we made eye contact, he slowly gave me a *companionable* grin – a really friendly look, as though he were overjoyed for us to be meeting each other again after being out of touch for ages. It took a moment for me to understand he was grinning at my terror.

'Oh . . .' I said.

I must have looked satisfyingly distressed – or to put it another way, scared shitless – to cause him to grin more widely now in some private pleasure at witnessing a muggee's dawning awareness of being *la* muggee.

Reality doesn't get realer than this, I remember thinking, though I couldn't tell you what I meant (although in that moment the thought seemed pregnant with significance).

My 'oh' apparently had appeal. The mugger repeated it falsetto, trying for a high-pitched staccato girlish voice. '*Ooh!*'

I was being mugged by a comic.

He was, I think, high on something, yet coolly and efficiently robbing me, with me simultaneously *in* the experience and observing it happening. He was both tense and calm, which despite my scared-shitless state I found excitingly interesting (and began mentally recounting the adventure to Mr Maki: 'So this guy comes up to me and jams this knife right into my throat – he didn't break *skin*, exactly, but . . .').

Outwardly I remained calm, remembering from somewhere that if he was psychotic you didn't want to unbalance him, or unhinge him, or destabilize him, or whatever it was you didn't want to do to such individuals when they were operating under the heavy stress of separating you from your valuables. And – and this is not news to an out-of-towner – in the Big

Apple it is sometimes very hard to tell who's deranged and who isn't, there being in New York more people per square acre than anywhere in the world who argue and yell at themselves as they walk down the street with arms oratorically flailing at invisible opponents in some kind of uphill struggle to convince them of something. Coming from Jyväskylä and Helsinki, this aspect of New York City life used to fascinate me at first but you see so much of it that after a while you stop noticing it.

Friendly-sounding or not, he was all for getting down to the business at hand.

'Now don't tell me you forgot to bring your mugger money.'

I flashed on Karl Malden, could hear his 'Don't leave home without it,' meaning plastic, and here I was flagrantly ignoring his sage advice and walking around with *cash* and finding myself, sure enough, in the process of losing it. I dug through pockets in various layers of clothing, searching for as much money as I could dredge up – and secretly *overjoyed* (forget Malden) that for *once* I had gone out without my Leica! (Talk about shit luck.)

He was pretty patient for a mugger, after all I've heard about their irritability and nervousness, and not having any suicidal wish to piss him off beyond reasonable limits (especially while the point of his switchblade continued to incite cooperation by giving my throat little reminder jabs), I hoped the minuscule haul he was getting wouldn't prove upsettingly inadequate for the fix he had set his heart on.

He was very businesslike. Accepting each small bit as I handed it over and stashing it uncounted (just another day at the office) in the pocket of a rather spiffy-looking camel's hair coat (an earlier, more successful mugging probably), he gave a cheerful 'Ciao, baby' and headed off into the sunset, or in this case broad daylight.

It was terribly brief, I thought. Was that it? I had been through a real-live mugging?

I was still thinking how ballsy the bastard was (I couldn't

help admiring the daring *outlawness* of the event, and its being done so publicly) when he stopped and looked back at me thoughtfully.

For several seconds I glared at him. Some instinct told me to high-tail it but I didn't move. (Give-no-quarter Inge.)

He called out in a peculiarly grumpy voice, 'Check it out, baby' – a grumpy but *concerned* voice – 'have I harassed you sexually?'

'Huh? No.'

'I don't buy into that macho shit, y'unnerstan? I'm not into abuse. Did I treat you OK, baby?'

What was this, an exit poll?

'I'm fine,' I lied.

'Because we're both living on the same planet and no sense in going around hurting people, y'unnerstan?'

I assumed the question was rhetorical and did not require any appreciation of his contribution to the quality of life.

'I'm just robbing you. I didn't stab you or nuthin serious like that.' Apparently a thought occurred. 'You think it's because I hate authority or you think it's because I need the money?'

Exit poll, all right.

'Because you need the money.'

He stared hard at me.

'Where you from, man? What the fuck kind of accent is that?'

I didn't think I *had* an accent. It had to be Finnish, whatever it was. He certainly had a sharp ear.

'*Finn*ish?' He smiled a flirtatious smile. 'Well, well, sweet thing.'

Oh shit, testosterone strikes again.

But he only said: 'Sorry about the mugging' – and strolled away. *Strolled.*

Turning his head back as he walked he said: 'In Noo Yawk you carry mugger money with you at all times.'

Instructions yet.

'*Never* go anywhere without it.' (The Karl Malden school of hold-up.) 'You're lucky you got *me* this time.'

Since I have never learned that there are moments in life when it's best to just shut up, I yelled after him angrily (and impotently, but what the hell), 'I'm going straight to the police.'

Fortunately he had more sense than I did. Judging by his sudden laughter, that was the funniest thing he had heard in ages. He let out a hoot, bent himself in half and kept cackling as he walked down the avenue. (No doubt it was the way I told it.) His laughter was so contagious I began laughing too. I decided I was becoming hysterical – relieved at no longer having a knife poking little dimples in my throat.

Apparently relieved in more ways than one, in fact: my crotch wasn't feeling too dry all of a sudden. It was only a small bit of pee (*not* a libidinal response), and I thought oh Christ! I'm losing it – and I'm too young to be that old.

What I like about life is . . . (Hang on, I had it here just a second ago)

I needed to be near people. The Bird in Hand was a couple of blocks away and it promised the two things I needed most just then, safety and a john. The 'women's room', aka john, at Rory's place was of four-star calibre, I'll say that for it (and her).

I entered at the café end of the Bird in Hand, which was hall-like and comfortingly buzzy with an afternoon crowd. Talk about safe: caffs – one of the greatest blessings of our post-Renaissance era.

There were so many people there that I had trouble finding an empty table. Finally I spotted a small one in a corner, which suited me perfectly: I wanted to be near people yet not too close.

Rory's place was catching on more and more, and it was rumoured she was planning to open another café cum eatery, a gay and lesbian bar in the East Eighties called The Unnatural

Act. (Other candidates for the name: The Sausage Mill, The Bearded Clam, The Naked Peacock, The Queens of Manhattan, The Navel Academy, and, my favourite, The Savage Butter, all recently proposed at one time or another by customers in various stages of inebriation – and all, alas, rejected.)

I ordered hot chocolate, my drink of preference in moments of crisis ever since I was a Junior Duck in my school camp's water-safety programme when I was seven. I'd been lost in the woods and was so terrified that I would never be found again that I did it in my pants. By the time someone found me I was bawling my head off and so inconsolable that I was immediately sent home, and nothing, no matter what anyone tried, would quiet me down until my mother in desperation made a cup of hot chocolate with double cream and that, for reasons unknown to all, did it.

The trip to the john showed no significant flood damage – false alarm, and both panties and pride eminently salvageable. Graffiti harvested from the john: none. The walls were bare, the only drawback to nice clean johns.

Back at the table, I sat sipping the hot chocolate and thinking about the mugging. Reliving it in safety, it seemed like an interesting New York City phenomenon now, a rite of passage. I thought of Hal and wished we were closer in some real way, meaning I wished he were someone I could talk with and who would have the patience to listen, especially at a moment like this. Empathic attunement. If there ever was a time when I needed someone's arms around me . . .

Forget it, I told myself, that was not Hal's strong suit and I wondered how long we would go on together, flashing on the thought 'Been there, done that, got those stripes on my back.' We were definitely not on the same page.

But was there anyone else for me? According to Roz, breaking up with a lover is no different from treating a minor infection: the best antidote is a fling with a candidate panting in the wings, 'of which there's an unlimited supply. And it's best done before the corpse is cold.'

It probably works for Roz, but easing out of a relationship with Hal only to slide into an affair with someone else had no appeal for me. I always thought that to do such a thing would mean I couldn't stand on my own two feet.

The chocolate was having the same effect on me as it had the day I got lost in the woods. Gradually a deep calm came over me and the murmur of a roomful of people around me felt reassuring.

The mugging was truly a staggering new experience and I went over it again in my mind. I felt violated, nothing less, and wondered if all muggings were like that.

But I was safe now and had lost nothing of value, and it began to seem funny. (*Reuters*) *Photographer* – no – I would be a 'mug-shot artist'. *MUG-SHOT ARTIST MUGGED. Finnish-American photographer Inge Saarinen, 26, of East 61st Street, Manhattan, was assaulted by a mugger holding a knifeblade to her throat as she was returning home from work yesterday afternoon.*

The waitress saw me staring in her direction and came over and asked if I needed anything.

'Thanks, no.'

She retreated with a friendly smile.

Threatening to 'slice her gizzard open', the unknown assailant, characterized by the victim as 'a stand-up comic with day-old crud in his beard', demanded cash in exchange for allowing her to go on living on the planet with him. 'A simple exchange,' the alleged perpetrator was heard to say, 'a quid pro quo.'

'Fortunately I had the presence of mind not to offer resistance,' the young woman told police, and was later quoted as saying to Manhattan psychoanalyst Martin Yeblon: 'He called me "sweet thing". Although I know that's a cliché greeting, I honestly don't believe he's dangerous – but I think he could probably use some psychotherapy. And a bath.'

Chief Inspector Murphy warned the public that the attacker, still at large, is armed and dangerous and if encountered should be approached with extreme caution.

Asked by reporters about the prostitution ring on East 34th Street (see p. 4, 'Call Girl Lust Bust'), Murphy declined comment 'pending further investigation'.

'However,' he declared, 'matters are being followed up and the public will be kept fully informed.'

He added that according to the latest available information, the legitimate tenants of the building had not voiced distaste for some time, but 'in affairs of this nature, something is inevitably bound to give'.

He had no further comment to make about the mugging of the young Finnish-American photographer, 'certainly not before further forensic tests have been completed'.

At last word, police were rounding up the usual suspects.

I realized I was being stared at. At a nearby table was the good-looking guy whose session followed mine at Martin's, the hunk who had said hello the one or two times we bumped into each other when my sessions ran late (tearful sessions, *damn*, me with puffy red eyes).

I was not in the mood to make any new acquaintances right then but when I glanced over again he smiled with a look of interest – and I thought, what the hell. He had nice dark eyes, they looked chestnut-brown from a distance – kind eyes. He got to his feet and came over.

A rose by any other name

'I've been curious,' he said, 'seeing you at Yeblon's. What's your name?'

'Inge.'

'Oh that's a very lovely name.'

(Early voting returns: he's a loser.)

'In certain parts of the world,' I said as a precautionary damper, 'it's a very common name.'

'In Scandinavia.'

'Yes, but I'm not Scandinavian. Finnish. What's yours?'

'Background?'

'No, name.'

'My name's Horatio.'

A small setback there. I didn't think any self-respecting woman could be expected to go through life saying, 'Horatio, dear, what time is it, please?' There are certain names like that – Cosmo, Junius – that make you wonder what comes over parents.

'Is that your first name?' (maybe a way out here – all may not be lost).

'Yes.'

(All was lost.) 'Do you have a nickname . . . or a middle name . . . ?'

'No nickname. My middle name's Hornblower.'

Jeez-us.

'. . . So . . . Horatio.'

(I was going from Prince Hal to Hamlet's sidekick. Was that moving up or down?)

'I was called Hooray in school but *hated* it.'

A tuft of hair at his wrist stuck out from under the cuff of his shirt, always a turn-on for me. Also I liked the quality of his voice, softly strong and smooth. It had the sexy essence of maleness, which for me is tenderness.

What surprised me was that I didn't feel disloyal to Hal – because it took about a minute and a half for me to start feeling that barring some obstacle like a clumsy move on his part, he was boffable. (Go figure.) Not right away though – just a candidate.

'I live around the corner,' he said.

A cut-to-the-chase guy. Maybe with a name like Horatio you have to move fast. In any case, I had to tell somebody about the mugging, so-o . . .

'How about a drink?'

Me, caution to the winds: 'Sure. Vodka.'

'No, I mean my place. It's very noisy here.'

He left enough money on the table to cover us both and

only then did I realize that I had ordered without a penny in my jeans.

Molten passion molto vivace

His apartment was the usual male zoo masquerading as living quarters, and as a setting for seductions absolutely nil. But perversely that appealed – maybe partly because of my own high standards of housekeeping.

It could have been that he was anticipating having me supinely stretched out on his bed before too long or it could have been genuine solicitude when I told him I had just been mugged, but whatever the reason, he suddenly couldn't do enough for me. Appropriately horrified, he wanted to know all about how the mugging had happened and where it took place, who did it, did I lose much money, was I feeling all right, and maybe I had better finish the vodka and have another. I had the impression that if I had pulled a Sarah Bernhardt fainting act and clutched for a (non-existent) cushion, he would have rushed right over to Bloomie's and bought two or three of them and, while he was at it, picked up some flowers on the way back, along with smelling salts.

He encouraged me to talk about the mugging until even *I* was bored – and said as much, and so, before long, he was telling me about Carlos Williams's poetry and also a poet named Wang Way (spelling?), putting on some new release of Jacques Loussier's that I *had* to hear (and he had to tell me who that was), and connecting that with *Nashville*, an Altman film I've never seen, and at the same time making at least a couple of passes at me. I admired his energy.

He taught me an Indian word: *Chaubunagungamaug*, which means 'You fish on your side, I fish on my side and nobody fishes in the middle, so no trouble.' It's Mohican, I remember that, but I don't quite recall how the information came up.

That kind of tidbit reminded me of Mr Nussl and I told Horatio about him, and I told him about Mr Maki and The Book. I didn't like Mr Maki's opening sentence, which he keeps insisting on despite my repeated misgivings – 'We are given a whole lifetime to discover what a whole lifetime is about' – to which Horatio said:

'Hey, that's not bad. Why don't you like it?'

'It's awkward. And platitudinous' – a word I had never used before though I run across it occasionally in a book. 'It tries too hard to be clever. And unfortunately makes it.'

I also told him about the geek at CompuMania and Viva Voce and he thought it was really smart of me not to put down my money and just buy the thing, take it home and *then* find out it doesn't work.

'Which is the sort of thing I would have done.'

It felt nice being admired for a change and, well . . . cut to the chase, as we say: the brain is our largest sex organ, and the easiest way to storm a woman's gates, speaking for myself, is through the mind (without, however, discounting a judicious amount of flattery if it at least borders on sincere compliment).

(I hate it when I come out sounding like Quent.)

In other words, I ended up feeling that 'the inevitable *eez* always' and we had a good afternoon boff – and *voilà*. I had been needing it, but then I was always needing it. Still, I was surprised by the intensity. I hadn't thought I was really all that horny, nor had I felt sexy for ages, which should have told me something about where I was – or wasn't – with Hal. I certainly would never have expected myself to be so easily aroused after a mugging, and I'm not quite sure how Horatio attained his goal (well, mine too, and rather swiftly), but we ended up enjoying it immensely.

When the guy is right, there's something inexpressibly satisfying about lying in bed with legs intertwined in that mellow post-coital mood I love so much and that the Romans thought so sad, poor bastards. For me it's the most calming and happy feeling there is. And in this case there was the added turn-on of a comfort-fuck (that is, post-mugging nerve-calming boff).

Half-way through the second vodka, I decided I needed to

take a shower, which, in one of those remarkable coincidences, turned out to be exactly what Horatio needed to do too. So it seemed like the most natural thing in the world to climb in together and squeeze up against each other. We spent more time than strictly necessary soaping up selected portions of lower torsos, with some supplementary time devoted to my top, and did such a conscientious job on each other that when we stepped out of the shower we found ourselves standing in a shallow tile-bottomed lake. The bathroom looked like the tide had come in and it made me think of those Hollywood movies where, just when Brando is about to boff the shyly yielding South Sea princess in all her Technicolor splendour, the camera discreetly pans away to a pounding surf accompanied by the orchestra crescendoing ever upward in C-major Dolby-stereo climaxes.

40

La vita nuova . . .

. . . or a fine mess. Well, in a manner of speaking.

It's pretty obvious what has happened to Karen though there's no proof. She is gone, lost, wasted. Finished. I would be deluding myself to think of it in any other way. Wherever she is, if she's still alive, Karen is dying and will die again every day, hoping against hope and the hope always and forever for nothing. Then the time will come when she will stop hoping and accept her life as the nothing it now is because it is all she has or can have before she dies physically. She will go on existing and no longer living.

As for Paavo and her family, what are they doing? What are they feeling?

Is there something *I* can do? There is nothing I can do. And how do *I* feel? (Don't be stupid.)

And poor Horatio: I had him as trapped audience – not fair to him, really. But he's a dear person and very good about listening.

We were dressed again, and I told him how anguishing 'this whole Karen thing' has been, about memories (and fantasies) that are tormenting. I told him about my letters to Karen and that I no longer wanted to write them, not believing them myself or seeing much use in it. He didn't say as much – he didn't have to: I could tell he was affected by what I told him.

'Don't look for relief,' he said. 'What*ever* happened, it'll gradually move to the periphery of your life. It'll always be there but your thoughts will be drawn less and less in that direction. Lucky for us, memories do fade.'

Sudden misgiving here: *et tu* Horatio?

'Are you saying I'll forget her?'

'No, no, you won't forget her, nothing like that.'

'Then what?'

'She will *always* be there. But she won't go on dominating your thoughts.'

I needed to mull that one over, though my first reaction was that he was right.

'You're blaming yourself,' he added. 'I suppose that's natural, at least I've heard it is but there's no reason for you to.'

Martin had said something similar, and now abruptly I wondered why Horatio was seeing him. And being me, of course, I asked. But he countered:

'I wondered about you too. I've seen you crying.'

'It started when Karen didn't come back,' I said. 'But then I found out it's not about her but about me.'

'What, about you?'

I thought of telling him about feeling down and not being able to do photography any more – then thought better of it.

'Not sure. I know that I haven't felt like doing anything recently, but that's probably temporary. Then when Karen vanished one day . . .'

'Are you depressed?'

Here we go again. Yes, I thought, it's that but it's not that. But he wouldn't understand. Just because he was *seeing* Martin didn't mean he would have Martin's empathy or understanding. There was more to it than that, and part of it was my anger at people, almost a disgust with them and their lives when I thought of Karen's life so brutally and cruelly wasted. I told him about the police and that I thought even the FBI had been drawn into it, although I wasn't sure about that, and that in any case there was still no word. The last anyone had ever seen of Karen and Frank together was their departure at the airport, on their way to Africa for a holiday jaunt. And the only thing anyone had ever said about that was: So what's the crime in that?

'So I withdrew. From a lot of people.'

He looked at me with brown, intelligent eyes and waited.

'OK, I'm depressed,' I told him, 'but it's more than that. It's hard to put a name on a dissatisfaction that gradually . . . that slowly *infects* your whole life.'

I guess I must have grown used to Hal and his reactions, because I was surprised that Horatio was willing to listen. I went on, telling him about the photography part and that it had not been going well for some time and about Hal and how *that* had not been going well either but that I owed him so much. But I didn't want Horatio to connect me with Hal, to think first it's Hal and then it's somebody else, that I was someone who goes around hopping in and out of beds.

'It's sort of over with Hal. Otherwise I don't think I could have . . .'

I didn't feel like explaining. Curious, an hour ago so many things in my life seemed so uncertain and now . . .

He picked up my hand, turned it over and stroked the inside of my wrist (I felt *that* in my gut). He had strong, straight fingers and his nails had tiny white flecks in them, microscopic snowflakes. Nice.

'Well, I don't exactly go around bed-hopping either,' he said. 'But then, I suppose, you would have no way of knowing whether that was true or not.'

That *sounded* good, but practically all men say things like that at the beginning. They lie so innocently – it's really testosterone: they're in its grip.

I asked again why *he* was seeing Martin.

'I had been involved with somebody and it had gone bad and I was feeling down about it, which is another way of saying I was feeling down about me, of course. It was pretty painful . . . but these things always sound banal when you talk about them.'

'Pain isn't banal.'

'Well . . . she was a friend, and I had been living with her a long time – too long. We both felt it wasn't right, but neither of us could break it off. To complicate matters, she wanted children and I didn't. I'm not ready for all that. And then one day I acted very badly to her, yelling and saying things I shouldn't have. And I thought, "I don't want to live this way," so I walked away from it. I simply left. And afterward felt tremendous guilt at just dropping her.'

He was silent as his thoughts drifted.

'That was the end?'

'No. We got together again. But we both saw it the way it really was, that it wasn't going to work out, and we called it quits. But the second time around at least she was less hurt. That time it was her idea to call it off. And it was right after that that I began seeing Martin. I didn't know what I wanted – or why I was so unhappy.' He added: 'One of the hardest things of all is to leave someone who is *almost* right for you. Because it's hard letting go even though you know it's wrong for you in the long run.'

I understood. Love has a shelf life. If things don't work out after a certain time, it perishes.

I was tempted to launch into the story of My Life and Loves, with special emphasis on Hal, but I really wasn't in a mood to go into all that. About Karen, I could see he was affected by what I told him, and *paska*, I felt little stirrings of love for the guy. But I heeded the warning signs that were already up: What do you know about him? What happened to the idea of living for a while without a man in your life?

I was enjoying feeling at ease with the way things were going but I also felt a vulnerable openness – so boundless it frightened me. But intense emotions never last, I knew, however much we may wish they could go on.

But right now I had a need to stay with the good feelings, revel in the moment . . . and savour Horatio's undoing my shirt again, button by button, unrushed, so considerate of feelings, as a charge of anticipation welled up in me, a giddy rush of lust and expectation.

Once you've made love with a man, your lives become joined together, even if only a single filament ties you, and even if the feeling quickly begins to fade. Because all feelings fade. But it doesn't matter as long as you are given that wonderfully revitalizing strength, which feeling loved does – as long as you can enjoy those unspoken little pleasures, as seeing a brightness come into the other's eyes when you catch him looking at you when he thinks you're not aware. No matter what else may happen, you've become special for each other.

I imagined his eyes had love in them, or the potential of love. But (surprising myself with the thought) I didn't want that. I didn't want him or anyone to fall in love with me. He would want more, I knew, because men did. But I would deal with that. For now I wanted something simple: moments together . . . with this nice person who listens and doesn't have all the answers – what a pleasure.

41

The Karen mystery solved?

Yesterday afternoon!!! Going to Mr Maki's, I stopped off at Great Scandinavia to see Mama. As I walked in, a man whose back was turned to me wheeled round and grabbed my two hands between his.

'Hey, I've been looking everywhere for you!'

Frank.

I felt my legs quaking. Where's Karen? *Where is Karen?*

But he was smiling! How could he smile? *Did that mean –?*

No, Karen was *not* back. Karen *was* missing. She had disappeared on him in Marrakesh.

Disappeared on *him*?

I stared, watching his smile fade, and waiting for him to go on.

'I left her to make a phone call and – unbelievable, but – she was gone. All at once the entire trip was a nightmare. I looked everywhere, searched and hunted for her, made inquiries of some of the locals, but no results. And it all happened so quickly too – right from the very moment of our arrival.'

And he spun out a long tale – obviously thinking I was interested in buying a piece of the Brooklyn Bridge.

He and Karen had taken an airport taxi to the heart of town, to the Hotel Mamounia, and had stopped at a large and crowded outdoor café before checking in because he'd remembered an urgent phone call he had to make. He left Karen at a table and was gone for only five minutes, but by the time he returned she was no longer there and their baggage was gone too. At first he assumed she had gone to freshen up, but after waiting a while, he asked the waiter and then the manager if they had seen her but they had been too busy to notice any particular young woman. The café was crawling with tourists.

He had then located the local gendarmerie and checked with them – they of course knew nothing – and alerted them she was missing. He questioned people on the street, reasoning that Karen would stand out among veiled Arab women and he hoped someone had seen an American woman (as he called her) but no one had.

'Do you think there might have been another man involved?' Frank asked as though I might help *him* to understand.

. . . Or maybe, he thought, she had run off to Rome with someone else . . . or Venice . . . she had mentioned Venice and the gondolas . . .

In less than five minutes, my initial excitement at finally seeing Frank turned to a sick feeling. I couldn't believe he really expected me to go along with the idea that Karen would go with him to Marrakesh merely to run off with somebody else.

Angrily I confronted him and he agreed:

'That wouldn't make sense, would it, unless there was – I don't know – maybe some prearrangement?'

He had no idea where she might have gone, and he had been hoping I or Hal or someone at Great Scandinavia would have news, or had heard something or had *some* clue.

He sounded desperate to find Karen. Our eyes locked. I

saw his bronzed athlete's features and almond eyes and grace-
ful lashes and felt how difficult it might be for a woman to
turn him down. I could see the accuracy of Karen's description
of him as 'very light-skinned for an inhabitant of Harlem' –
but also the inaccuracy about his origins. He had the colouring
of middle-period Michael Jackson – and his handsomeness
had true film-star quality, and I recalled now her telling me
she was attracted to the strange beauty of African-Americans
– 'l'exotique' she had said finally in French, searching for the
right word. But with this up-close look I saw she was wrong.
I remember Mama telling me earlier he was Egyptian-
Polynesian, not African-American – not black at all.

All the while I was staring at Frank he was returning my look.
Without embarrassment. When I remained silent he said:

'You've had no news, I suppose.'

Frank and the dream of the New World first encountered

Perhaps not too sure about me or what I might be thinking,
he went on with his story. Seeing him and listening to him, it
was easy to understand Karen's being drawn to him: the lure
of adventure away from family, far from the old Baltic culture
at the other side of Europe. Frank was America, a new life
– the thrill of Manhattan with its thousand high-rises and
skyscrapers, its museums and cinemas and expensive shops,
and cafés and people, and avenues that swarmed with buses
and cabs. Karen told Leena (or Marita or Paula) she had no
idea life in New York could be so much *fun*, and though the
au pair girls themselves worked long hours, they agreed it
was exciting being away from Helsinki, where nothing much
ever happened.

Karen had never felt loved by any man as deeply as she felt
loved and desired by this lover and his (in her unintentional
pun) 'gentle manly manners'. He was not just elegantly
groomed but a talented songwriter – a creative person, sensitive.

Karen had grown more and more fond of Frank and in the

few weeks they were seen together she was always so very much at his side that Mama said she suspected he had sexually awakened her. And I suppose that could be true, even though ordinarily Finnish women don't need much awakening after the age of about twelve and a half. By the end of their first week Frank was spending nights at her small East Side hotel and showing her Manhattan, from the Rainbow Room to the Village Vanguard, from the Cloisters to the Statue of Liberty. As someone self-employed, his time was hers and his. The Met, the Modern, the Guggenheim: each day she was not working they had gone somewhere new and ended at Great Scandinavia for happy hour before having a meal somewhere and heading back to her room.

Karen had told me how much she liked his generosity. He bought drinks for the regulars of Great Scandinavia and even treated Mama and Mrs Jaaskelainen to an occasional round. One time, Karen once told Mama, she offered to buy Frank handmade Italian shoes at six hundred dollars a pair but he would not permit her. He said he was not in any kind of financial need and hinted he would be getting a large sum of money in a few weeks. He'd been vague about it but did say that one of his songs was to be played by a big-name band whose musicians were friends, a song that would be featured on a television programme in the spring. He played her a tape of himself singing it, with his own soft piano accompaniment, a melancholy love song called 'Never-Ending Time'. She had fallen in love with it at her first hearing and knew it would be a success. She adored Frank's silken voice and felt it confirmed what she already knew, that (as she thought) African-Americans are known for the beauty of their singing voice.

I thought of all this, and I thought also of a slew of unanswered questions in what he told me but I didn't raise any of them. I didn't want to hear any more of his lies. Why would he and Karen, still with their bags, stop at a café *before* checking into their hotel? If the phone call was so important, why couldn't he have made it from the hotel room? And on returning to New York, if he had been searching for me *everywhere*, why hadn't he tried Hal's studio, where we had met several times? And where has he been for the past several weeks?

I felt horribly sick. Barely able to speak, I left – just walked out, and found myself wishing *he* would vanish from the earth.

He called after me: 'Let's see each other again.'

I made it round the corner – just – and for the first time in my adult life threw up.

As matters turned out, that was just the beginning. I went back to Great Scandinavia that evening, thinking Mama would be on duty and I could tell her of the meeting and compare notes. But Mrs Jaaskelainen was there, pinch-hitting for Mama, who was home with a bad cold. I said hello to Lasse, at his usual spot in the middle of the bar, Lasse the fixture: not really there but always there (like death, I thought).

As I took a sip of my drink I saw Mrs Jaaskelainen in the mirror slyly regarding me, unaware that I could see her watching me. Thoughts were turning in her mind as she murmured:

'Karen is not coming back. They kidnapped her. I saw it happen. You might as well not think about it any more.'

I turned and looked at her directly, saw her eyes appraising my reaction as she dramatically paused.

'I saw it happen,' she repeated.

I waited.

'You not shocked?' A prompt.

'You saw *what* happen, Mrs Jaaskelainen?'

'You were right, you know. Frank kidnapped that girl to Africa and he sold her. You von't see her again.'

I thought back to the time when she told me she knew nothing about Frank. There was nothing left in my stomach, but it threatened another performance anyway. Especially when she recited that old dumb Finnish saying:

'After too much laughter, tears.'

'You saw it happen . . . and did nothing?'

253

Her smile was almost sweet. The words were rational.

'You think things like that don't happen?' I could see her enjoying my unhappiness. 'You're so naïve?'

'Why didn't you do something to stop it?'

'Do vat? Call the police because he's sitting here having good time with his friend? You think maybe now *you* can do something? Now *you* know. So vat now *you* go be doing?'

After a silence, during which we regarded each other, she went on.

'Some people are like dat. You vant to stop life? Hah. Yoost you try.'

No, I thought: not life. Killings, and hurting and destroying things. 'Only the horrible things,' I said.

'Yes, but da horrible things, dey iss part of life.'

So confident she was.

'You make it sound as though the whole thing had been inevitable.'

'Dey *iss* inevitable.' She made a look of disgust. 'Yeah, you try and stop dem.'

She moved down the bar to serve someone and came back and stared at me again.

'But how can you be sure she was kidnapped?'

'That's vat's the best part,' Mrs Jaaskelainen said. 'Ven there's no witness nobody is sure. The kidnappers are not so dumb. *I* know vat happened, but there's no proof, only vat *I* see. So the police, you know – they can do nothing. You know Frank?'

'Not very well.'

'They say he is not a black man. Everybody *thinks* he's a black man. He's from Africa but born in Egypt. One half Egyptian and one half from South Pacific, Polynesia.'

'Yes,' I said. I'd heard that. A beautiful combination, Egyptian-Polynesian.

'Don't believe it,' Mrs Jaaskelainen said. 'He's not Egyptian or Polynesian or South Pacifican. Only *black* people do such a thing to white people.'

42

My new place is beginning to feel lived in, almost homey. A few minutes ago it was sleeting outside. It sounded like someone pouring gravel against the windowpanes – a terrifying roar. I worried for the glass.

I had come back from a walk – and just in time. I love to go walking on nights when storms blow down from Canada, all the way down along the long sweep of the Hudson valley, and feel it come gusting through Manhattan's empty streets. I like being pelted by wet, heavy snowflakes that pile high in hummocks and cover the pavements, which you know are there but can't see and there are no shoeprints to guide you as you make a path through the smooth wavy drifts. When even the last taxis have gone home because of the weather, the streets are so hushed you can hear the feathery sound that snowflakes make as they fall. They actually make a *sifting* sound as they float past your ear, the softest sound imaginable.

My new place is a tiny studio apartment, a one-room place to hole up in, and except for my walks, I have no urge to go out. 'Out there' is something that can be frightening sometimes. Of course I know that's not really true and soon I will have myself convinced of it, as before.

Since installing my gear, the fuses have blown twice and the super thinks if the problem is not in the fusebox it must be in a switch somewhere. As an electricity illiterate, I believe anything anybody tells me. It all sounds plausible because it's so meaningless.

The maintenance in my new building is Operation Overkill, the opposite of the service provided by Mr Nussl. I called the super on the intercom and he in turn called in a union electrician. The union electrician arrived within minutes, accompanied by a lanky colleague, the assistant electrician. Mutt and Jeff. They were both apparelled in spotless white overalls with blue-logo monograms emblazoned across their (no doubt hairy) chests.

Briefly they contemplated the dial of a gadget from which two wires sprouted, then thoughtfully called a conference. The problem needed brainstorming. The chief electrician wondered aloud to the assistant electrician if the problem might not be the up-and-downy parts of the framis, or might it be the gizmo with the wobbly bit? Silence, pondering that. Then they went back to staring moodily at the dial with the wires, and the chief electrician pointed to a nearby light switch and said to his assistant:

'Is it on "On" or is it on "Off"?'

'It's on "Off".'

'Put it on "On".'

'Right. It's on "On".'

Fuse blows.

'Shit. Put it on "Off".'

(Verbatim.)

Coffee break, Mutt to Jeff:

'I was reading today where the Dutch now have acoustic wallpaper.'

'What's acoustic wallpaper?'

'I don't know, but it's a new advance.'

(Verbatim.)

Later: afternoon. I told Martin of last night's dream, which was my first entirely in English, with no trace of Finnish in it. I saw graffiti that said '*Anger!*' and watched it become transmogrified into '*Inge!*' I thought that was rather witty of my unconscious, an opinion I voiced as a prompt. In return I got a grunt, or possibly a throat clearing, from behind the couch, a discreet, barely audible, unreproducible sound.

'. . . rrgh . . .'

(Verbatim.)

I mentioned Horatio. Ah, a sexual topic? Stirrings behind my back? No – more silence.

Martin is a discerner of themes. Floundering the other day, I began telling him about the curious detritus of my life. I told him I collect things the way a bowerbird builds a nest except that I don't build nests. I just collect the bits – thoughts, ideas, factoids – and then unload them on the nearest unsuspecting person. My own Oral History of Our Time.

I was of course being wise-ass, using up valuable time with jokes – spendthrift me, with my new mail-order-catalogue income. I informed old Martin that for obvious reasons, a croupier's suits have no pockets –

'– and I'm sure you didn't know that. Nine persons out of ten in New York City don't know that croupiers' suits have no pockets.'

The central European serenity from his direction was almost palpable. (He was born and raised on Flatbush Avenue, Brooklyn – source: himself – but there's something Viennese about analytic silences.) I switch to Italian.

'*Capisc*' "croupier"?'

A rich, peaceful Central European silence. I'm sure my anger in all this doesn't escape him. (He sometimes detects anger before I feel it, and that's when I have to hand it to him.)

Nothing daunted: 'Do you realize that it's not possible to open a can of "Oregon air"? The moment you open it, it ceases to be Oregon air.'

More rich silence. Ah, but a stirring in his seat! Maybe there's something sexual about Oregon air? Yes?

No. Silence.

'I'm seeing Horatio.'

Silence.

'He's a patient of yours too.'

Silence.

'We compare notes about you.'

Silence.

'We're *fucking*.'

Silence.

'We *talk* about you in *bed – discuss* you.'

I wheel my head quickly to see the expression on his face. With relief I note that he doesn't make cathedral fingers, like the Great Stone Faces in Hollywood films. He has an amused smile, which he turns towards me in a friendly way. And of course: silence.

Martin seems to have a lot of patience with me and can go for sessions at a time without saying much beyond 'Please continue,' which he says when I arrive and stretch out and at the end lets me know the ritual is over with 'Till next time.' Between these two sound bites, these morsels of human communication, there are many intelligent throat clearings in Rachmaninov's Variations on Harumph.

Lately, though, he's been practically jabbering. On this occasion, after the bit about Oregon air, he waited a minute before circling back to the phrase 'ceases to be'. Evidently piqued his interest. Apparently I've been saying 'ceases to be' frequently without being aware of it. I'm sure it's Karen, I tell him. She has ceased to be. And I did some associating: cessation of being, cessation of growing, no longer developing . . . the only crime in life is to stop someone's development . . . murder is only an obvious and extreme example of stopping someone's development . . . but short of murder, there are thousands of ways of stopping development, as for example kidnapping –

Martin: 'What about stopping one's own development?'

Right. Hmm.

I like him, except when I'm pissed off at him – personally pissed off, I mean. But he of course interprets my being personally pissed off as transference, which, like any self-respecting patient, I categorically deny. (Why have denial if you don't use it?)

Sometimes he makes sense, though, and when he hits home I feel a rush of love for him. Those are the moments when I actually feel a change happening in me, a sort of shift into a new mode of seeing things, of new feeling.

That may sound like an exaggeration but when emotions on a given point do change, they come with a sudden conviction that's unshakable. Each time that happens it alters my view of Martin and reminds me of the story of Mark Twain's, how at fourteen he thought his father was so ignorant he could hardly stand to have the old man around, but when he reached twenty-one he was astonished at how much the old man had learned in seven years.

A good day for reading

Brought home books by Gould, Darwin, Dyson, Dennett and Hawking (the well-known international law firm). The books happened to be side by side at the front desk of the library in a prominently displayed bookrack marked 'Recommended Nonfiction'. Took the shebang – a reading blitz.

As I knew before I brought them home, the books were not my cup of tea, so the kick was not really any cause for alarm. My reading enthusiasms have as short a duration as my attention spans. I hoped in this case I was dealing with a feeling of intelligence that would last a few hours but it didn't. Dutifully, I dipped into Darwin, found him interesting but not exactly light summertime reading in the hammock. Gould by comparison was a page turner. I cracked the others and after a while, deciding it would be best not to break faith with the easy pleasures of life, put the books on the floor in a nice neat pile. To return to the nice bookshelf.

But a dilemma: I was on a reading jag, maybe not for science but for words on paper, *any* words on paper (but not if they were about the first three seconds of the universe). Hungrily,

I went out and brought back a whole stack of newspapers and magazines and climbed into bed again with a cosy little glass of chablis. Old habits die hard – we should count our blessings.

New cuttings for the scrapbook:

Item: (Anthropology Report, Part MMMCCCXXXII) In New York City three different people were decapitated in three unrelated subway accidents in one night. I found that hard to believe. But even the *Times* reported it (in a local-interest column). Or maybe this was sociology. (Whatever.)

Item: A woman died of typhoid fever after drinking water from a carafe at a sidewalk café in Madrid. She was proving to a friend that it was safe to drink the local water.

Item: A retired Hindu-American living in India had been receiving monthly annuity cheques from Boston and, as is the custom there, endorsing them by thumbprint. A credit-rating firm in Massachusetts discovered on a routine examination that he had died two years before and his Bombay relatives had buried him without his right thumb, which, for endorsement purposes, they had prudently preserved in alcohol.

Then this gem:

AP – SYDNEY. There have been reports of an outbreak in Papua New Guinea of a psychiatric condition known as Koro. The syndrome is triggered by acute anxiety that the genitalia are shrinking and in danger of disappearing . . .

Jesus: *more* disappearances.

. . . The delusion can affect both sexes but is much more common among men than women, who may believe that their nipples are vanishing.

Koro can become an epidemic as anxiety spreads through a community. One man, convinced he would die if his penis shrivelled into his abdomen, decided not to await the dreaded fate and committed suicide.

It only takes one man to claim that he can see his manhood shrivelling before his eyes for all his friends to hastily inspect their members and see how they themselves are faring. They all become similarly convinced they are no longer the men they once were, and this adds to the alarm that spreads through the village. To avert the worse catastrophe of complete genital loss, some stick safety pins through their organs and weight them down with rocks or attach them to doorframes or household furniture. This temporarily calms their anxiety. The other men then go searching for a scapegoat and finally bring the calamity to an end by tracking down the local medicine man and lynching him.

Start as you mean to go on.

And this just in . . .

I poured another glass of chablis and made myself comfy, thinking I might as well get drunk. That's what being Finnish is all about.

For old times' sake, I also enjoyed a medicinal spliff, some of that good California sinsemilla Hal brings back from the Coast, and started feeling *que sera*. Fuck it.

The next item, coming *right after the above*, made me think I had somehow stumbled into the middle of National Penis Week:

Reuters – BANGKOK. A jealous Thai wife cut off her husband's penis as he slept at home in a northeastern town, tied it to a helium-filled balloon and let it fly away, the victim, a rickshaw driver, told police after being rushed to a hospital. The police were seeking the woman for questioning.

And no doubt the poor man was seeking his penis as it went floating across Asia, the Quest being one of the oldest themes of man.

Not so flamboyant but no less interesting:

> AP – LONDON. The Imperial Cancer Research Fund recently reported in the *British Journal of Cancer* that a study of 4,800 Swedish women showed that mothers of twins had an increased resistance to breast cancer.

Made a mental note to try for twins when the time comes. ('What's yours?' 'I'll have the twins, please – hold the epidural.')

Story in the *New Yorker*: a view of marriage:

> 'I'm really *excited*!' she exclaimed. 'Aren't *you*?'
> Yes, he said.

Obviously someone has fictionalized Hal.

Facts. Alexander Graham Bell wanted to name his daughter Photophone. Imagine: Photophone Bell. Unfortunately (or perhaps fortunately) the poor girl died young. Send not to ask for whom the bell tolled free.

Another chablis. Each glass tastes better than the last. Which is the way life should be.

A *Times* article mentioned Weston's *Daybooks*, which whetted my appetite, so I got them out and riffled through volume two, about California, then switched to Ansel Adams's *Autobiography* and skipped around, here and there, and before I knew it, I was in the mood to go out photographing. So, faithful to the muse, I went to the docks, ferries, Staten Island, the Village, Minelli's. Especially Minelli's, needing renewed warmth as provided by more chablis.

But not for long – and soon back again where I belong: bed. And well supplied with wine. I had spent a long day outdoors 'working', with not much to show for it. The trouble is, these cold and snowy days the muse has an affinity for Minelli's – and it's definitely Minelli's rather than Great Scandinavia. The muse shies away from my Finnish home-away-from-home ever since the other day, when I saw Frank sitting at the bar and chatting with Mama. We exchanged hi's, his warm, mine icy.

I could tell he wanted to talk to me, and me, I didn't even want to acknowledge his existence. I sat at the other end of the bar. Our eyes met once and I quickly looked away. Mama told me not to believe the filth that Mrs Jaaskelainen came out with. Frank definitely was Egyptian-Polynesian and not African-American. The Harlem detail was pure Jaaskelainen racial hate – which aroused in Mama a few choice comments about bias and ignorance. But I didn't give a damn what his background was, black, brown, white or whether he was from the South Seas or the Near East – I no longer wanted to know him. I got up and headed for the door, reminding myself that it's altogether possible that he had nothing to do with Karen's disappearance, but I knew that nothing could persuade me of that. It *had* to be him.

Mama asked Frank if he would like another drink. He said yes he would, actually. Mama said it looks like we go be have rain maybe.

43

The bed as decompression chamber

Got a bit chilled by the trip to Lower Manhattan, so my GP (Dr Inge Saarinen Strangelove, the lovable old country doctor) ordered more bed rest and another sip or two of wine. I haven't been relaxing enough lately, it seems. Need *loads* of bed rest.

So, piling fresh reading material on the bedcovers and plunking down a bottle of chablis beside the bed for convenient replenishments without leaving bed warmth, I began skimming through the events of the world as we know it. According to the good doctor, this is the only way to live: take world disasters lying down and you won't get knocked down by them. Would I care for another round? I most certainly *would* care for another round, and keep 'em coming.

> TO THE EDITOR. In a report last week headed 'Grave Robbers' you cited the fascinating information that 'one of New York's largest cemeteries was looted and a life-sized angel has disappeared'. I wonder if you would not mind telling your readers how big a life-sized angel is. *Theresa Baxter, Queens.*

> TO THE EDITOR. Thanks for your story on armies and modern warfare. But is there a country in the world that can match the feat of Liechtenstein, fifty of whose soldiers went off to fight in the Napoleonic wars and fifty-one came back. They had recruited a member of

one of the other armies. *William Millennaire, Yonkers.*

LOCAL NOTES. A Westchester woman, Mrs F. P., reports that she always gives her son $20 'mugger money' to stop a robber from becoming angry and violent. She has expressed suspicion of late, however, about the frequency with which her son was being mugged.

An article about Dostoyevsky, and this *wonderful* quote! (Or Why I Read Newspapers):

I no longer think, as other writers do, that a description of trivia is 'realism' in writing. Consider what you can read in the daily newspaper: you come across reports of authentic events that are quite extraordinary. Why don't writers take account of them? Because they feel they are too fantastic and therefore 'lacking in universality'. But I feel just the opposite. I hold these unusual events to be the 'real truth' about life. At every moment of every day, in fact, *these are what is happening in life.*

Yes!

What caught my interest next was something called the Oddest Book Title of the Year Award. It was won by (second place) *Proceedings of the Second International Workshop on Nude Mice* and (third place) *Highlights in the History of Concrete.* The prize-winning title was: *Greek Rural Postmen and Their Cancellation Numbers.*

I thought I'd send that one to my father. The winning entry won a bottle of champagne – and that of course called for another chablis. This was living. I need to do this more often.

A team of New Testament scholars is starting an unusual, five-year project called the National Seminar on the Historical Jesus to determine exactly what Jesus's actual words were. The 14 participating scholars are to meet three times annually over the next five years to examine each of the gospel sayings to decide which are authentic.

Jesus's sayings will be determined by majority vote.

That should settle it.

With that happy thought I snuggled down and dozed – and dreamed I don't know what but woke up with the sudden realization that if Mrs Jaaskelainen 'saw it happen', then almost certainly Lasse saw something too. Maybe he was there and might be willing to tell me what he knows.

I threw on some clothes and hotfooted it over to Great Scandinavia – and luck was with me: Lasse was there, at his usual spot.

He studied me with an attempt at interest and said yes, he had seen the person called Frank. No, 'nothing had happened'.

'Nothing?'

'Nothing at all. They were out having a good time.'

Struck out again.

As you were

So, *paska*, back to bed.

(AFP) WASHINGTON: The US Food and Drug Administration has been told that a pill to help balding people to grow hair or stop losing it is effective. But 4 per cent of men in a study reported side effects including a loss of interest in sex and problems with erections.

Headline about a man sentenced to death on a murder charge:

KILLER SAYS JAIL SMOKERS ARE A THREAT TO HEALTH

Impatience leads to taking things into your own hands (if you know what I mean)

I read another prison report, this one from Italy:

PALERMO. The arrest of a woman prison governor charged with having sex with male inmates was seized on yesterday as proof that conditions in Italian prisons are 'now completely out of control', reported regional authorities.

Ottavia Parlagreco, 41, prison governor for the past three years at Malfatto, Sicily, was arrested for alleged 'obscene acts and lascivious behaviour'.

A convict said he saw her 'amicably fondling' inmates through the bars of their cells. Signora Parlagreco denied these charges, claiming she was being victimized because she was a woman. But several witnesses testified they saw the governor having sex 'in cells, the infirmary, the laundry room and the kitchen'.

An investigation into her conduct was begun after a prisoner testified that she regularly 'sold her favours to convicts who offered her "gifts" in exchange', including money. In addition to enjoying sexual relations with her, the favoured ones were served 'quality' food and received 'day passes' to the outside. No prisoner was ever known to use 'weekend leave' to escape. In fact, one prisoner who had served his time insisted on going back to serve more.

Modern penal reform.

One that was close to home:

A man aged 76 died from a heart attack after chasing a mugger who had made off with $4 from his wife's handbag. Llewellyn Marsh collapsed near his home in Smithtown, New York, after his wife of 56 years was robbed as he escorted her to her weekly bingo session. Marilyn Marsh said her husband ran 20 or 30 yards before collapsing. 'He was the sort of person who would try to do something about things,' she said.

It's you and me against the world, Llewellyn. I hope I don't collapse of a heart attack while doing something about things.

And I like this one, again from Italy (*molto* activity on the Italian front):

ROME. Carlo Tagliavini, 42, of Lucca, is bringing suit against his mother because 'she remarried without consulting me', he said. He was 20 years old when she married her new husband and the son claims that this has caused him 'lasting psychological damage'.

Then this filler:

A child goes missing every 18 seconds in the US.

Thank you for sharing that, and I could have lived very happily without this one too:

PARIS. Polish officials have acknowledged the existence of a white slavery ring linking the old Communist Party in Poland with the Mafia.

Exiled Polish dissident groups say the admission merely hints at a history of long-standing connections with corrupt party officials and Western organized crime.

Members of the Party have been accused of taking payoffs in a traffic involving 1,500 to 2,500 teenagers, sent to Belgium, Italy and Greece, where local Mafia chiefs have forced them into work as bar 'hostesses'. Money is paid into large Swiss bank accounts held by highly placed Polish Communist Party figures.

Exiled Romanian dissidents allege similar ties between their country and large-scale international prostitution rings.

44

Getting near the end of April now, and nearly four months since I last saw Karen.

Question: How long can you go on worrying about someone who isn't there? Answer: Feelings have a statute of limitations.

Scene: Minelli's Bar and Grill. Time: The Present. Now that Bill's opening is passed, Roz is heading back to Hollywood and then off to location in Thailand, where she's looking forward to some fabulous pot. Right now we're listening to Bill holding forth on life and death, all three of us greatly aided in our various roles in life by little sips of alcohol.

'I really don't see the need to make reference to some paltry and probably adolescent idea of the vastness of space and its so-called indifference. That's just an anthropocentric idea and one of the worst of pathetic fallacies, isn't it?' (Words more or less to that effect – talk about touching the ground running.)

There are moments when I don't want to hear *stuff* any more (*many* moments when I don't want to hear stuff any more), 'stuff' as defined by Quent as The Higher Twaddle. But here we sit, prisoners of circumstance, trapped in the postexistential here-and-now, living out reprieveless and forlorn little lives. (I worry that I sound a little like Quent at times. This is especially true right after I've left him.) (Worse, though, would be to sound like Bill. That would *really* worry me.)

Bill is bound to talk himself out if we let him carry on, or anyway that thought gets us through many a ho-hum stretch.

Right now he takes in our *ponderous* silence and serenely-affably-cheerfully sips his drink, gently puts his glass down philosophically and says, 'Doesn't anybody read Cuh-*moo* any more?'

Greenwich Village artists like to feel they're more intellectual than even the most intellectual of uptown intellectuals. That's because they think *intuitively*, see? (Dun't esk.) And that's what's so *vital* about them. (Anyway that's what they want you to believe.)

Me, I go through life wondering what the hell everybody's *talking* about.

Another instalment now from Bill:

'The obvious suggestion is to modify our collective philosophy of life.'

Meaning what? I wonder.

'The fact is we live in a way that guarantees unhappiness.'

Oh.

'Well,' says Roz, 'that's one good reason to offer your friends another round of these.' She holds up an empty glass and shouts down the length of Minelli's at double the volume needed to effect communication: 'Hey Sam! *Una mas* of these, *por favor*.'

At the bar, affable, forever unperturbable Sam gives a nod. He's Italian and why she keeps addressing him in Spanish remains a modern mystery. And we won't even go into her grammar.

Sam assembles Paralysers, based on Roz's instructions late one night, and then on his own initiative and perhaps even enthusiasm, daring soul that he is, adds maraschino cherries as trimming, along with toy paper umbrellas just to spruce things up a bit and make life more joyous. The drinks look like birds of plumage in the Central Park Zoo: they look like Paralysers as invented by a South American cha-cha band playing a conga. Smiling-Sam brings them over in a small round tray that advertises Blatz beer and serves us before I've finished my first two Paralysers, both drinks still sitting there barely an inch down from the brim and our black tabletop scattered with a half-dozen toy umbrellas and a couple of reprieveless cherries living out what's left of their forlorn little lives.

'There is more to life than life.' Roz

In all these discussions with Bill it's Roz I enjoy. It doesn't ever matter what Bill is saying, you take his statements as having merely emotional significance, however private, especially when he gets on his karmic investiture kick. My whole pleasure in their combined company is in Roz's irrelevant interruptions – Roz the hole puncturer. She either kills the twaddle by stepping all over some of his less penetrable lines or she brings them to life with irrelevant wisecracks that undermine his efforts. I've seen her do this with Quent too, like the time he got drunk after his divorce became final and he spent the night soaring into the empyrean. Quent kept saying all evening long, 'I know this sounds like the world's shallowest cliché, but time really *is* very much like a river in that it never stops flowing and we are all merely a part of that flow, one great perpetual flux' – stuff that doesn't qualify even as Twaddle, let alone The Higher (or even the Lower). I was feeling a little embarrassed for him, but then it got even worse when he said (voice swelling grandiloquently, with maybe even a slight tremor), 'For as Emerson asked, "Who looks upon a river in a meditative hour and is not reminded of the flux of all things?"'

Roz: 'Me.'

I miss Roz for her taking the whole world as straight man with her as Groucho. Which is maybe the way life should be lived (or so I think at times – lately, much of the time). Barry Hammer, the artist who was mistaken for Bill by the uptownik who fled his studio leaving her underwear behind, once said to Bill and Roz: 'There's more to life than just fucking.'

Roz: 'For example, there's fucking.'

*

271

Roz sips this new (third edition) Paralyser and regards Bill with such intensity that she looks almost distrustful of him. (But it could be myopia.)

Only Bill can reach her, I know I can't, and since Bill likes being listened to, they make a good team. He can see as well as I can that her kidding is a cover for a deep-down, sappy-drunk but sincere love. A baby love. I always feel Roz is going through life a little girl looking for Mother but finding only Bill and showering him with all the love left over from childhood. But I envy them, really and truly I do. They get along with each other better than most couples do.

Roz takes the floor: 'Why should I sit on top of a cold goddamn mountain like what's-his-ass in Japan you're always telling me about?'

'China,' says Bill.

'Whatever. As a human being I enjoy the company of other human beings much more than goddamn mountaintops. I can be true to myself and live right here in our normal everyday fucked-up world – in fact even truer. What the hell is there to sitting on top of mountains and eating rice cakes?' At this point she turned around to me so abruptly I thought the question was meant for me. ('Oh, uh . . . ,' I was prepared to say.)

'If the truth be told,' Bill said, 'I prefer a woman's crotch smell to Western civilization. But fortunately I don't have to make that choice.'

Roz turned to me again, this time with a 'Huh?' look.

'It's a koan,' Bill explained, horseshit mode in full sway now. 'You can't explain a koan' – a friendly wink here for my onlooker's benefit, adding: 'Wouldn't it be funny if those turned out to be my dying words: "I can't explain it."' He laughed and tried it on again for size: '"I can't explain it." Not bad,' he said, 'not bad. That'd make a good epitaph for me. "I can't explain it."'

'What's my epitaph going to be, baby?' Roz asked.

'"*Una mas*!"' he shouted.

Sam looked up, surprised.

'No, no,' Bill called over to him. 'Just talking. Jesus, no more *mas* of these. We have two cocktail parties to go to, and before that, remember that we're supposed to meet the Watersons for drinks, and then we're stepping out for the evening.'

'All this boozing it up has gotta stop,' Roz said, grinning happily.

'Did you know Dick Waterson is lusting after your ass? Can't blame him, you know. You've got a gorgeous ass.'

'I wouldn't let him come anywhere *near* my ass. Let him *dream* about my gorgeous ass.'

Bill said he had to go point percy at the porcelain. As he stood up, Minelli's house phone rang and Roz called over to Sam, 'We're not here. Nor have we been seen.'

Sam gave her a friendly wink as he picked up the phone, and Bill walked off chuckling, looking for the john and starting to unzip his fly as he walked.

Epitaphs: Mr Nussl's should be: 'Dun't esk.'

(Mine? Dun't esk that either.)

45

I would never have discovered Hal's diary if it had not been for his West Coast trip. He went to San Diego on a four-day shoot for a swimsuit ad and his agent Roberta and I were holding the fort: headquarters staff.

On Day One, Roberta made some inevitable googoo eyes at me, out of habit probably, but after that there were no further attempts at conversion. I was strictly Hal's friend and we got along fine. Or it could have been my imagination.

She has Sapphic chic. Her very attractive mouth verges perpetually on a smile and she has wide, appraising eyes and glistening long dark hair, which she periodically rakes back with her long fingers. Her nervous gesture of raking her hair back enhances her look of intelligence. An act maybe? It doesn't matter. She's a pleasure to look at.

I was tempted to move into the studio for a few days but didn't, contenting myself with being studiositter (non-sleep-in) and important-mail-answerer and Roberta as chief bottle washer and problem solver. She is a consummate pro at that last (thank God) and we make a compatible team.

I enjoy our long chats together. She lights up a small cigar after making us both some hot wine with cloves, cups her glass in a slender hand as we talk shop, she sitting cosily cashmere-sweatered, knit-suited among the large odalisque cushions of the low couch that Hal uses for model-boffing. (For one fleeting moment I think of us all as his harem. This is not a thrilling thought.) I'm learning from Roberta that apparently the same relationship problems occur no matter what your sexual orientation. I wondered if she knew that before switching to women – but then, how could she?

Roberta reps (aside from, occasionally, me as a personal favour) only three non-competing clients. The other two are a top-of-the-line graphic artist and a Danish fabric designer. Her combined income is in the low six figures: not bad. Hal says he could not have achieved his success without her knowhow and her relentless breaking down of Madison Avenue doors.

I discovered the diary when I was in the 'harem' room. The first afternoon he was gone, I went rummaging through some 8 × 10s and saw a large artist's drawing book, something I had never seen around the studio before, and out of curiosity opened it. And – like an actor in an old silent movie (close-up of heroine's horrified eyes) – I clapped it shut out of pure guilt reflex and slammed the book down with a bang. Mary Tyler Moore couldn't have done it better.

And then got it out again of course. (She would have too.) I turned to the opening page, thinking, 'Piss on guilt' and hoping Martin would approve of my great daring and appreciate my overlooking my own perfidy (perfidiousness – whatever). Anyway, I successfully conquered all neurotic sense of decency and integrity and other such useless trappings and started reading.

Hal's diary: or something sensational to read in the train
The opening section had a title: 'Indecent Exposures'. (Hm, I might even like this, I thought.)

Quickly – furtively – I read bits here and there as though Hal might stroll in from San Diego at any moment and catch me spying or could somehow magically see me from three thousand miles away. Martin says I sometimes have a superego that doesn't know when to quit. (One thing that irks me about analysis is that *before* I started it, I felt pretty normal. Now the longer I see Martin, the more things we find in me that don't seem to be working quite as they should be.)

Hal's interest in poetry took me by surprise. He'd never mentioned anything. But it did not surprise me that his writing was so visual – very photographic: and it was romantic-surrealist, another hidden side of him. For example: 'Title for a poem: *Sarabandes and Rubber Bands*.' (Sort of nice, though a bit cleverish.) And: '*Winterpoint: A Sustenance of Mist*.' And, more amusing: '*A Desperation of Parsley*.' I wish I could think of things like that.

'Stand firm in the middle'

I liked what I thought was a list of phrases on an otherwise blank page. But when I read the words a second time, I thought they might be intended as a poem, a kind of description of a trip:

> *an exasperation of cities*
> *voyage through a cobalt cool*
> *sea clouds over crooked brooks*
> *a fishy mist of coast*

Or maybe not a poem. But whatever it was, I liked it.

There was also (inevitably) Hal raunch: '*The Gladness Bush*' and '*The Cock as Standing Invitation*' – in short, familiar ground. I liked them both, though, especially *Gladness Bush*.

But most of the diary seemed to consist of notes on friends. I flipped over a few pages and came to a section called 'Portraits' – and was a little shocked by what I saw. (Me shocked? Never, right?)

ROBERTA: '*I used to drive men mad teasing them, then became honest and turned lesbian, which actually I had always been without knowing it until Susan "taught" me. "Corrupted" me is how Susan puts it, Susan the ironist.*'

Roberta's frisson on the word 'corrupted'. But the

frisson was meant to be amusing, a little act put on for my benefit. She admits me into her world, which implies trust and closeness. I feel complimented.

ROBERTA: or ways of knowing a young woman who dislikes a world of standardizing tastes. Enjoying watching her (me, appreciative observer) through the peephole as she pisses (pee-hole, peephole), thighs spread wider than I would have thought. She reaches far down and under, back to the delicacy of taint, and then a quick-casual sniff of the fact-gathering finger while pretending now, even though she's alone, that she's merely scratching her nose. Her face blanks out as her mind follows an interior drift. The beauty of seeing women when they're being themselves, thinking they're unobserved. They don't know that that's when they are at their most beautiful: to men.

Roberta leaves the can, is back again in the studio and dressed Fifth Avenue sharp, sleek, suave, to go out and do battle in the Madison Avenue wars, Making Money being what counts, bless her. She doesn't know that part of my liking her is for having seen her, crotch exposed, on the can. I don't know why women can't see that. They're so shy.

I felt horribly guilty at reading that, like a voyeur myself. I snapped the book shut again but, as I did so, out of the corner of my eye saw 'KAREN'.

KAREN: her saying openly: 'I weell peess forr you. There, voilà. (She laughs.) You like dot?' Then, for me, she smilingly pretends to caress herself with a quick clitty quiver of finger, and smiles at the joke, in friendship. 'Girrls – een school.'

Slices of life.

Good grief. I didn't like knowing these intimacies. Not about Karen and not about Roberta. I had no idea I had been living all this time with a piss freak. It wasn't the pissing so much as his doing it apparently with every woman he meets. It was quintessential infidelity, even if all it was was peeing.

'Inge': a page turner

Yet I couldn't stop, especially when on the next page, *bang*, there it was: 'INGE'. Heart in mouth (and now I know how *that* feels), I read on:

These twitchings, these images of Inge.

Twitchings? I hoped this wouldn't be another pee- or peephole act (what is it about men?).

Straddles the bidet and lathers her bush, chatting through the open door. The naturalness of a woman who loves the man she's with.

Not twitchings. More like narrative rape of sorts.

Inge's soap and bath oil smells in the steamy bathroom and then a pleasant morning laughing together about nothing as we breakfast in a sunny breakfast nook.

Well . . . that part's nice.

Inge, nude, dialling a telephone number, and with each energetic, nervous jab of finger, her breasts nervously quiver.

Her lion-blonde hair.

Watching her dress, I take 'pictures' of her: one hand outside her bra and one inside she recentres a wayward nipple. To her a banal gesture, to me a fascination of tit, to handle the globe so casually.

Below, pubic hair edging panty crotch. Strips off panties that are now hours and hours old and tosses them to a chair. Gets a clean pair, accidentally dropping them and bending over to pick them up: and the loveliness of the view from behind. Would she understand I like her all the more because of the few unmatted hairs in the perineum? I don't say a word, of course: never seek to tell thy love.

Jeez-us. This – *this* – was the famous 'Inge diary'? (But there was no stopping now.)

Saw Inge on the street, her winking, blue-denimed auth-oritative ass cheeks commanding both sides of 58th Street. This knockout, this mythic tail.

Life sketches

Inge reading:

Gets up from peacock chair, crosses room reading a book and eating an apple. When she stands, the impres-sion of her cunt lips remains in the crotch of her blue-jean shorts, like plump ghosts. Holds apple in mouth with a big bite clamped on to it, jaws grimaced wide, eyes screwed into a helpless stare at the printed page still being read over the top of the apple. Free hand disappears to front, jean shorts slip down, slim Finnish buttocks come into view, pantyless now, as she reaches john, turns inside door, sits, eating apple while reading, and then a hishing sound of piss whistling past labia, and then a velvety trumpeting blast, plup! turd-into-water sound. Drops the tiniest remainder of apple core into the bowl between legs that swing apart and lazily shut, wipes from behind (well trained), one-handedly rinses self with soap, water and wash cloth, washes the one hand, and, still reading, tugs up blue-jean shorts, zips, buttons. Without looking, flushes, recrosses room and sits again in peacock chair, one gangly leg seriously swinging up to lie on chair arm. Turns page with interest. On her studious face solicitude now, eyebrows intelligently arched, eyes caring (about a character in the story?), eyelids fluttering briefly at the printed page: 'Shit.' Something wrong, something terrible happening in the book? Eyes leave book, stare off at wall. Murmurs: 'Forgot carrots for the soup.' Eyes return to page, priorities revealed: 'Fuck soup.'

At Great Scandinavia, Inge coming in dressed in a short coat with the fur inside and white pelt outside, the fur of the hood a pale grey circle framing her face: a Finnish Eskimo. As she sat down she opened the coat: a T-shirt underneath said TITS *across her chest. Sat, though, so only I could see it.*

Inge. Lying in a Persian silence, that unaffected lascivious smile and a pointing to her opened crotch, a split-beaver shot in a mime of animal welcome. A gazing come-fuck-me look filled-to-overflow with love. I gaze at the darker-fleshed cunt of Japanese ink-drawing beauty and up into Finnish unblinking eyes.

Her bird's nest . . . the smoothed-down warm tuft of hair, the surprising heat there, 'So gentle,' she murmurs, parting her thighs wider for more caressing, then my slipping it in and soon her huffing sweating grunting, her ass heaving, teeth clenched, body quivering, a pleasurable tremor-held-back breathing, belly and thighs taut-straining while hips mindlessly undulate like a flesh machine, with the freshet coming down in a shuddering sobbing helpless come.

(Turns me on.)

. . . that first time, in Central Park, her unbelievable throes, hips lunging like an ocean liner in heavy seas, nearly bending my cock off and crying and whimpering, coming profoundly.

. . . that time I finally fell asleep and woke up again fearing my nightmares, and lay motionless not to awaken her and began thinking of ways to get sleepy again,

couldn't sleep, thought of Inge's long white thighs and the flat honeydew of her belly, the darkish-haired red-plum slit of diffuse pungency, breasts the delicate lavender of the palest pigeons, feeling a renewed stirring for her and wanting her but not enough to want to disturb her sleep. Then the glow of excitement slowly changing into drowsy dullness as I lay asleep listening to the night and the city's faroff sounds, a police siren distantly wailing, happening almost in another time, in the soft passage of time that at night never moves forward but always rounds back towards daybreak in one long perfect curve.

Inge dressing. She walks purposefully across the room, her lithe lean-legged walk flexing a bare cleft-melon ass. Pert ass cheeks winking up and down impertinently, almost insolently, left-wink, right-wink, left-wink. Ponytail flicking at the silk round haunches over which panties now slip on, inch wide at the hips. Sheathed in the sheerest of panties, the furrow of her ass becomes an unpolished-silver crack. The dress, a pale turquoise-and-white jersey print, upward now, above her head and sliding down her arms, shoulder, body, curtaining the flesh, her nakedness still there below, secretly, with the thinnest film of dress over it. Dressed up is nice too: the dress is to go out to the street with. Inside it comes off as easily as it goes on, as if not meant to be on for too long. Indoors a piece of jersey gets easily removed from around that blonde Inge body, and at the top of the body a shyly downward-looking smile of happiness, as now (fluttering eyes averting from me), interrupting her dressing and moving up against me ('You're really staring at me'), her eyes caressing my face, now her mouth kissing my mouth, neither of us saying anything, and anyhow, say what?

If you could say such a thing as 'I was slowly stunned,' I would. Because I was.

Here is the difference between Hal and me, presented *graphically*:

He and I went out to Connecticut one beautiful September afternoon and had brunch at an inn, then drove along empty roads beside a meandering stream, the last part of the trip a chancy low-gear grind across a field of short wild grass, until we stopped at the river's edge. I got out of the car and went down the bank and looked at the slow-moving stream under a peaceful Sisley sky, thinking how beautiful everything was. Along the stream were bottle-green bushes growing up to the water's edge and millions of small yellow flowers like a soft haze on the grass. Over a line of faraway trees a tiny puffball of a white cloud travelled swiftly past, alone, hurrying on some errand. The scene was so idyllic I enjoyed just being in it. It was one of those happy-to-be-alive moments and I threw my arms around Hal to enjoy a warm hug, I was that glad. There was no one in sight so I slipped out of my clothes and waded shiveringly into the stream, dived around like a fish and splashed water all over the place and, trembling, came right out again, dried off quickly and got dressed feeling cold and shivery and exhilarated. I told him it was *wonderful* and hugged him again and asked if he loved me and he said yes, of course, could there be any doubt about it? I told him how happy it made me feel to hear him say that. We opened one of the bottles of plonk we had brought along, drank several elaborate toasts to us, chugging it straight from the bottle and getting sillier by the swig, and hating it when the afternoon ended and we had to get back to town.

Hal's version of that same afternoon, *in toto*:

That river scene and her dimpled butt, svelte and lithe.
Inge coming out of water, goose bumps covering her ass

as she stumbles drippingly out of the river and shivers
in the cool September air, her nipples fiercely puckering
as though suddenly aged.

By the waters of Connecticut I sat down and wept

It gives pause, to say the least. I could barely recognize myself.
It's O K that men are a *little* crazed by testosterone, in fact,
viva testosterone, but what sets me back was that *that was
the entire entry.* Glad as I was about having a lithe and svelte
ass (Is your ass lithe? No, but it gets svelte a lot), I was
disappointed that that was what he retained of the day. I
could see something poetic in it for him – the puckered nipples
amounted to a haiku, or almost. But still.

Are all men like this or only Hal? Or is it me?

Pissing in action

It saddened me because it spoiled a very special memory I had
of the two of us – from that same picnic day. About half-way
through the second bottle of plonk, after many good long
pulls from it – *Finnish* drinking – and feeling in fine fettle,
which is to say absolutely painless, I cornily declared the little
patch of ground where we were eating as forevermore a sacred
spot. No one else would ever *ever* be permitted to picnic there.

'How do you plan to stop them?'

Ho-ho, a challenge (chugalug, swig).

'Watch *this*!' I wiped my mouth, squatted down and cere-
monially peed (the two of us now, deep crocked, breaking up
over our own antics), 'Territory established!' – and he laughing
and, not swaying particularly dangerously, ritually peed a
healthy spattering piss on the same spot, dancing the stream
all over the area in a union of the waters and saying, 'Signed
and sealed.'

'Not to mention delivered.'

'Sealed with a piss, in fact,' he said.

'Do we sniff it now? What's the protocol?'

'No,' he said, 'we just leave it. A gift to the soil. *Others* come along and sniff it. And stay away from here. That's the whole point.'

It was a goofy event that stayed with me as a happy memory every time I thought of the two of us having picnicky fun together. That is, until now, with the dawning awareness that good Prince Hal was, well, well, well, a piss freak. And me, I had unwittingly contributed to some imaginary piss album. Who'd a thunk it?

I don't know about your bimbos, I reflected as I continued riffling through the rest of his diary, but you've seen *me* piss for the last time – though if I know him, he'll probably not even notice. Or care, given that half the population of New York remains as yet unlaid, unpeepholed, not to say full of piss.

Somewhere around the middle of the manuscript I saw his brainstorm of a title: *My Memoirs* (which was as imaginative as naming his cat Pussy). But to me it all sounded more like *My Twitchings*. I read on, now as an act of pure compulsion.

Joy of woman's desiring

Inge, slightly drunk, listening to a cycle of mournful Finnish songs from Brentano's, one of them a sweepingly sad ballad complete with Russian-chorus background, at window-rattling volume, and her eyes suddenly rocket upward and lips purse in emotion, head swaying in melancholy wagging rhythm and her nude body violently dipping and then shooting up again as the music takes her to the forests of Suomi in those long winters of frozen lakes and endless northern flatnesses at which her eyes now stare as though the walls were the ice of Lapland. Her clothes are scattered everywhere, pantyhose lying on the floor like a curl of smoke, and in the corner an empty bottle of Finlandia vodka.

'Come here.'

Husky-voiced, she pulls me over to the couch for a change of pace, to bed down beside her along its length. Lying sideways she nuzzles her mouth against my neck to suck my body and enfold me self-comfortingly in her arms, hands lazily planted on my butt and pressing my groin into hers with a that's-nice feeling, yes like that, then a sudden purposive wriggling away, ducking down on the couch, hot-mouthing my cock, too late the thought of freshening up, but it's only drunken affection, a gift, not arousal, and coming up for air she kisses and moves her lips against mine, 'I want you so much,' but her alcoholic fatigue all at once sapping impetus. Her heavy head slides down the long sloping mountainside of the cushion as she sinks down down into sleep, nosetip in my ear, her hot breathing whistling through hairs deep inside her nostrils like an icy howl through Finnish pines, the desolate low moan of the arctic north.

Next day up very late, past noon, opening my eyes I see no one there, but turn and find her sitting at the open window in the buttercup sunlight of afternoon, among the tall spike-leaved dracaena marginata, sober, content, sipping coffee, in complete ease. Barefoot in the old microlength summer dress she wears around the studio, her knees up, pantyless, deep-slitted petal-soft lips squeezed between pressed thighs. In a single view her triangular face and between buttock-thighs, in the nipped-in hollow, the lightly furred lips, their hairs puffing in the breeze. Blonde hair above, darkish hairs below surrounding a brown pudgy slit.

She sees me looking over (never fails to catch me at it) but is elsewhere, head tilted towards the sun, eyes narrowed, in her hair a broad peach-coloured ribbon cascading down her back, and she just smiling at the pure pleasantness of the afternoon air. I wonder where her mind is.

'You're a freaked-out cunt-viewer,' she softly says.

That's where her mind is. Inge sober. But she doesn't really mind, my Humper Inge: my non-judgemental, patient, accepting, ever-suffering Inge.

The new squeeze

Evidently that was it for patient ever-suffering me, or at least I didn't see any more entries about me. I don't know whether I felt glad or sad: at least for several pages I had held centre stage. The very next entry, evidently of recent date, was (and you can't imagine how 'delightful' it made me to read this):

DOLORES: At the Met: unbelievably, she looked at the Monets through yellow sunglasses. Which, if anything, is worse than keeping her sunglasses on while boffing. But, an unexpectedly hot one. Dolores/Dolorous. One to make your balls ache.

Dolores an Unexpectedly Hot mo-DELL? Dun't esk. (Ah – got it finally: the *party* – of course.)

Now I was beginning to understand how I could feel two ways about Hal and be unable to reconcile them. It was all there, in the writing. There was an obvious parallel with his personal work and his private life, the same division between them. He perceived (how else to say this?) narcissistically – yet there was poetry in it – better than any early attempts of mine, though God knows that would not be difficult. I could love it for its music and dislike it for its take on life, and I wasn't even sure about disliking the take. Except for his view of me – and also a *serious* emphasis on peepee (!) that really might be looked into by a qualified professional, as we say.

I liked the pantyhose 'on the floor like a curl of smoke' – another haiku:

> *her pantyhose on the floor*
> *like a curl of smoke*
> *but waking up alone . . .*

. . . because Hal, my newest feeling is, will wake up alone no matter who he has spent the night with. And of course I realized that I too have been waking up alone when I've stayed over and listened to his peaceful snoring (once past the initial leg-twitching stage).

Do I judge him too harshly? I could be wrong. Hal has me *almost* convinced that I'm usually wrong, but I disagree with him. I'm sometimes more right than he thinks, I mean about myself and about things of importance to me, though I don't ever expect him to see that. Which is understandable: the only me he sees is *him*. (Credit Martin Yeblon.)

46

Missing (not) in action

It was I who discovered Bill's body. I had gone over to show him some prints of painting shots I'd recently made and that I thought he or Sue might be able to use somewhere.

There was no answer to my knock. I tried the door, found it unlocked and let myself in.

There was nobody in the vast and draughty loft. In fact, in the silence, the place felt so empty I had the crazy feeling that no one had ever lived or worked in this ghost-y barnlike space.

I needed to use the toilet and – there he was, legs sprawled on the filthy wooden planks and his shoulders and head curled under the sink, facing an ugly, cracked full-length mirror. A pool of his blood had dried into a brown oval and his eyes, opened unnaturally wide as if he had just reached an astonishing insight, stared at the glossy spinach-coloured walls from which peels of paint, some as large as beer coasters, had flaked off, exposing yellowing white plaster.

Another person vanished from the scene: life the vanishing act, all right.

Even so, I didn't really react except to think, almost in passing, that I should not touch anything but first phone the police, which I did. While waiting for them, I tugged Bill's sweatshirt down a bit to cover what seemed a surprisingly soft and vulnerable stretch of midsection. 'Love handles,' Roz used to tease, 'a-k-a, pure flab, baby.'

On the kitchen table there was an unopened container of milk with a sell-by date at the end of the week. He hadn't even outlived the milk.

Cause of death: life

The medical examiner's report said he had fallen and bled a considerable amount but that that was not the cause of death. The cause of death was perhaps the paracetamol in his system but, more significant, he had enough alcohol in him to get a roomful of people pretty stinko ('inebriated'). According to the report, it was not possible to say if he had killed himself or if it had been an accidental death caused by a mix of alcohol and paracetamol.

'Death by misadventure,' one of the policemen murmured knowingly.

I went back again the next day – just to be there. I was surprised that the paintings were there still (were they safe?), what with the door unlocked. Maybe word was not yet out. I would have expected dealers and friends to descend on the loft in their postmortem scavenger hunt.

I sat on the john seat, my feet where his head had lain, and thought about his life growing up in Wyoming. His mother had died just after he began school and his father, who never remarried, was so brutal to him – some said it was because Bill resembled his mother – that sometimes neighbours were called in. It was not surprising that before he met Roz, Bill found a wife named Alice, a large plain woman who was alcoholic, unstable, violent and pathologically dishonest. They got married while on a binge, declaring an undying love for each other that did not survive the first hangover. She was later diagnosed as suicidal, paranoid and hypochondriacal and at the age of thirty-one suffered a stroke that left her aphasic. A few weeks later she died of cardiac arrest.

I sat and just thought for a while, feeling a need to learn to face things as they really are. Not beginning with Karen – that was still too tough a nut to crack – but now, starting with Bill. I was beginning to understand that 'this whole Karen thing' would probably require, at my current rate, a whole lifetime. (But then we are given a whole lifetime to find out what a whole lifetime is about.) But meanwhile, for openers, I knew as a fact that Bill didn't die accidentally, nor was it death by 'misadventure', as poetic as that sounded, unless life itself is the great misadventure (and here Mr Nussl would nod his head in agreement). To me nothing was more obvious than that Bill had made the conscious choice to kill himself. The only thing missing was a goodbye note.

I took the phone from the windowsill to see if it had been disconnected or not, found it still worked and rang up Roz, on the Coast. I told her about the coroner's report, which I knew was all wrong: they didn't know Bill. Paracetamol had nothing to do with it. Even if it was the drug that killed him it was not a drug that killed him.

I explained that the coroner said a tremendous amount of alcohol in his stomach had not been absorbed at the time of death. I could just see Bill chugalugging a whole bottle at the very end, purposefully losing consciousness and slipping calmly, insensibly into his beautiful nirvana.

'There's no doubt that Bill killed himself.'

I did not know what reaction I had been expecting, but all Roz said was, 'I know.' Gently, not surprised. But I continued to hold my breath, braced for – what, denial, anger, despair? 'I knew it long before he did it. His whole life was a suicide.' As an afterthought: 'Drinking was merely a postponement of it. Maybe that's why I never stopped him. Bill drunk was better than Bill dead.' The closest she was to come to expressing grief was to add: 'But what a stupid fucking thing to do.'

I was so relieved at her reaction – relieved not to have to

test my new resolve, or ability, to face up to reality, to see things as they really are, at least not immediately (though in retrospect, a challenge might have been good for me).

I remembered Bill's 'epitaph': 'I can't explain it' – and recalled the gag, the night of the party, about the 'story of his life' and 'if you talk it all out, you lose it.'

We agreed, Roz and I, that that wasn't prophetic, which was the kind of thing a tabloid would make of it. ('Or Californians – don't forget the airheads.') It was just coincidence. His suicide wasn't planned – except unconsciously, in Wyoming decades earlier.

'Right,' Roz added, remembering that evening, 'except that now the poor sonuvabitch has lost the entire plot. You know, I thought he was hallucinating at times that night but he was just happy drunk. I said, "Are you sure you're all right? You're sounding a little crazy, you know," and he laughed because that sounded like a pleasant thought to him. But he said, "You can send for the white coats when I start getting Radio Tibet on my back teeth."'

I took a last look around the studio and found an old canvas he had begun back in his student days in England, which he had allowed me to see once 'as a special favour'. No – *wanted* me to see it (in an elaborate seduction scene that charmingly misfired). The small painting showed a split beaver, life size, done in the manner of Rembrandt, with layers of rich impasto. A really luscious cunt: gorgeous, resplendent, life-giving, sensual. 'Like Courbet's but mine is better: mine's spread open wide, and welcoming.' It was obvious that a lot of time had gone into it and, I'm sure, love too. He said he had laboured on it for years and considered it still unfinished.

The canvas just fit inside my carryall bag and I took it with me. I would tell Roz later but felt sure it was all right. Besides, more than once Bill had asked me to pick out a painting if I saw something I liked.

Just behind where the small canvas had been stashed I

discovered what the police, in a new line of inquiry, were now calling the 'missing suicide note'. They could not have searched carefully because a bit of it stuck out from between the canvases leaning against the wall. Probably it had fallen there or been blown from the table by a draught and gotten stuck. Its entire message was:

I regret that I did not lance a huge boil of pure venom within me before giving so much pain to others. But I am doing this now.

It was dated Tuesday, which was the day before I had found the body.

Bill would have hated the triteness of the act but I sat down and wept. For him, for Roz, for Hal, for Karen, and finally – for me.

47

I went home and got into bed for the rest of the day and stayed there all the next day, when, towards evening, the phone rang: Horatio, asking if I was doing anything and to see if I was feeling OK.

'Yes, fine.'

'You should take good care of yourself.'

'Parts of me are excellent already.'

He didn't want the kidding.

'How about coming over and I'll make us both some dinner.'

'Naa, I'd only whine and complain.'

'So come over and complain.'

He made a meatball spaghetti that reminded me that the art of cooking is a matter of infinite hope. It also exploded one of my mother's myths: 'Spaghetti is one dish you can't ruin.'

As a change from Jacques Loussier, we listened to Smetana and Vaughan Williams, but at nine o'clock, I suddenly felt I couldn't stay. I didn't understand myself why I needed to get away. He was extremely nice about it.

Back in my safe cocoon, I had to admit I was feeling better for the evening (but convinced that spaghetti sauce with turmeric and parsley doesn't make it). I lay in bed drowsily thinking that Horatio was possibly somebody I could count on in need. Time would tell, I thought sagely as, getting cautious about life, I summoned up clichés, which is another form of cocooning, I suppose. I didn't think he'd keep a piss diary either, which was in itself a calming reflection.

We hadn't boffed that evening, a novel experience for me considering he definitely 'give me the hots'. I fell asleep without even so much as a sip of wine and thought virtuously how healthily self-nurturing I was being. And I was living the celibate life too (for one night anyway).

In the morning I called the Missing Persons Bureau.

Oh yes, they recognized the name. Her brother had called, but no, there were no developments to report.

Paska!

I calmed down before I called the police, about Karen and about the futility of going through the Missing Persons Bureau, and asking what could *I* do.

'Sorry, lady, but there's nothing anybody can do.'

'But there *must* be something.'

'Did you ever stop to think she might not want to come back?'

'What do you mean?'

'It's been our experience that many women of Karen's age have boyfriend problems and resolve it by taking off. Maybe she doesn't *want* to be found. She may be happy where she is. That happens more frequently than people think. You may *think* she's lost but for all you know she's having a good time.'

I tried to think about that. How much effort would it take to believe that Karen isn't in danger, that she's living happily off somewhere on her own?

Maybe if I gave myself this pep talk enough times I could end by believing it.

'There's nothing you can do, then.'

'Lady, in my honest opinion, no. There has been no body found, no crime's been committed, no threats have been made, and there are no witnesses – what do you expect us to do?'

But I could tell he sensed how much this was affecting me because he added:

'Look, in a kidnapping you might contact the FBI –

although quite frankly I don't know what they can do either. They get calls like this all the time, especially kidnapped children between divorcing parents. You have no proof that this girl's been kidnapped. So my best advice is to give it time. She may yet show up. Sometimes people show up months later, years later.'

I tried not to slam the phone down after telling him, 'And sometimes they never do,' and added: '*Fuck!*' – but only after I had hung up.

Paska. Getting hungry for lunch, I warmed up a bowl of menudo and was sitting down at the kitchen table when Karen's luggage caught my eye. It was still sitting in the corner where I had left it. I had not wanted to open it out of respect for her privacy.

It was a large suitcase – some very famous brand or other (so much for advertising) – one of those matched-luggage jobs you see on TV where an eighteen-wheeler drives over a suitcase that just happens to be lying on the Long Island Expressway and it doesn't leave a scratch on it, let alone squish it into polymer pulp.

I opened the bag, hoping it would offer a clue to Karen's whereabouts. But aside from a handbag, gloves, a diary, a few postcards and some postage stamps, it contained bits of her wardrobe: pairs of underwear, a pale-blue cashmere buttoned sweater and a beautiful Kelly-green silk scarf I had never seen her wear (it was new, probably something she had recently bought). On the sweater there was an attractive silver lapel pin illustrating the Mother Goose rhyme: 'The Dish Ran Away with the Spoon.' I put the pin in my pocket.

It felt strange going through Karen's belongings as if she were dead, feeling the softness of materials that had not very long ago clothed her body and loving the faint fragrance issuing from the interior of the travelling bag. I closed my eyes and imagined Karen had come back and I was going out after lunch to meet her. I would tell her how I had feared for her very existence, and she would tell me about her crazy adventures in Rome and we would laugh and have a good time together again.

48

Start as you mean to go on. The next thing that happened was that no sooner did Hal, my soon-to-be ex, get back from the trip to San Diego than he was sent off on another quickie assignment, this time to Cancún. Would I sit his studio again?

Obviously I was still Inge the Resident Gopher, and to him, I suppose, I always would be, but it was an emergency and I said yes as long as he promised to kick the habit when he got back. He had to leave in so much of a hurry that his 'No problem!' had not the slightest shred of truth in it, and by the time I got over to the studio, he was gone and his answering machine was flashing like a pinball machine.

I decided not to bother with messages. That's what the machine was for, and people would have to wait till his return. I felt sure he had left his usual recorded message about being away, but in any case I could always check that later, and ditto for any Extremely Important Please Call Back Im*med*iately messages.

First things first: a raid on his king-size refrigerator, which, as luck would have it, harboured three bottles of Mumm's and two of Moët & Chandon (and *orchids*? – hmmmm . . .). That was a more than generous two-day supply of champagne for me and Iris.

I rang her up but got her father, Aristotle –

'Iris is *not HOME*' –

– and hung up on the old charmer. So I could have a *four*-day supply, if I chose, especially since Roberta was off on a junket, I think in Tobago, and even if she showed up unexpectedly, she was practically a teetotaller, not having had a drink, except for an occasional hot wine, since the day of her coming out with Susan.

While I was at it I grilled a couple of frozen South African 'lobster tails' (OK, giant crayfish) and removed their handsome shells and buttered them and squeezed lemon on the succulent chunks. I loaded champagne and the lobster on to the tray I had given Hal last Christmas and had my snack in the harem dressing room, perched a little uncomfortably on the edge of the Eames chair and gazing up from time to time at Hal's Cistine Ceiling of spots, wondering in what circumstances champagne could be spritzed that high.

Life as a long mulling over

The old mood of shaking up my life was still there except that now the shake-up included Hal the Boff. The glooms, which had never entirely gone, were threatening to return full force despite two times a week with Motor-mouth Yeblon. Mr Nussl's 'so-*cold* civilization' was sounding more and more like mature insight, not Baltic mispronunciation.

Aside from the phone ringing occasionally and having the sweet manners to answer itself, it was a nice quiet afternoon and I let my thoughts drift, remembering one by one everybody I knew and deciding I *liked* them all as fellow human beings but felt fondness or love for only one or two of them. Some I doubted I would miss if I never saw again.

49

Still down. Forever down? I hoped not.

I went over to see Mr Maki and he talked to me of the 'life unlived': a lovely phrase, and a sad thought (and almost identical to Mr Nussl's 'unlived life').

'In a sense, you know, it's true of everybody. It's the idea of what we do *not* become in life. There are many lives we don't live. In a sense we sacrifice them all to the one we do live.'

Though that may be true, I doubt that I can ever accept it. It would take away from Karen, who, if she is not dead, is living a *destroyed* life, which, yes, *is* a life unlived, but it's more horrible than that, much worse than that.

But maybe worst of all was the *unknowability* of her fate – and our impotence before the frustrating uncertainty.

I had to stop thinking such thoughts. In fact I felt I had better leave rather than try to work, and telling Mr Maki I was not good company and could we continue next time, I said goodbye.

Heading back to Hal's studio I suddenly felt an urge, a *need*, to get my hair cut. It obviously had to do with more than hair – it was a necessary break.

At the Bird in Hand I ordered a good jolting double espresso and opened the Yellow Pages for a hairdresser I had never been to before, because that seemed important now too: it had to be a new person.

The names were a kind of marketplace poetry, and I

couldn't believe the profusion of Crowning Glory, A Cut Above, The Cutting Edge, Take It Off, The Brush Off, Head to Head.

Short Cuts, Hair Today, The Hairafter, Hair and Gone – no thanks. I liked Bangs and Tail. Not of personal interest but amusing was Toupee or Not Toupee. And the same for Yours Permanently. As for Curl Up and Dye, I'd give that a miss. I liked Hair Peace, though.

I ended up choosing Snippets, not just because it happened to be the nearest salon but because the snippets/jottings connection resonated with the way I was currently living my life.

At the hairdressers I read an article about a lovely swan named Casino who had entered the *Guinness Book of Records* by returning to Britain after a two-and-a-half-thousand-mile flight from Siberia for her twenty-seventh consecutive winter – astonishingly: the normal lifespan of swans of her breed is fifteen years. A research officer at the Gloucestershire Wildfowl and Wetlands Reserve commented that she is looking very good and added, 'There is no reason to believe she will not come back to us again.'

O undying hope.

Found missing

There was a story about Bill, too. The tabloids were already reinventing him as something ghoulishly interesting: 'Famous Artist's Death: Suicide or Dealers' Foul Play?' But I learned from this trash that what I had feared had in fact happened: his studio had been mysteriously cleaned out, ransacked. Enormous canvases, the kind that would require a huge van to be hauled away, were missing (yet more disappearances), and an investigation 'is currently under way'. Some commissioner has expressed the fear that a massive daylight robbery has taken place under the nose of the police and in the barn-door syndrome ordered that the studio be placed under police seal. He said the estimated worth of the 'fabulous

Joachim estate' amounts to tens of millions of dollars, 'according to Rupert Damson, financier and socialite, husband of dealer Susan Damson'.

The reporter's story was a confection of sleaze about Bill's life with 'Hollywood idol' Lorna Beach, and I was just reacting to the muck when I suddenly went all dizzy for a few minutes and almost fainted. I didn't know what was happening to me. The smell of hair lotions began to nauseate me and I could barely sit still. I wanted to crawl away somewhere and shut out the world.

The next morning, on waking up I vomited. That was it! I was pregnant! Which cheered me no end – having *Hal's* baby. This sitoo-ation obviously required thought. But maybe the baby wouldn't inherit his nervous traits or that (booby) prize-winning temperament.

But first I had to make certain I *was* pregnant before I let myself get carried away (as is sometimes my wont). I dashed out in search of a pregnancy test at the local pharmacy, and meanwhile – just in case – began telling myself that every baby is a good baby no matter *who* the father is. The baby would be cute and adorable (it would, after all, be *my* baby, and besides, Hal does have *some* redeeming qualities), and I decided I had better mend my ways and start drinking warm milk at bedtime, cut back on vodka and maybe I wasn't getting enough bed rest.

The pharmacist sold me the best pee test of three ('This one is one hundred per cent sure, just about') and I brought it back to Hal's studio. It seemed very appropriate to do a pee test for the presence of Hal's baby in the very room that figured so largely in Himself's piss diary.

The test was a cutesy-looking thing, with splash guards over the tiny result windows. If I was pregnant, I would see a pretty blue line show up in a *heart-shaped* (!) patch. I was so convinced I had a nice little baby growing inside me that I plunked myself down on the john seat to conserve strength. It was going to be a long nine months, during which I would have to make serious – and long overdue – adjustments in lifestyle.

As I waited for the test result to appear I planned on looking into various brands of diapers and checking with mothers' groups and La Leche League to see what they recommended. And maybe I had better call up *my* mother and break the happy news that she would soon be called Grandma.

After the requisite ten minutes passed, I took a peek – and got the good and bad news simultaneously: Hal was not going to be a father (well, anyway, not by me).

And (on second thought): phew!

The phone rang and, with the voice thing turned on, I heard a very annoyed Hal: this was his *third* attempt to reach me, for *God's* sake . . . ek-cetera, ek-cetera, blahblah. He was calling his trusty gopher for help with gear he had absent-mindedly left behind. Also he forgot his large Moroccan leather wallet, in which he keeps his collection of at least thirty thousand charge cards (one for each morning).

The lens was the 121mm Super-Angulon, his favourite lens (and truly a gem). It would probably be on the table where he mounted prints, close to the dry-mount press, and would I please package the lens and charge cards, grab a taxi and rush them out to JFK, at the British Air desk, insure the sonuvabitching package and see that it got off on the next flight. Yes *sir*.

Sometimes a relationship is like knitting a scarf: you never seem to get anywhere, and suddenly it's long enough

By then I was pissed off enough at life to feel a great urge to tell him, in the best Iris tradition, to go take a flying fuck but realized how immature that was. (Unfortunately.) So I simply said, 'OK, goodbye' and hung up. I'm getting good at hanging up phones with a nice satisfying slam.

Shit, *merde*, *paska*. I raided his refrigerator again and filled a glass with I forget which champagne, as if it matters, and downed a half a tumbler of it for a quick jolt. Hell, not being pregnant, I could drink all the champagne I wanted. That in itself called for a refill.

Five minutes later, Hal again – calm Hal, wise Hal, the old familiar Humour-the-Kid Hal, a style of male discourse that women love.

It was a nudging phone call. 'Look, there's time if you leave im*med*iately. There's a flight leaving in an hour and a half. So please.'

The 'please', a sop born of desperation, actually lost him points. Sad that he still didn't know me enough to understand I didn't need bribery to deliver the goods. Sadder still, I didn't think he ever would understand. But on the plus side, it no longer mattered.

I found the lens neatly encased in its black soft-leather, green-velvet-lined bag, packaged it and the charge card wallet together and grabbed that in one hand and the neck of the open champagne bottle in the other (after stashing bottle *numero due* in my handbag for taxi-ride enjoyment across the concrete wilds of Long Island) – and I was off and running.

A day in the life of a New York cabbie

I sprinted to the elevators and grabbed the first one that stopped, banged every 'Lobby', 'Close Door' and 'Down' button I could find and, feet running the moment they touched the lobby, hit Lexington Avenue yelling at the nearest cab at the kerb: 'Kennedy!' I was barely seated when I heard a satisfying screech of tyres as we plunged into a wide torrent of taxis, cars, buses – the usual Friday afternoon traffic madness. Going from zero to sixty in ten seconds, in an impressive display of Keystone Cops' slaloming through the traffic, the driver corralled vehicles sheepdog style to both sides of the avenue in territorial demonstration that Lexington Avenue *did* in fact belong to him, arousing a road-rage blaring of horns as cars slammed on brakes and cabbies flung various 'Mother-fucker!'s and 'Asshole!'s at him and me sinking into the back seat feeling deeply thankful I hadn't told him to step on it.

'Doan worry, lady,' he said as, I *swear*, he took some paint off a bus we were passing (more furious beeping, horns blaring, two 'Shit-for-brains!' and a surprising 'Hey, *Gon*ad!'). 'We'll make eet in good time, lady' – and *bang*!

Halt – standstill – dead calm: a motionless sea of vehicles. We were surrounded by a mass of taxis, buses, *two* armoured cars, an art-movers van, delivery trucks, an incongruous R V out of *Arizona Highways* that had probably taken a wrong turn at Philadelphia. Through the window all I could make out as far ahead as I could see were idiotic 'Dig We Must' signs and a barrier of grey sawhorses: 'Police Line – Do Not Cross.' The cause of the delay was too far forward to determine, but the avenue had become indistinguishable from the proverbial Long Island Expressway parking lot. In an act of desperation you *could* free yourself of the mess by walking over the tops of the stalled vehicles, but that would be the only way.

'A traffic jam?' – I said to the driver – 'so early in the afternoon?'

Major shrug from up front: disgust beyond description. I noticed he didn't say, 'Go figure.' A glance at his ID card (Mendelsohn? Goldstein, Goldsteen?): No: Vasquez. First name: Jesus (or as Roz would say: Hey Zeus!).

I wondered if I should do the normal cowardly thing and get out and find another cab and leave him stuck on Lexington Avenue. But I couldn't, not with Jesus – or Zeus.

'Mr Vasquez?'

Polite, inquiring eyes viewing me in the rearview mirror – my first real look at him: a nice Puerto Rican family man, at a guess.

'As soon as you can, take any street or avenue going in *any* direction as long as you get us off Lexington. And then keep going.'

I broke out bottle number two (glad to be sharing it so that I would not get totally blotto), and after he took a courtesy swig and a regretful rain check for the rest, I settled back, thinking the worst-case scenario was we wouldn't make it in time for the flight immediately leaving and no amount of worrying would magically make that possible. And if I did miss that flight there would be another later, and it would be a bad day for Hal at the far end, not for good old me at this end.

I felt an unaccustomed (and quite refreshing) absence of involvement. Selfish, perhaps, but I was still a bit pissed (probably in every sense of the word, at this point), and anyhow, I could always ship things overnight express, so no big deal.

But Mr Vasquez had talents in reserve. Or maybe it was his changing his mind and taking a second, long pull of the Moët & Chandon that did it, ending with a huge happy mouth-wipe on his sleeve. Making a deep sigh of contentment, he handed me back what remained of the bottle and was ready now to take on the midtown traffic wars. Where, until then, the cars and buses inching ahead in teasing increments had been testing his limits, now a dam broke. A sudden yell of '*Cabron!*' from the front seat, and I felt the taxi lunge full force into an opening he miraculously wedged between two vehicles on our immediate left and, with a series of manoeuvres that the other cabbies took in with traffic-becalmed boredom, he insinuated us by degrees towards the extreme edge of the avenue, where he violently humped our front wheels up on to the sidewalk, panicking a small scattering of shoppers. Wobbling the rear wheels up, hump-*bump*, he purringly slithered the taxi through the thinning group of freaking-out pedestrians startling to our left and right and edged us around a corner, where a bank dick, alarmed by the sensation of car bumper grazing his uniform, idiotically reached for his holster. Having become free of Lexington Avenue, the driver vaulted the taxi from the sidewalk back to the street again and tore off eastward, his foot implacably flooring the accelerator and my back getting sucked deep into the upholstery with the force of a jet approaching takeoff speed.

I feel fairly certain that the time it took us to get to JFK qualified us for some record or other, and as we screeched to an abrupt stop at the British Air terminal, Mr Vasquez, grinning, turned his head and announced:

'I have never meess a plane yet.'

'If you do not get it from yourself, where will you go for it?'

With the package on its way (*a first-class seat for a bloody package* – dun't esk), I felt all my problems melting away. I had seen the lens and credit cards off, watched them pass through the gate and disappear into the BA system. Appearances, disappearances. There was now only the matter of getting back to town and for that there was loads of time – the words suddenly making me think of Frank's song, 'Never-Ending Time'. (Had it been played yet? Did I give a happy fuck?)

To relax after the taxi from hell, I picked up a photo magazine at a news-stand and found an empty booth in the adjoining bar lounge. Living it up – in fact, feeling pretty damn good with all the liquid happiness gurgling inside – I ordered a coupe of champagne (go for broke) and began reading an article that bored me so much it took a while to become aware I wasn't taking in the words. Then I realized I wasn't drinking the champagne either – in fact was feeling surprisingly sober.

I tossed the magazine aside and began thinking about Hal. It was over and I no longer needed to be involved with him. As I allowed myself to think that previously unacceptable thought, I felt purged and unburdened. I felt my body relax and had a palpable sense of letting go of something that actually, now that I looked at it, had been long gone. We would always be friends, meeting at parties and going to Rory's every once in a long while, or maybe trying out Rory's new place, The Unnatural Act. I owed Hal much and was grateful for what I had learned – and earned too: there would be more money coming in soon, for yet another catalogue job. That would provide loads of time for my own work – and about that I suddenly felt new stirrings: to get back to work, which was a yen, a passion, I had lost along the way.

It felt so good letting go of things, disappearing the bad experiences. My anger was gone, and with it the Glooms too, and I felt an enormous relief at leaving behind all melancholy thoughts, as well as a self-pity disguised as sorrow over Karen. Now I would have the freedom to mourn Karen honestly, not confusing her losses with any losses of mine. The sorrow, which I thought would probably never leave, at least became more manageable. If I was right about her (and I was fairly certain there was no 'if' any more), then constricting *my* thirty thousand mornings to match hers wouldn't help either of us. Far better to make the most of mine as she would have hers. Did it honour or did it dishonour Karen to just go on living? And did one have a choice about living on?

On a television screen, a news reporter said that the cemetery strike had ended. There was an imbecilic sound bite of a gravedigger grinning at the camera and saying: 'Dig we must.' A tombstone salesman remarked – with a straight face – that sales 'showed signs of reviving'. The Ferguson-Ames Report presented an 'in-depth' interview of a funeral director, who said that the convention of the New York City chapter of the Southern New England Embalmers' Association, to have been held in Atlantic City, was being temporarily called off this morning 'in view of events'.

In the terminal I watched a couple in their forties going by struggling with suitcases and bags, both wearing identical baseball caps and sweatshirts that read: '*GOTTA BELIEVE – Quantum is REAL!* Jan-Conf '98 / MIT'. As they searched for the right gate, the youthful slogan on their jackets seemed as incongruous with their age as their toddler, rubber nipple in hand, doggedly stomping along behind them, yelling, 'Wait for Baby! Wait for Baby! God*damn* it, wait for Baby!'

50

Thirty thousand mornings

Yesterday, in a reflective mood before going to bed, I leaned out the window and felt the pleasantness of the crisp evening air veined with city smells. The icy breeze was a smooth liquid flowing over my cheeks. Underneath it I could sense a warmth – the long winter was breaking up.

My thoughts wandered back to people I've known and I began thinking that they were like my aunt Leena's goldfish. As a little girl visiting her in Ii, I used to crawl up to the dining-room table and tap with my fingertips against the goldfish bowl to see the fish startle away in a lovely pattern of flight – a one-inch darting-off panic. But in less than a second they would return to the spot they had fled. If I tapped again they would startle and dart away in the same one-inch pattern and again return to the same spot. I was fascinated by the behaviour. I could tap any number of times and never see the slightest variation in the reaction, as if memory were something that lasted only a second. It was out of sight, out of mind – back to square one. That made me think of Karen, who had been a part of our lives, and already our concern was fading. She was gone and we had our lives to live.

Maybe, after all, feelings do have a statute of limitations, but Karen's feelings, whatever they are – I'm sure the most dreadful imaginable if she is alive and held against her will – will never come to an end as long as she remains in life. I don't know where she is or what is happening to her, but if she is someplace where she will never again be free, she is alive only as a zombie, as much a member of the living dead as those slaves in work camps who are cynically worked to death. In what sense could she remain fully a human being if someone (as I imagine it) were forcing her to be a woman-as-toy, displayed in lavish seclusion for the periodic servicing of someone's glandular need and then led away from the presence once the repulsive passion had spent itself in that seventeen-year-old body? Her only tie to life would be her will, the universal will to live at all costs.

But if the point should come, as more time passes, when that will shrivels, destroyed from having been so beaten down that she no longer cares to remain in life – in *that* life, in alien surroundings, in alien hated comfort and among alien objects, mere *things* of another world – she will almost surely welcome the paradox of a great liberating death for her sanity's sake. She will wake up each morning in dread of what the day will bring – imprisonment, a familiar longing, the hated despair. It will no longer matter how many thousands of mornings would yet remain, and anyway, they wouldn't be mornings, which are the renewals of day, but reminders of a prolonged dying.

If she does not come back, I will have to let her go because whatever the circumstances, she has been murdered. I will have to think of her as dead because only that would be merciful – not for her, perhaps, but for me. If I go on seeing photographs of her from time to time, I will have to say to myself: 'I can't bear to think of her in any other way than dead. Prove to me she's not. Tell me where she can be found so we can bring her back.'

Because if she *is* alive somewhere and is being kept in some loathsome hole – or palatial comfort – she is dead in the worst possible way. She is suffering the ineffectual sorrow of all prisoners tasting the bittersweetness of memories of a former, happier life. That is the most frightful end of all, the suspension of a life in full flower – like my mother's mayfly trapped in amber, which was once alive and free as we know by the irony of seeing its delicate beauty preserved forever in death.

Maybe the others are right, that Karen is happy in some other place, living a new life somewhere with some new friend. It's possible but I don't believe it. My friends tell me they're certain that something like that could have happened and I'm being foolish to deny it merely because I don't like to think it.

I don't know how to counter that except by saying there's no reason to believe that Karen will ever show up again . . .

Morning now, the sun shining brightly.

I picked up my camera and headed (inevitably) to the bottom of Manhattan, where I admired the East River, that labouring river, a rough work beast, not like the Seine at the Cité, which is a medieval tapestry, or the Tiber at Sant' Angelo, which is an old slow serpent of mud compared with East River's shipyards, basins, piers, bridges, slips and docks. I stood at the river's edge and watched it make its wide-sweeping arc that flowed towards the bay and the great Atlantic beyond. It was the changing of the tide. I looked at the water moving in two directions at once, in a stationary rising flood, the roiling flow reversing itself as water rode on water, the rippled surface slipping backward while flowing peaceably out to sea.

Back home again there was a call from Horatio: to go for a walk. It had begun to rain, the first real rain this year, washing away the snow except for a few icy black patches – but they won't last.

I said yes, if it stops raining, and if it doesn't, to just come on over. I'd fix us a nice lunch.